THE ICE DUCHESS

SCANDALOUS REGENCY WIDOWS, BOOK TWO

AMY ROSE BENNETT

COPYRIGHT

The Ice Duchess

Copyright © 2016 Amy Rose Bennett
First Edition Publication: September 2016
Revised Edition Ebook Publication: April 2023
Print Publication: July 2023

First Edition Editor: Cathleen Ross
Revised Edition Editor: Emily EK Murdoch
Cover Artist: Erin Dameron-Hill

ISBN Print Book: 978-0-9954283-1-7

PRAISE FOR AMY ROSE BENNETT

"Amy Rose Bennett is a fresh new voice in historical romance with a flair for historical atmosphere."

> — ANNE GRACIE FOR *HOW TO CATCH A WICKED VISCOUNT*

"Amy Rose Bennett is a charming new voice in historical romance."

> — ANNA CAMPBELL FOR *HOW TO CATCH A WICKED VISCOUNT*

"A sweet and spicy read full of sly wit and rich with delicious details that pull the reader into the scene. A delightful confection of ballroom banter and bedroom seduction."

> — SALLY MACKENZIE, *USA TODAY* BESTSELLER FOR *HOW TO CATCH A WICKED VISCOUNT*

"The perfect blend of sexiness and humor... Amy Rose Bennett has created a lush, vibrant love story, her characters sharing a fabulous sensual chemistry that fairly scorches the page."

> — CHRISTINA BRITTON, AWARD-WINNING AUTHOR FOR *UP ALL NIGHT WITH A GOOD DUKE*

ABOUT THE ICE DUCHESS...

The Duchess of Darby never thought she'd meet a man who could melt the ice around her heart...until she crosses paths with Lord Markham. But will the past come back to burn them both?

Georgiana Dudley—the "Ice Duchess"—has just emerged from mourning after a nine-year marriage of convenience to the Duke of Darby, her twin brother's lover. Deeply hurt by a scoundrel a decade ago, Georgie swore she would never turn her head for any man, let alone another rakehell. But then she encounters the wickedly handsome and all too charming Rafe Landsbury, the Earl of Markham and against her better judgment, her interest is reluctantly aroused. An affair may be impossible to resist but dare she trust Lord Markham with her most intimate secrets...and her heart?

Society believes Rafe to be a diplomat but for many years he has been working on the Continent as a spy for the Crown. Leaving the shadowy world of espionage behind, he returns to London with the intention of finding a wife. When he is paired with the frosty yet fascinating Duchess of Darby at the piquet table during a ton ball, he is intrigued. Do-or-die man that he is, he's certainly not going to let her cool demeanor dissuade him from pursuing her.

When Rafe's dark past returns to endanger Georgie, he is determined to protect her at all costs, even if that means hiding who he once was. With the stakes so high, both Georgie and Rafe must decide if love is a risk worth taking...

DEDICATION

For the love of my life and hero, Richard.

CHAPTER 1

Latimer House, Mayfair, London
18ᵗʰ October 1816

"Jonathon, I can't believe that you and Helena have managed to talk me into this hare-brained scheme." Georgiana, the widowed Duchess of Darby, turned her back on the crush in the ballroom of Latimer House and threw a baleful glance at her twin brother. *He should at least have the decency to look a little shamefaced.*

But Jonathon merely smiled broadly at her, setting her on edge even more. "Come now, Georgie dearest," he cajoled in the exact tone that always made her want to poke him in the ribs. "You know very well why Helena and I have embarked on this mission. You have been holed up in the Wolds for far too long." His expression altered slightly, his smile taking on a melancholy tilt, his blue eyes so like her own, softening. "Your mourning period was officially over a month ago. Allow yourself to have a little fun for once. Teddy would have wanted you to." Jonathon didn't need to add that life was far too short.

The last year had definitely shown them both that it was indeed the case.

Georgie closed her eyes as a sharp bite of grief pierced her heart. She was more than just a little relieved to be lurking in a secluded alcove behind an elaborate floral arrangement on the edge of the ballroom. She really didn't think she could bear the prying eyes of the *ton* upon her right now. Thank the Lord her acquaintances were keeping their distance, obviously out of respect for her widowed status.

Poor Teddy. A husband in name only, but my best friend.
The love of Jonathon's life.

"I know, Georgie-bean," Jonathon said in a low voice, squeezing her arm gently. "I miss him desperately too. But life must go on. And twenty-eight is far too young to be acting the part of a dowager."

"Humph. Yet I'm far too old for this nonsense," she replied, her voice starch-stiff with an annoyance that bordered on resentment. She knew she sounded ungracious—not at all like a duchess—but she couldn't help it. She wasn't ready for this return to society. Heavens, after ten years, she'd truly had enough of this tired old parade. The false gaiety. The appraising glances and facile flirting. The ceaseless whispering of the *ton*. She really didn't want to don her social mask again. The famous Ice Duchess. Poised, remote, unshakable.

Untouchable.

But she must. Especially since matchmaking seemed to be high on the agenda of both Jonathon and Helena, Georgie's dearest female friend.

Jonathon raised a dark eyebrow. "Speak for yourself, Georgie. I certainly don't intend to spend the rest of my days as a monk." Reinforcing his point, he threw a calculated smile toward a beautiful young dandy with an elaborate cravat Beau Brummel himself would have been proud of.

"Be that as it may, I seriously doubt that Teddy would

have wanted you to procure a lover for me." She caught her brother's startled gaze and narrowed her eyes. "Because that's exactly what your intention is this evening. And Helena's. You can't deny it."

This time Jonathon did squirm beneath her penetrating stare. His cheeks reddened and he cast his gaze downward as he pulled at his cuffs. "Hey ho, that's a bit strong, sis." Apparently finished with adjusting his apparel, he slid a glance her way again. "Teddy did ask me to make sure that you were happy. You know that as well as I."

Georgie barely suppressed the unladylike urge to roll her eyes. "How many times do I have to tell you that taking a lover —or indeed, finding another husband—will *not* make me happy, Jonathon?"

Her brother reached forward and stilled her hand that had been busily flicking her fan against her azure silk skirts. "But maybe it will."

Georgie made a moue of displeasure, deciding then and there she was going to summon her carriage and leave. No matter that she had only arrived ten minutes ago. No matter that Helena and her husband Phillip Latimer, the Earl of Maxwell, had gone to such pains to throw such a grand ball even though it was October. No matter that both her friends and Jonathon had engineered the evening so that several of the *ton's* most eligible bachelors were here for her delectation. They could deny it all they liked, but Georgie knew the truth.

Jonathon's grip tightened on her gloved wrist. "You're not going to cut and run are you? That would be poor form. Especially now that Helena is headed our way."

Oh heavens, no. Georgie followed her brother's gaze and spotted the dark-haired Countess of Maxwell weaving her way through the throng—her flame-red satin ball gown made her impossible to miss. Mercifully, she was by herself. No darkly handsome Lothario or Viking fair rake accompanied her. Georgie released the breath she'd been holding.

"Georgie, darling. There you are." Helena's wide smile lit her beautiful face before she turned her attention to Jonathon. "Why are you letting your sister hide away like this?" she admonished playfully. "I've been searching everywhere for her, Sir Jonathon."

Jonathon huffed out a sigh that was clearly affected. "She's taking her widowed duchess status far too seriously, I'm afraid. Before long we'll find her sipping tea or lemonade in the ladies' retiring room with a cold compress across her forehead, claiming her tired old bones ache far too much."

Helena laughed and touched Georgie's arm. "Surely not." But Georgie's attempt at a smile didn't fool her friend. After searching her face for a moment, a look of compassion replaced the twinkle in Helena's eyes. "Oh, my dear, there is a frightful crowd here tonight, isn't there? I completely understand if you are not quite ready for this. Phillip did warn me that this ball might be a bit too much too soon. If you *do* want to retire—"

Georgie shook her head, suddenly feeling guilty that she had planned to abscond. "It's all right, Helena. I can see how much effort you and Phillip have gone to this evening." She patted her friend's hand still resting upon her arm. "Just don't expect me to dance. You know how I loathe it."

Helena's dark eyes sparkled with mirth. "You're going to claim you're wearing the wrong sort of slippers again, aren't you? New ones that pinch?"

"She already mentioned her toes hurt on the way here," added Jonathon.

Georgie's mouth twitched with a reluctant smile. She clearly needed a new repertoire of excuses. "I'll stay for a little while," she conceded. "But both of you *must* promise not to introduce me to any remotely eligible gentlemen. I know what you are up to, no matter what you say."

Helena sighed dramatically. "As you wish. I promise I won't introduce you to anyone fitting that bill. But you can't stay hiding in the corner. Everyone will talk. Why don't you come and play cards? I know Phillip has been looking for a worthy piquet opponent. He's still smarting over the last time you trounced him."

Piquet. Georgie hadn't played cards since Teddy had died. He'd taught her everything there was to know about the game and she prided herself on her prowess. He'd also understood that to her, the cards were both a shield and a weapon during *ton* social events. And she wielded them well. It meant she didn't have to dance or cultivate mindless conversations with men who might have seduction on their minds. She could just play. But it hurt too much to think of the games she had played with Teddy. The challenge, the good-natured verbal sparring, the laughter...

But Helena wouldn't know that. Swallowing past a leaden lump in her throat, Georgie pasted a smile on her face and inclined her head. "That sounds absolutely perfect."

Helena's smile was as dazzling as the rubies and diamonds about her neck. "Wonderful. I'll go and find him."

As Jonathon claimed Georgie's arm and began to escort her out of her bolt hole and around the edge of the ballroom, he murmured in her ear. "As I've said before, dear sister, life goes on. Enjoy yourself. Win this game for Teddy."

Georgie nodded and squeezed Jonathon's hand. "I will. For Teddy."

Georgie took her seat at one of the piquet tables in the card room and removed her gloves, hoping that Phillip, Lord

Maxwell, wouldn't notice her slightly trembling fingers when he joined her. It seemed absurd to be so nervous. Where was her famous sang-froid?

It probably didn't help that a hush had descended over the card room as Jonathon had escorted her in, and at this very moment she could feel at least a dozen pairs of eyes, if not more, upon her. The unvanquished Ice Duchess—the woman who barely ever lost a game—was about to play cards again. Of course people were going to notice.

Curse her brother and Helena. She would have attracted much less notice if she had simply decided to dance after all. Lemonade in the ladies' retiring room seemed more appealing by the second. And where in heaven's name was Phillip? She glanced about the room but could not spy Helena's husband anywhere.

Not only that, she could see Jonathon disappearing out of the card room, no doubt chasing the dapper young buck he'd been making calf's eyes at earlier.

If Phillip didn't appear within the next thirty seconds, she *would* cut and run.

"May I join you, Your Grace?" A soft baritone drew Georgie's attention away from the ornately arched doorway of the card room and back to the table.

She glanced up. And it was all she could do not to gasp.

A dark-haired, lean-jawed rake was smiling down at her. Her dastardly brother and friends had set her up after all.

Blast them all to hell.

Drawing in a steadying breath, she summoned a slight smile. Her well-practiced, cool duchess's smile—a smile that had sustained her for almost a decade in the face of such obvious raw masculinity. Thank God she still had it.

"And you are?" she asked smoothly, arching an eyebrow. "I believe we've never been introduced." She thought she knew most rakes of the *ton* and she had only been away from

6

London for a year. But this tall, handsome man with smoke-gray eyes and a dark velvet voice she didn't know at all.

The corner of his wide, well-shaped mouth lifted into a smile. "Forgive my boldness, Your Grace. I am Rafe Landsbury, Lord Markham. Lord Maxwell has been...detained and offers his apologies. He asked me to stand in, in his stead." His eyes held hers—a question or perhaps it was a spark of challenge flared in their gray depths. "If you don't mind, of course."

As if she could refuse with everyone watching. She'd gleefully strangle Phillip, Helena, and Jonathon later for putting Lord Markham up to this. They probably thought she'd build up a rapport with the man over cards. Then he'd suggest they dance or perhaps peruse the supper table together. His large hand would touch her elbow, the small of her back. His fingers would brush against hers as he passed her a glass of champagne... She knew all the ploys he would use to try and get her hot and bothered. But she wouldn't fall for any of them. Never again. Just because she was a widow, it didn't mean she was fair game.

Lord Markham was still watching her expectantly so she affected a small tinkling laugh and shrugged a shoulder. "Of course I don't mind. Please, take a seat."

"Thank you, Your Grace."

Georgie tried not to stare as the nobleman folded his long, lean frame onto the damask covered Adams chair opposite her. *Markham, Markham.* No, not a memory of him stirred at all. *Where had such a man been hiding for the last decade?* He exuded such a quiet self-assurance as he watched her reach for the deck of cards, a completely unexpected and most disconcerting wave of heat swept over her face.

She hadn't blushed in years. *What is wrong with me?*

"Shall I cut first?" Her voice had a breathy edge to it and she forced herself to sit up straighter, praying that the extra air entering her lungs would fortify her for when she next spoke. But all the movement seemed to do was draw Lord Markham's gaze toward her sweeping neckline.

Why on earth had she dressed in such a frivolous, indecorous gown? So what that it was *à la mode* and the azure silk precisely matched the color of her eyes—or so Madame Dupuis, her modiste, had declared. What she wouldn't do for a fichu to hide the rise and fall of her bosom right now. Another blush scalded her cheeks.

Lord Markham's eyes returned to her face, his mouth tilting into another half-amused smile. The wretched man knew she was rattled, damn him. "By all means, cut away, Your Grace."

Georgie forced what she hoped would pass for a sophisticated smile on her face and managed to smoothly shuffle the deck. Placing the cards in the center of the table, she then made her cut. The queen of hearts was exposed.

Not the best card to start with but it would do.

She glanced at Markham and the rogue cocked an eyebrow at her, his mouth tipping into that decidedly irritating, knowing half-smile again.

Wonderful. The man was *going to flirt with her.* Probably for the entire card game. He obviously didn't give a fig that she'd just emerged from mourning. And he must know—the entire *ton* knew. Jonathon, if not the Maxwells, had probably told him that she was ripe for the plucking.

Unless flirting was just a ploy to put her off her game. Lord Markham struck her as a man who liked to play games in the true sense of the word. And to win. She would show him though. Georgiana, the Duchess of Darby, never lost. Ever.

Markham reached for the deck, his long fingers covering the cards before he took his turn to cut them. With a small jolt of surprise she realized the knuckles of his right hand were scarred, misshapen even. She stole a glance at his face and noticed further evidence of past physical altercations—a slight deviation to the bridge of his nose and the faint line of a scar running through one dark eyebrow. Was he a pugilist, or a military officer perhaps? But she had no more time to speculate on the man's recreational habits or profession.

Markham turned over the ace of hearts.

Oh, Lord no. She was already at a decided disadvantage, unsettled by Markham's good looks and devil-may-care manner. And now he'd claim all the subsequent advantages that came with being the younger hand during the first round.

"I'll deal." Markham flashed her such a confident grin, if Georgie had a drink at hand, she'd be tempted to throw it at him.

Instead, she simply smiled back and unclenched her teeth with an effort to reply, "Of course."

Markham reached for the cards. "What stakes shall we play for, Your Grace?" he said, his voice running over her like rich, thick treacle, making her shiver. His disconcerting gaze slid to her lips for the briefest of moments before returning to meet her eyes. "I am open to whatever you suggest."

Georgie blushed hotly again. Why did Markham make it sound as if they were playing something infinitely more dark and dangerous than cards? She would never be able to concentrate with his stare focused so intently on her, sexual innuendo lacing everything he said.

Provoking man. That's when Georgie had a premonition that she was in deep trouble. What if she, the Ice Duchess, lost? Oh, she would never live it down.

∾

"I'm satisfied with playing for points, nothing more, Lord Markham."

Rafe couldn't help but smile inwardly at the frosty reply

of the stunning woman before him. She was doing a sterling job at affecting a calm demeanor, but he knew that deep down she was flustered. By him.

His reputation in particular covert circles as one of Britain's premier spies hadn't been without good reason. Reading people was his stock in trade. His life had depended upon it for so long it was second nature to him. He'd have been killed a dozen times over during his years in Spain, France and in the Russian Court if he hadn't been able to accurately deduce someone's emotional state and thoughts. Anticipate their every move.

And right now, he knew beyond a shadow of a doubt that the newly widowed Ice Duchess—who as rumor had it was a card player extraordinaire, a woman who had rarely been beaten in the last decade and by no one at all in the last three years—was more than a little bit nervous being around him.

Intriguing. It was the first time in a long time that a woman had so effortlessly and completely aroused his interest. He had been back in England just over a year and had heretofore managed to avoid most of the *ton's* lackluster whirl of social events. Until his bloody friend Maxwell had persuaded him to turn up this evening.

At least it was going to be more entertaining than he'd previously anticipated.

He began to deal the cards. The Duchess of Darby obviously despised flirtations. Her beautiful blue eyes were still narrowed with annoyance as she waited to see how he would respond to her request to play for points alone. Maxwell had warned him she would be pricklier than a gooseberry bush when he'd proposed that he, Markham, take his place in this *partie.*

Now seeing the heightened color in the duchess's cheeks and her slightly elevated rate of breathing, Rafe was going to flirt with her like mad. He could never resist a challenge. She might have a tart tongue and a glacial blue gaze, but one thing was certain: the delectable duchess was going to be the most exciting challenge of the feminine kind that he'd come across in a long time.

"Points alone it is then, madam," he said at last with a deliberately provocative smile. To his amusement, he was rewarded with an even icier glare, entirely at odds with the deepening flush across the duchess's high cheekbones. "Although, if you'd like to up the stakes at any time..." Cad that he was, he dropped his gaze to her tightly compressed, rose-pink lips again.

"Just deal, Lord Markham," she replied in the most delightfully clipped tone, he had to bite his cheek to keep from chuckling with glee.

But she was right. They should get down to the business at hand. Win or lose at piquet, he was going to have the time of his life.

CHAPTER 2

L ord Markham had trounced her. Well and truly.
So much for winning for Teddy...

The damp, cool night air was welcome after the stifling crush of the ballroom. And the terrace was completely deserted, thank God. A recent shower of rain had obviously put off those guests who usually sought illicit assignations from venturing outside. Georgie quietly took her first glass of champagne for the evening over to the farthest corner of the terrace and stared out into the dripping, lantern-lit courtyard garden. Her blue satin slippers would be ruined—she could already feel dampness creeping up through the soles—but she didn't care.

She still couldn't believe it. She'd lost at piquet for the first time in three years. All because of that devil, Markham. She took a large sip of champagne to prevent herself grinding her teeth with frustration. The gossip would be all over *ton* circles by midday tomorrow—that the indomitable Duchess of Darby's famous composure had slipped.

They would think it was because she'd just come out of

mourning, no doubt. But that wasn't the case at all. She couldn't bear it.

Now that Teddy was gone, her reputation as a ruthless card-player was the only defense she still had against men like Markham. And now it was all but shattered. Just as her heart had been shattered ten years ago.

She lifted the cool and slightly dewed champagne flute to her flushed cheek. Maybe she was coming down with something. That might explain her inability to keep count of the cards and her poor decision making throughout the game. Yes, that must be it. Aside from feeling infuriated with herself and Markham, she also felt edgy, feverish. Her pulse was racing, as if the champagne she had just been sipping was fizzing through her veins. She was not herself at all.

"Your Grace?"

Georgie turned her head, knowing before she saw him that it was Lord Markham. Damn the brazen devil back to hell. She supposed he had followed her out here to gloat.

He crossed the wet terrace toward her with an unerring stride, obviously sure of a welcome reception from her. She slid her gaze over him. She supposed many women, perhaps even Jonathon, would find him attractive. He had a lean, muscular build, and as he drew closer she was struck again by how tall he was.

But so what if he was broader across the shoulder and more powerfully made than most other men of her acquaintance? So what if he was roguishly handsome? He was only another man.

In the end, he would be bound to disappoint her.

He paused but a foot away, leaning a hand nonchalantly on the stone balustrade. "May I join you?"

She steadfastly tried to ignore the vibration the rich timbre of his voice sent through her just as she futilely attempted to suppress the wild thudding of her heart. She couldn't account for her body's wayward responses to this man.

Stop it, Georgie. You are reacting like the foolish girl you used to be.

"If you like," she replied, pleased that her voice sounded even and non-committal, despite her inward discomposure. She took another sip of champagne and turned to stare out into the dark garden again. Let Lord Markham state his business and be done with her. She wasn't going to play along.

She felt his gaze upon her.

"I'd heard that you hardly ever lose, Your Grace. I've come to offer my apologies for spoiling your run."

She sensed the undercurrent of smug amusement in his voice. Yes, he was definitely an arrogant peacock.

Steeling herself against any further errant physical reactions, she angled herself toward him and summoned a slight smile that she hoped conveyed a lack of concern. "It's no matter," she lied.

His wide mouth tilted into a smile. "Hmm... Your brother didn't think you'd feel that way."

She bristled. "So Jonathon put you up to this," she accused, unable to hide the sharp note of irritation in her voice. "Well, it won't work, you know. I'm not interested in engaging in flirtatious banter as you make a futile attempt to woo me."

Markham lifted a dark eyebrow and the corner of his mouth quirked. "So cynical, Your Grace. But I like a challenge." He slid a little closer to her and sought her gaze. Even though the terrace was only dimly lit by patches of light spilling through the salon's main door and the softly glowing lanterns placed at strategic intervals around the garden, she thought she detected a sincere light in his dark gray eyes. "However, it seems I have put you out. Again, I apologize."

He paused and leaned a little closer, his shoulder touching

hers, the tantalizing scent of his expensive cologne wrapping around her. His breath warmed her ear. "Perhaps I could even offer you some recompense for ruining your winning streak. Make it up to you."

He was much too close. Georgie's mouth went dry and she fought the urge to take another sip of champagne. Instead, she placed the flute on the balustrade and faced him, readying herself to quit the terrace. "I assure you that's not necessary, Lord Markham. Besides, I'm certain that I wouldn't be interested in anything you had to offer."

"Are you sure?" His gaze pointedly fell to her lips before returning to her eyes.

She only just repressed a most unladylike urge to snort. "It sounds like whatever you have in mind would be rather more for your benefit than mine."

His mouth curved into a slow, sensual smile. "I'm sure it would be mutually beneficial. In fact, I promise you that you'll thoroughly enjoy what I'm offering."

Damn him. She realized that despite her urge to berate him for his audacity, part of her knew she probably would enjoy what he was so clearly proposing to do.

His gaze roamed over her face before dropping to her mouth again. He angled his head a little, moved imperceptibly closer. He was going to kiss her she was sure of it.

But then he drew back. Frustration as well as an unexpected surge of desire flared. "You're teasing me, Lord Markham."

"Just heightening your anticipation, trying to turn the odds in my favor. Besides, I'm still waiting to hear if you'll actually accept my offer of recompense. You won't be disappointed."

She shot him a heated, hopefully withering look. "You are so cock-sure of yourself."

He smiled and shrugged a wide shoulder, clearly unperturbed. "So?"

"So what?"

"May I kiss you, Your Grace?"

Georgie narrowed her eyes, resisting the urge to let her gaze drop to his suddenly all too tempting mouth. "I've a mind to say no."

"But you won't."

No, she wouldn't.

Markham knew it too. That utterly enticing, languorous smile appeared again and she felt breathless. Almost lightheaded. She grudgingly acknowledged that it had been a long time since she'd been so affected by a man. Been kissed by a man.

She was such a fool to crave something that could only be bad for her.

Markham closed the small distance between them and raised a hand to wind one of her brown curls around one long finger. "Beautiful," he murmured, watching it slide off before he gently brushed the back of his hand across her fevered cheek. Her breath caught and his gaze returned to hers. "You're nervous," he said, a note of surprise in his voice.

Georgie swallowed. Yes, she was. But she didn't want to acknowledge the real reason why. "We... I need to be discreet, that's all," she lied.

He frowned. "Of course." He glanced over to the salon door before he gently reached for her arm and drew her into a dark corner behind a screen of potted firs. Even that simple touch—his hand on the bare skin between her sleeve and glove —sent a strange shiver of heat through her.

Heaven help her. She mustn't be in her right mind to be letting him do this, drawing her closer, his large hands on her all but bare shoulders. And how strange that she suddenly wanted him to kiss her so very much. She closed her eyes—

raised her hands to his wide chest, and then felt his firm, warm lips angle across her own.

His kiss was surprisingly light at first, undemanding—it was almost as if he was anticipating she would change her mind. But it wasn't enough. It wasn't what he had promised. He was holding back, teasing her, provoking her.

Arousing her.

Without conscious thought, she leaned closer into him, inviting him to take more. At last, one of his hands rose to cradle the back of her head and he drew her closer still. She willingly yielded to the increase in pressure against her mouth.

Yes. Her lips parted on a sigh and his tongue entered to softly taste her. Warm, drugging desire began to heat her blood, pulse insistently between her legs. Now even this gentle exploration wasn't enough.

She could scarcely recall ever feeling this way before.

Needy, hungry. *Insatiable.*

She realized she wanted more. So much more.

Her hands curled into the lapels of his superfine jacket and she felt the kiss change again. Markham groaned against her mouth and pulled her hard against the long, hard length of his body. Then pushed her up against the wall. His tongue plunged farther, deeper and this time she answered with a bold sweep of her own tongue. Then another. Her hands tangled in his hair.

He tasted like cognac and heaven. He tasted like everything she used to desire.

Foolish, Georgie.

She abruptly pulled her mouth away, panting. Markham was breathing heavily too, the look in his eyes soft yet smoldering like hot, dark smoke.

He had been right about one thing. She hadn't been disappointed.

"So, Your Grace." Markham removed his hand from her

nape and ran a finger along her undoubtedly kiss-swollen lower lip. His gaze was intent, his voice a soft caress in itself. "Did I succeed? Are you appeased?"

Appeased? Georgie felt anything but appeased. She felt restless and ruffled. Reluctantly aroused. She pressed her lips together, not willing to concede her enjoyment. The man was already far too conceited for words. "It was just a kiss, Lord Markham." She started to disengage herself from his hold, but as she stepped back, he caught her gloved hand.

"So it's not enough then?" Markham raised an eyebrow in query as he lifted her hand to his lips. Even the light contact of his mouth through the silk of her glove seared her, deepened the hot ache inside her. "Perhaps more kisses are in order." He turned her arm slightly, then placed another teasing kiss just above the crook of her elbow, on the sensitive skin between her glove and silk sleeve. "I am at your disposal," he murmured softly, drawing her closer. Another kiss fell at the juncture between her neck and shoulder. "For whatever you require..." He rained a trail of light kisses from her ear, along her jaw, toward her mouth. "Or want..."

Dear Lord. Her bones might be as soft as melted candle wax and her skin aflame beneath Markham's assured caresses, but what her body wanted didn't matter.

What she *needed* was to get away.

She drew a shaky breath, trying but not succeeding to summon a voice that didn't quiver. "Really, Markham. You presume far too much." She pulled herself from his hold and thankfully, he let her go. She hardened her voice. "As if I'd even consider—"

"Georgie?"

Jonathon!

Markham sighed then muttered what she thought might be a curse. "Your brother has impeccable timing, Your Grace."

Georgie threw him a wry smile. "Yes, he does. I trust you'll be a gentleman and remain here until I've gone inside."

Markham smiled and inclined his head. "Of course." He caught her hand and kissed it as she attempted to brush pass him. "Until we meet again."

"I wouldn't count on such a circumstance eventuating, Lord Markham." Raising her chin and gathering as much icy hauteur about her as she could, given that her cheeks were flushed and her lips were kiss-bruised, Georgie pulled her hand away then stepped out from behind the screen of firs. "Here I am, Jonathon. I was just taking a turn about the terrace."

Jonathon raised an eyebrow as she approached him by the salon door. "Of course you were." A mischievous smile played about his lips. "I trust Markham has been keeping you entertained."

Georgie scowled and lightly swatted his arm. "Is that what you call it?" she snapped. "Well, I don't need *entertaining* by men like him, Jonathon. And I don't appreciate being lied to by you and the Maxwells. I've had enough of being a source of amusement to you all. Will lonely Georgie get a good swiving tonight because, Lord knows, she must need it?"

"Now, now, Georgie-bean." Jonathon took her arm to escort her back inside. "There is nothing wrong with a good swiving. And no one is laughing at you, just as no one set you up with Markham."

"Liar." Georgie held her ground. She hadn't finished with her brother, by any means. "You and Helena made me sit down to cards on the pretext of playing with Phillip and then he didn't show. Not only that, Markham all but admitted that you sent him out to placate me for losing, or some other such nonsense. You are all treating me like a child." She was so cross she wanted to stamp her foot, but she didn't, knowing it would appear just that—childish. "If Teddy were here..." She couldn't finish. She swallowed, tears suddenly stinging her eyes. *If Teddy were here right now, he'd be doubled over with laughter at my fit of temper, and in the process he'd have made me laugh at myself also.*

But then if Teddy were still here, none of this would have happened. He'd always known how much she despised rake-hells. And Jonathon knew very well that she did too.

Jonathon's expression sobered. "I'm sorry to have upset you, sis. It was only meant to be a bit of fun because there's been little enough of that of late. Surely you must agree. As for setting you up... I will admit that I did point Markham in your direction when I saw you step out here. But please don't blame our friends. Phillip was actually called away by Helena at the last minute. Little Phillipa is being particularly fractious tonight and they've sent for the physician, I believe."

"Oh dear." Georgie immediately felt a sharp twinge of contrition for assuming the worst about Phillip's withdrawal from cards. "I hope it's not too serious."

Jonathon frowned. "I'm not sure. But come inside, Georgie. Aside from being cold and wet, it's now windy out here and you haven't a shawl. We can't have you falling ill now."

Unspoken were the words, *like Teddy.* Teddy's sudden illness—a virulent ague—had descended without warning and had taken him within the space of a week last autumn. "I'm fine, Jonathon," she reassured her brother, all of her rancor suddenly dissipating like mist in the morning sun.

"Not quite." Jonathon reached up and pulled a fir needle from her hair. He smiled gently. "That's better."

Georgie blushed. "Thank you."

"You're welcome. Now why don't we get some supper? I'm famished."

She sighed heavily in resignation. "As you wish." As much as she wanted to leave, she couldn't without saying good night to Phillip and Helena. She prayed their daughter, who was only two, would be all right.

As Jonathon escorted her back into the noisy, glittering ballroom, she chanced a backward glance at the screen of firs. There was no sign of Markham. At least he had been a gentleman in that regard.

But would he be a gentleman next time they met?

Somehow, she rather doubted it.

Rafe leaned back against the wall, arms crossed, waiting for the delectable Georgie to quit the terrace with her brother before he emerged—like he'd promised. He could definitely do with another cognac right now. Aside from warming him—a chill wind had suddenly picked up—it would help to put out the fire surging through his veins straight to his cock. God, how fine had that woman tasted? And such a contradiction—positively glacial on the outside yet all fiery passion beneath. What he wouldn't do to have her underneath him. Or on top of him. Or whatever way she damn well wanted.

When he'd said *until next time*, he'd meant it.

Snatches of conversation between the duchess and her brother drifted to him on the wind. Her acerbic comment about the need for a good swiving would have been amusing except for the fact that she'd also hinted she was lonely. Many a true word was spoken not only in jest, but in anger. If he were a better man, he wouldn't file that tidbit away for future reference.

It certainly seemed that the Duchess of Darby was as multi-faceted as a diamond of the first water. But he was an expert at delving beneath layers, at unraveling mysteries. He knew she would be a challenge to seduce—or swive, as she'd so delightfully put it—but he was definitely up to the task.

Reprobate that he was, he was going to enjoy working out his plan of attack.

A sudden gust whipped through the dark garden. Shadows stirred and raindrops pattered from leaves onto the wet ground. Senses suddenly on high alert, Rafe squinted at a patch of darkness, perhaps inkier than the rest beneath the horse chestnut in the far corner. Had there been a flash of something paler against the black trunk? A movement separate from the swaying lower branches?

Stop starting at shadows, Markham. You're retired, remember? It's probably just a trick of the light. You're not in Madrid or Paris or St. Petersburg anymore.

But his instinct to investigate anything the least bit out of place was still strong. At the sound of the salon door snicking shut, Rafe eased away from the wall and keeping to the shadows, edged toward the balustrade, studying the darkness, but nothing else caught his eye. Perhaps it had just been a stray cat. The mews ran alongside that side of the garden wall. Nevertheless, the spy in him insisted that he should investigate further.

A squall of rain hitting the garden made his mind up for him. Lifting up his collar against the freezing droplets, Rafe made a quick dash toward the salon doors. Whatever, or whomever had been out there was going to get a soaking, that was for damn sure.

Searching the mews could at least wait until the rain stopped.

CHAPTER 3

J onathon escorted Georgie through the throng toward the supper room. "So, aside from feeling chagrined about being cornered by Markham, how are you coping with your loss at the card table?"

Georgie grimaced. "Everyone's talking about it, aren't they?" She hadn't failed to notice the susurration of voices behind fans, the turning of heads toward her and Jonathon as they passed by. The occasional smile of sympathy from someone she knew. Or smirk.

Jonathon smiled. "A little. But it's not every day that you see the Ice Duchess defeated so spectacularly. And by someone as mysterious as Markham. But don't worry"—Jonathon paused by one of the decadent buffet tables and began piling a plate with all manner of delicacies—"it's only because the *haute ton* have no one else to gossip about at the moment. Lobster patty?"

Georgie declined the proffered treat with a small shake of her head. She was still too out of sorts to even think about eating. "No thank you, dear brother. I think champagne will be sufficient." And it might make her feel less disgruntled.

She took a flute from a passing footman, then led Jonathon over to a small table and pair of chairs situated in a quiet nook beside a potted palm. She imagined that it wouldn't be long before some of their myriad acquaintances wandered over to pay their respects. Already, Georgie could see Lady Billington glancing their way as she simultaneously fussed over the attire of her two daughters; she was obviously making sure they were presentable.

Georgie sighed with a weariness that was bone deep. It was time to slide on her mask of composure again. To appear cool and collected when she felt anything but that.

Jonathon seemed oblivious to everything around them as he munched his way through his plate of hors d'oeuvres. "You know, these lobster patties are exceptional, sis. You really should try one."

A decided hush suddenly descended upon the whole gathering. Even the orchestra ground to a jarring halt.

Georgie craned her neck in attempt see what had caused such an astounding thing to happen. Jonathon, having no hesitation in being a busybody, stood up to peer into the next room. "It's Helena's brother, Lord Rothsburgh, and his new wife. They've just arrived." Jonathon smiled down at Georgie. "See, I told you it wouldn't be long before there was someone else to talk about."

The orchestra started up again as did the hubbub of excited conversation. The Marquess of Rothsburgh, renowned for being a great snubber of society, had set tongues wagging like mad when he'd wed the newly widowed Countess of Beauchamp, Elizabeth Harcourt. The *ton* was agog with the scandal.

Jonathon continued to unashamedly spy for Georgie. "Oh. It's all right. Phillip and Helena have reappeared and are chatting to them. Along with Markham and the equally scandalous Lady Rosemont." He slid her a glance and waggled his brows. "You might have some competition, dear sister. Shall we go and join them?"

As much as Georgie wanted to avoid Markham and his smug, knowing stare, now was as good a chance as any to bid adieu to Helena and Phillip. She really did wish to go home. Especially since Markham was still hovering around.

Catherine, Lady Rosemont, she knew next to nothing about—aside from a pack of malicious and quite outrageous gossip. It had been long rumored that the very beautiful, enigmatic Catherine had once been an "actress" who'd snared the attention of the elderly roué, the Earl of Rosemont. After only two years of marriage, the earl had passed away, leaving Catherine with a sizeable inheritance and a young son. Some elements of the *beau monde* even dared to whisper that Catherine was nothing more than a grasping jade—a woman who'd once been held in notorious Newgate Prison on suspicion of murder—so she must have had a hand in her husband's demise. Georgie had never been formally introduced to the woman, but she seriously doubted that any of the salacious tales were true. The last time she'd crossed paths with Lord Rosemont—and it would have been several years ago— he had the look of a man with one foot already in the grave.

"All right," Georgie agreed, standing and smoothing her skirts. She took one last sip of champagne before putting the glass aside. "Elizabeth is such a lovely thing. I should like to see how she is before we go. And as for Lady Rosemont, she is welcome to Markham."

Jonathon quirked a dark eyebrow as he offered his arm. "Giving up so soon?"

Georgie cast him a disdainful look before she placed her hand on his sleeve. "There's nothing to give up. I was never going to play along, no matter how much you and Helena wanted me to."

As they wended their way through the tight knots of chattering guests, Jonathon wisely steered the conversation to safer ground. "You know, I expect Elizabeth is much happier with Rothsburgh, despite all the gossip surrounding her. Her first husband was nothing but a scoundrel."

"Now that is something we can definitely agree upon," replied Georgie with a wry smile.

As they approached the small group—and Georgie steadfastly refused to make eye contact with Markham—she couldn't help but admire what a fine pair the marquess and his wife made. Swathed in diaphanous, silver-gray muslin and silk, and a mine's worth of diamonds, the fair-haired Elizabeth looked as ethereal as an angel. Lord Rothsburgh, impossibly tall and strikingly handsome—one might even say diabolically good-looking—stood close by her side, his dark gaze daring anyone outside their present circle to give him or his wife the cut direct.

Of course, he was nothing but charm personified when Georgie and Jonathon exchanged greetings with him and his new marchioness. As was Catherine, Lady Rosemont.

The elegant countess certainly commanded attention. Georgie was immediately struck by the confident glitter in Lady Rosemont's lavender-blue eyes as she scanned the room, and the slightly feline smile curving her lips whenever she regarded members of the opposite sex—including Lord Markham. Georgie couldn't help but revise her opinion of the woman. Perhaps some of the rumors about her—those related to her past profession—might be true after all. But then, surely Helena wouldn't have formed an attachment to the countess if she were actually guilty of the things whispered about her.

Phillip soon claimed her attention, diverting her thoughts. "I'm so sorry to have reneged on our game, Georgie," he said with a rueful grimace. "I hope you don't mind that Markham stepped in."

"Not at all," lied Georgie with a smile. Out of the corner of her eye, she could see Markham—to the other side of Jonathon—watching her. "We shall simply have to arrange a round between us another time."

Phillip returned her smile. "Most definitely."

Markham leaned her way, as if about to speak, but Georgie turned to Helena. If he wanted to flirt with a woman so badly, he should transfer his attention to Lady Rosemont. She was certainly casting a great deal of appreciative glances his way. "So Jonathon tells me that poor little Phillipa is unwell," she said to her friend. "I hope it is not too serious."

A slight crease appeared between Helena's elegantly arched brows. "Just a bad cold the physician thinks, compounded by the fact she's cutting another tooth. But with this infernally cold, wet weather we've had all year—and because it so easy to catch something dreadful in autumn—I just thought it would be best if..." Helena clutched Georgie's hand. "Oh, I'm so sorry. How inconsiderate of me to be blathering on so."

"It's all right, Helena." Georgie glanced briefly at Jonathon, but he was talking to Lord and Lady Rothsburgh and appeared not have noticed their line of conversation. Swallowing to ease the tight ache in her throat, she returned her gaze to her friend. "It is the season for it. And it never hurts to be careful. I pray that Phillipa is feeling better soon. Now, tell me all about how your charity work is going with the Widows of Waterloo Trust. I understand Elizabeth has now resumed her role as one of the patronesses."

As Georgie spent the next quarter of an hour chatting pleasantly to Helena and then Rothsburgh and Elizabeth—or Beth, as Rothsburgh now called her—it was clear how in love the marquess and his new wife were. The way they looked at each other, shared smiles and touched, anyone could see they were absolutely smitten.

Although she'd long ago sworn off the idea of ever finding

love, Georgie couldn't help but be a little envious of their happiness. But then, she'd had nine contented years being wed to the best friend one could ever hope to have, which was much more than others ever experienced in their married lives. She'd been fortunate—nay blessed—to have someone like Teddy in her life. She would always be grateful for what he'd done for her.

"It seems that luck is still smiling on me tonight. We meet again, Your Grace."

Georgie started at the sound of Markham's deep voice so close to her ear. Glancing about, she noticed—belatedly—that Jonathon had moved slightly away from the group and was now chatting with the Beau Brummel look-alike. Lady Rosemont had also drifted away and was conversing animatedly with another nearby group of gentlemen.

Hell and damnation.

"But not for long I'm afraid, Lord Markham," Georgie managed to return with a falsely polite smile. "Jonathon and I were just about to leave."

"Oh no, we weren't." Jonathon leaned back toward their group. "I've just challenged Lord Farley here to a few rounds of *vingt-et-un*. We might be a while. You should join the others, dear sister, and have a dance or two."

The expletive that flashed through Georgie's mind as she watched Jonathon and his newfound friend depart was much stronger than the last curse. Especially when she turned around to find Phillip and Rothsburgh escorting their respective wives out into the middle of the ballroom floor to ready for the next dance.

It seemed there was another attempt afoot to throw her and Markham together. She compressed her lips and clenched her fists, trying to stifle the uncharacteristic and unseemly urge to swear long and profusely at the whole lot of them.

She felt Markham's superfine clad shoulder imperceptibly

brush against hers, but she kept her eyes firmly fixed on the dance floor. By the positions being assumed by all of the couples, it appeared the next dance was a turning waltz. The music swelled—definitely a waltz. And there was no way on earth she was going to waltz with Markham.

"Would you care to dance, Your Grace?"

Georgie kept her gaze dead ahead. "I don't particularly like dancing." Why wouldn't the abominable man take the hint that she was not interested in furthering an acquaintance with him?

"Well, I suspect another round of cards is out of the question." Before she could even take another breath to respond, Markham gathered her into his arms and swept her onto the edge of the floor. "Or a good swiving."

A furious blush scorched Georgie's whole face. How dare Markham haul her about like this, and how dare he mention such a thing? "You were eavesdropping," she accused, barely aware that Markham was expertly steering her about the floor. The man literally made her blood boil. "You really have no manners or morals whatsoever."

Lord Markham grinned down at her. "Oh, how I love your tongue lashings, Your Grace."

A vivid memory of how his tongue had stroked and wound around hers not a half hour ago burst into Georgie's mind, and her blush spread downward, staining her décolletage as well. She must look like a beet.

Markham spun her in a particularly complex turn and she had to focus on her feet for a moment. She wouldn't focus on the fact that he'd also gathered her closer and one of his muscular legs had pushed indecently between hers.

"For someone who professes not to like dancing, you are exceptionally graceful," he said in a low voice. "Why won't you look at me?"

Because I'm afraid of men like you... Georgie quickly

buried the brutally honest thought and at last met his gaze, determined not to show how perturbed she really was. "Because you're insufferably arrogant and you irk me no end," she said instead with false sweetness as if bestowing a compliment rather than a blatant insult.

Markham's grin broadened, and he tightened his hold at the small of her back. "You didn't seem irked when I kissed you earlier. Perhaps we should go out to the terrace again."

∽

Georgie's eyes flashed with blue fire. "You're baiting me on purpose, aren't you?"

Rafe smiled. Yes, he was. And he really should stop torturing her. "I can't help it, Your Grace," he teased. "You look so delightful when you're ruffled."

To his surprise, Georgie's tight-lipped smile curved into a dazzling grin of triumph. "Aha, so I was right. That *was* your stratagem during cards—employing deliberate flirtation to put me off."

Rafe couldn't resist pulling her closer into him so their hips gently collided as he took a deeper than necessary step in another turn. "You mistake my motives for flirting," he murmured against her shell-like ear. "And besides, we're not playing cards anymore, are we?" The blackguard within him was gratified to feel her shiver in his arms.

"Well, you can put the thought of playing at anything else right out of your head, Lord Markham," she grated out, her smile now more of a forced grimace. "I'm tired of your games."

"What about my kisses?"

She turned her head away and looked down the room. "Ugh. You're impossible."

He couldn't help but chuckle. "I won't disagree."

They danced in silence for a while longer. Indeed, Georgie remained aloof and stiff in his arms as they made another whole circuit of the ballroom floor. Markham knew she was seething beneath her apparently calm exterior. Perhaps he had miscalculated and had pushed her too far. He realized, with an entirely unexpected pang, that he didn't want her to go.

He needed to come up with another tactic to keep her engaged.

The music came to an end with a flourish and Georgie immediately began to pull away. Rafe tightened his hold. "Play cards with me again, Your Grace," he said with grave sincerity. "On my honor, I won't flirt."

She arched an eyebrow, her expression imperious. "I don't think so. Two bouts of piquet and a waltz in one evening? I really don't want to become the main topic of tomorrow's scandal sheets." She took a decisive step away.

Markham reached for her arm and tucked it into his to escort her from the floor. "Coward."

She sucked in a shocked breath. "I beg your pardon?"

"I said you are a coward, Your Grace."

Her glare was scorching. "How dare you—"

"I didn't think you'd be the type to swoon at the prospect of a little gossip. You're just afraid that I'll beat you again." He began to steer her toward the end of the ballroom where the card room awaited, trusting his bait would have the desired effect.

"No. I'm not," she all but hissed. "Now that I've worked you out, I'm immune to your ploys and dubious charms, Lord Markham. I seriously doubt you could beat me a second time."

Rafe stopped outside the card room's entry and gave her his most charming smile. "Then play with me. I dare you..."

∾

He trounced her. Again.

She must be in some sort of nightmare.

Georgie stormed down the stairs onto the pavement in front of Latimer House, Jonathon following in her wake.

"Georgie... Wait."

She rounded on her brother, her silk skirts swirling and hissing about her legs. "I've waited long enough, Jonathon. In fact, I've been waiting to go all night."

"But it's drizzling and we're standing in puddles. At least wait in the vestibule until the carriage is brought round."

Georgie scowled at him. He spoke sense, but somehow that made her feel even worse. "I wouldn't care if I had to wait knee deep in the Thames. The idea of seeing any more of...of that man, even for a second—"

"I take it you mean me, Duchess?"

Markham. Here he was yet again, sauntering toward her like some large beast of prey. Why wouldn't he leave her be?

"I suppose you've come out to *appease* me a second time," she snapped, then immediately regretted her waspish behavior when Markham flinched. To her added mortification, tears pricked her eyes. It wasn't just the sting of humiliating defeat, or the fact she was continuing to behave like a fishwife that had her so distressed. It was the fact that she'd let a man like Markham affect her so badly, in ways she didn't want to think about. She swung away from him and Jonathon, and faced the street so they wouldn't see how upset she really was.

Thankfully, Markham kept his distance. "No, I was simply taking my leave as well, Your Grace. It has been an eventful evening."

Georgie ignored him and pulled her shawl more tightly around her shoulders. The rain was icy cold and she could feel it trickling down the back of her neck. She started to shiver.

Jonathon cleared his throat. "Would you like a ride, Markham?"

Georgie wanted to kick Jonathon, but she was saved from displaying more unseemly emotion by Markham himself. "Thank you, but no, Sir Jonathon. My residence is but a short stroll away. I bid you good night. And you too, Your Grace."

Georgie turned her head a little and inclined her head. She was relieved when she managed to reply without her voice cracking. "Good night, Lord Markham."

Just then, their carriage rounded the corner and halted before her. Steadfastly ignoring both the footman and Jonathon's outstretched hand to help her in, she lifted her damp skirts and climbed the steps herself. She didn't dare turn back to glance at Markham, although she fancied she could feel the weight of his all too perceptive stare upon her back.

The dark interior was indeed a welcome relief. She sank into the Moroccan leather seat, leaning her head against the squabs as she closed her eyes. A moment later she heard Jonathon settle himself on the seat opposite before he knocked on the front wall of the carriage to indicate to the coachman they were ready to drive on.

Thank heavens their Hanover Square residence wasn't far. She pressed a hand to her temple—her forehead had begun to throb in earnest. All because of Markham. She didn't want this attraction, this stirring of lust within her. Between her friends and her charities, her properties and affairs in general to manage, she had more than enough to fill her days and nights. She didn't want a man like Markham, or any man for that matter, to make her feel this way—like something was missing from her life. She suddenly felt as brittle and empty as the discarded champagne flute she'd left sitting on the Maxwells' terrace. And she didn't like it one little bit.

"Penny for your thoughts, sis?"

Georgie opened her eyes and sighed wearily, a shaky, rattling breath that clearly betrayed how close she was to tears. "There's nothing for it, Jonathon..." To her dismay, her voice trembled too. She took another quick breath, grateful for the near darkness inside the carriage. "I'm going to return to Harrow Hall tomorrow." The depths of Lincolnshire had been a much-needed sanctuary during her mourning period. There was no reason why it couldn't be again.

"Tosh. All because you lost a couple of piquet rounds to Markham? No one will care, Georgie. No one that matters. I won't let you disappear down a rabbit hole to lick your imagined wounds." Jonathon reached forward and squeezed her hand.

"You know it's not just about the cards." She paused and pulled her shawl tighter about her shoulders, as if wrapping herself up could somehow contain her pain. "Without Teddy..."

"You're worried that you'll be beset by unscrupulous suitors who think you're desperate for a man. Who'll use you and then discard you like yesterday's scandal sheets. I know, Georgie, believe me. But not everyone is like that bastard Lord Craven."

Georgie sucked in a sharp breath and her heart stuttered oddly. Painfully. A toxic combination of shame and fear roiled about in her belly and she had to swallow down a sudden wave of nausea. "Please don't mention that man's name to me," she whispered, her voice edged with such harsh bitterness, she almost didn't recognize it.

Jonathon sighed and he reached for her again, but she kept her hands clenched tightly in the damp silk at her chest. She was too furious and heartsick to even accept that small gesture of comfort.

"I'm sorry, Georgie-bean," he said softly and sat back again, clearly accepting that she'd retreated behind a wall of sullen anger. "That was unthinking of me. But I honestly don't think Phillip and Helena would have introduced you to Markham if he was a complete cad. Or worse."

Georgie snorted. "I'd never even heard of the man until he sat down in front of me and bold-as-you-please introduced himself. How much could Phillip and Helena really know about him? He could be exactly like Lord Cra—" She couldn't finish the word and she glared at Jonathon through a haze of hot, stinging tears. The light from a lamppost revealed his guilt-stricken face for a fleeting moment, and her heart twisted a little more—this time with her own remorse. Jonathon meant well, she knew that. She swallowed past the ache in her throat then drew in a steadying breath before attempting to speak in a gentler tone. "How much do *you* know about him?"

Jonathon's shoulders heaved with another weary sigh. "Only what Phillip told me, to be honest. Markham's recently become the heir to the Marquessate of Avonmore. His older brother, who was much given to living quietly in the country, passed away about a year ago without issue—a hunting accident—so Markham's now an earl and next in line for his father's title."

Georgie nodded. She only vaguely recalled the details of the marquess's son's death because it had occurred about the same time as Teddy's. But still... She frowned. Rafe Landsbury, the new Earl of Markham, was almost a complete stranger in the realm of the *haute ton*. And she was intrigued as to why that should be so. She knew nearly everyone. "That still doesn't explain why you and I have never laid eyes on him before tonight."

"Apparently Markham's been overseas in diplomatic service for some years. Russia, Sweden and the like. Though I believe he attended Cambridge at the same time as Phillip and Rothsburgh. However, he would have been known as Lord Rafe Landsbury then."

Georgie sighed and lessened her vice-like grip on her shawl. That piece of information reassured her a little. Perhaps Markham wasn't rotten to the core. But nevertheless, he was still very much a rake. And for that reason alone she should avoid him. One broken heart was enough for one lifetime. She'd never risk giving it to anyone again.

"Well, all of that hardly signifies," she replied stiffly, "as I'm not interested in cultivating any sort of relationship with another man. Least of all someone like him."

"Really?" Jonathon's voice quivered with sudden mirth. "Then why did you let Markham kiss you?"

Georgie huffed out an exasperated sigh. There was no point insisting that Markham hadn't kissed her when Jonathon had seen her emerge all flustered from the shrubbery-screened corner of the terrace with fir needles in her hair. As to why she'd let Markham talk her into such an encounter... No, she still didn't want to think about it. "It was the champagne and well... Markham is devilishly handsome." She was willing to concede that much. "But it was only one kiss. And that is all there will ever be between us."

"But what if you could have more? You might not want another husband but surely—"

"I don't need *more* of anything, Jonathon," she bit back. "Why won't you drop this subject? I don't want to talk about Markham any longer. Besides, I have a fiendish headache." She leaned back against the squabs again and rubbed her fingertips up and down along her temple to prove her point.

"All right. I'll drop it...for now. But promise me you won't hare off to Harrow Hall tomorrow. You need to rest by the looks of you. I pray you're not coming down with something after all."

"You are such the mother hen," Georgie chided but without any real venom this time. She opened her eyes and attempted a small smile. "And I promise I won't bolt. Not tomorrow, at any rate." She really did feel unwell. Shivery with an achy back, and the beginnings of a scratchy throat. Perhaps she had caught a simple chill. Probably from lingering on cold, wet terraces and standing in the rain. But she wouldn't mention how she truly felt because she didn't want to worry Jonathon unduly.

Jonathon reached out and touched her hand again. "Good."

Perhaps having a cold could work to my advantage, thought Georgie as they entered Hanover Square. She could hardly attend any social events if she was unwell. And then she could legitimately claim she needed to retreat to Harrow-on-the-Wold to take the country air.

With any luck, Markham would have disappeared to resume his mysterious overseas duties—whatever they may be —by the time she returned to London for the Season proper next year.

The carriage slowed and Georgie glanced out the window. By the glow of the streetlamps she could clearly discern the marble Corinthian columns flanking the portico of Dudley House, their rather grand four-story townhouse—an unentailed bequest from Teddy. The new Duke of Darby—a distant cousin of Teddy's—was apparently still living abroad and wouldn't be taking up residence in Darby House in Grosvenor Square until Christmastide.

After Georgie had alighted from the carriage, Jonathon took her arm. "It's lovely to see you smiling again," he said in a low voice as they ascended the stairs into the inviting warmth of the vestibule, "although I suspect it's not just because we're home."

Georgie arched an eyebrow as she shrugged off her wet shawl and handed it to Reed, their stalwart butler. "Oh? Whatever do you mean?"

"Despite what you said before, you're hatching an escape plan. I know it," he murmured after Reed had disappeared with their wet things.

Georgie yawned theatrically behind her gloved hand. "The

only place I'm escaping to right now is my bedchamber. Good night."

Jonathon's blue eyes suddenly twinkled with mischief. "Good night to you too, sis. I'm sure you'll have sweet dreams."

Georgie didn't miss his cheeky jibe. She sniffed then stalked off toward the stairs with as much poise as she could muster given her body was aching more with each passing moment. She'd send Constance, her maid, to fetch some warm milk or even better, an urn of hot water and her tea caddy so she could brew some of her favorite herbal tea, a special blend of chamomile and valerian that never failed to soothe her. Hopefully, she'd sleep soundly and have no dreams at all.

She certainly wasn't going to dream of the mysterious, odious, Lord Markham.

Well, at least she could lie to herself until she fell asleep.

CHAPTER 4

A fter the duchess's carriage pulled away, Rafe sighed then pulled up the collar of his greatcoat against the insistent, pattering rain.

The Duchess of Darby was royally mad with him. You didn't need to be an agent of the Crown or even a keen observer of people in general to notice that obvious fact. She'd been fairly sparking with anger. If he'd struck a match, he was positive the Ice Duchess would have flared up like a bonfire on Guy Fawkes night.

And he only had himself to blame. He'd kept his promise and had behaved with the utmost gentlemanly decorum throughout their second game. Even though she was undoubtedly a brilliant player, he'd read her as easily as the cards. Winning at piquet—whilst not quite child's play—had been a relatively straightforward exercise. But in the process, perhaps he'd lost his chance to win the duchess, even for a night.

He could be such a fool sometimes.

A sense of heavy disappointment settled over him as he made his way down the narrow laneway leading to the mews behind Latimer House. He could kick himself over his arrogant stupidity later when he got home. But right now, he needed to make sure that he really had seen nothing of concern in the garden.

Save for the weak glow of an oil lamp hanging at the very end of the lane, it was as dark as Hades. Rafe stepped with care —the cobblestones were slick and no doubt riddled with patches of mud and sodden horse dung. Whilst another lamp would have helped in his investigation, he also didn't want to draw attention to himself. After a good decade of skulking about in the shadows, staying hidden was still second-nature to him.

The low rumble of male voices—most likely grooms and carriage drivers—along with the general bustle and clatter of a busy stable, echoed off the surrounding walls. The mews would be packed with the horses and equipages of the Maxwells' guests. In fact, Rafe was surprised that there wasn't more activity in the lane, given the crowd attending the ball.

He ran his hand along the rough brick wall as he progressed, and about halfway along, he located what he'd been looking for—the garden gate, tucked away in an alcove. It was constructed of sturdy wood panels and reinforced with iron brackets and hinges—but it was unlatched. Even more concerning was the fact that the lock was broken—it was bent and hung at an odd angle.

Rafe frowned deeply, his skin prickling with unease. That was odd, decidedly odd. He was sure the Maxwells' gardener wouldn't leave the gate in such disrepair. It was an invitation to trouble. The gate had clearly been forced open. But why and by whom? Common footpads?

Perhaps. Or has someone been watching me? And the duchess...

Muscles tightening, eyes and ears straining for even the slightest hint of another's presence, Rafe pushed at the gate and it swung silently inward—the hinges were well-oiled, at least. He stepped through into the shadows beneath the dripping, horse chestnut canopy and studied the darkness. But there was no one. Whoever had been lurking here had gone.

He glanced toward the house. From the lights spilling from the French doors and nearly every window, he could clearly see the terrace was still deserted. The sound of chatting and bright laughter overlaid the dulcet tones of the orchestra —the ball was nowhere near to drawing to a close yet.

Rafe sighed and ran a hand across his face, wiping the chill rain from his eyes. Whilst part of him hoped he was simply being paranoid about the broken latch and what he thought he may have seen earlier in the garden, he couldn't let it rest. Accustomed to a life of subterfuge, being suspicious of others and trusting his gut instincts were integral parts of his nature.

He'd hoped that somehow he could leave the dark shadows of his past behind him. But maybe he couldn't. One thing was certain: he wouldn't let his desire to lead the life of an ordinary English nobleman compromise the safety of those he cared about. There was no excuse for naivety or stupidity. He needed to go back inside and speak with Phillip.

The mahogany longcase clock in the corner of Latimer House's library heralded the hour of one as Rafe took a seat in the leather wingback chair before the fire. The last guests had departed but an hour ago and he really should have been on his way too. But Phillip had insisted he stay for a drink. A tumbler of warmed cognac in one hand, Rafe looked over to his friend. "So all is secure now?"

Phillip nodded. "Yes. My head groom has put a temporary padlock in place and one of the burlier stable hands has been posted to keep watch until morning. At first light I'll send for a Bow Street Runner to investigate." He took a long sip of his own cognac before catching Rafe's eye again. "But I really wouldn't worry too much. I'm sure it's just the doings of a local thief. You should sit back and enjoy your retirement from His Majesty's service. Old Boney's safely locked away and his cronies—if they weren't killed or captured at Waterloo —have been driven to the four corners of the earth."

As long as one of the corners wasn't Mayfair. "Hmm. I'm trying, believe me." Even though Phillip worked for the Foreign Secretary, Lord Castlereagh, and was one of the few men who actually knew of his spying activities, Rafe thought his friend was being more than a little naïve. He sipped at his cognac, focusing on the searing heat at the back of his throat and the subsequent loosening of tension in his shoulders and limbs. "Old habits do tend to die slowly though," he added. *Like old enemies.* And Rafe would be a fool indeed not to realize he had a fair number of those.

Phillip's forehead creased into a deep frown. "I have no idea what you've really been up to for the last decade—I've only seen a few of your reports that have come through Castlereagh's office—but I imagine it would be difficult to put it all behind you."

You have no idea. Rafe raised his glass and studied the deep amber glow of the liquid against the firelight as memories he could never quite bury surged to the forefront of his mind— dark, shocking images of deeds enacted for king and country. The sharp stab of guilt for the unforgiveable hurt that had befallen others because of him. Things he would never forget, no matter how hard he tried. But like always, he easily feigned a nonchalance he didn't feel. "Certain things, yes." He shrugged and smiled at his friend. "But you learn to live with it. After all," he took another sizeable sip of his drink before continuing, "it was all for a good cause."

Phillip seemed to take him at his word. "Yes indeed. You are a true hero, Markham, yet only a few know it."

Rafe snorted. "Hardly. It's not like I fought in the Peninsular Wars or under Wellington at the Battle of Waterloo like our friend Rothsburgh. And all the rest he's had to endure. Now that's heroism for you."

Phillip nodded. "Agreed. He's lucky to have found a woman like Beth. He certainly deserves some happiness." He put down his cognac and leaned forward, his forearms resting on his thighs, his gaze intent. "Speaking of good women, tell me, what do you make of the Duchess of Darby? You did seem rather taken with her, don't deny it."

Rafe smiled. At last, the chance to discuss something—the someone—who truly interested him. Someone who could perhaps help take his mind off the past, at least for a little while. "She is... intriguing."

"Ha!" Phillip slapped his knee in triumph. "Helena was right. She said you'd be smitten by her."

"Did I hear my name?" Helena, her tall slender figure wrapped in a rich silk shawl, crossed the Turkish rug toward them. Rafe stood, but she gestured for him to be seated again as she took a seat on the sofa beside her husband. She laid her hand over Phillip's and smiled at him. "I hope you don't mind me interrupting."

"Of course not, my dearest. I'm surprised you're still up. Can I get you anything? A sherry, perhaps?"

Helena shook her head. "No, thank you. I've been up in the nursery with Phillipa, and at long last she has settled. But I'm too wound up to retire yet, so I thought I'd see what you were up to."

Phillip shrugged. "Just discussing this and that." He hadn't told Helena about the possible break in, then. He obviously didn't want to worry his wife when it could be nothing at all, especially when she was already anxious about their sick daughter. Rafe could understand that.

Helena smiled and her dark eyes twinkled as she shifted

her attention Rafe's way. "Hmm. This and that." She looked back at her husband and gave him a mock frown. "That's not a very polite way to speak about Georgiana though."

Georgiana. *Georgie*. Rafe wondered if the duchess would ever permit him to use her name, let alone touch her again. "I was just telling Phillip how much I enjoyed the duchess's company this evening."

Helena tilted her head, studying him. "I'm glad. You two would be good for each other, I think."

Rafe raised his eyebrows whilst Phillip gave a nervous laugh.

"Now, now, Helena," her husband chided. "Georgie and Markham have only just met. Though if it were up to you, you'd have them married off by Christmas, wouldn't you?"

"Whatever are you thinking, Phillip? A Yuletide wedding? Perish the thought." She threw Rafe an arch smile. "Everyone knows a *ton* bride must wed in the spring."

Rafe nearly choked on his cognac. Lady Maxwell was clearly not timid about making her opinion known. "Good Lord," he said at last when his voice had recovered sufficiently. "The duchess and I barely know each other. Besides, I'm not all that certain she reciprocates any interest."

Helena smiled, clearly amused by his discomfiture. "Of course she does. She just doesn't want to acknowledge it. And as for not knowing anything about her, I'm sure Phillip and I can remedy that. So ask us anything. Anything at all. All we ask in return is that you keep your newfound knowledge a secret. Georgiana is very dear to us and... Well, we just want to see that she is happy."

What a veritable hornet's nest of a statement. Rafe was sure he could make the duchess very happy if he could persuade her into his bed. But as for anything else... He simply smiled and inclined his head. "Of course. I definitely know how to keep confidences, Helena." He took another long sip of cognac, thinking on what he already knew and what he'd like to know about the duchess.

Everything, if he were honest with himself. She truly was the most fascinating woman he'd encountered in a long time.

He'd studied her as she'd chatted with Helena and her other friends before he'd swept her off for a waltz. She may have been frosty toward him, but she was clearly amiable with others and well-liked in return. When she smiled—really smiled—and laughed at quips her friends or her brother made, her eyes, indeed her whole lovely face lit up like the brightest of summer's days. He suddenly realized that he wanted her to smile at him like that.

But she obviously loathed rakehells. And for some unfathomable reason, he suspected she saw her fearsome reputation at cards as a way to keep men like him—interested men —at bay.

And he wanted to know why.

"The duchess's late husband. Tell me about him and their relationship," he said at length. Had she been married to a scoundrel who'd failed to give up his wild ways? He'd been away from England too long—he could scarcely recall a single thing that he knew about the former Duke of Darby.

Helena and her husband exchanged a speaking look before Phillip replied. "I don't know if you remember, but Darby was formerly known as Teddy Dudley, the Marquess of Harrow, when we were at Cambridge. He was a few years below us and, ahem...shall we say, shared a close acquaintanceship with Sir Jonathon Winterbourne, Georgie's brother."

"A *close* acquaintanceship. That's an interesting choice of words." Rafe frowned. Although he couldn't be sure, Sir Jonathon struck him as a man who was attracted to members of his own sex. He hid it well, but Rafe was sure he'd seen a keen light in Jonathon's eyes when he'd interacted with the young and very pretty Lord Farley in the ballroom, and then later when they'd played cards together.

Christ Almighty. What was Phillip suggesting?

Rafe fought to keep his tone even as the maddest of scenarios took shape in his mind. "Helena, please forgive me for bringing up such a delicate subject, but now that I think on it..." He turned to Phillip. He suddenly had more than an inkling that Georgiana's former husband hadn't been a rake at all. "When we were at Cambridge in our final year, wasn't there a rumor going around that Lord Harrow was partial to the company of other men? And I sense that Jonathon is that way inclined as well."

Helena laughed. "You don't need to beat around the bush on my account, my dear Rafe. Are you asking if Jonathon and Teddy formed an attachment?"

Rafe raised his eyebrows, more than a little surprised at Helena's directness. "Yes. I am."

Phillip cleared his throat. "They hid it remarkably well. But yes. You've come to the right conclusion. Teddy and Jonathon Winterbourne were—shall we say for the sake of propriety?—involved in a relationship. And not just at Cambridge. Afterward as well."

Bloody hell. Was Phillip implying that the Duke of Darby and Georgie's brother were lovers throughout the duchess's marriage? Rafe's mind reeled with the implications of such a revelation. He ran a hand down his face, then shook his head, struggling to take the astounding news on board. "I don't understand. Why on earth did the young Lord Harrow marry Georgie? I mean, nothing surprises me much anymore, but..." He set his cognac down on a side table. "Are you seriously telling me that the duke and Georgiana Winterbourne's marriage was one of convenience only?"

Phillip nodded, his expression deadly serious. "Yes."

Why in God's name would she—or any woman—agree to

such an arrangement? Rafe stood then paced toward the fire-place. Bracing his arms against the mantel, he stared down into the leaping flames. *Poor Georgiana. Only living half a life for the last decade. Just like me...*

He turned back to his friends, frowning. "I'm mystified as to why you would openly share such personal information about Her Grace with me."

Helena glanced at her husband before her solemn gaze returned to meet his. "Because we trust you, and given your background and experience in diplomatic affairs, we suspect you would be more understanding of Georgie's situation than others. That you wouldn't judge her for choosing to lead a different type of life." Her wide mouth curved into a knowing smile. "Besides that, Phillip and I rather thought you might be looking to settle down now you have returned to England. And you may correct me if I'm wrong, but I strongly suspect the usual pretty young things flooding the marriage mart at Almack's wouldn't be your cup of tea."

Rafe gave her a wry smile. "You are not wrong at all."

Silly, eighteen-year-old virgins were of no interest to him whatsoever. Of course, the life he'd led up until this point had made it impossible to cultivate any kind of lasting relationship with any woman. Brief, uncomplicated liaisons with courte-sans or widows had been *de rigueur* for him. Then there had been the affairs with wives of certain individuals of interest. Those entanglements Rafe didn't want to think about. At all.

But he'd never fallen in love. That was a luxury he'd never been able to indulge in.

Until now. Perhaps...

When he'd first spied the Duchess of Darby this evening, he'd seen her as nothing more than another conquest. Another beautiful woman to take to his bed for a short while before moving on. But what if he could have something more with her? He was right in his earlier summation—Georgiana had

47

many facets. And secrets. The more he learned about her, the more determined he was to work her out. To know her.

But love her?

He was getting ahead of himself, thinking about love. He wasn't the type to be completely besotted at the bat of a pretty eyelash. And he suspected the duchess would rather walk across broken glass than see him again.

He returned to his seat and downed the last of his cognac. "I have one last question before I go."

Phillip inclined his head. "Ask away."

"I don't suppose you know—or that you'd tell me—why Georgiana agreed to wed Teddy, knowing that he was committed to her brother and not her?"

Helena met his gaze directly. "I think it would be best if Georgie shared that information with you. But don't think for a minute that she wasn't content with the arrangement. Teddy and Georgie... They cared deeply for each other. They were the best of friends."

Rafe nodded. Friendship was all well and good, but to turn away from love—physical love—there had to be a very good reason for the young Georgiana Winterbourne to have made such a significant decision. Someone had hurt her. A rake. And he'd hurt her deeply. Rafe would stake his life on it. And for some reason he didn't want to examine too closely, he felt compelled to discover more about her past. "Whoever it was that broke her heart, I will find out," he stated with soft, deadly assurance.

Helena paled. "Rafe. It was a long time ago. She doesn't need a champion. She needs..."

"Someone to care for her?" Rafe smiled. "I can but try my friends. I must say though, after tonight, I'm certainly not in the duchess's good graces."

Helena's eyes twinkled with mischief. "Send her flowers in the morning. Pink roses are her favorite. I will send a footman to your townhouse with the direction to the best florist in London." Her smile took on a sly tilt. "And Georgie's address. I'm sure she will give you a second chance."

Rafe inclined his head then stood to take his leave. "Thank you. Now, I really should bid you both adieu. It is half past one and well past everyone's bedtime, I should think."

Phillip saw him out.

Shrugging on his greatcoat again, Rafe waited until the night footman had retreated to a discreet distance before speaking to his friend. "When you send for a Runner, ask for John Townsend and mention my name. He will take the matter seriously."

Phillip's eyebrows shot up in surprise. "You know John Townsend? Doesn't he arrange protection for the King, Prince Regent and his family?"

Rafe kept his expression neutral. "Amongst other things." He didn't mention that Townsend had recently sought him out to act as a consultant on matters of royal security. It seemed he was only semi-retired at the moment. He patted Phillip on the shoulder. "Now go, man. Your wife and a warm bed awaits you. I shall see you much later."

As the door closed behind him and Rafe strode out into the cold, wet night again, he wondered if he would ever be fortunate enough to have Georgiana in his bed. Helena had not so subtly intimated that he could even be the one to make her happy.

Only time would tell if he and Georgiana were suited— and if either one of them would be willing to take a chance and fall in love. But sending the Ice Duchess roses seemed like a good place to start.

CHAPTER 5

R oses. He'd sent her dark pink roses—too many to count. The bouquet was so large the footman had struggled to bring it into the morning room of Dudley House.

Georgie sat in her favorite shepherdess chair before the fire, staring open-mouthed at the ridiculously large arrangement on the cherrywood sideboard for at least a minute before she crossed the room and reached for the parchment envelope with trembling fingers. What on earth was Lord Markham thinking by sending her such a gift? To say the man was wildly extravagant was an understatement.

He's attempting to seduce you, Georgiana, you dolt. It's nothing more than a rake's ploy to charm his way into your bed. She swallowed past her still scratchy throat, took a deep breath then pulled out his brief, hand-written note.

Dear Duchess,
I assure you, these roses have not been sent with the intention to appease.
They are for your pleasure alone.
Markham

Humph. She'd been right. He was a cock-sure devil. There was no mistaking Markham's not so veiled reference to their kiss and the attendant physical pleasure associated with it. She should cast his offering onto the cobbles outside and throw his more than forward card into the fire.

"Hey ho, sis," Jonathon called as he strolled into the room, looking particularly stylish in his latest purchase from Savile Row. When his gaze fell on the roses, he raised an eyebrow then grinned. "Well, what do we have here? Flowers from a not-so-secret admirer, if I'm not mistaken."

Georgie tucked Markham's note into the sleeve of her lavender-hued morning gown before tugging her pale gray cashmere shawl about her shoulders. Although she still felt unwell, she'd made the effort to rise and get dressed so she wouldn't worry Jonathon. "Yes, they're from Markham," she confirmed. "But judging by the color of the roses, I imagine Helena's had a hand in this as well." Georgie didn't know whether to smile or scowl at her friend's blatant meddling.

"They are quite impressive, you must give Markham that." Jonathon stroked one of the soft petals before he turned back to her, his brow furrowed with concern. "Are you all right, Georgie-bean? You sound a trifle croaky today."

Georgie cleared her throat. "I think I've caught a bit of a chill." She forced a bright smile. "Nothing to worry about, I assure you. A few days' rest, plenty of tea, and I shall be quite fine." She ran her gaze over her brother's walking apparel—a pale gray tailcoat and powder blue and silver-striped waistcoat were paired with ivory breeches tucked neatly into shiny Hussar boots. "I'm afraid I won't be able to join you for our usual stroll in the Park though."

Jonathon took a few steps closer and felt her forehead. "Hmm. You are a little warm. Perhaps I should send for the physician."

Georgie caught his hand and pressed it between her own.

"It's nothing, truly. I've just been sitting by the fire too long. Now go, before it begins raining again." She arched an eyebrow. "Besides, you don't want to keep Lord Farley waiting, do you?"

Jonathon chuckled. "Am I that predictable?"

Georgie smiled back. "Yes. But we *are* twins. I always know what you are thinking."

"Which is why I'm convinced that you're probably still planning to decamp to Harrow Hall on the pretext of needing the country air to recover from your case of the sniffles." Jonathon raised an admonitory finger when Georgie began to protest. "Now, don't try to deny it. I know you desperately want to avoid Markham. Especially now he's obviously paying court."

Georgie scowled. "He knows very well I don't want him to. He's more persistent than a fox in a hen house. Lord knows what the gossipmongers are saying this morning about us."

Jonathon smiled as he pulled on a pair of gray kid gloves. "Trust me, there's barely a mention of your exploits from last night in *The Times*, or the scandal sheets being passed about on the streets this morning."

Georgie groaned and buried her face in her hands. "I don't want to know."

"There, there, Georgie-bean. I understand if you need to go to ground for a few days until someone else becomes the favorite topic for the latest *on-dit*." Jonathon patted her shoulder. "Just promise me again you won't up and leave."

Georgie dropped her hands before clasping them behind her back. "All right," she said with a resigned sigh. "I promise."

Jonathon's eyes narrowed with suspicion. "Now promise again but uncross your fingers. Don't think for a moment that I can't tell what you're doing."

Georgie only just resisted the childish impulse to poke out her tongue before she held up her hands so he could see her fingers. "I promise to stay here in London. Happy now?"

Her brother smiled. "Yes. Now why don't you take a seat by the fire again and I'll order some tea for you before—yes, Reed?"

Their butler hovered near the open door. "Excuse me, sir. Your Grace. Lady Maxwell has called to see the duchess." Reed turned in Georgie's direction. "I encouraged her ladyship to leave her card, ma'am, but I'm afraid she's most insistent on seeing you."

Georgie sighed. There was no putting off Helena—she could be like a force of nature. Besides, there really was no point in delaying the inevitable examination of each and every detail related to the ball...especially Georgie's encounter with Markham. "Show Lady Maxwell in, Reed. I shall receive her here. We shall take luncheon as well."

Reed bowed. "Very good, Your Grace."

Jonathon began to take his leave also. "As much as I would like to stay and join in your *tête-à-tête* with Helena, I will bid you adieu as Lord Farley awaits." He kissed her forehead. "Don't be too harsh on her for her attempts at match-making. She cares for you like a sister, you know."

Georgie gave a wry smile. "I know."

Within a matter of minutes, Helena was ensconced in the matching shepherdess chair positioned directly opposite Georgie's. Smartly dressed in a walking ensemble of claret wool trimmed with black, military-style frogging, and a beaded black reticule on her arm, she was the epitome of elegance. Georgie, on the other hand, dressed as she was in one of the gowns she'd worn during half-mourning with only her shawl, a crumpled kerchief and a red nose as her accessories, felt quite the frump. However, she had little time to dwell on her wardrobe's shortcomings.

"So, tell me what you think of Lord Markham," Helena

53

began without preamble, her dark brown eyes dancing with mischief. "Isn't he one of the handsomest men you have ever seen? And obviously taken with you." She waved her hand toward the roses. "I've never seen such beautiful blooms."

Georgie stifled the urge to groan. It seemed her interrogation was to begin even before the tea arrived. But she wasn't going to be the only one subjected to an examination. Helena had a bit of explaining to do. She narrowed her eyes. "How do you know that it was Lord Markham who sent them?"

Helena only flushed a little as she continued to meet her gaze. "Well, it's obvious isn't it? I mean, he did play cards with you twice. And waltz. Why, the man couldn't take his eyes off you. It's even in *The Times*."

Georgie curled her fingers into the ivory brocade covering the arms of her chair. "Hmph. It must be true if it's in *The Times* then." She glanced over to the flowers before settling her gaze on Helena again. "Strange how he knew pink roses are my favorite."

Helena's blush deepened. "Yes... Well—"

At that moment, a pair of chambermaids appeared with the tea trolley laden with a Wedgwood tea set, a silver urn and tea caddy, and plates bearing an assortment of cakes, biscuits and sandwiches. Once everything had been deposited on the low table gracing the hearthrug between herself and Helena, Georgie dispensed the tea for both of them. She was about to take a fortifying sip from her own cup when Helena surprised her with a question.

"Why do you dislike him—and others like him—so much, Georgiana?"

Georgie put down her tea untasted. The cup rattling against the saucer revealed all too well how perturbed she was by Helena's question. She glanced to the door to make sure it was fully closed—it wouldn't do for any of the servants to overhear their conversation. "I don't know what you mean."

Helena put down her cup as well. "Of course you do, my darling friend," she said softly, the expression in her eyes gentle. "The only time you give a man like Lord Markham a glance is when he's sitting across a card table from you. And even then, it's usually with cool calculation in your eyes."

Helena was being kind. It was more likely to be a look of disdain. But Georgie only shrugged. "I like to win." Her mouth lifted into a rueful smile. "Or at least I did until last night."

Helena inclined her head, studying Georgie's face. "Markham rattled you, didn't he? More than anyone has before."

That was true. Georgie couldn't deny it. "Yes. But perhaps it's because I'm widowed now. I must confess to feeling quite vulnerable without Teddy by my side."

Helena laughed. "You mean, you don't have your personal guard dog with his razor-sharp wit and hard black stare scaring any potential suitors off anymore." Her brow suddenly creased in thought. "All the years of your marriage, you never did take a lover, did you?"

"No." Helena was perhaps the only person in the world—apart from Jonathon—who would dare venture such a personal question. Indeed, Helena and Phillip were the only friends who'd known about the true state of her marriage. And the clandestine—illicit—relationship between her husband and Jonathon. There were few who could be trusted with such a powder keg of a secret.

Georgie fiddled with the tassels at the end of her shawl and stared into the fire as she spoke. "To be perfectly honest, I occasionally contemplated the idea. Teddy and Jonathon even suggested that I should find someone. They reasoned that it wasn't unusual for a married woman of some years to do so. Aside from that, Teddy assured me that he wouldn't have minded in the least if I'd produced an heir that wasn't actually his. But in the end I just couldn't." Georgie couldn't disguise the sudden rough edge to her voice. Clearing her throat, she reached for her tea, blinking away sudden tears as she took a careful sip. She had lost so much. Too much. And all because of a scoundrel of the worst kind.

The worst part—the part that hurt the most and still kept her awake and fretful in the dead of night—was that she didn't know if she would ever recover what had been stolen from her. Even after a decade.

But what if Lord Markham was her remedy? *Remember his kiss, Georgiana. How he made you feel deep inside. Alive.* Her cheeks burned so fiercely as she recalled the feel of his mouth and hands on her, she had to take another large sip of her tea to mask her unease. Or was it sexual frustration?

"Georgie, darling," Helena said softly. "I don't know who wronged you, or how exactly, but I'm sure Lord Markham is different. Phillip has known him for quite some years and swears he is a man of honor. A good man. He is not the rogue you suppose him to be. You should give him a chance."

Georgie bit her lip to stop her lower lip trembling. Helena saw far too much. She drew in a shaky breath and shook her head. "Despite what you or Phillip say, I don't think I can. Markham's far too..." Too arrogant, too clever, too devil-may-care, too handsome.

Too dangerous. She lifted her chin, determined to make Helena understand she would not be swayed. "He's not the type of man I would consider a suitable suitor."

Helena sighed heavily and picked up her tea again. "Pity. I happen to know that despite appearances, and what you may have heard, he is looking to settle down in England. And he has quite a sizeable income and inheritance headed his way— not that you need worry about that—but he's certainly not a fortune hunter. So perhaps he's more suitable than you think."

Oh. Georgie frowned. "Jonathon told me he was in diplomatic service in Russia or perhaps it was Sweden. At any rate, I assumed he would be returning to his post before winter set in."

Helena smiled at Georgie over the rim of her cup. "No. He's here to stay. His days gallivanting about the Continent—and gallivanting about in general—are well and truly over, I'd say."

Georgie leaned forward and absent-mindedly selected a piece of shortbread then placed it on her plate. *Damn and double damn.* Markham would probably be dogging her heels until she left London. Her cold was definitely about to become much worse. Pulling her lawn handkerchief from her pocket, Georgie raised it to her nose and sniffed delicately.

"Oh, my dear. Are you all right?" asked Helena, her brow furrowing with concern. "I thought you sounded a little under the weather. I hope you haven't caught the same cold as Phillipa."

Georgie sighed for effect. "I'm sure it's nothing but I should probably rest for at least the next few days." *Or weeks. Perhaps months.*

"Of course. And I should go." Helena put down her cup and reached inside her reticule. "You must get better so you can attend the dinner party I have planned for next week. A small, intimate affair." She handed Georgie a heavily embossed ivory envelope bearing the Clan Maxwell family crest and Helena's initials—her personal stationary. A mischievous smile quivered on her lips. "Markham shall be there. As well as a card table or two."

Georgie took the proffered invitation as if it were an offering of hot coals. "It's a *fait accompli* isn't it? You really are quite determined to pair us off."

Helena laughed. "Guilty as charged. But I only have your best interests at heart."

Georgie would like to debate that, but for now, she chose not to. A sudden wave of weariness washed over her and another headache was beginning to pulse in her temple.

"You can beat him, you know."

Georgie sharpened her gaze on her friend's face. Trust Helena to choose exactly the right type of lure to tempt her. "How?" Headache or not, she was burning to know.

Helena's mouth curved into an enigmatic smile. "I have a plan."

CHAPTER 6

Latimer House
A week later...

Inwardly ruing the need to keep a clear head, Georgie accepted a glass of ratafia from one of the Maxwells' footmen, all the while wishing it was champagne or even claret she was drinking. Maybe then the sudden pounding of her heart and the unfamiliar feeling of breathless anticipation in her throat would ease. Perhaps her cheeks wouldn't be aflame and her skin wouldn't tingle with awareness. For across the room, standing in the doorway to the drawing room, was Lord Markham. And despite the fact that Helena and Phillip were in the process of greeting him, he was looking directly at her. The intensity of his gaze followed by the sudden flash of a roguish smile triggered a shiver—a strange combination of arousal and fear—that coursed through her entire body. Tightened her belly. He reminded her of a hungry lion sizing up his next meal.

God in heaven, she should run now. She had foolishly thought she was fully prepared for this encounter. But she wasn't. Not at all. In the space of a week she had forgotten how devastatingly handsome the man was. How the very air around him seemed to vibrate with a strange energy, giving an overwhelming impression of leashed power barely contained beneath an urbane façade and superbly cut evening wear.

Stop imagining things, Georgiana. Perhaps the ratafia had been laced with something stronger than brandy—an opiate of some kind. With a trembling hand she deposited the barely tasted drink onto the tray proffered by another nearby footman. She clearly wasn't in her right mind. But she needed to be if she was to have any hope of salvaging her tarnished card-playing reputation. And sanity.

Jonathon's hand was at her back. "Breathe, Georgie-bean," he murmured into her ear. "Markham won't bite, you know." He suddenly chuckled. "Well, maybe he will considering how scrumptiously dressed you are this evening. I swear you are making *me* blush. And you know I don't blush easily."

"Be quiet, Jonathon," Georgie hissed under her breath as she attempted to feign a composure she did not feel in the least. She'd regretted Helena's plan from the moment she had donned this ridiculously risqué gown in her bedchamber at Dudley House. The burgundy satin clung indecently to her curves and barely covered her plumped up breasts; she looked more like a courtesan than a duchess of the realm. "With comments like that, you are *not* helping."

She tore her gaze from Markham's strangely spellbinding stare and searched the elegantly appointed drawing room for someone else to speak with. To distract her. Phillip and Helena had only invited a relatively small number of guests for tonight's dinner—perhaps a dozen couples in total—most of whom she knew. Lord and Lady Rothsburgh chatted with Baron Dunwood and his wife, but they were too close to the Maxwells and Markham on the other side of the room. However, not too far from where she and Jonathon currently lingered by the white marble fireplace stood Lord Farley and an attractive, fair-haired woman who looked to be in her early twenties. She so obviously resembled Farley in coloring and features, the pair must be siblings.

"We need to circulate," Georgie whispered to Jonathon with an urgency she couldn't disguise. "Introduce me to Farley's sister. Now." Markham was headed in their direction and she didn't want to speak with him. Not until she absolutely had to—hopefully much later during a round of post-prandial piquet. A game she would win. Somehow between now and then she needed to regain some of her much-vaunted composure.

"You can't elude him forever, you know," said Jonathon as he took her arm and escorted her toward their intended conversational partners. "He wants you. "

"Don't be vulgar, Jonathon," she scolded before assuming her polite social smile in preparation for the introductions to Farley and his sister.

She resisted the strong, almost overwhelming urge to glance back at Markham. The real reason for her shaken equilibrium—if she were brutally honest with herself—was that perhaps, she wanted him too.

Incomparable.

That was the word that had immediately sprung into Rafe's mind the moment he'd laid eyes on the Duchess of Darby this evening. She had, quite literally, taken his breath away. He'd heard via the Maxwells that she'd been indisposed with a chill for several days following the ball, but tonight she looked absolutely stunning. *Provocative.*

His gut told him she was up to something.

Now, as he observed her—she sat diagonally opposite him

at the vast dining table—there was no doubt in his mind whatsoever. For a woman who professed to eschew rakehells, it seemed decidedly odd that she'd worn such a revealing gown; a gown that would obviously invite male attention—especially from men like him. Yet her manner, toward him at least, had been completely standoffish throughout the entire dinner service.

It was as though she'd set out to deliberately tease him: *You may look at me, but don't address me. You may desire me, but I despise you.*

If it was her intention to drive him wild with wanting what he couldn't have, she was succeeding.

Indeed, over the last few hours it had taken every ounce of self-control he possessed to prevent his cock from hardening at the sight of her. He thanked God he was seated with a napkin over his lap. With her glossy, spun-sugar brown hair piled into an artful arrangement of curls, and her full, rounded breasts almost spilling from the neckline of her lush red gown, he felt like he was dining in the presence of the goddess Aphrodite. Or perhaps Artemis, the feisty huntress, would be more accurate.

His mouth quirked into a slight smile. On another, less sexual level, her continued ire secretly amused him. From the way the duchess's sapphire blue eyes darted fire whenever she glanced at him through the space between the silver candelabra and a rather elaborate floral centerpiece, he could tell she hadn't yet forgiven him for his behavior at the Maxwells' ball. Or the fact he'd defeated her at the card table. The roses obviously hadn't soothed the sting. Not that he'd really expected them to.

Yet even though the duchess was clearly as cross as a hellcat with him beneath her aloof exterior, he was still determined to have her. The question was, how the devil was he even going to engage her in conversation at this point, let alone attempt to seduce her, given she continued to openly snub him?

He sipped at his claret, contemplating his stratagem. There would be no dancing this evening. And he doubted she'd take a turn about the room with him after dinner. Or the terrace. So all that he could feasibly do was invite her to play piquet with him again. On his arrival, he'd noted that several card tables had been set up at one end of the drawing room. Surely challenging the duchess to another bout to win back her crown would appeal to her pride, if nothing else. He could but try.

Perhaps sensing his speculative gaze, the duchess—Georgiana—suddenly flicked him a glance from beneath her long dark lashes. He cocked an eyebrow and bright color flooded her cheeks.

Interesting. Although she'd been pretending otherwise, she was undoubtedly aware of his avid attention. Maybe he wasn't quite dead in the water yet. Holding her gaze, he reached for his glass of claret again, then ventured a smile at her over the rim as he took a sip. And for one long moment she didn't look away.

Christ, she's beautiful. Rafe's heart rate kicked up a notch as her telltale blush spread all the way down to her bountiful breasts. When he deliberately lowered his gaze, he swore he could see her nipples hardening beneath the satin of her bodice. Was she even wearing stays? His cock jerked in appreciation and his smile widened. Oh yes, the Ice Duchess wasn't completely immune to him.

He could hardly wait for dinner to be over.

"It is such a pleasure to see you again, Your Grace. You are looking well this evening."

And so the game began. Strategically installed on a velvet upholstered chaise-longue by the fire, slightly apart from the other ladies of the company, Georgie willed herself to take slow, even breaths when she lifted her gaze and smiled up at Markham with deliberate nonchalance. "Thank you. And may I say, so are you, Lord Markham."

He smiled. "You may."

Ever since the ladies had retired to the drawing room to let the gentleman dally over their port, she'd been steeling herself for this moment. And she was inwardly pleased that she'd managed to reply to Markham without blushing or stammering. She just prayed that she could remain as cool as a cucumber in his presence throughout the remainder of the evening. And that Helena's dashed plan to beat Markham at cards would work.

But remaining calm was easier said than done when Markham's blatantly admiring gaze roamed over her indecently exposed bosom. *Don't you dare lose your nerve now, Georgiana. Isn't this what you wanted? Markham to be hopelessly distracted by you?*

Yes, but she had not counted on the effect his focused interest would have on her. A warm, heavy ache pulsed between her thighs and she shifted uneasily on her seat.

Lord Markham's eyes immediately lifted to meet hers; something like triumph flared in their dark-gray depths and he smiled like a cat who hadn't just found a saucer of cream, but had been presented with an entire pitcher. He was enjoying the fact he'd made her flustered far too much. Somehow she had to turn the tables. Say something clever and amusing.

But what? She suddenly felt as caper-witted as a kitten. To her added chagrin, Markham spoke first. "I was sorry to hear from Lady Maxwell that you have been...indisposed following the ball last week," he said in a low voice clearly meant for her ears only. A lover's voice.

A flush warmed Georgie's cheeks. Curse the man's confidence. But she mustn't show any more weakness. He was the one who was supposed to be thrown off balance tonight, not her. She tossed her curls and drew in a deep breath, yet again drawing Markham's attention to her chest. "Just a tiresome cold, but I am now fully recovered." She smiled and looked up at him through her eyelashes just as Helena had suggested. "I must thank you for the roses you sent. They were both beautiful...and pleasurable. As you intended."

Markham's eyebrows shot up in surprise before he quickly recovered his composure. He inclined his head, amusement sparking in his eyes. "My male pride is appeased, Your Grace."

Georgie's breath snagged in her throat. Dear Lord. The man was too handsome for words, even with his facial scars. They marked him as a man of action—a man who quite possibly was too much for her to handle. What madness had possessed her to make her think she could actually flirt with him like this? Let alone gain the upper hand? She was clearly out of her depth. Somehow, with a great effort of will, she made her voice work. "I'm glad."

Markham smiled but then his gaze slid from her face and began to wander about the room. He suddenly seemed withdrawn. Preoccupied. Unexpected panic gripped Georgie's chest as an awkward silence descended between them. Surely he couldn't have lost interest in her already? But what if he had? What if he was seeking out another diversion—or someone else like Lord Farley's sister, the very pretty Lady Lucinda Tisdale—to entertain him? What if her utterly ridiculous plan to vanquish Markham in this underhanded way was all for naught?

But then, how arrogant it was of her to assume she would be able to retain Markham's undivided attention. *He was a rake, after all.*

The thought stung her feminine pride, more than she

cared to admit. She should feel beautiful and desirable and powerful in this *couture* version of a Cyprian's gown but instead she suddenly felt like a shabby fraud—someone undeserving of Markham's admiration. Perhaps she should make her excuses and go before she embarrassed herself further. She couldn't continue this farce of pretending to be someone she wasn't.

Beneath the cover of her burgundy silk skirts, Georgie clutched the edge of the velvet seat as a surge of bitterness she thought was long buried rose up inside her. *Damn Lord Craven to the hottest corner of Hades for all eternity for making me feel less than I ought to be. That I'm somehow lacking as a woman.*

But why in God's name was she even thinking about that contemptible excuse for a man right now?

Closing her eyes, she desperately tried to ignore the familiar swirl of anguish and anger in the pit of her stomach at the mere thought of him; tried again to crush the insidious memory of him to dust and scatter it like ashes in the wind.

Markham was not like him. She had to believe that.

And she was the Duchess of Darby. The ghost of her own self-doubt be damned as well. She was worth Markham's—indeed any man's—attention. And tonight, she intended to have it.

"Are you all right, Your Grace?"

Georgie's eyes flew open. Markham watched her, concern creasing his brow.

She sucked in a shaky breath and forced herself to smile. "Yes. Of course," she replied with false brightness. She took a moment to smooth her skirts then somehow rose with studied grace from her seat. "I think perhaps it is a little too warm by the fire. Perhaps we could take a turn about the room...or play cards?"

She quickly scanned the drawing room as Markham had

done. By now, everyone else had split off into various groups. Lord Rothsburgh and the Dunwoods were gathered about the pianoforte, listening to Lady Rothsburgh as she played a rather complicated nocturne. Jonathon chatted with great animation to Lord Farley, Lady Lucinda and their aunt, Lady Talbot, by the doors leading out to the terrace, whilst at the far end of the room Helena and Phillip played a rowdy game of loo with the quite jovial, newly wedded couple, Lord and Lady Palmerston.

Markham offered Georgie his arm. "Duchess, I was also going to suggest we play piquet again. However, after last week, I wasn't certain how such an invitation would be received."

"Well, worry no more, it is received with pleasure." Georgie smiled—a coquette's smile, she hoped—then placed her bare hand on Markham's forearm. Even beneath the layers of fabric she could feel the firmness of taut muscle and bone. The memory of those same strong arms wrapping around her, those hands cupping her face and skimming over her arms made her shiver.

Markham smiled and bent toward her ear. "I think I know how to make the evening even more pleasurable."

Oh, my Lord. Georgie swallowed, her mouth suddenly dry and her pulse racing with panic. Or was it anticipation? "What are you suggesting?"

Markham began to lead her in a slow promenade down the length of the room toward one of the vacant card tables. "How daring are you feeling, Your Grace? I propose heightening the stakes this time. Let's make this match worth both our whiles."

Daring? Up until tonight, Georgie had never considered herself to be anything of the sort. But the way Markham looked at her right now—his gray eyes alight with amusement and sharp interest—she suddenly felt daring indeed. An uncharacteristic and entirely indecent bolt of excitement shot through her. How silly she was to think Markham wasn't interested in her. Markham was a man who liked the thrill of the chase and she represented a challenge to him. He'd all but admitted that last week. "I'm listening."

Markham's mouth tilted into a no-doubt calculated half-smile. "I propose a wager. If I win this game, you must attend my house party at the end of next week, even if it's only for a few days. I've recently purchased a property at Richmond. On the Thames. Rivergate House. It will be the first time I have received guests."

Georgie arched an eyebrow in skepticism. "A house party? Really?" Everyone knew there were two types of house parties: those that members of polite society attended, and then there were other affairs that were nothing more than a thinly veiled excuse for licentious behavior.

They paused by the card table and Markham chuckled, a low throaty rumble that seemed to vibrate right through to her very toes, making them curl in her satin slippers. "Don't worry. Phillip and Helena shall be there. It will be all above-board, I assure you."

Georgie gave Markham a narrow look, still suspicious. The idea of spending several days under this man's roof—even if her friends were there—sounded much too dangerous to contemplate. For her it would be akin to entering a lion's den. Her reward for winning tonight would need to be sweet indeed for her to agree to such a bargain. "And if I win?"

Markham's smile grew enigmatic. "I will tell you how I beat you fairly and squarely, both times last week."

Georgie sniffed. "If I win tonight, then that should hardly matter to me."

"Perhaps. Although I would hazard a guess that you are still dying to know, all the same."

Yes, damn you, I am. Georgie's eyes met his. It was a deal she could hardly refuse and he knew it, judging by the arrogantly amused expression on his face. He was tempting her with exactly what she wanted—the very something that had bothered her all week and would continue to irritate her until she knew.

She lifted her chin. "I should say no."

He cocked a brow, dark mischief dancing in his eyes. "But you won't."

Double damn him. She wouldn't.

≈

Yes. He had her.

His gambit had worked.

Markham couldn't help but smile to himself as he pulled out the duchess's mahogany Hepplewhite chair so she could take her seat at the card table. Not only had she taken the bait to play cards again, but he was quite sure he knew what her scheme was—play the siren to befuddle him. It explained why her customary, frosty demeanor had apparently melted away after dinner.

Her seductive smiles and sighs, the flirtatious banter, even the way she'd positioned herself on the chaise-longue so that he was afforded a breath-stealing view of her amply displayed cleavage—these behaviors, whilst intriguing, had completely thrown him at first. Right up until the moment she'd made an assuredly out of character, innuendo-laden quip about the roses being pleasurable—then the truth had hit him like a thunderclap. The Ice Duchess wanted to win at piquet so badly, it seemed, she would go to great lengths to achieve her goal. Even if deep down inside she was uncomfortable playing the role of seductress.

But forewarned was forearmed. No matter how many times Georgiana Dudley fluttered her pretty eyelashes at him, or heaved a bosom-swelling sigh, she wasn't going to put him off. In fact, two could play at this game she'd started.

Markham took his own seat opposite her, keeping his gaze locked with hers and away from her tantalizing décolletage. *For the moment.* "Duchesses first. Would you like to shuffle then cut the cards?"

Georgie took a deep breath, her breasts straining against the fabric of her gown before giving a nod. "Yes. Thank you."

He studied her as she reached for the pack. Her smile might be steady, but her fingers trembled slightly and he could see the pulse fluttering in her neck. Yes, she wasn't as confident as she appeared.

If he were a better man, he wouldn't take advantage of the fact.

Whilst she shuffled, he deliberately raked her with an appreciative gaze, his eyes shamelessly lingering on her face, her delicious mouth and then her breasts. As he'd anticipated, color immediately rose to her cheeks. She glanced away from him, suddenly very interested in the cards in her hands.

Leaning forward a little, he drew her gaze to him again. "Because the rest of the company are otherwise engaged and we are still somewhat...alone," he said in a low voice, "I thought I should take this opportunity to tell you how beautiful you look this evening, Your Grace."

She affected a little laugh before she placed the cards on the table. Something hot and bright flashed beneath the cool blue of her eyes. Anger or desire, he couldn't tell. "Heavens, you are full of compliments this evening, Lord Markham," she said. Although she sounded a little breathless, she arched an eyebrow. "But you must realize by now that flattery will get you nowhere when it comes to playing. Only strategy will."

Cutting the cards with a decided flip, she revealed the seven of clubs. Not good by any means. Her lips flattened, her displeasure clear.

"It would seem a modicum of good luck doesn't go astray either," Markham ventured with a wicked grin. He took his turn to shuffle and added, "I don't know about you, Your Grace, but I'm feeling rather lucky tonight." His cut revealed the knave of hearts. Although he wouldn't have first choice from the talon in this first round, the advantage would be his in the sixth and final round of the *partie*. "I shall be the younger hand to begin with."

"Of course. I wouldn't have expected anything less." The duchess observed him from beneath her eyelashes as he started dealing. "Playing with you again will be quite a romp, I should expect, regardless of the outcome."

The seductress was back. He couldn't help but play the rake. "I can think of no lovelier woman to romp with than you, Duchess."

This time, when she blushed, it was to the roots of her hair. There could be no mistaking what he meant by romp. He was a devil, but if she wanted to play with fire, she should expect to get a little burned. As soon as the last card hit the table, she hastily picked up her hand and began to study it in earnest.

Grinning, Rafe picked up his own cards. But his smile immediately fled. *Bloody hell.* His hand was shocking; not a single face card amongst the whole twelve. He would almost assuredly have to declare *carte blanche*.

He waited until the duchess had made her exchanges from the talon in the center of the table—five cards from the eight, leaving him little to choose from—then made his call. The duchess's mouth lifted into a bright smile when he gave her a glimpse of his cards.

"Thank you," she said with a nod. "Perhaps luck isn't on your side after all, Markham."

"We shall see." *Minx.* The duchess had begun to toy with the ruby necklace she wore; it hung just above the shadow of her cleavage. Trying his best to ignore the play of her fingers and the building tension in his balls, Rafe returned his attention to the cards. He couldn't afford to be distracted when he had so much lost ground to make up.

As the usual declarations and initial tallying of points commenced, an audience began to gather about them. The Maxwells and Lord and Lady Palmerston looked on from their nearby table; Jonathon, Farley, Lady Lucinda, and Lady Talbot took up positions behind the duchess; and the remaining couples including Rothsburgh and his wife, Beth, gathered to his rear. They obviously all thought they'd be in for a good show.

Not that Rafe minded. The audience actually worked in his favor. As he'd suspected—and to his immense relief—the duchess assumed her usual, dignified persona again. It seemed she was not quite game enough to play the coquette in front of so many interested gazes.

The playing of tricks commenced, and as he'd anticipated, the duchess won the first round easily. Triumph gleamed in her blue eyes as she took the last trick on a perfect run of diamonds. She'd also managed to score a pique of a bonus thirty points.

Their audience began to clap.

"Well played, Your Grace," Rafe offered.

"Thank you," she acknowledged with a gracious inclination of her head.

He sat back in his chair and puffed out a small sigh. Five hands to go yet. He wouldn't lose sight of the prize; the opportunity to have the duchess—Georgiana—nearly all to himself for a few days. He just needed to keep his head and concentrate on the task at hand rather than flirting.

As the duchess gathered the cards and tapped them into a neat pile, Phillip leaned over and passed him a cognac. "You might need this, my friend," he murmured. "Go slowly though."

Rafe had to agree.

~

After three, very close, heart-hammering rounds—to Georgie's immense relief she'd won two—Helena insisted they all break for tea.

Georgie gratefully accepted a steaming cup of Darjeeling from Helena. The tension of concentrating so hard had taken its toll—the beginnings of a headache pulsed in her right temple.

When Helena had finished dispensing the tea to the other guests, she took up a seat beside Georgie at the fireside. "You are doing well," her friend murmured with a conspiratorial glint in her brown eyes. "And I'm sure that after tea, a number of our guests shall take their leave, which means you will be free to distract Markham again."

Georgie pursed her lips. "Hmm. I don't know about this tactic of yours, Helena. I'm not even certain it achieved much in the first instance."

"Fie. What nonsense. You absolutely flogged him in the first round didn't you?"

"Yes, but that was more to do with how the cards fell—"

"I disagree. Never underestimate the power of feminine wiles. Once a man's member is engaged, his brain all but ceases to function."

Georgie gasped, shocked at her friend's frankness. "Helena!"

She laughed. "It's true, mark my words, Georgie darling. If you want to be certain of winning, you must be prepared to do whatever it takes. Remember, the rules of fair play do not always apply in love and war."

AMY ROSE BENNETT

Georgie's frown conveyed her skepticism. "Even if that means acting like a harlot?"

"Georgie, that is something you could never be. And there's nothing wrong with playing the temptress." Helena winked at her over her teacup. "In fact, it can be quite fun."

"But your situation is entirely different," Georgie protested. "You're married to a wonderful man."

"There's no reason why you shouldn't be wed to such a man too." Helena leaned closer and touched Georgie's hand before adding *sotto voce*, "If you give Rafe a chance, who knows...perhaps he might amount to more than just a paramour for a season. He might even be the one to win your heart. But first you need to decide he's worth the risk."

The one.

Georgie was not fool enough to deny that others were fortunate enough to find their perfect match in life. Phillip and Helena obviously had. So had Lord and Lady Rothsburgh. And Jonathon and Teddy had been the picture of bliss during their years together.

However, she was not like other people. If her past had been different—if she were different—then perhaps Markham might have been that special someone.

But not for her. Not now. She doubted that even someone like Lord Markham—Rafe—would ever be able to convince her otherwise.

And any further speculation was pointless because in her heart of hearts, she knew she would never take such a risk.

CHAPTER 7

T he assembled company had thinned considerably by the
time the ormolu clock in the drawing room heralded
midnight. Only the Maxwells, Jonathon and Farley remained
to witness the final round.

Which meant that Georgie could at last attempt to flirt
with Lord Markham again.

At this stage, she dealt from a position of relative strength.
She'd won three out of the five rounds played and had gained a
quite respectable score of seventy-six. Markham, on the other
hand, had a running total of sixty-four.

With only one hand to play in this *partie*, victory was definitely within her reach. She was certain she could easily make
one hundred or more. To beat her, Markham would have to
earn an incredible number of points. His only advantage at
this point was that he was now the elder hand and had the first
choice of the cards from the talon.

The wicked, uncharitable part of her prayed she dealt him
something dreadful. And that she had the bravada to flirt as if
her life depended upon it.

As she shuffled the cards, she moistened her lower lip with

her tongue, then gently pushed her teeth into the soft flesh. The effect on Markham was immediate. He sucked in a sharp breath and Georgie risked a glance at him. His gaze was riveted to her mouth.

Helena had been right, curse her. But could she keep up the performance?

She had to. She couldn't bear the idea of spending a whole day, let alone several, in Markham's company.

With a deep, bodice-straining sigh, she deftly dealt out their hands then spread out the talon.

Thankfully Markham had transferred his gaze back to the cards, giving her time to both sharpen her concentration and muster her strength for her next series of moves.

She fanned out her hand of twelve—more spades and clubs than the red suits. A decent run and a trio of jacks. There was potential there, but she would need to work hard. And as Helena advised, do whatever was needed. God forgive her.

She slipped Markham a glance. His brow furrowed in concentration, his mouth set in a determined line, he seemed focused—too focused—on what was in his hand and the exchanges he made. She had to unravel him. Crushing down a wave of nervousness and a bothersome pang of guilt for using grubby tactics, she set about twirling a curl of her hair around her finger whilst biting her lip, as if deep in thought.

Markham's gaze was instantly on her again, a decided glint in his eyes—whether it was amusement or sexual interest, she couldn't tell. "Your turn to exchange, Your Grace," he said, his lips tipping into a smile.

Is he laughing at me? Oh God, she hoped not. Releasing her curl, she reached for the remaining three cards in the talon. "Thank you."

Oh no. Nothing but red. And not a single face card. Panic squeezed her heart for a moment whilst she fought to keep a neutral expression. She could still win this. She had to believe it.

Discarding what she'd picked up from the talon, she ventured another look at Markham. It was time for the declarations. Would he be honest, or would he try to sink her at this juncture by not declaring everything he had?

He cocked an eyebrow. "Point of six."

She arched an eyebrow in return. She had a point of seven in spades. An additional seven points that raised her score to eighty-three. "Not good," she replied smoothly.

"Hmm." Markham frowned then rubbed his thumb along his jaw—a completely masculine gesture, no doubt designed to make her heart flutter—then declared again. "Sixieme."

Oh no. He had six cards of one suit in a sequence. She did not. And that gave him an additional sixteen points making his score eighty—only three points behind her.

Her heart began to hammer. This would be a close game after all. "Good."

Markham smiled slowly. "Quatorze of aces."

Oh God, no. Four of a kind. Fourteen more points. And she only had a trio of knaves. Markham was now at ninety-four and he hadn't even won a single trick yet. She would undoubtedly be lost if the cards didn't fall her way in the course of play. Swallowing, she found her voice and forced herself to make the required response. "Good."

Markham inclined his head. "May the best hand win, Your Grace."

"Yes," she agreed faintly. There was nothing for it. She was going to have to pull out her last dirty trick to stop him reaching one hundred points first. Beneath the cover of the table, she eased off her slipper then reached forward with her stocking–clad foot and found Markham's ankle just as he played his first card, the ace of hearts.

Markham jumped. His gaze flew to hers. Then smiling, he

leaned back a little and moved his leg forward so that her toe brushed against him again.

The cad. He knew what she was about. And he *was* laughing at her.

Heat scalded her cheeks and she jerked her foot away.

God help her. She was mired in the mud on the wrong side of one hundred and it seemed there was nothing—bar a miracle—that would save her.

As expected, her miracle did not eventuate and Markham won six sequential tricks. Within a matter of minutes, he effortlessly reached one hundred, claiming victory with a flourish and a wolfish smile.

Helena, Jonathon and Farley clapped and Phillip handed his friend another cognac. "Well done, old fellow."

Georgie dropped her gaze to the table and quite unnecessarily gathered the cards, attempting to make a neat pile; anything to avoid Markham's too observant eyes.

Don't be so sensitive. It's only a game at a private party. It doesn't matter. That's what Jonathon and Helena—even Teddy, if he'd been here—would say.

But it did matter. She'd gambled and she'd lost. And the price was heavy. Her reputation, her confidence, and her self-respect lay in tatters all around her. Three times she'd played Markham and three times he'd soundly thrashed her. Not only that, this time, she'd all but prostituted herself into the bargain.

And to make matters worse, he knew what she'd been up to. The wicked smile curving his mouth after she'd attempted to tease him beneath the table had said it all. How could she possibly attend a house party hosted by him? She'd rather die.

"Your Grace?" Markham's voice was soft with concern. "Are you—"

"Congratulations, Lord Markham," she offered crisply. She didn't want his pity. She didn't want anything from him.

Plastering a smile on her face, but keeping her gaze averted from him and everyone else, she pushed away from the table. Her vision blurred and her throat tightened so much she could barely breathe. The humiliation was too much. She had to get out of this room before she lost control of herself. "Excuse me."

Thankfully, no one followed her as she rushed from the room into the hall then up the stairs that led to the ladies' retiring room. Praise God it was deserted at this late hour. Collapsing onto a settee before the dying fire, Georgie buried her face in her hands and at last gave herself up to a flood of angry tears.

She was such a fool. And she only had herself to blame. Hopefully Markham would be gone by the time she was ready to emerge.

If she never saw him again, it would be too soon.

Rafe lounged against the balustrade on the upstairs landing, pretending to peruse a finely rendered painting of the Palace of Holyroodhouse with a backdrop of Edinburgh's Salisbury Crags. Save for the ticking of the longcase clock farther along the passage, all was deathly quiet in this part of Latimer House.

He permitted himself a deep sigh. He'd been waiting half an hour for the duchess to emerge from hiding. To his surprise, it had been Helena who'd suggested he go after Her Grace to see if she was all right—and Jonathon had readily agreed. Whilst Rafe appreciated their match-making efforts, he rather thought that Georgiana wouldn't.

Indeed, he suspected this whole evening had been engineered to throw them together again. No wonder the duchess was livid. And fool that he was, he'd made it worse by bruising her pride yet again; not only had he beaten her, but he'd teased her mercilessly. He'd definitely pushed her too far.

This time, even a simple apology wouldn't be enough.

The longcase clock struck a quarter to one and Rafe started down the hallway, counting doors. At the risk of increasing the duchess's wrath tenfold—and having a chamber pot hurled at him—he was going to have to invade the hallowed sanctuary of the ladies' retiring room. Although he was generally a patient man, he really didn't want to wait all night. And he wouldn't leave the Maxwells until he'd made peace with her.

Fourth door along on the right, Helena had informed him. He stopped and listened, his ear to the wood panels but all was silent within. He should knock. But then he wasn't like other men. Breaking rules like uncovering secrets, was as natural to him as breathing.

He turned the handle and stepped into the small, dimly lit room.

It took a moment for his eyes to adjust—the almost extinguished fire, and a pair of low-burning oil lamps in wall sconces on either side of the chimney were the only sources of light. And then he saw her, huddled on a low settee, staring into the dying embers in the grate.

"Your Grace?"

Her whole body jerked. "Markham. What in God's name are you doing in here?" She rose and even in the poor light it was obvious she'd been crying. Her voice was husky with tears and barely suppressed fury, her toffee-brown hair a disheveled halo. "Get out. At once."

"No." He advanced toward her. "We need to speak."

"No. We don't," she bit out. She took a step back, then another, edging away from him toward the other side of the room.

"I beg to differ." He followed her around the settee as she continued her retreat.

"You can beg all you like." Her blue eyes glittered with cold derision. "I don't want to hear your gloating condescension dressed up in pretty words. I don't want an apology. And I certainly won't be mollified or *appeased* or anything else you want to call it this time."

She bumped into the oak-paneled wall and before she could fire another verbal shot at him, he crowded her in with his arms, one hand at the level of her shoulder, the other beside her head; his body almost pressed against hers, but not quite. At these close quarters, the scent of her floral perfume teased him. The heat of her body aroused him, made his pulse race, his cock twitch.

"How dare you? Leave me be," she hissed. Her chest heaved and judging by the hard set to her jaw, he wouldn't have been surprised if she was contemplating clawing his eyes out. "Your attentions are not wanted."

"Are you sure?" he murmured thickly as he pushed a wayward curl behind her ear. "Because it didn't seem that way at all during the game. And you're wrong, you know." He trapped her furious gaze again. "I didn't come here to gloat or apologize. Or to appease you..." He dropped his eyes to her mouth. "I came here for this."

Before she could even utter a sound of protest, he captured her tear-stained face with his hands and ruthlessly claimed her mouth. She gasped beneath him. Her hands clutched at his shirt, her fingernails biting into him even through the linen. But she didn't push him away.

Far from it.

She moaned then swept her tongue into his mouth, even before he could taste her. Kissed him back with needy, almost desperate abandon. Her hands slid up to his neck and she speared her fingers into his hair, dragging him closer. Lust immediately roared through his veins, thickening his cock, at the thought she was actually mad for him too. He devoured her, sucking her tongue further inside him, thrusting himself into her in return.

God in heaven, she tasted divine. Hot and sweet and salty. Honey laced with tears. And entirely addictive. More potent than cognac or even opium. He could easily get drunk on her, and perhaps he was so already.

Suddenly ravenous for the taste of her fragrant, satiny skin, he slid his mouth from her lips and traced a line of kisses along her jaw to her throat, and then lower. His tongue delved into the sweet cleft between her breasts as his fingers pushed aside the slippery satin of her bodice to expose her nipple. When his lips closed around the hardened bud and he suckled, she gripped his head and a low moan tumbled from her throat.

Her breath came in ragged gasps. "I shouldn't... You shouldn't..."

"Shouldn't what? Do this?" Cradling the plump mound of her breast with one hand, he circled his tongue around and around the tight, rose-colored flesh. "Or this?" He then delivered a light volley of flicks with his tongue tip before covering her with his mouth, suckling again.

"Any of it." She tugged at his hair, pulling him away.

"Why not?" He searched her eyes, hoping against hope she'd answer him truthfully. Given the way she kissed him, pushed her body into his, he didn't think she was a virgin. But perhaps he was wrong—and that might explain her reticence to go further. "Tell me."

"Because..." She drew in a shaky breath. "You are exactly what I don't need. And I cannot be what you want me to be."

"And what is that? Speak plainly." He narrowed his gaze, suddenly exasperated with her for always thinking the worst about him. "How can you possibly know what I want from you?" he demanded. "And maybe I'm exactly what you need."

She laughed, a mirthless sound, then arched against him, her belly grazing his already throbbing cock. "So arrogant. And I know what *you* want, Markham. It's obvious. The problem is..." She closed her eyes and bit her lip. Then shook her head. "It doesn't matter."

A tear escaped onto her flushed cheek and a strange combination of guilt and anger pierced Rafe's heart. Whoever had hurt this woman, he wanted to throttle him. "Georgiana—"

"I haven't given you leave to use my name," she whispered, but there seemed to be no more fight in her. She tugged her bodice back into place, her movements jerky. Then she sagged against the wall. Away from him. The fire in her eyes had died.

"Georgiana. Why do you fight me so? I want you. And if I'm not mistaken, a moment ago you seemed to want me too. We're both free." He fisted his hands to stop himself touching her because he knew she would rebuff him. "Why shouldn't we see if there could be anything between us?"

She sighed, and to his surprise she reached forward and cupped his jaw with trembling fingers. "Find someone else, Markham. I'm not for you."

He dared to place his hand over hers. He wouldn't let her go so easily. Not when his heart thundered like this and his whole body ached for her. "Promise me you'll come to Rivergate. We had a deal."

Another sigh. Infinitely sad. "All right. I'll come." Her hand slipped from beneath his and she gently poked at his chest like he was a naughty schoolboy. "But only if you give me your word that you will behave yourself."

At least the light had returned to her eyes.

"I give you my word," he said, inclining his head, trusting his expression was sincere. He suspected his definition of behaving himself was quite different to hers, but she didn't need to know that.

She drew up straight and narrowed her eyes. "And don't expect me to play cards."

Rafe sighed, but he couldn't hide a smile. "So many rules, Your Grace. A house party is supposed to be entertaining, you know."

Her mouth twisted. "Do you want me there or not?"

He raised his hands in a placatory gesture and took a step back. "I promise. No more cards either."

She nodded once. "Good."

"Well," Rafe took another step away and gave a slight bow, "I shall bid you adieu until next week then, Your Grace." He turned to go.

"Wait." The duchess closed the distance between them and laid her hand on the sleeve of his evening jacket. "I...I need your assistance."

"Of course." He waited.

"Where are the others?"

Rafe frowned. "Farley departed shortly after our card game. I left your brother and Phillip in the library, but that was a little while ago. And Helena, the last I heard, had headed up to the nursery. Another one of their children is unwell, I believe. Young Charlie."

"Oh..." The duchess worried at her bottom lip for a moment. "Would you mind terribly if I asked you to help me escape unnoticed?" She gestured at her hair—her curls had tumbled into further disarray during their amorous tryst and her gown was noticeably creased. "I fear I am in rather a state. I can't be seen by anyone. And I'm loath to disturb Helena or call on her maid at this late hour. I have a redingote—a black velvet one—in the cloakroom downstairs."

In Rafe's opinion, Georgiana looked nothing but beautiful even if she was delightfully rumpled, but he understood her need for discretion. "I will fetch your coat and ask for your carriage to be brought round immediately. Shall I also tell your brother to meet you outside?"

"Yes. Yes, thank you so much."

She began to draw her hand away but Rafe caught it and raised it to his lips. "Whatever you want, you have only to ask," he said softly. "And I shall make it so."

Her forehead creased into an apparent scowl but she couldn't quite hide a twitch of amusement at the corner of her mouth. "You are a persistent devil, Markham, I'll give you that much. But your charm won't sway me into your arms again, you must know that."

Pleased to see her spirit returning, he couldn't resist throwing her a deliberately roguish grin. "Well then I shall just have to rely on my good looks, intelligence and wit to sway you instead. I shall see you shortly." Then without further ado, he slipped from the room before the duchess could react. Judging by the flash of annoyance in her eyes, he suspected she might just actually be thinking about launching a chamber pot at him.

CHAPTER 8

As soon as the door clicked shut, Georgie sighed heavily then paced over to the looking glass positioned by the fireplace. Lord, she was a mess; her cheeks were tear-stained, her lips were kiss-swollen, and her fingers trembled as she vainly attempted to repin some of her tumbled tresses into a semblance of order. But worse still was the tumult of wild emotions and thoughts careening around inside her.

Curse Markham.

Why was he making it so hard to continue despising him?

He was arrogant, undeniably so, but he was also more than a rake; Helena was right. Handsome, witty, intelligent— he did indeed possess all of those qualities he'd jested about. But he also seemed—and she hardly dare think it—caring. Not only did he make her heart race and set her stomach flutter, he made her ache and feel far too much.

He makes me want far too much.

It would be far easier for her to dislike him if she'd been able to hold onto the anger she'd felt when he'd first invaded the room—when she realized he'd sought her out with the sole purpose of seducing her.

But then when he'd kissed her—ravished her—her traitorous body had responded to him in a way that had shocked her. Still shocked her. She could no longer hide from the irrefutable fact that she wanted him, just as much as he clearly wanted her. Even now she could still feel the slickness between her thighs and the insistent pulse of unfulfilled lust low in her belly. The problem she hadn't wanted to admit to him—the thing she could barely admit to herself—was that she would always be unfulfilled. Desperately wanting yet never able to achieve satisfaction.

She hated feeling this way. Only half-alive. Half a woman.

Markham could never find out.

The idea of spending so much time in Markham's company next week, beneath his roof, was daunting to say the least. The possibility of exploring if there might be anything between them—as he'd put it—terrified her even more so. And she didn't believe for a moment that he would hold to his promise to behave. The way he'd looked at her after he'd kissed her, when he'd declared that perhaps he was exactly what she needed—she hadn't only seen passion in his eyes. There was a promise of...more.

He was tempting her down a treacherous slope, and only untold frustration and bitter disappointment awaited her at the end.

And she just couldn't put herself through that. Or him.

Georgie, you would be a fool indeed to think anything could come of this.

But how was she to get out of this mess? A deal was a deal. Markham was a determined man and he wouldn't let her renege, no matter that his own promise to behave was likely a lie.

At least she had a week's grace to think on it.

By the time Markham entered the room a few minutes later, she'd managed to compose herself a little more. Her hair and dress might still be in a disastrous state, but at least the cool and dignified Ice Duchess had resurfaced. "Thank you." She was relieved her voice sounded steady when Markham helped her into her coat. He'd also brought her a light muslin shawl of Helena's to drape over her hair. "Your thoughtfulness does you credit."

"You are most welcome, Your Grace." Markham offered her his arm, then escorted her from the room. "Your brother is waiting for you outside in the carriage. He bid Phillip farewell for both of you. And you'll be pleased to find that no one is about in the vestibule at the moment, not even the night footman."

Georgie peered over the wrought-iron railing as they descended the stairs and confirmed that was indeed the case. "Thank you again, Markham."

"It's the least I can do."

When they reached the silent vestibule, he released his hold on her arm to open the front door for her. "I know you are concerned about appearances, but it's very foggy out there. I should escort you to your carriage."

Georgie peered out into the night. Sure enough, a thick gray fog swirled about. The gas lamps flanking the bottom of the stairs were barely discernible and she couldn't even see her carriage. Nevertheless, she shook her head. "It's only a few feet away. My footman will be waiting to hand me in. I shall be fine."

"Are you sure?" Markham's brow creased in concern. He stepped closer—too close—and the rich, spicy scent of his cologne enveloped her, immediately reminding her of the kiss they'd shared.

Georgie had to stop herself from leaning into his large, warm body. "I'm sure." That was a lie. She wasn't sure of herself at all; she really needed to leave right now before she changed her mind and threw herself into Markham's arms. "Goodnight then."

He bowed his head, a mysterious, almost regretful smile curving his mouth. "Goodnight, Your Grace."

Georgie lifted her skirts and stepped carefully down the stairs into the roiling, gray miasma. The dark shape of the carriage loomed ahead. She'd only taken a few steps across the pavement when something—someone—crashed into her, almost knocking her down. A startled cry escaped her as a man roughly clutched her arms. Helena's shawl fell away.

"Pardon me, Fraulein."

She had a fleeting impression of a male face obscured by a scarf and a mess of dark hair, and then he was gone. The swiftness with which he released her sent her flying again. She stumbled back, grabbing the wrought-iron railings to stop herself falling.

"Are you all right?" Markham was suddenly at her side, gently grasping her about the shoulders. "What happened?"

"Georgie." Jonathon, with a footman close behind him, appeared behind Markham. "What in God's name? Markham, what's going on?"

Georgie's gaze darted between her brother and Markham. "A man bumped into me. That's all... I'm quite all right. Maybe a little shaken." She rubbed her upper arm and grimaced. "And perhaps a little bruised. But nonetheless fine."

Markham's gaze was as hard as steel. "Describe him. Which way did he go?"

Georgie frowned, puzzled at the intensity of Markham's concern. "He was tall. Dressed in a greatcoat and scarf. Black. Oh, and he was foreign—he spoke German. I think he went that way." She gestured with a nod of her head. "Toward Grosvenor Square, I imagine. But it was only an accident, Markham. Don't fuss."

Markham ignored her and directed his next comment at

Jonathon. "See her safely home." And then he was gone, sprinting off into the fog in the direction she'd indicated.

Georgie's mouth fell open. "Why on earth...?" The man had been rough, but it wasn't as if he'd collided with her on purpose. It was impossible to see anything in this fog; he'd obviously been in a hurry and hadn't seen her. Markham was completely overreacting by haring off after him.

"Georgie," Jonathon grasped her arm and attempted to steer her toward the carriage. "Come. Let's get you home."

Giving up on trying to see anyone or anything at all through the impenetrable, chill gray cloud surrounding them, Georgie sighed then followed her brother. Although she believed Markham's act of gallantry was unnecessary, she couldn't help but be flattered by his concern for her.

The carriage had just started to pull away when a wholly unpleasant thought burst into her mind: what if Markham was putting himself in danger? A sharp spike of panic speared her heart. What if the stranger who had barreled into her was a nefarious character after all?

Their collision had been accidental, but why had he been in such a hurry on such an inclement night at such a late hour? There could be a hundred reasonable explanations for his haste and brusqueness, but still... If he were up to no good and then Markham caught up to him, what then? Even though she knew little of Markham's past, he appeared to be the type of man who could hold his own in a physical altercation. But what if he and the stranger came to blows, all because of her? She couldn't bear to think of it.

"Jonathon, get the driver to stop the carriage."

"Whatever for—"

"I'm worried about Markham."

"Georgie, I'm sure—"

She sat forward and rapped sharply on the carriage wall behind the driver. "Stop, Benson."

The carriage immediately drew to a halt. As Georgie reached forward to grasp the handle of the door, Jonathon gripped her wrist. "Markham will be fine."

"You don't know that. Let me out, Jonathon. I don't know why Markham felt the need to chase after that man, but at least we could ask our footman, even the Maxwells' staff to assist. What if...what if that man is dangerous?"

Jonathon's forehead furrowed into a deep frown. "I seriously doubt that. This is Mayfair after all..." He sighed and released her arm. "But if it makes you feel any better..."

"It will." Perhaps, like Markham, she was overreacting too. She certainly wasn't going to leave here until she knew he was all right. Her heart still thudding uncomfortably in her chest, she unlatched the door and waited impatiently for Perkins, the footman, to attend her, all the while scanning the fog in the direction the stranger and Markham had headed toward. But she could see nothing. Not only that, all was deathly, eerily silent save for the rattle of the steps as Perkins let them out, and the jangling of the horses' harnesses. She really didn't know if that boded well or ill for Markham. Either way, she must find out.

Alighting on the pavement again, she picked up her skirts and started back toward Latimer House. "Tell Perkins to head for the Square, I'll speak with the night footman," she called over her shoulder to Jonathon.

"Georgie... Wait."

Ignoring her brother, Georgie increased her pace, anxiety gnawing at her belly. Her breath puffed out in short, ragged spurts. Latimer House was just up ahead—the gaslights shone like beacons through the mist.

And then a large shape materialized out of the fog, directly in front of her. A man. Gasping, she stumbled to a halt.

Markham. Thank God.

He grasped her firmly by the shoulders as if to steady her

before pulling her close to his hard, lean body. A dark scowl creased his brow as he stared down at her. "Your Grace, why haven't you gone home like I instructed?"

"I..." She wanted to say she'd been worried for him, but the words jammed in her throat. What on earth had she been thinking? Of course Markham could protect himself. Animal strength and steely assurance literally radiated from the man. Heat flooded her face; she suddenly felt foolish and more than a little embarrassed. And vulnerable beneath his intense scrutiny.

"You shouldn't be here. Where is your brother?" he continued when she didn't answer; there was a rough edge to his voice, and he seemed different somehow. *Annoyed.*

A matching spark of irritation burst into life inside her. She lifted her chin, determined to brazen this awkward encounter out. "I won't be ordered about by you."

A muscle worked in Markham's jaw. "Duchess or not, if we were anywhere but here, I'd tip you over my knee and—"

"Markham. You're all right." Jonathon appeared beside them. "See, Georgie, I told you he would be fine—"

"Be quiet, Jonathon," Georgie snapped, pulling away from Markham's hold. She didn't want Markham to hear any more about her misplaced concern. Instead, she glared back at him, the irritation she'd felt a moment ago blazing into full-blown anger. The temerity of the man was unbelievable. She couldn't let him get away with his previous comment, incomplete or not. "What was it that you were saying, my lord?" she demanded with false sweetness. "That you'd like to tip me ov—"

"Enough," he growled before taking her firmly by the elbow and marching her back toward the carriage. "Whilst I'm flattered you are concerned for my welfare, you really have no need to be."

"Just as you have no need to be concerned about mine,"

she retorted, trying but failing to wrench her arm from his firm grasp. "Why did you set off after that man? Did you actually catch up with him? Demand he make an apology to me? Chivalry is all well and good, but your actions...well, they do not make sense."

Halting by the coach, Markham shook his head. "It's half-past one in the morning and I really don't wish to discuss the matter with you right now," he bit out in a clipped tone; he was clearly exasperated. "Please, just get in, Your Grace."

She turned and faced him, standing her ground. She knew her contrariness was now bordering on absurd, but she couldn't seem to help herself. "You are so...high-handed."

The corner of Markham's mouth suddenly twitched with amusement. He drew her close, one hand still at her elbow, the other at her waist. "You have no idea," he murmured, his gray eyes glinting with a devilish light. "Right at this moment, I'd like nothing more than to lift up your skirts and apply my hand to your delectable arse for potentially putting yourself in harm's way again. So you'd best get in the carriage before I do."

She gasped. "You wouldn't."

The hand at her waist slid downward to cup her buttock. "Oh, indeed I would," he whispered in her ear, squeezing her gently. "But rest assured I'd offer to soothe the sting later with a kiss."

A potent combination of shocked outrage and white-hot desire flashed through Georgie. Her breath caught and her lower belly quickened as she imagined Markham doing exactly that—slapping her, then placing his lips on her bare behind as she lay across his lap with her skirts around her waist. Splaying her hand against the wall of Markham's impressively wide chest, she only just managed to crush the urge to press herself into his crude embrace. Lord, the man was turning her into a wanton of the worst kind. How could that be when another part of her also itched to slap him back for his impudence? She must be going mad.

The sound of Jonathon and the footman returning pulled her out of her lust-induced stupor, and she immediately scrambled up the steps into the carriage away from a chuckling Markham. Thank God the interior was dark so he couldn't see her burning face.

But Georgie could see his large frame, silhouetted in the doorway, even if she couldn't see his expression. "Goodnight again, Duchess," he said in a velvet-soft voice. Then he was gone.

"Lord, what a night. Too much excitement all round, what?" Jonathon declared a few moments later as he threw himself into the seat opposite her. "I'm done in."

And I'm undone. Her pulse racing, the secret place between her thighs throbbing again, Georgie squirmed on her seat, pressing her legs together in a futile attempt to try and ease the pressure. She'd never, ever felt this way before. Markham had teasingly threatened to slap her *delectable arse* but instead of being affronted, she was aroused. In fact, it felt like she'd been aroused for hours—perhaps all night. She couldn't bear feeling this frustrated for much longer. When she got home, she was almost tempted to touch herself where she ached most, to see if she could relieve the agony.

"Georgie-bean. Did you not hear a word I just said?"

She started guiltily. "No. I'm sorry I didn't, Jonathon..." Forcing herself to sit upright and perfectly still like the lady she was supposed to be, she then focused on her brother. "Tell me again."

"I said, Markham will call tomorrow about three o'clock."

Tomorrow? Oh God. She didn't want to see Markham tomorrow, next week at his Richmond house, or ever again for that matter. "Did he say why?" Her voice sounded strained and breathless but her brother didn't seem to notice.

He shrugged a shoulder. "He didn't say specifically. I imagine it would be to see how you are faring after the accident. And perhaps he wants to seek my permission to formally court you, Georgie. He seems quite infatuated with you."

Infatuated. Georgie could no longer deny feeling that way about Markham either. However, she didn't say anything, just looked out the carriage window, although it wasn't dark, mist-shrouded streets she saw. It was a wickedly handsome man tempting her to engage in all manner of wicked, wanton things. Things that made her yearn for more from this life.

If anyone in this world could melt the icy core within her body as well as her heart, it would be Lord Markham. *Rafe.*

The question was—as it had always been since she'd first laid eyes on him—was she willing to take the risk and give him the chance?

Rafe strode through the blanket of fog in the direction of his townhouse in South Audley Street, ears and eyes alert for the slightest indication of activity. The foreign stranger—whoever the hell he was—had disappeared without a trace.

Which was deeply frustrating on a number of levels. Rafe bunched his fists and paced faster as he skirted Grosvenor Square again, scanning the murky, shifting darkness. Not only was he precluded from exacting revenge on the brute for hurting the duchess, he also hadn't discovered the man's identity—and whether or not he was someone from his past.

A threat.

Georgiana might believe it was an accidental collision, but Rafe's gut told him otherwise. It seemed odd that a German-speaking man just happened to barrel straight into a woman mere inches from him. It might have been foggy, but gas lamps illuminated Latimer House's entrance. That coupled with the unsolved broken gate mystery meant that in the space of a week, two decidedly unusual incidents had occurred in the vicinity of the Maxwells' residence. And on both occasions, he and the duchess had been together; on the rear terrace and then on the front steps of Latimer House.

Someone had been watching him with the duchess. He could sense it.

It would be easy to shrug off both occurrences as being insignificant and unrelated. However, for a man like himself— someone with a good deal of skeletons in the closet—complacency was a luxury he could ill afford. He needed to exercise the utmost caution, if not for his own sake, then for others he cared about.

Like Georgiana.

It was a sobering notion indeed to realize that in the space of a week he'd been completely entranced by this woman. And he would be a fool to dismiss his desire to look out for her as being nothing more than an extension of the wild lust he felt for her—both in and out of her presence. He knew the protectiveness he felt toward her, the need to be near and to please her, were the symptoms of a growing *tendre*. And he hadn't even bedded the woman yet. Christ, how far gone would he be when that happened?

But did she want to be with him? It was encouraging to find out that she'd been worried for his safety. Even so, whilst she may care for him, even just a little, one thing was clear— seducing Georgiana was still going to be a challenge like no other.

He'd been thrilled when she'd first responded to his kisses and bold caresses with eagerness. But then she'd pushed him away, both physically and emotionally. Fear of being hurt undoubtedly held her back to some extent. Helena and Phillip had told him as much a week ago. Recalling the tears in her eyes, the catch in her voice when she'd told him to find someone else to pursue, made his heart twist in the strangest way. Finding out who had harmed her in the past—and how deeply—would be the key to understanding her. He wouldn't rest until he knew.

Leaving the Square, Rafe entered South Audley Street, then immediately ducked into the pitch-black shelter of a narrow laneway. He may have lost the suspicious foreigner, but that didn't mean the man had lost him. Folding his arms across his chest to ward off the biting cold, he leaned against the wall and waited to see if anyone should happen by.

Fifteen minutes passed, but aside from the occasional clatter of a cab rolling past and then the more distant sound of discordant singing from a group of drunken men stumbling through the streets, all was quiet as the grave.

Time to go home and get some rest before tackling the problem again tomorrow. Slipping back onto South Audley Street again, Rafe walked quickly, hands buried in the pockets of his greatcoat. He might need to sleep, but he wondered if he would be able to given that whenever he had time to think, his thoughts drifted straight to Georgiana—her in that sinful red dress, with one of her full, beautiful breasts exposed, writhing beneath his mouth and hands. Then there was her delightful intake of breath and dilated pupils when he'd teased her about spanking then kissing her arse. It was a risk provoking her in such a fashion, but his instincts told him she secretly enjoyed his boldness—that he dared to tread where perhaps others feared to.

God, he needed to stop thinking about her. A stiff cock and aching balls were not conducive to a peaceful night's slumber. As soon as he was alone in his rooms, he was going to have to take matters into his own hands if had any hope of getting any rest at all.

Although Georgiana had declared that she wanted him to find someone else, he didn't want another. He wanted her.

And he was going to damn well have her. Once he set his mind to something he wouldn't be swayed.

Georgiana, the Duchess of Darby, would most definitely be his.

∽

She couldn't sleep. Lying in her bed, staring at the walls and how the flickering firelight danced over the blue-striped wallpaper and rose-patterned plasterwork, Georgie groaned then threw her arm over her eyes.

Sweet heavens above. She'd never been this miserable with desperate need before in her entire adult life. As she'd earlier suspected, she was going to have to try to ease the throbbing ache inside her if she was to get any sleep. The problem was, even the very thought filled her with sheer panic if her racing heart was anything to go by. It had been four years since she'd tried such a singular thing, and it had been an epic failure that had only brought her to tears rather than satisfaction.

Like tonight, it had been lustful thoughts about another man that had brought on her fit of neediness—a handsome, quiet, scholarly young man with soft brown eyes and a gentle smile. He'd been a friend from Teddy and Jonathon's club, Sir David Gilbert. Over the course of that long ago season, she'd played cards with him, chatted with him, even danced with him. Let him kiss her once when they'd got lost in the maze at Harrow Hall one summer's afternoon. It had been a soft, gentle kiss—a sigh like the touch of a butterfly across her lips, or the kiss bestowed by the prince at the end of a fairytale. Her body had been stirred by desire and she'd believed that perhaps at long last she would be able to achieve fulfillment, at least by her own hand. She definitely wasn't going to embark on an affair with Sir David unless she could.

However, her attempt that same evening when she'd been

alone in her bed had been all for naught. As soon as she'd touched herself, the longing within her had died as quickly as the snuffed-out candle on her bedside table. And she hadn't been game enough to try again since.

But what she'd felt when she'd been with Sir David was nothing compared to what she felt with Markham. Closing her eyes, she relived the experience of Markham kissing her, freeing her breast and claiming her nipple. A flash of heat shot straight to her quim and she shuddered, aflame with such acute longing it was like a physical pain. Dare she try?

She had to know. The lonely years of widowhood yawned before her like a dark abyss. Whatever the consequences, it was now or never. She slid the hem of her already twisted, rucked-up night rail farther up over her hips, exposing herself to the cool night air. With trembling figures, she then reached between the juncture of her thighs and tentatively touched the seam between her tight curls—then gasped on discovering she was wet with dew.

Sopping.

Don't think of anyone but Markham. Holding her breath, Georgie feathered her fingertips along the sensitive crease again then slid one finger between her folds. *Oh.* She jumped, her other hand curling into the sheet. For the first time in such a long time, it felt wonderful to do something so illicit. So wanton.

What would it feel like if she touched her aching core? Would she still feel this aroused or would the sensations die again? There was only one way to find out. Holding her breath, she flicked her fingertip over the hardened nub at the apex of her folds then whimpered as the burning, clenching need inside her womb intensified. *Oh yes.* She could do this. She had to or she'd die. And it was all because of Markham. *Wonderful, wicked Markham.*

She emptied her mind of everything but him as she danced

her fingers in and around her swollen, slick, throbbing flesh. His smile, the rich scent and taste of him, the feel of his hard, muscular body beneath her hands. Imagined how he would look divested of his shirt, his breeches... How it would feel to be pressed against him as he explored her with his hands and mouth, touched where she now touched. Stroking, teasing...

The coil of need inside her pulled tighter and tighter as she rapidly flicked her fingertip over and around the rigid, oh-so sensitive bud. Something was happening deep in her womb. Something inexorable, like a building inferno. Georgie lifted her hips, clenched her jaw, thought of Markham thrusting inside her, whispering deliciously naughty things in her ear.

Oh, God. She exploded. Cried out. Tears spilled down her cheeks as wave after wave of searing pleasure swept through her quaking body.

A miracle had happened. Her body had been as lifeless as an arctic wasteland for ten long years, but now it was if the heavens had opened and she was awash with warm, pulsating satisfaction. She was whole again. And filled with glorious, budding hope.

Dragging in a deep, shuddering breath, she curled onto her side and closed her eyes. Achieving climax by her own hand was one thing. Being able to push all her long-held fears and inhibitions aside when she was with another—perhaps someone like Markham—was an entirely different matter altogether.

There was plenty of time to think about that dilemma tomorrow. Right now, she would fall into sleep's waiting arms with blissful, contented abandon. And if she dreamt of Markham, so be it. Perhaps that wicked devil of a man would be her savior after all.

CHAPTER 9

After alighting from a hackney cab at the edge of Hanover Square, Rafe paused and surveyed his surroundings. It was five to three and the Square and surrounding thoroughfares appeared relatively quiet, the light passing traffic unremarkable for a Saturday at this hour. He would have much preferred visiting the duchess and her brother under the cover of darkness, but such were the conventions of the *ton* for social calls. At least no one appeared to have followed him. Even his man, Cowan—a former Bow Street Runner with an excellent reputation—was nowhere to be seen. Rafe would be most interested to hear his report later on.

Judging it safe to approach Dudley House for now, Rafe turned up the collar of his coat against a sudden shower of icy, drizzling rain, then walked smartly across the Square to the impressive residence. The stony-faced butler relieved him of his damp coat, hat and gloves, then promptly ushered him into the library before he could even produce his card. He was obviously expected.

Sir Jonathon Winterbourne was alone; he smiled broadly and extended his hand in greeting. "Welcome to Dudley House. Miserable day to be out and about though. Shall I send for tea or coffee," he gestured at a mahogany sideboard where an impressive array of spirits and liqueurs sat atop a silver tray, "or do you fancy something a little stronger?"

I would prefer your sister. Pushing the distracting thought aside, Rafe answered smoothly. "Coffee, if you don't mind." As much as he would love to see Georgiana, it actually better suited his purpose that she wasn't present during this discussion.

After dismissing the butler with an instruction to fill his request for coffee, Jonathon indicated they should each take a seat in the pair of matching leather wingback chairs gracing the Persian hearth rug. "First of all, let me say that my sister wishes to extend her thanks for the roses you sent this morning."

Rafe inclined his head in acknowledgement. He'd sent deep red roses this time, the exact shade of the alluring burgundy dress she'd worn the night before. "I hope this day finds her well, considering what occurred last night."

The corner of Jonathon's eyes crinkled with amusement. "I take it you are referring to what happened on the doorstep of Latimer House and not to the events preceding that."

Nice attempt at fishing, Winterbourne. Rafe's mouth twitched but he wouldn't be drawn on what had occurred in the ladies' retiring room. And he rather doubted that Georgiana had divulged any details of their encounter to her brother. Schooling his expression into seriousness again, he met Jonathon's gaze directly. "I want you to know that I highly esteem the duchess and have nothing but the best of intentions where she is concerned."

"I don't doubt that for a moment, Markham. I trust the

Maxwells implicitly and if they deem you a worthy candidate to attempt to snare my sister's—shall we say interest?—who am I to stand in the way? I just wished Georgiana would..." Jonathon rubbed his chin, studying Rafe for a brief interval before he added, "She can be prickly, but I want you to know that you have progressed much farther than I would have thought possible in such a short space of time. She likes you. I was surprised by how genuinely worried she was about your safety last night."

Rafe was, again, secretly pleased to hear the duchess had been concerned for him, but he hadn't come here to have his ego stroked. He'd come here for information. He fixed Jonathon with a hard stare, determined to find out what he needed to know—to help him understand Georgiana. "I must confess that I have been more than a little surprised at the support I have received from both you and the Maxwells. Which begs me to ask, why are you doing this?"

"Encouraging your suit?"

"Yes."

Jonathon sighed then got up and poured himself a brandy. "Care for one?"

Rafe consented. *Why not?* If it helped him to build up more of a rapport with Georgiana's brother and encouraged the inviting of further confidences, he wouldn't say no.

Jonathon passed him a rather full tumbler, then with his own glass in hand, returned to his seat. He took a long sip before catching Rafe's eye. "My sister, although she would be loath to admit it, is in a word, unhappy."

And lonely. After a nine-year marriage of convenience, Rafe didn't doubt it. Time to take a gamble and make use of what he already knew. "I know how things really were between her and Darby." He held Jonathon's suddenly sharpened gaze. "And you."

Jonathon paled. He swallowed then licked his lips. "Who told you?"

"No one. I worked it out for myself. From bits and pieces I'd heard from my Cambridge days. From things Helena and Phillip did or didn't say. And I'm very good at reading people. But don't worry. I assure you, your secret is safe with me."

Jonathon nodded then his shoulders heaved with a deep sigh of resignation. "I believe you." He stared into his brandy, clearly mulling over what to say next before he returned his attention to Rafe. "So you know how lonely Georgiana really is?"

"Yes." Rafe let the silence between them extend for a few moments. "But it's not only her loneliness that I've noticed."

Jonathon frowned. "What do you mean?"

"Forgive me for speaking so frankly, but I also sense your sister has a very real and very deep fear of being hurt. Again."

Jonathon's jaw dropped but then there came a knock at the door and a footman entered bearing a tray with the coffee and an assortment of light luncheon delicacies.

By the time the footman had arranged everything on a nearby table and had then departed, Rafe's host seemed to have recovered his equilibrium. Ignoring the coffee and array of sandwiches and savory pastries, Jonathon pinned him with a narrow look. "You are shrewder than I thought, Lord Markham."

Rafe shrugged. "It was not so difficult to deduce the truth of the matter. Why else would Georgiana continue to view most male suitors with such antipathy? And why else would someone as remarkable as her wed someone like Darby, a man who could only ever be a friend to her? She must have known how things were between you and the late duke."

Jonathon paled again; he looked drawn. And perhaps guilty. "Yes. She did."

Rafe put down his brandy and leaned forward. He was so close to hearing the truth, he wouldn't let go, no matter how uncomfortable Jonathon grew. "A young woman entering Society would need a very good reason to agree to such a marriage, I would think. A compelling reason."

Jonathon huffed out a large breath and ran a hand down his face. "I know you're a capital fellow, Markham. But I don't feel comfortable going into...detail. It's Georgie's business."

"I understand your reluctance and you are wise to be wary," Rafe said, whilst somehow pushing aside the urge to pummel Jonathon for more information. "But please do not doubt my motives. I said before that I esteemed your sister. Actually, I should confess my feelings are much stronger than that. I also strongly feel that if I am to move forward with Georgiana, I need to understand the reason behind her...hesitancy. I only need a name."

Jonathon's blue eyes grew a shade darker as he assessed Rafe. The set of his jaw hardened when it appeared he'd made up his mind. "Oliver Cantwell, Lord Craven," he said roughly as though it was hard for him to speak the words without choking on them. "A bastard to his very bones."

Craven. Rafe knew the name. *Why?* Whilst he inclined his head in thanks for Jonathon's concession, he scanned his memory for any recollections. Craven was undoubtedly a rakehell. Probably one of the worst of his kind. That was it. He'd run with the late Earl of Beauchamp's pack—the Sapphire Club—the most soulless group of reprobates he'd ever come across. *Oh, God. Poor Georgiana.*

He tried and failed to stop the muscle tic in his clenched jaw.

"You know him." Jonathon's tone was flint-like. Angry.

"Of him," Rafe corrected. His name had come up when he'd been discreetly investigating the sordid private life of the

Marquess of Rothsburgh's first wife, Isabelle. Whatever Craven had done to Georgiana, it had to have been deplorable. Despicable.

He drew in a measured breath as he reached for his brandy. "I have a question for you, Sir Jonathon." His voice was as hard as the cold knife of rage slicing through him. "Do you want Craven to pay?"

Jonathon's eyes widened momentarily before his mouth flattened into a grim line. "For how he made Georgiana suffer, yes. Yes, I do."

Rafe nodded once. "So be it."

"Your Grace?"

Georgiana cursed beneath her breath at the sound of Markham's deep voice directly behind her. *Trapped in the vestibule.* How ironic considering she'd been hiding from Markham for the best part of an hour. But then it had been silly of her to try to sneak from the drawing room and back up to her own apartments when she knew very well his interview with Jonathon was probably due to finish.

After surreptitiously running her suddenly damp palms down the gauze skirts of her pale blue day dress, she drew in a fortifying breath then turned to face him.

"Markham." Sliding what she prayed was a cool smile into place, she extended her hand. "My brother mentioned you may be calling on him this afternoon." She really should have added how lovely it was to see him, but as he took her bare hand in his and bent over it as any gentleman would, the words caught in her throat. Dear Lord, how was she to observe the expected proprieties when all she could think about was how the very fingers he held had been buried in her quim last night as she'd fantasized about him?

Despite her best efforts not to react to his touch or her own libidinous thoughts, a hot blush washed over her cheeks.

Markham, as she expected, looked amused when he straightened and released her hand. A smile tugged at the corner of his mouth, but strangely, his eyes held a soft light rather than a devilish twinkle. "I also came to see you."

Of course he has. He sent you roses again, Georgie. Don't pretend you didn't expect this. She broke away from his gaze to glance behind one of his wide shoulders, but the vestibule was deserted. Where on earth was Jonathon, or Reed or Perkins for that matter? Seeing no way to extract herself from Markham's company without appearing supremely rude—or worse a coward—she dredged up something customary to say. "I trust you have already taken tea with my brother."

"Yes." Markham glanced back over his shoulder—perhaps to check the vestibule for occupants as well—before his eyes returned to meet hers. "Even though it is perhaps presumptuous of me to ask, I wondered if we might speak somewhere privately for a few moments?"

Georgie's heart kicked into an unbridled gallop. Jonathon had thought this call had been arranged so Markham could seek approval for continuing his courtship, despite the fact her brother's permission was not really necessary given she was a widow; and despite the fact she'd clearly told Markham to pursue another. But Markham didn't seem the type to play by any sort of rules except his own. She'd be naïve indeed to believe he'd continue to behave as a gentleman should when they were alone. Especially after last night.

Her wariness must have shown on her face.

"I have no untoward designs on you, Duchess, if that's what you are concerned about." He suddenly leaned closer, his eyes alight with the mischief she'd been expecting to see. "Although when we're alone, if *you* would like me turn you over my knee—"

"I thought you said you only wanted to speak with me," she accused.

He smiled. "True. But I'd be happy to oblige if you requested anything else of me."

She sighed in resignation, and tried not to smile back, her irritation dissolving as quickly as a lump of sugar in her tea. "You're impossible."

He grinned back. "So you told me when we first met."

"Follow me." She turned on her heel and led Markham into the drawing room. If she ignored the racing of her pulse, and considered the situation with a cool head, what wickedness could he possibly get up to in broad daylight whilst her servants and Jonathon were within calling distance? Nevertheless, she left the door ajar after they'd entered the room.

Markham's gift of red roses was on prominent display atop a small mahogany table in the window alcove facing Hanover Square. Their heavy scent filled the room; much like him, they couldn't be ignored.

"I have been remiss in not thanking you in person for the bouquet you sent," she said with as much gracious aplomb as she could; not an easy feat given the wild fluttering of her stomach. Indeed, it felt like a battalion of butterflies swarmed around inside her.

"It was the least I could do, considering the events of last night."

Markham's comment was as layered as a *mille-feuille* pastry. So much had happened at Latimer House, it was impossible to know which specific event or events he referred to—trouncing her at cards again, attempting to seduce her, the accident with the rude stranger, or making crude suggestions to her on the street. Georgie certainly wasn't going to ask him to elaborate.

And she wasn't going to offer him a seat. Instead, she

hovered at the edge of the room, not far from the open door. "You wanted to speak with me," she prompted.

"Yes." Markham took several steps closer and she stepped back. His advance and her retreat reminded her of their encounter in the ladies' retiring room.

"Markham," she said in a low voice edged with warning.

He stopped his approach immediately and his brow creased into a deep frown. "I wanted to make sure you were all right, after the collision." His gaze drifted to her right shoulder and upper arm, however her sleeve hid her flesh from his eyes. "You said you'd been bruised."

She couldn't resist arching her eyebrow. "That's odd coming from a man who keeps suggesting he wants to spank me."

His eyes darkened to a stormy gray. "I'm serious. Did he hurt you?"

"A little," replied Georgie, taken aback by the depth of his concern. "It's nothing."

Markham moved closer and before she could utter a word of protest, he gently pushed up the silk gauze of her sleeve. His lips tightened into a hard line when he saw the livid purple marks—fingerprints—on her upper arm. "You're sure he spoke German? What did he say?"

His hand lingered at her elbow, his touch gentle, his fingers warm. She should admonish him and tell him to remove it, but she didn't. "He...he called me Fraulein. His speech was heavily accented."

"Do you recall anything else about him? Anything at all."

She shook her head. "Not really. It happened so quickly."

"Even a minor detail."

Markham's intense interest puzzled her. Nevertheless, she closed her eyes for a moment and summoned the memory. "He had dark hair. Messy. Low on his brow. I couldn't see his eyes properly." She opened her eyes and shook her head again.

"That's all I remember, Markham. I don't understand your fixation. Do you know this man?"

Markham dropped his hand and the expression in his eyes became shuttered. "Forgive me, Duchess. I cannot help but feel responsible that you were hurt. I should have escorted you to your carriage."

"I asked you not to. You should not blame yourself. I certainly do not."

Markham inclined his head and stepped backward a pace. "Thank you. You are indeed gracious. Now I really should bid you adieu." Bowing over her hand, he brushed a light, almost perfunctory kiss over her knuckles. "Until we meet again, Your Grace."

And then he was gone. Just like that.

Georgie pressed herself against the wall behind her, feeling unexpectedly flat with disappointment. How ironic that she'd been fending off Markham's advances and playing the affronted Ice Duchess, but when he didn't press her for anything more, she felt put out.

What did you expect, Georgie? That he would offer to promenade with you in Hyde Park? Or that he would attempt to kiss you again? After you'd warned him off?

Do you really want him to pursue you?

For once the answer that sprang to mind wasn't a decided no.

She closed her eyes and pressed her fingers to the soft flesh of her lips—dry and cool. *Untasted.* He'd awakened her. She couldn't ignore that fact. No matter how much her body trembled, or her heart frantically pounded with an apprehension that bordered on terror at the thought of being with him, she owed it to herself to at least *consider* exploring what could be. She'd be a fool to turn away now.

She smiled, realizing that instead of dreading the idea of Markham's house party, a small part of her thrummed with anticipation. How strange to think she might actually be counting the days until she saw him again.

~

"There's been no activity in 'anover Square today at all, milord or in Limmer's Hotel on the corner. An' the duchess an' 'er brother ain't left their 'ouse, not even for a jaunt about 'yde Park. Which is no' at all surprisin' given, it's still rainin' cats and dogs."

Just like every other day and night for the whole week. "Thank you, Cowan." Rafe sighed and ran a hand down his face. He was slightly relieved that his team of men had seen neither hide nor hair of anyone—at least no one fitting the description of being tall, dark and foreign—watching his own movements, the Maxwells or more importantly, the comings and goings of Georgiana. But then, constant pouring rain would discourage most, except for the very determined, from conducting outdoor surveillance.

Rafe wouldn't let down his guard though—not yet. The watcher, whoever he was, might simply be biding his time. To do what, Rafe didn't know, but he'd been in the spy game too long to let go of the matter prematurely. *A viper always strikes when you least expect it.*

Cowan cleared his throat, claiming Rafe's attention again. "As for the other matter..."

Craven. Markham's gut tensed. "What have you managed to find out about him?"

Cowan's shrewd, pale blue eyes lit up. "The last few nights 'e's been seen frequentin' some of the less reputable gamin' dens around Soho 'an the Strand. As well as spendin' 'is coin on the company of several—shall we say cheaper—ladybirds from Tothill Fields."

"It sounds as if our Lord Craven is a little down on his

luck then," mused Rafe. He rubbed his chin. A well-heeled gentleman's playground of choice was usually the more exclusive gaming establishments and high-end brothels around St James's or Pall Mall.

"It would seem so, milord," agreed Cowan. "One of my contacts says the earl walked out wi' naught but vowels from a cockfight two nights ago. Do you want me to make discreet enquiries about Town regardin' 'is accounts, an if 'e is known to any of the moneylenders or debt collectors?"

"Yes, that would be a good idea." Rafe would also enlist Phillip's help in gleaning additional information from the *ton* bucks frequenting White's, Boodle's and Brooks's. Rafe had already learned that Craven had sold off a good portion of his estate's unentailed assets in the past year, and he'd also given up his rented townhouse in Curzon Street during the Season proper. By all accounts, it appeared the man was desperately short of funds at present. And there was nothing Rafe would enjoy more than pulling the purse strings a little tighter to make Craven squirm just that bit more.

And if in the process, the bastard ended up living in penury, even better. It would undoubtedly be poetic justice for one of the *ton*'s worst hellions. If Craven had ruined Georgie—and everything he had learned so far indicated the cur had—Rafe would ruin him.

Hauling himself out of his dark musings, Rafe turned his attention back to Cowan. "If you find out anything of import, you know where to find me." The house party at his Richmond residence was due to start tomorrow. However, due to the abysmal weather, he suspected that many of the invited guests would be put off. Ruthless man that he was, as long as the Duchess of Darby kept her promise and attended, he really didn't give a fig if anyone else came.

After issuing a few further instructions he dismissed Cowan, then abandoned his desk in favor of gazing out the rain spattered window to South Audley Street below. But it wasn't the teeming gutters and cobbles Rafe saw, or the passing traffic. All that filled his mind's eye was the image of a lithe, toffee-haired siren with rose-pink lips and sapphire blue eyes, and how she would look in his bed.

If only Georgiana would let him take her there.

CHAPTER 10

Rivergate House, Richmond
1ˢᵗ November 1816

"This is madness, Jonathon." Pushing aside the plum velvet curtains, Georgie peered out of her carriage window, but saw little more than sheets of driving rain hammering down upon the swollen, murky brown surface of the Thames. "What does Markham think we are all going to do for the entire party? Play charades and chess whilst we watch the river rise?" She knew she sounded terse, but as their destination drew closer, her nerves had begun to wreak havoc upon her body. Her pulse raced and her stomach churned. Even her cheeks felt warm. A whole two days and nights, perhaps more with Lord Markham. In close quarters. The prospect was both exhilarating and terrifying.

Jonathon snorted and stretched his legs out, crossing his booted feet at the ankles. "Well, perhaps you might have those pursuits in mind Georgie-bean, but I, for one, will be seeking out other diversions."

"Well, I hope for your sake, and mine, that Lord Farley

attends with his sister and aunt," sniped Georgie. Her brother seemed far too *laissez-faire* considering the potential for social disaster. "We already know Phillip and Helena have sent their apologies because they and little Charlie are both unwell, and Lord and Lady Rothsburgh have beaten a retreat to Scotland before the snows set in up north. What if there's no one at Rivergate but us? I'm telling you, we should turn back now."

Jonathon regarded her with a considering look. "You've got cold feet haven't you, sis?

She puffed out a small, exasperated sigh. Her brother's ability to read her so easily was annoying in the extreme. "Perhaps a little," she admitted. *Well, perhaps a lot.* It seemed as if a lifetime had passed since she'd last seen Markham at Dudley House, and like the rising Thames, her old insecurities had returned to overwhelm her. She might have wanted his kisses —perhaps even more than that last week—but now, she wasn't so sure.

There was a decided glimmer of mischief in Jonathon's blue eyes even though his forehead lowered into a frown. "I thought you promised Markham that you would come. You really shouldn't go back on your word."

Georgie sighed again, this time in defeat. "I know." And there was the rub. She'd never be able to face Markham again if she bailed out now. She just prayed there would be so many other guests attending that he, as host, would be sufficiently busy with entertaining them, rather than spending time with her.

"Here we are." Jonathon tugged back the curtain from his window to reveal they were approaching an impressive set of black, ornately fashioned, wrought-iron gates. "Oh, I say..."

Georgie's breath caught as her gaze drifted across the large expanse of emerald-green grass to a magnificent, three-story Palladian style manor. Flanked by groves of golden-leafed lime and beech trees, Rivergate was stunning. Even though the drive and grounds were awash, and the lowering sky behind it was a canvas of sullen, dark gray, its beauty was in no way diminished. The simple geometric lines and white-washed façade of the house, the formal parterre-style garden beds gracing the lawn before the circular drive, all conveyed an air of understated elegance.

Georgie caught herself smiling despite her nervousness. One thing was certain: she couldn't fault Markham's taste.

In no time at all, their carriage and a second coach which conveyed Georgie's lady's maid, Jonathon's valet and most of their luggage, negotiated the streaming gravel drive and stopped before the entrance. Two sweeping flights of divided stairs led up to a covered portico and the main doors of glossy black wood. As Georgie peered upward, a small retinue of liveried footmen materialized as if from nowhere, armed with what appeared to be a forest of wide umbrellas.

"Someone's prepared for your arrival, dear sis. And is obviously keen to impress." Jonathon winked at her before tugging on his black kid gloves and checking the fastenings of his great coat.

"Pish," she retorted. "A display of good manners is hardly a sign that Markham—"

"Wants to win your heart?" Jonathon grinned. "We'll soon see. As the expression goes, *'faint heart never won fair lady.'* And Markham doesn't strike me as faint-hearted or a man that's easily dissuaded once he's set his mind on achieving something. I'd suggest you be prepared for a well-mapped out campaign."

Before she could even draw breath to protest—she was certain Markham's primary mission wasn't to win her heart— the carriage door swung open to reveal Markham himself, smiling up at her from beneath a vast green umbrella. Even simply dressed in a well-cut, navy-blue tailcoat over a white linen shirt, form-fitting buff breeches and Hessians, he was heart-stoppingly handsome. He bowed and offered his hand. "Your Grace, welcome to you and your brother. Please, let me assist you inside."

Georgie consciously smoothed her brow and painted a polite smile on her face. "Why, thank you, my lord." She gathered her blue-gray merino wool skirts and matching pelisse in one hand before placing her other gloved hand in Markham's. His fingers clasped hers firmly but gently as he helped her alight, then his hand slid to her elbow, drawing her in close to his side beneath the cover of the umbrella. "Just making sure that you don't get too wet," he murmured into her ear.

Georgie pressed her lips together, trying desperately not to dwell on the double entendre his choice of words brought to mind—especially after the week of restless nights she'd had since she'd last seen him at Dudley House. She definitely did *not* want to think about being *wet* in any way, shape or form around Markham right at this moment. But it was hardly his fault if she was the one having errant thoughts.

As Markham escorted her up the slippery stone stairs, she was painfully aware of the closeness of his warm body and the scent of his expensive cologne. Huddled beneath the umbrella, his arm and thigh occasionally brushing against her, she was becoming increasingly hot and flustered. She was nothing but relieved when they at last gained the shelter of the portico and she could step away from him into the elegantly appointed vestibule.

It was an eye-catching, elegant room—an airy space, which was octagonal rather than square or rectangular. The floor was laid with black and white parquetry tiles, and the white walls and high ceiling were decorated with delicate plaster work. A large arrangement of exquisite hot-house flowers stood on a walnut table in the center. Retreating to the opposite side of the room to regroup, Georgie shook the raindrops off her skirts and then removed her gloves, hoping beyond hope that she didn't appear as she felt—both breathless and flushed.

"Are you all right, Duchess?" Markham's forehead was etched with the lines of a concerned frown as his gaze traveled over her.

"Yes. Of course." Hadn't she uttered those same words in the carriage? Dear Lord, could she not think of anything else to say? "I mean... I'm a little damp... Only my boots are... Nothing else." Fierce heat scorched her cheeks. *Oh, God. Stop speaking, Georgie.*

Markham's wide mouth curved into a rakish grin. "I'm sure I can soon remedy that."

Does he mean what I think he means? Georgie's mouth dropped open but she was saved from being subjected to any further inappropriate quips as the butler appeared to take her gloves, bonnet and pelisse.

Grateful that she had an excuse to avoid Markham's disconcerting gaze, she turned away and set about making her suddenly clumsy fingers undo ribbons and buttons, her mind buzzing desperately all the while. *Where on earth was Jonathon? Or anyone else for that matter? Hadn't there been a whole army of servants about only moments ago?*

As she handed her damp clothes to the butler, she heard a man's voice calling—was that Benson, their coach driver?—followed by the sound of carriage wheels crunching on the drive. Still no sign of Jonathon. Then one of Markham's footmen appeared in the doorway.

"Excuse me, my lord." The young man bowed to Markham before he turned to Georgie and bowed again. "I have a message for you, Your Grace. From your brother."

"Yes?" Heart hammering, Georgie forced herself to retain a dignified stance rather than fleeing the vestibule to chase after Jonathon. She knew what the footman would say before he spoke. *He's abandoned me.*

"Sir Jonathon wanted to inform you that he has taken the carriage in the hopes of assisting Lord Farley."

"What do you mean?" Markham took a step forward, frowning deeply. "Is Lord Farley all right?"

The footman turned to his master. "I believe so, my lord. He has simply been stranded at the White Swan Inn. As you were escorting Her Grace inside, a messenger arrived on horseback with a note for either you, my lord, or Sir Jonathon, requesting an alternative means of conveyance to Rivergate. Lord Farley's carriage has apparently been mired in the mud and the inn does not have any other suitable transport. Sir Jonathon said he would return with Lord Farley as soon as possible. Although, according to the lad from the White Swan, the river is rising and there is some local flooding on many of the laneways that lead to the inn."

Georgie's hand flew to her throat, her heart freezing in her chest. "Oh, heavens." *If anything happened to Jonathon...*

Markham crossed the vestibule and took her other hand between his. "Your brother will be fine, Your Grace." His voice was low, his tone, like the gentle clasp of his fingers about hers, was reassuring. "I'm sure if conditions were not safe, Jonathon would turn back rather than put himself and your staff in danger."

"Yes. Yes, you're right." Jonathon was sensible and Benson was an experienced coachman. She offered Markham a small smile, touched that he so obviously cared that she should have peace of mind. "How far away is the White Swan? I do not recall passing it on our way here."

"Only two miles. Ordinarily it would be less than a half hour's journey, but considering the conditions"—Markham gestured toward the doorway and the pouring rain just beyond—"I would say it will take longer than that."

Georgie nodded and attempted to withdraw her hand, but Markham simply tucked it into the crook of his elbow. His thumb brushed across her bare knuckles and a shiver of aware-ness ran through her. Whether the brief caress was by accident or design, she wasn't sure. Either way, she was effortlessly aroused and she didn't like it. When she glanced up to meet Markham's gaze, he smiled at her—a knowing gleam in his eye —and her heart tripped over itself. *Not an accident then.*

"Now, let me escort you through to the main hall," he continued as if nothing had just passed between them, "where my housekeeper, Mrs. Chalmers should be waiting to show you to your rooms upstairs. I'm sure your luggage is being conveyed there as we speak. And when you are feeling restored, might I suggest you come to the drawing room to take tea? Say, in half an hour or so if that suits you?"

She inclined her head and attempted to return a smile— Markham might have promised to be a gentleman, but beneath his veneer of concerned civility, he was an out-and-out rake and she must always remember that. Nevertheless, she would take his offer at face value. For now, she would give him the benefit of the doubt that he meant well. "Yes, it will," she replied. "Thank you."

As he led her from the vestibule, into the adjoining hall where the main staircase—a grand, gleaming mahogany affair —was located, she couldn't help but notice how quiet River-gate seemed. *Deserted.* Not even Mrs. Chalmers, the house-keeper, could be seen. A nervous fluttering recommenced in the vicinity of her stomach. "Will the other guests also be joining us?" she asked, attempting to feign a lack of concern.

Markham paused at the bottom of the stairs. Warning bells clamored in Georgie's head when he smiled a little sheep-ishly. "Until your brother and Farley return, I'm afraid you are my only guest, Duchess."

What? She swallowed and forced herself to hold Markham's gaze, determined not to show one iota of trepidation. "I know

Phillip and Helena, as well as Lord and Lady Rothsburgh are not coming. Do you mean to say the other parties have not arrived yet? Given the appalling weather, I suppose that does not surprise me..." She looked at her host expectantly.

A brief emotion—was it guilt?—flickered in Markham's gray eyes. "I shall explain all—"

Horror gripped Georgie and she wrenched her hand away from him. "No one else is coming, are they?" she accused, her anger rising swiftly, tightening her chest and stealing her breath. "I... I knew it. You've...you've engineered this situation, haven't you? Lured me here under false pretenses. And somehow you've roped Jonathon and Farley into your scheme."

Markham's brow creased. "I assure you, Your Grace, I have done no such thing. I only received word this morning that the Palmerstons are not able to attend as, very sadly, Lord Palmerston's cousin, just passed away. And Lord Dunwood was injured in a hunting accident—a suspected broken arm— only yesterday. There would have been a dozen of us here otherwise. And there is still a very good chance that Lady Lucinda and Lady Talbot will be accompanying Lord Farley. I understand you are apprehensive, but I swear to you, a genuine house party has been planned. There is definitely no scheme afoot."

Georgie regarded him through narrowed eyes, assessing him. His gray eyes held a sincere light. But her instincts told her that just like a cup of rich, hot chocolate, Markham was too smooth for words. Georgie doubted she could trust him any farther than she could throw him.

"I would like to take you at your word," she said at length after she'd managed to tamp down her ire enough to regain a little of her composure. "But after our encounter at Phillip and Helena's, you cannot blame me for being suspicious. One can never be too careful, especially in matters concerning one's reputation."

Markham inclined his head, his expression grave. "Of course. Please believe me, it was never my intention to place you in a compromising situation. I apologize if I have made you uncomfortable." The corner of his mouth lifted into a slight smile. "If you recall, I did promise to behave myself."

Georgie arched an eyebrow. "Yes, you did."

"So will you still take tea with me?"

It was a straightforward question, but the now familiar glint of devilry in Markham's eyes made it seem as though he was asking her to do something quite illicit, rather than simply joining him in a quite ordinary—albeit pleasant—type of activity. It was almost as if he was challenging her to another dare.

Her mouth twitched. Despite her wariness, she was finding it very hard not to smile. Markham's mischievousness was becoming frighteningly infectious. "I take it you'll let me pour?"

"I wouldn't have it any other way." His gaze broke from hers and lifted to the first-floor landing above. "Ah, Mrs. Chalmers. Her Grace, the Duchess of Darby, has arrived."

The gray-haired housekeeper dipped into a deep curtsy. "Your Grace. Welcome to Rivergate. If you would like to follow me, I shall show you the way to the Rose Suite. Your maid and luggage are there already."

Suite? Markham was indeed playing the magnanimous host to the hilt. "Thank you."

Georgie lifted her skirts in preparation to climb the stairs but Markham laid a hand on her arm, staying her. "Promise me you won't bury yourself in your room. After tea, I would be happy to give you a tour of Rivergate—the interior at least. I have quite an extensive library, and, well... I would very much like to spend more time in your company, Your Grace."

There. He'd revealed his intentions. He did indeed wish to be alone with her and she didn't for a minute think that taking tea and taking tours were the only pursuits on the agenda. Heart pounding, Georgie glanced up the stairs, but Mrs. Chalmers had retreated a discreet pace or two and seemed to be engrossed in studying the Persian runner at her feet. She looked back at Markham and was struck by the intensity of his expression. He was holding his breath—hanging by a thread as it were—waiting for her answer.

He's nervous. Somehow, seeing a chink in Markham's armor, tugged at Georgie's heart in a wholly unexpected and peculiar way. "I... All right." She couldn't mask the slightly breathless quality of her voice, effectively betraying her own nervous state. "I should like a tour."

Markham smiled so softly and disarmingly, her heart stumbled. "Excellent. I'll be waiting in the drawing room. It's through the set of mahogany doors, just to the right of the stairs here."

Releasing her, he then stepped away and bowed briefly before turning and disappearing through the doors he'd indicated.

Georgie let out a shaky breath then gathering her skirts again, she climbed the stairs to follow Rivergate's housekeeper. One thing was certain, whatever lay in store for her, it was not going to be a dull afternoon.

Half an hour later, Georgie, with the assistance of her lady's maid, Constance, had refreshed her appearance to her satisfaction. Her hair had been styled into a becoming Grecian arrangement with curled tendrils escaping about her neck, and she'd also changed her dress. Her creased and damp traveling garb was abandoned in favor of a dusky pink day gown of shot silk, trimmed with ivory ribbon and lace. Whilst she was now suitably attired for taking tea, she rather doubted she was suitably prepared to face Lord Markham and his all too potent charm.

When she glanced in the looking glass above the dressing table, she could see her cheeks were almost as pink as the dress she wore. Blowing out a deep sigh, she pressed her hands to her hot face. The problem was—as it always seemed to be when it came to Markham—she was constantly in two minds about him. To run or to stay? That was the question.

"Can I help you with anything else, ma'am?" her maid asked quietly. "I'll have your dove-gray silk gown aired and pressed in plenty of time for dinner at seven."

Georgie met the young woman's gaze in the mirror's reflection. "No. I don't require anything else for now." Constance was an intelligent, efficient girl and Georgie quite liked her. More importantly she knew she could trust her implicitly. She had been in her service for four years and during Georgie's marriage, the maid had never once remarked upon the fact that Teddy had never spent a single night in his wife's bedchamber or vice versa. "After you've attended to my gown, why don't you have a late luncheon in the kitchen? Tell Mrs. Chalmers, the housekeeper, you have my express permission."

"Yes, ma'am."

After dismissing Constance, Georgie pulled a soft, cream cashmere shawl about her shoulders then crossed to the wide window in her bedchamber. A third-floor room with an adjoining sitting room, it overlooked the grounds, the drive and the Thames beyond. The rain continued unabated and the sky—if anything—had grown darker; the clouds looked bruised and brooding. She frowned when she saw the Thames was even higher—a churning, fast-flowing muddy brown. The banks of the river were quite low here and she suspected some areas would be prone to flooding. Anxiety for Jonathon gnawed at her insides again. She prayed he would keep safe.

However, staying buried in her room—as Markham had put it—wasn't going to stop the rain or the river from rising. With a resigned sigh, she tugged her shawl about her more tightly. It was time to stop worrying and take tea.

She set forth from her apartments and easily found the stairs that led back to the main hall and the drawing room. As she descended, she noticed the door had been left ajar, as if beckoning her inside. Markham was in there, waiting for her; it was almost as if she could sense his magnetic presence.

Taking a deep, fortifying breath, Georgie stepped into the room beyond but then stopped immediately at the edge of the Aubusson rug, a small gasp of delight escaping her lips. Like the exterior of the house, her rooms and the vestibule, Rivergate's drawing room was breath-takingly elegant. Delicate plaster work—predominantly scrollwork, and intricate vine and flower motifs—adorned the high ceiling, and a pair of wide windows afforded a sweeping view of the grounds and the Thames beyond. Exquisitely detailed Chinoiserie wallpaper featuring peonies, cherry blossoms and exotic birds in muted hues of blue, pale pink and soft green covered the wall at one end of the room. At the other end, before a white marble fireplace, stood an inviting arrangement of Chippendale armchairs and settees also in the Chinoiserie style. A sumptuous afternoon tea had been set out on a low mahogany table in the center.

Also looking more than sumptuous was Lord Markham. He stood facing away from her, staring into the brightly burning fire. With a booted foot resting on the hearthstone and one arm resting on the white marble mantel, he was a study in aristocratic nonchalance. And almost too beautiful for words. The way the leather of his Hessian's hugged his calves, how his breeches seem molded to his muscular thighs, how his coat fitted his broad shoulders then tapered off highlighting his narrow hips, he was as captivating as any fine work of art. She suddenly wondered if the musculature beneath his clothing was as well-defined as that of any male marble statue. Blushing with shock at the waywardness of her thoughts and ill-mannered behavior—she had never, ever ogled a man in such a way before—she gave herself a mental admonishment. *For shame, Georgiana Dudley. Why, you're no better than a rake yourself.*

Immediately ceasing her blatant perusal of Markham's body, she swallowed then cleared her throat. "Rivergate's drawing room is delightful."

Straightaway, Markham lifted his head and met her gaze. His mouth lifted into a welcoming smile. "Ah, there you are," he said as he stepped away from the hearth. "And yes, the room is lovely, isn't it? I'd like to take the credit for having such good taste, but I'm afraid much of what you see before you, bar the furniture, is courtesy of the former owner, the Marquess of Melton."

Georgie frowned in confusion. "But doesn't Lord Melton and his family reside in—" *Oh.* She felt another blush creep up her neck to stain her face. She had been about to say Grosvenor Square or the marquess's country estate in Cheshire, but then she recalled Lord Melton was rumored to have had a very spoiled mistress—Lady Bascombe, the widow of a baronet—whom he kept just outside of London. Rivergate had obviously been her residence.

Markham grinned and moved toward the arrangement of armchairs. "Fortunately for me, but perhaps not so fortunately for Lady Bascombe, Melton was in the process of selling the property just as I was looking to acquire one. And it suits my needs exactly."

Georgie wasn't game enough—or silly enough—to enquire what Markham's exact needs might be. Instead, she simply smiled and nodded toward the tea tray; a silver urn, teapot and blue and white Wedgwood china stood in readiness beside several plates of small cakes, biscuits and delicate sandwiches. "Perhaps we should have a cup before it grows cold."

Markham inclined his head. "Yes. And your timing is impeccable. The tea trolley arrived not five minutes ago so I would say the water in the urn is still piping hot." He then gestured toward the arrangement of chairs. "Please take a seat, Your Grace."

Georgie chose an armchair upholstered in a pastel-hued floral brocade whilst Markham took the ivory and pale blue striped settee opposite her. As was customary, she then busied herself with dispensing the tea as per Markham's stated preference—black with a lump of sugar, before she poured herself a cup with only a little milk added. Aside from the crackle of the fire, the occasional clink of silver against fine bone china and the constant drum of rain upon the windowpanes, all was silent.

As Georgie took a small sip of her tea, she felt Markham's gaze upon her. She dare not contemplate what he was thinking. She suddenly realized this was the first real opportunity that she'd had to properly converse with him. However, now the occasion was upon her, she found that her tongue was tied in knots and her mind was as blank as a newly cleaned slate. Awkward didn't even begin to describe the way she felt.

Why doesn't he say something? "I've heard—"

"I wondered—"

Their voices collided and Markham laughed. "Ladies first."

Georgie returned his smile and put down her cup. "Helena mentioned you have been in diplomatic service for some time, but have perhaps returned to England for a longer sojourn. Whilst travelling abroad can be stimulating, I imagine there must have been times when you missed home."

Markham regarded her steadily. "Yes. The life of a diplomat is a solitary one for the most part and there certainly were occasions when I"—his mouth lifted slightly at one corner into a wry smile—"longed to be back in our fair land. I am pleased indeed that my wandering days are now over. In fact, I've recently retired and am keen to set down roots. My father's estate is in Hertfordshire, but I have lately realized that I've a very strong desire to establish a home of my own."

Markham's gaze trapped hers. She couldn't mistake his meaning just as she couldn't stop heat flooding into her cheeks. Helena had been right. Perhaps Markham was indeed in the market for a wife. But a man like him would want an equal partner both in and out of the bedroom, she was certain of it.

Surely he doesn't want someone like me...a widow... And a broken one at that. Scrabbling through the tumble of panicked thoughts in her head for something to say, she voiced the first thing that came to mind. "I...was sorry to hear about your older brother." *Where is your tact, Georgie? Why bring up something that must pain him?* Her blush deepened and she hastily reached for her barely touched cup of tea.

Judging by his response, Markham didn't seem to mind. "Thank you. It seems we have both suffered recent losses," he said in a low voice, soft with compassion. "Although I had not seen your husband for many years—since Cambridge actually —I remember him as a very generous, noble man."

Georgie lifted her eyes back to Markham's face and was surprised to see genuine understanding in his expression. "Yes. He was." She blinked away a sudden rush of tears and took a sip of her tea to mask her discomposure. *If you only knew...*

"You met him through your brother? I understand they were firm friends at Cambridge."

Such a simple enquiry on the surface, but one that had the potential to be dangerous. Heart racing, Georgie's studied

Markham's face again. He might be displaying all the outward signs of sympathy, but she had the distinct impression he was watching her reactions carefully. *Why?* Did he know something about her and Jonathon's situation? And her arrangement with Teddy? He was close friends with the Maxwells, but would they have divulged such a volatile secret? Jonathon would not have done so.

Georgie suddenly felt like one of the exotic butterflies pinned beneath the glass in the picture on the wall directly opposite her. "I take it you have been discussing my marriage with Phillip and Helena." She'd tried to reply in a mild tone but there was no mistaking the acerbic edge to her voice. Unease was transforming her into a short-tempered shrew again.

Markham didn't even blink; his disarming gaze remained steady. "Yes. At the risk of appearing indecorous, I must confess I am more than a little intrigued by you, Your Grace. To be perfectly frank—and as I intimated earlier—I should like to know more." His gaze flitted to her mouth before returning to meet her eyes. "Much more."

Oh, dear Lord. Markham's meaning couldn't be misunderstood this time. Panic and excitement swirled around inside Georgie's chest like a flurry of autumn leaves caught in a gale. "I..." Hands trembling, she placed her cup back on the table. "I must warn you that you are in danger of pressing me too far, Lord Markham. As I keep saying, I really don't know how far I wish to further my acquaintanceship with you...if at all." She drew in a steadying breath to firm her voice and threw what she hoped was a quelling look at him. "I am certainly not in the mood to play verbal cat and mouse games with you. What is it that you want from me exactly?"

Markham's mouth twitched with amusement. "Forgive me. It was not my intention to make you feel uncomfortable. It's just that... This is the first time you and I have had the opportunity to openly engage in intercourse. Indeed, I had harbored hopes that you would come to regard me more favorably—that perhaps you would see me in a better light—if we spent time in each other's company, simply learning about one another." His expression sobered. "I swear to you again, on my very honor as a gentleman, you are in no danger of being verbally pounced upon."

Georgie raised an eyebrow. "Your words, at face value, are somewhat reassuring. Although, given your behavior last week, I would feel better if you had reassured me that I'm not in danger of any sort of pouncing, verbal or otherwise."

Markham threw back his head and laughed, a rich, deep chuckle. Georgie couldn't help but admire the strong column of his throat, the subtle bob of his Adam's apple above the snowy white linen of his cravat. How had she never noticed that a man's throat could be so appealing? *Distracting.*

Markham rubbed his jaw, as if attempting to wipe the grin from his mouth. "Forgive me again, Duchess. I should not have laughed so. But you truly astound me sometimes." His smile softened. "I like that about you."

Georgie pursed her lips and gave him a measured look. "And you still exercise far too much practiced charm for my liking, my lord."

Markham's expression became grave. "You think me insincere. Untrustworthy."

Georgie fought against the impulse to squirm in her seat. His directness confounded her. "I hardly know you. I do not wish to slight you, but I believe trust is earned over time. And I will not dispense it just because you wish it to be so."

And to share her body, her secrets, perhaps even her heart, she would indeed need to trust Markham implicitly. *If only that were possible.*

~

Trust. Rafe barely suppressed a smile as he studied Georgiana over the rim of his teacup. She didn't realize it, but she'd just handed him one of the keys to unlocking her. She'd been badly hurt a long time ago and the scars were undoubtedly deep. He was an absolute dolt not to have grasped the full significance of that until now.

"I completely understand your reticence. Your need to take care," he said as he carefully placed his now empty teacup on the table. "And up until this point I will readily admit my behavior, whilst in your company, has been far from impeccable." He paused and sought Georgie's wary gaze. "Whilst on the subject of trust, I should be completely open and honest with you, and confess I have sent a groom and footman out to locate your brother. They will render any and all assistance, if required. If I can ease your mind—or do anything else at all to make your stay at Rivergate as pleasant as possible—you have only to ask and I will do my best to make it so."

Georgie gave him a small smile. "Thank you, very much. I must, too confess, Jonathon's whereabouts and his safety are weighing heavily upon my mind. I have never seen so much rain. The Thames looks fit to burst."

"There should be news within the next hour or so. Until then, I believe some sort of distraction, aside from drinking tea, may be in order." It was a delicate balancing act Rafe was undertaking—an exercise in gaining Georgie's trust and challenging her to take a risk, to step outside of her safe sphere of existence. Somehow he had to simultaneously ruffle and beguile her, tease and coax her, and break down her walls of resistance without frightening her away.

Somehow, he had to tempt her to stay.

God, he hoped he was up to the task.

Georgie didn't appear suspicious of his motives—*yet*—as her smile had widened in response to his comment. "Ah, the tour," she remarked and placed her cup on the table. "I should like that very much."

Rafe stood and bowed, the perfect gentleman. "If you are ready, Your Grace..."

"Yes. Indeed." Georgie rose and when she pulled her shawl about herself, hiding the creamy, delectable flesh above the neckline of her gown, Rafe had to stifle a disappointed sigh. *Patience and gentle persuasion with a dash of excitement are the tactics required, Markham. Not a full-frontal assault like last time. If you play your cards right, it won't be long before she'll let you discard more than her shawl.*

After offering the duchess his arm—and Rafe was heartened that she readily accepted it—he guided her about the drawing room, pointing out the various pieces of art and curios on display: a set of Ming vases; a cherrywood cabinet containing an array of figurines carved from jade; an intricately carved, ivory Chinese puzzle ball; and beside it, a delicate Boulle table inlaid with brass, mother of pearl, tortoiseshell, and lapis lazuli.

"How long have you owned Rivergate, if you don't mind my asking?" Georgie queried as she traced a pattern on the tabletop with one elegant fingertip. "For a residence that you have only recently acquired, well I must say, you seem remarkably well settled. I'm truly astonished at the beauty of this room, indeed the whole house."

If Rafe had been more certain that she wouldn't rebuff him, he would've remarked it was her beauty alone that truly astonished him, but he set the comment aside. Instead, he simply answered her question with a conventional response. "I purchased the property at the beginning of this year. Whilst I have a townhouse in Mayfair—South Audley Street to be exact—I also have a great desire to escape Town on occasion. And this residence is perfect. Whilst it possesses a rural aspect, it is still relatively close to London which makes it easy for me to attend to any Crown business that occasionally comes my way."

Georgie's brow furrowed. "But I thought you had retired."

Ah, but she was quick. And obviously a little bit curious about his background. Encouraged by her interest, Rafe smiled. "Yes, for the most part. I sometimes need to deal with a few odds and ends from time to time. Such is the nature of the beast."

"Hmm. Your work sounds altogether too mysterious, my lord," Georgie said with a sly look from beneath her lashes. "You haven't even told me where you were posted. In fact, I'm beginning to wonder if the term 'diplomatic service' is really a roundabout way of saying you were engaged in some sort of espionage. I know Phillip works in Lord Castlereagh's office and I suspect you do too." Her lovely mouth suddenly curved into a coquettish smile as she looked at him directly. "I think you'd make a rather good spy for the Crown. Tell me, was charm one of your chief weapons?"

Far too quick. Rafe needed to deflect her line of questioning. Leaning closer, he murmured beside Georgie's shell-like ear, "Of course, but I'm also particularly adept at deep cover work. Shall I show you?"

As he'd anticipated, Georgie immediately stepped away and fixed him with a frosty glare. "So much for your assurances that you would act with gentlemanly decorum."

Rafe simply shot her a rakish grin. "If you are going to flirt with me, Your Grace, you need to expect that I will flirt with you in return. It seems only fair."

"I wasn't—"

"Oh yes, you were, and you know it."

She blushed all the way to the roots of her hair. No doubt her obvious embarrassment was mixed up with a good deal of indignant anger at being caught out. The way her body had tensed—she'd fisted her hands and her back had grown ramrod straight—he had the distinct impression that she would dearly love to stamp her foot. Or slap him.

He pressed his lips together for a moment to suppress another smile. "Come now, Duchess. Surely a little harmless flirtation is permitted. And as much as I would love to ravish you, I shall only do so at your invitation. Shall we continue the tour?" He offered her his arm again.

Georgie scowled. "You are a scoundrel to your very bones. Your comments and actions in no way inspire the trust you wish me to place in you."

"I would suggest to you that most men are scoundrels when it comes to the fairer sex, Your Grace. At least you are left in no doubt of what is on my mind. Furthermore, I have just admitted you are safe from any attempts at seduction unless you so desire it. Is it not better to know where I stand on the matter rather than pretend an indifference? Surely you must give me credit for being honest."

Georgie studied his face for a moment. Her blue eyes gleamed—whether with amusement or anger or both, he couldn't be sure. "Yes. I suppose I must," she acknowledged grudgingly. "But even though you have been quite frank, you try my patience, Markham. Heaven knows, I've made it abundantly clear where *I* stand on the matter of flirtation."

Rafe quirked an eyebrow. "Contrary to all appearances."

"Ugh." This time she did stamp her foot. "Just show me the rest of the house, or I *will* bury myself in my room."

Rafe bit the inside of his cheek to stop himself chuckling as he moved toward the door. "This way if you please, madam," he said with polite solemnity as he opened it wider and gestured toward the main hall beyond.

Chin raised and her shawl wrapped firmly about herself, Georgie swept past him.

Rafe didn't dare offer her his arm this time.

CHAPTER 11

The Boulle clock on the mantelpiece was striking three o'clock when Markham escorted Georgie into Rivergate's library. Perhaps to dispel the gloom of the afternoon, Markham's staff had built up the fire and many of the candles and lamps had been lit. Even though it was tempting to select a leather-bound volume from the oak shelves and take a seat before the fire, Georgie ignored the impulse. Crossing to one of the windows, she peered out through the rain-lashed glass to the driveway below. There was no sign of activity. No sign of anyone at all.

"I can see how worried you are, Duchess," said Markham softly from behind her. "I anticipate that my footman and groom should be back very soon."

Georgie released a shaky breath and wrapped her arms about her middle to contain a shiver. It seemed as if the cold bleakness of the day had penetrated her as well. As Markham had shown her through the main living areas of the house, her apprehension had risen steadily, to the point where she could no longer concentrate on anything he said to her. And he'd obviously noticed. "I really hope so," she replied. Even her voice trembled, but she didn't care. "Better still would be the return of Jonathon himself. Wait—"

Markham moved to her side and drew the claret-red velvet curtain back. "Speak of the devil, it's Ridley and Fanshaw." Two men on horseback had appeared between the wrought iron gates.

But not Jonathon.

Before the men had even made it halfway up the drive, Markham had taken her hand, threading his fingers through hers. "Come," he said, tugging her toward the door. "Let's see what they have to say."

Georgie didn't even think to protest about Markham's familiar hold on her hand. Her heart pounding, she simply rushed out into the hall with him, past Rivergate's astonished looking butler in the vestibule and then straight out to the covered portico. Within moments, a sodden and very breathless footman appeared at the top of the stairs.

"My lord... Your Grace," he began.

"Is my brother all right?"

The footman turned to her and bowed. "Yes. I believe so."

Georgie released a sigh as heady relief washed over her, but Markham frowned. "You believe so?" he asked tersely.

"Yes. All thoroughfares between Rivergate and the White Swan have been cut off by local flooding, and we did not see any sign of Her Grace's carriage, my lord. We believe Sir Jonathon must have made it across. One of the local landowners—a Mr. Chapel—who was in the process of sandbagging his property, Lowood House, also reported seeing a fine carriage pass by about an hour and a half ago before the roadway became impassable."

Markham nodded. "That would also fit the time frame I had in my mind." He turned to Georgie and after curving his hand about her elbow, drew her gently to the other side of the portico, out of earshot of the footman. "Your Grace, I'm sure your brother has made it safely to the White Swan. The road on the other side of Lowood House leads to much higher ground. If your carriage was able to cross earlier in the afternoon, there is no doubt your driver would have been able to negotiate the rest of the short journey. It seems that Jonathon may be spending the night at the inn with Lord Farley."

Georgie frowned as a different kind of panic fluttered within her. "Surely not the whole night." She really didn't want to be spending the entire night alone at Rivergate with Markham. Not at all.

"I doubt the waters will subside between now and nightfall. And it would be foolish indeed for your brother to try to cross a flooded road in the dark. Rest assured, I'm sure Jonathon is swigging ale and claret and feasting on the inn's very good beef and suet pudding as we speak."

Georgie closed her eyes and sighed heavily. Jonathon was safe. And she could easily imagine he was making the best of the situation with Farley. She should at least do the same. It was no one's fault unforeseen circumstances and the elements had prevented so many of Markham's invited guests from attending the party.

"Your Grace?"

Georgie opened her eyes to find Markham studying her face intently, a concerned light in his gray eyes.

"I am fine," she reassured him. "Just very relieved that there is some encouraging news about my brother."

"I'm sure he and Farley's party will join us as soon as they are able to."

Georgie nodded. "Yes." She offered Markham a smile. "Thank you for all you have done. Your concern and your help, mean more than I can say. You see, Jonathon is the only family I have..." Her breath hitched for a moment and she swallowed to clear the tight feeling from her throat. "I am truly grateful."

Markham returned her smile. The light in his eyes was soft. "You are quite welcome, Your Grace." He then turned to the sodden footman. "Thank you, Fanshaw. Now go and get warm and dry, man, before you catch your death."

Fanshaw bowed. "Yes, my lord."

Markham gestured toward the door. "Shall we return to the library?" he asked. "And if looking through Rivergate's substantial book collection doesn't take your fancy, I have a very nice chess set if you'd like to play. Unless," he smiled devilishly, "chess, like cards, is also not permitted."

Georgie really didn't think she was up to playing any sort of game with Markham right at this moment. He might have declared she was safe from any further overtures from him, but given the look in his eye, she wasn't so sure. Especially since he'd boldly stated seducing her *was* on his mind. Finding a book and then taking refuge in her room suddenly seemed very appealing. Her reply was guarded. "Hmm, perhaps another spot of tea would be a better option for now."

"And something to eat," Markham added. "You didn't have a single bite of anything in the drawing room earlier. You must be ravenous. I know I am."

Before Georgie could even respond, he caught the eye of the butler then placed his request for tea and a light luncheon for two.

"Thank you," Georgie said as Markham gently steered her back toward the library. Now that she knew Jonathon was all right, she realized she was actually famished. Breakfast seemed a long time ago.

She approached the arrangement of chairs before the fireplace and hovered uncertainly behind a settee upholstered in burgundy damask. Should she take a seat or peruse the shelves? Just like before when they had taken tea, she felt painfully self-conscious and couldn't think of a single thing to say, especially now she could sense Markham watching her.

He'd crossed to one of the ebony oak bookcases beside the fire. With one arm resting along one of the shelves, he appeared quite relaxed as he frankly studied her.

Annoying man. Why was it up to her to initiate a topic of conversation? She glanced about the room, desperately looking for something—anything—to remark upon. She'd been quite cold when she'd been out on the portico earlier, but now an uncomfortable warmth enveloped her. Her cheeks began to burn and it wasn't because she'd drawn closer to the fire. Swallowing to moisten her suddenly very dry mouth, she ventured the first, most mundane question that sprang to mind. "Is the collection of books here yours, or did they come with the sale of Rivergate?"

"Some of them came with the house, yes. Mainly the older volumes you see on the wall behind you. All of the books on these shelves"—he gestured at the bookcase he stood next to and the matching one on the other side of the fireplace— "come from my own collection at Avonmore Park, my family's home."

Georgie crossed to the opposite shelf and ran her gaze over the titles at her eye level. *Choose a book and leave,* she told herself, but she asked aloud, "Do you enjoy reading?"

"Yes. Amongst other things." When Georgie glanced at Markham, his gaze had become so dark and heavy, she couldn't mistake his meaning.

And she couldn't bear it. The building irritation inside her burst forth. "Why do you do that?" she accused angrily. "Turn everything I say inside-out and upside-down? Turn a perfectly ordinary conversation into something so...so—"

"So entertaining?"

"So vexing!" Georgie snapped. "Laden with unseemly undercurrents and double meanings. I swear you could turn even a discussion about the weather or this Turkish carpet beneath our feet into something quite vulgar."

His mouth tilted into a thoroughly wicked smile. "Would you like me to?"

"No!"

"Your Grace, I can hardly see how making the simple comment that I enjoy other pursuits besides reading could be misconstrued as vulgar." Markham placed a hand upon his chest. "You wound me."

"What rot. It's not what you say exactly." Georgie paused as past conversations about swiving, tongue lashings, and spanking sprang into her mind, and she amended, "Well, sometimes it is... But more often than not, it's *how* you say things."

Markham raised his eyebrows. "*How* I say it?"

"I will not explain further as you know precisely what I mean." She threw her hands up in the air. "If you are not going to converse properly with me, perhaps we should just play chess after all."

He grinned. "I knew you would succumb eventually."

"See? You—oh, I give up." Now Markham had turned her into an inarticulate dolt. Clutching her shawl tightly about herself, she stalked over to the chess table that was set in an alcove by one of the windows. She'd play a game—and hopefully bring the conceited, frustrating so-and-so down a peg or two—perhaps stay for tea and toast or whatever else arrived, then beat a retreat to her bedchamber. She was certain to have a megrim coming on that would last until Jonathon returned.

Before Markham could assist her with her chair, she sat down and picked up one of the finely carved, blond wooden pawns directly in front of her. Boxwood perhaps. "Is it a Calvert?" she asked as she reached for a glossy, red knight from the other side, probably rosewood.

"You have a good eye," remarked Markham as he sat down opposite her.

"Teddy has...had one." Keeping her gaze lowered, she

returned Markham's piece to its rightful place before replacing her pawn. She didn't want to look up and see compassion in his eyes again. Not only would it bring on another wave of sadness, she suspected it would make her regard Markham 'more favorably' as he'd put it earlier. And she still wasn't sure if that was a good idea.

When Markham didn't say anything else, she murmured, "The style of the pieces is very distinctive." Despite her best efforts to remain impassive, her voice cracked a little.

"I can see you miss Teddy terribly, Duchess," Markham said softly. "Did you play chess with him often?"

Georgie needlessly straightened her king and queen as bittersweet memories flooded her mind. "Yes... He used to say it was one of the few games he could actually beat me at." She took a deep breath and at last looked up, a falsely gay smile plastered on her face. She didn't want to talk about her marriage anymore. Too many inconvenient questions—about Teddy, Jonathon and her past might arise. She needed to distract Markham, and quickly. "So, how good a chess player are you?"

Interest flared in Markham's eyes. "Good enough."

She maintained her smile, still pretending nonchalance. "Care to lay a wager?" It was a risky maneuver, but it was a gamble she was willing to take if it kept Markham focused on other things.

"You should know by now that I would never say no to such a proposal, Your Grace. What do you suggest we play for?"

Aha. Her strategy was working. It suddenly occurred to Georgie that perhaps she could take advantage of the situation. She tapped her chin, as if in thought. "If I win, you *will* tell me how you trounced me at piquet."

"And if I win?" Markham asked, his eyes gleaming.

She shrugged a shoulder. "You don't have to tell me."

Markham crossed his arms over his wide chest and she tried very hard not to notice the substantial outline of his upper arm muscles beneath the fine woolen fabric. "That hardly seems fair," he replied gravely, however there was still a glint of amusement in his eyes. "I don't *have* to tell you *now*. You will have to offer me better terms than that."

Oh, heavens. What can I possibly offer him other than... Georgie glanced at Markham's mouth and blushed hotly. *Stop it, Georgie. Don't even think about it.* Somehow, even though her pulse leapt erratically, she managed to speak with a relatively clear and confident sounding voice. "I will dine with you rather than requesting a tray in my room."

Markham rubbed his chin in apparent contemplation. "Tempting. But still not enticing enough."

Georgie straightened in her seat. "What do you suggest then, my lord?" she asked stiffly. "Keep in mind that I might very well get up and leave if you propose anything remotely improper."

"Hmm. If I win, you will dine with me, staying for the four-course meal planned. And then..."

"Markham," she warned.

"Wait." He raised a hand. "Please, hear me out. You will dine with me *and* I will tell you how I trounced you at piquet afterward."

Georgie frowned in confusion. "But why? You just said you didn't have to tell me. So why would you offer such terms? Terms that are from your perspective, even a little unfavorable."

"On the contrary, they're not unfavorable at all," Markham said in a low voice as intimate as a caress. "It's simple really. My terms guarantee that if *I* win, I will be able to enjoy your delightful company for the entire evening. Contrary to what you might think, winning at cards or chess is not that important to me, but..."

~

But winning you, is. Rafe had to bite his tongue to stop the words slipping out.

"But," Georgie prompted. Her expression had grown wary again and he couldn't blame her, considering that seduction was uppermost on his mind.

"But ensuring you have a pleasurable time is," he finished. "I live to serve, Your Grace." That admission was true at least. And in more ways than one.

"How very noble of you, my lord," replied Georgie in a crisp tone. She picked up one of her blond pawns and made the first move in the game. "However, I think only time will tell whether your last pronouncement *is* true."

Rafe moved one of his own pawns. "I look forward to proving myself," he said with deliberate softness. "Your good opinion means a lot to me. More than I can say, in fact."

Georgie's cheeks grew a delicious shade of pink and she kept her attention focused on the board. "I hardly see why."

"Perhaps, as you say, time will tell."

She didn't respond to that.

They fell into a companionable silence as the game continued. Georgiana was indeed a skilled player. When their tea and a tray of light savory dishes arrived, they took a small break from the game and Rafe was pleased that the conversation began to flow easily between them. It probably helped that he had decided to play the perfect gentleman. For once he refrained from engaging in overtly sexual banter with Georgie and kept to safe subjects even the sternest of society's matrons would be happy to discuss. At long last, it seemed the duchess was comfortable in his presence.

He noted her smile was genuine rather than forced. Her beautiful blue eyes were alight with good humor rather than sharp glints of annoyance. Her cheeks were flushed with laughter instead of embarrassment or anger. And the most encouraging sign of all was that she'd stopped clutching her cashmere shawl about her like a shield. She'd let it slide from her shoulders and it was now draped over the back of her chair, entirely forgotten.

Such simple pleasures, taking tea, chatting and playing chess, but Rafe decided this would count as one of the most enjoyable afternoons he'd ever spent. When he and Georgie eventually resumed their game, his body seemed to be filled with a warm buzz of happiness, as if he'd been drinking cognac. Somewhere, at the back of his mind, the habitual warning to crush his tender emotions lurked, but he chose to ignore it. He was fast becoming utterly enthralled with Georgiana and for the first time in his life, he didn't want to avoid the feeling. Didn't *have* to avoid it. He could embrace it.

As play continued, the light outside the room began to fade. At some point, perhaps because Rafe kept losing his concentration—the base male in him couldn't help but notice the tantalizing swell of Georgie's breasts every time she leaned forward to move her chess pieces—or perhaps because he didn't much care about the outcome of the match, he completely lost control of the game. When Georgiana triumphantly called 'checkmate', he wasn't surprised in the least.

"Congratulations, Your Grace," he said, inordinately pleased to see her smiling at him so brightly. "Well played."

"Thank you," she replied with a gracious tilt of her head. "You play very well also. However, I believe my victory may partly be due to the fact that you seemed to lose your focus toward the end. As if your mind were...elsewhere?"

As he couldn't very well confess he'd been imagining how he would pleasure Georgie in bed when he finally got her there, Rafe thought it wise to dissemble. "No, I think it's more the case that you are unquestionably the better player."

"I'm not sure about that, Lord Markham." Georgie's smile slipped and her expression grew serious, perhaps even a little remorseful. "And I must add, you are considerably more gracious in defeat than I have hitherto been. I want to offer you a sincere apology for my less than amiable—nay, ill-mannered behavior—last week and, indeed, when we first met."

On an impulse, Rafe reached forward and covered one of her elegant hands with his. "I did not make it easy for you, Your Grace. The way I teased you afterward, on each occasion, I was a complete cad. If anyone deserves an apology, it is you."

As he expected, a blush crept across Georgie's cheeks. "I...I don't know what to say." She didn't pull away and Rafe's pulse rate kicked up a notch at the thought she might enjoy his touch.

"You do not have to say anything," he said softly. "However, I would be most pleased, and honored, if you joined me in a celebratory-cum-reconciliation drink."

Georgie glanced at the clock on the mantel and he held his breath, praying he hadn't pushed her too far. To his relief, she smiled and inclined her head in agreement. "Even though half-past four is a trifle early for me, I will not say no."

"Excellent." Rafe assisted her to rise before crossing the room to a small cabinet beside his desk. "May I offer you a glass of sherry or Madeira?"

"Sherry, thank you. Canary, if you have it."

"I do." He poured each of them a small glass, then after passing her one, sought her gaze. "May I propose a toast?"

She smiled. "Of course."

He raised his glass. "Let us drink to our health and happiness but most of all, to our mutual passion for a good game."

Georgie raised an eyebrow, no doubt because of his choice of wording for the toast, but nevertheless, she touched her glass to his. "Indeed." She took a small sip then fixed him with a cool, uncompromising stare. The frosty Ice Duchess had returned in full force. "So enough hedging about with pretty words, Markham. It's time to deliver what you owe."

❧

Even after a week, Georgie was still dying to know precisely how Markham had roundly vanquished her not once or twice, but three times at cards. Heavens, it was only because of her defeat last week that she was even at Rivergate.

It might be irrational, and she really shouldn't give a fig about how others in the *ton* saw her, but in her heart, she knew she would never again have the confidence to play a public game of piquet until she discovered what her vulnerable spot—her Achilles heel—actually was. It was definitely time for Markham to pay the piper.

And it seemed Markham wasn't about to disagree. "Yes, you are absolutely right, Your Grace," he said easily. Leaning back on his desk, he finished his sherry in one long smooth sip, then fixed his disturbingly intense gaze on her. "During my years as a diplomat, I became quite adept at studying people. Not just their overall expressions, but subtle things such as the movements of their eyes, the rate of their breathing, a twitch of a muscle, a sigh, a small gesture. You might be surprised at how easy it is to accurately glean what is in another's mind just by being able to interpret these tiny clues. For instance, I *always* know when someone is lying, or bluffing. When we played piquet, I knew when you had misled me with your calls. And I was able to deduce what you would or wouldn't play and adjust my play accordingly. Every single time."

Georgie frowned, entirely skeptical. *That was all there was to it?* "But...I have been playing for years, Markham. I know how to school my features. I didn't earn the title Ice Duchess for nothing, you know."

"I'll admit you are good and your reputation as a remarkable player is well deserved, but you couldn't hide from me. There were certain things you unconsciously did that betrayed you."

Suddenly intrigued, Georgie's next question slipped out before she'd even considered the consequences. "Such as?"

"Little things." Markham's fingers brushed hers as he took her glass of sherry and placed it upon the desk. "Let me show you."

Both fascinated and petrified, her heart pounding furiously against her ribs, Georgie found herself rooted to the spot as Markham pushed away from the desk. He slowly lifted a hand then gently stroked the back of his fingers down the side of her neck.

"The flutter of your racing pulse just here," he explained, studying her flesh as if it were the most fascinating thing he had ever seen. His fingertips then traced a path along her quivering skin to the base of her throat. "The movement here as you try to swallow past a throat tight with nerves. The increased pace of your breathing." His gaze then drifted upward and focused on her mouth. "The way you press your lips together after you've told an untruth, as if wanting to take it all back." He brushed his thumb across her trembling lower lip then at last he raised his smoldering gray eyes to hers. "The nervous dart of your tongue."

Georgie tried to summon a feeling of outrage at his presumption, tried to marshal the will to turn on her heel and go, but she just couldn't. Not when her whole body was trembling with a paralyzing combination of apprehension and acute longing. Whether she was spellbound or trapped, it hardly mattered. Either way, she knew that if she stayed, Markham would soon be ravishing her just as he'd wished. And the most frightening realization of all was that part of her wanted him too. Very, very much.

"You seem to be able to read me as easily as any book." Her voice sounded strange. Husky, yet strained. Brittle. "What am I thinking now?"

"You're wondering if I am going to kiss you. You're nervous, perhaps even a little afraid that I might. And you're also afraid that I won't." Markham's eyes, heavy-lidded with blatant desire, searched hers. "Am I right?"

She twisted her fingers into her skirts, resisting the urge to grip Markham by the lapels—to shake him or draw him closer, she could hardly tell. "Yes, damn you."

His mouth curved slowly into a devastating, bone-melting rake's smile. "Such language, Your Grace. But I don't mind at all. In fact, I rather like seeing you this way."

"What, bristling with rage?" she managed to grit out.

"No. Tempted. Perhaps even a little reckless and on the brink of stepping out of your self-imposed cage of propriety. But it's your choice entirely, what happens next. What do *you* want, Duchess? A kiss or—"

Georgie didn't let him finish. She simply reached up, grasped him by the shoulders and pressed her lips to his.

Markham responded to her invitation immediately. With a deep groan, he dragged her against his body, his arms wrapping around her, binding her to him, his hot mouth sliding frantically against hers. Desperate for more, her entire being aching with a wild desire held in check for far too long, Georgie arched into him, her hands spearing into his short, dark, silky hair, pulling him closer still; wanting, craving, seeking the pleasure she'd been denying herself all afternoon, perhaps forever, the pleasure she sensed only he could ever give her.

When Markham pushed his tongue against the seam of his lips, Georgie parted for him instantly, a satisfied moan escaping her at the very moment he entered her mouth. Assailed by delicious sensation—the flavor of black tea and sweet sherry and Markham himself—she tasted him back, her eager tongue twining with his.

As one breath-stealing kiss melded into another, and then another, all thought fled. Her long-held fears and inhibitions seemed to be rapidly dissolving in a torrent of dizzying, all-consuming lust. A furious lust that made her quim slippery and her nipples throb as they never had before. Nothing existed except Markham and her burning need for him.

And it seemed Markham needed her too. At some point during their frenzied bout of kissing, he'd sunk back onto the desk and she was now positioned between his muscular thighs, one of his large hands gripping her nape. And there could be no mistaking the insistent jut of his rock-hard cock against her belly. When he tore his mouth from hers and began to devour her jaw and neck with nips and ragged, sucking kisses, she let him, even encouraged him; inclined her head and swept her tumbling curls to the side to allow him unfettered access.

The moist sweep of his tongue across the sensitized flesh at the edge of her neckline momentarily roused Georgie from the sweet madness engulfing her. Pulling gently on his hair, she breathed his name. "Markham..."

He immediately raised his head; he looked dazed, his eyes a dark shade of gray, the pupils dilated as though he were intoxicated. Breathing heavily, lips swollen, cravat askew and his hair ruffled, he looked thoroughly disreputable—and so handsome, he stole her reason and her breath all over again.

"Do you want me to stop?" His voice might be rough with lust but she knew he would do as she asked. That he was letting her choose what should happen next touched her deeply; the remaining core of cold fear and doubt inside her started to melt completely away.

"I... You offered a kiss, but..." Georgie paused, unsure how to put into words what she really wanted. That maybe this time she would find fulfillment instead of the stultifying, soul-destroying torment that had been her lot for so long. Perhaps Markham truly could help her to tear down the barriers within her mind and her heart.

Please, dear God, let it be so. Heart in her mouth, she drew a shaky breath. "I don't want you to stop... I want more."

"Then more you shall have, madam." With a low growl, Markham effortlessly swept Georgie off her feet into his arms and within moments, she found herself draped sideways across his lap on the nearby settee.

"Tell me what you want. More of this?" he murmured before burying his face in her neck again. She felt him inhale deeply as if drinking in the scent from a bouquet of the sweetest, summer blooms, and then his mouth was on her, his lips and tongue tracing a path from her ear down to her heaving breasts. "Or would you prefer this?" With a deftness that should have shocked her, Markham loosened the ties and buttons fastening her bodice, eased away her stays and linen chemise from her breasts then set his mouth over one protruding nipple and suckled.

Georgie couldn't speak, only gasp as a flash of pure, molten desire shot through her veins straight to her nether regions. She was vividly reminded of Markham's attempted seduction the week before, but this time she wasn't going to stop him. Holding her steady with one strong arm, Markham taunted her breasts with tongue and teeth and lips and fingers until she was panting and clutching at his bent head as if holding on for dear life. It wasn't long before the pulsating throb between her thighs had intensified to the point of discomfort and she began to move restlessly upon Markham's lap.

Markham groaned, the gust of his warm breath against her nipple making her shiver. "Christ, Your Grace." He raised his head and kissed her briefly on the mouth again. "You'll have me spending in my breeches like a youth if you continue to squirm like that."

"I cannot help it," she protested, pulling at his cravat, suddenly wanting to see and kiss his throat. Inhale his potent masculine scent—spicy bergamot cologne and the essence of the man himself. "You're driving me mad with wanting."

"Good." Before she could finish untying the linen folds at his neck, he pushed her down onto the cushions of the settee. Bracing himself on one arm, he leaned over her, his gaze trapping hers. "Now you know how I've felt since the very first moment I laid eyes upon you."

Without preamble he claimed her mouth again, thrusting his tongue deep inside her as he tugged up her skirts and slipped a hand beneath...then groaned. "Thank God you're not wearing drawers. Bloody annoying things," he murmured hoarsely.

If she wasn't so far gone, Georgie knew she would have blushed. But as Markham's wicked fingers skimmed past the top of her silk stocking, then traced a light, teasing path up her bare leg, all the way to the excruciatingly sensitive skin at the top of her inner thigh, she really didn't care.

"Markham," she whimpered, straining toward his hand. "For the love of all that's sacred..."

He chuckled against her mouth. "Is this what you want?" His fingertips gently ruffled through the curls just above, but not quite touching her slick, aching cleft. "Do you think this will help to ease your torment?"

She wanted to berate him for being so cruel, making her wait for his touch right where she craved it the most. But all she could do was part her legs and gasp into him, "Yes. God damn you, ye—"

The moment one of his long fingers slid between her wet folds and unerringly found her throbbing core, the only sound that left her lips was an inarticulate moan. Touching herself had felt glorious, but this... This feeling was sublime. Sweet Lord, why had she resisted this amazing man for so long?

Markham lowered his head and began feasting on her breasts again, and all the while his clever fingers circled and stroked, expertly building the hot, sweet tension inside her. Her inner passage began to wind tighter and tighter. So tight. And then somehow, everything went wrong.

A noise—a log falling in the grate—made her jump at the very moment Markham slid a finger deep inside her. She gasped at the unexpected intrusion, her sheath clenching in protest. And her pleasure began to ebb away. *No. Oh no... Don't think, Georgie.*

"Your Grace," Markham withdrew and caught her gaze; a deep frown creased his brow. "I'm sorry. Did I hurt you?"

Georgie shook her head. "No. You just took me by surprise. It has been such a very long time since..." She closed her eyes, determined not to revisit her last time. *Shut it out. Don't think of him. Not his name, not anything. There's only Markham.* She forced a smile and reached past the tangle of her rucked up skirts to Markham's hand that now rested on her thigh. "It's all right. I want... What you were doing before, I want that."

"This?" Markham bent forward and placed a tender, almost chaste kiss at the corner of her mouth as he renewed his erotic finger-play between her thighs.

"Yes," Georgie whispered and closed her eyes. But it was no good. It didn't matter what Markham did—kiss her mouth, her neck, pleasure her breasts, circle or rub or stroke any part of her quim—or how much she tried to empty her mind and relax. Rekindling the spark of desire within her was a hopeless exercise. Her body had become as unresponsive as one of the lumps of wood stacked in the pile beside the fireplace. Bone dry and completely lifeless.

Georgie's stomach knotted with humiliation and bitter

disappointment. Hot tears stung the back of her eyelids and she crammed a fist to her mouth to stop a sob escaping. *Oh God, even Markham can't help me. I can't bear it.*

"Georgiana?" Markham's fingers stilled. He'd obviously noticed something was amiss. How could he not? The evidence of her desire had all but dried up.

"I'm sorry. I can't do this." Georgie swallowed, trying in vain to dislodge the hard lump of embarrassed anguish jamming her throat, but there was no disguising the fact that her voice was thick with tears. Pushing Markham's hand away, she sat up, twisting away from him.

"I *did* hurt you." The rich timbre of Markham's voice was tinged with remorse.

"No. You didn't. It's not anything like that. Or you." Her fingers trembling, her movements frantic, Georgie clumsily jerked her clothing back into place. "It's definitely not you."

"Well then, if you're worried about becoming pregnant if we take things further, I swear I'll take care so that won't happen." The touch of Markham's hand on her shoulder made her flinch. He must have felt her recoil as he immediately let go. "I'm sorry if you thought—"

"Please. Don't apologize." Somehow Georgie found the strength to stand. She couldn't look at Markham. Instead, she simply tried to concentrate on doing up her bodice. Tears dripped onto her fingers. "I need to go."

"Georgie." Markham stood and tried to catch her hand but she snatched it away.

"Don't." Still unable to meet Markham's gaze, she stepped away, heading toward the door. The gathering ache in her throat was almost unbearable. "Just let me go. This. You and I. It was a mistake. God knows, I tried to tell you as much last week."

"No." Markham closed the short distance between them

and grasped her by the shoulders. "Look at me. Talk to me. I can't let you leave like this, Georg—"

"Don't call me that! I've *never* given you permission to use my name," Georgie snapped, wrenching herself away. It was a completely ridiculous thing to say, given the liberties she'd let Markham take with her body only moments ago, but right now, blind anger was the only thing stopping her from dissolving into a blithering mess upon the floor at his feet. "And don't follow me."

She bolted for the door and as it slammed behind her, the flood of scalding tears she'd only just been keeping at bay, gushed forth. She'd meant it when she'd told Markham she needed to go. She couldn't stay at Rivergate. Not now.

Ignoring the gaping footman in the hall, Georgie made a dash for the vestibule and the front door.

CHAPTER 12

C hrist, I'm a fool.

Rafe stared at the gleaming mahogany panels of the library door—the door Georgie had soundly slammed on him —then dropped his head. Pinching the bridge of his nose, he tried to control his ragged breathing and riotous thoughts.

No, I'm wrong. I'm worse than a fool. I'm an arrogant, selfish arse, too busy thinking with my cock instead of using my brain.

He *knew* Georgie had been deeply hurt by Lord Craven, but he'd been too quick to dismiss her initial reluctance to share any degree of intimacy with him. A reluctance that was no doubt, entirely justified.

No, reluctance wasn't the right word. It was more than that. In the moments just before Georgie had fled the library, Rafe had sensed deep-seated anxiety, perhaps even fear within her. Bitter anger and despair. The same emotions that had flared up during their fraught encounter at the Maxwells' last week. Yet on both occasions, he'd callously disregarded her apprehension and like an inept, horny adolescent, he'd charged in anyway. God, he'd even thoughtlessly quipped her propriety was self-imposed.

But it wasn't.

Be honest with yourself, man. You didn't want to consider the full ramifications of what might have befallen Georgiana at Craven's hands because it didn't suit your prick's agenda.

Shame welled within Rafe's chest as he contemplated how his own roughshod indifference had hurt Georgie. He knew at least on some level she desired him. The sweet, breathy moans that had escaped her as he'd pleasured her wet quim were clear enough evidence. But when he'd entered her, her arousal had died almost immediately. And she'd been devastated.

One thing was certain: whatever fragile trust Georgie had previously placed in him, it was now shattered. Although she'd stated he didn't need to apologize for anything, the pain in her voice, in her tear-filled eyes—he couldn't help *but* feel responsible. He'd pushed Georgie too far, too fast without due care or regard. What he'd done was unconscionable.

Rafe dragged a hand down his face and sighed. Standing about mentally flagellating himself wasn't going to repair the damage he'd done. He needed a clear head. Ignoring the throbbing pain in his groin, he crossed over to the cabinet beside his desk and poured himself a good measure of the strongest, peatiest whisky he owned, then downed it in one gulp. The alcohol burned his gullet, but ironically it also helped him to regain control of his body, as well as master the dark and turbulent emotions still roiling around inside him. *Stow your lust, guilt and thirst for vengeance, Markham. They won't help Georgiana.*

Rafe tossed back another whisky then proceeded to remove his loosened cravat. The memory of Georgie wild with desire, tugging at the silk to get to his skin suddenly filled his mind. Yes, she definitely wanted him. However, even after a decade, her past—whatever Craven had done to her—it was still holding her captive. He'd stake his life on it.

With a plan already taking shape in his mind, Rafe strode to the library door, determined to find Georgie. As he suspected the hall was deserted; she'd most probably retreated to her room. He headed for the staircase.

If Georgie needed more time to feel comfortable with the idea of being with him, she could have it. Indeed, after living the life of a spy for near on a decade, patience was one attribute he possessed in spades. He most certainly wasn't going to give up on her now, not after he'd tasted such sweetness in her arms. He *would* have her. No matter how long it took.

"My lord."

Frowning, Rafe turned around to find one of his footmen hovering in the vestibule. The lad's brow was also creased with a deep frown.

"Yes, Harris?"

The footman swallowed. "Ah, it's probably not my place to say anything, but the duchess... After she left the library, I saw her rush out of the front door, my lord."

What? Surely not.

Rafe shot a look past the footman to the half open door. Rain still teemed down in buckets. Christ, was Georgie that upset that she'd decided to bolt altogether?

"Did you see which way she went? Did she take a coat?" Rafe's voice was harsher than he intended but sharp panic was shooting through his veins.

Harris blushed a little. "I didn't like to pry, my lord. But no, she didn't take a coat. However, I did see her turn toward the portico stairs on the left. I don't know why, but I thought she might be headed for the stables."

One glance at the footman told a different story. His periwig, the broadcloth upon his shoulders and the emerald satin of his waistcoat were rain-splattered. He'd no doubt followed the duchess at least part of the way, but Rafe wasn't about to berate him at this point for that or his slight variation upon the truth. He liked to think the man was motivated by concern rather than the desire to collect a tidbit of salacious gossip to share with the other staff. But he would have to deal with that later.

Rafe thanked Harris then dashed out to the portico and down the stairs into the driving sheets of freezing rain. There was no sign of Georgie on the drive. And it was rapidly growing dark. He could barely see the gates or the Thames beyond.

Jesus, what was the woman thinking? Would she really attempt to leave in these conditions? Heart already thundering against the wall of his chest, he broke into a flat out run, heading toward the rear of Rivergate where the stables were located. She only had a ten-minute head start on him at most. He had to believe that given the appalling weather, she wouldn't venture far, if indeed she dared to venture out at all.

Perhaps that depends on how desperate she is. Anxiety and guilt might be twisting his guts, but one single thought dominated Rafe's brain. *I have to find her.*

Damn it all to hell.

Georgie bit her lip to stop the coarse expletive escaping from her frozen lips. The precious minutes she needed to make good her escape were fast slipping away and there was nothing much she could do about it. Blinking away tears of frustration, she continued with her all but useless attempt to tighten the bridle on one of her own carriage horses. But her numb, wet fingers shook so much, she couldn't manage it. She glanced around the dimly lit stables, hoping beyond hope that there might be an acquiescent stable lad lurking about in the shadows who might help her, but aside from the occasional equine snuffle and quite whicker, nothing else and no one stirred.

Georgie let out a shaky sigh. There was nothing for it: she was going to have to ready the horse all by herself. She was already soaked to the bone so taking a ride through the rain to find an alternative place to stay for the night was a small price to pay if it meant she didn't have to face Markham again. There *must* be some other lane or thoroughfare she could take that would lead her to the White Swan. At the very least she could entreat the owner of Lowood House—Mr. Chapel, if she recalled correctly—to accommodate her until it was safe to cross or get word to Jonathon.

She was definitely *not* going back inside Rivergate. The thought of seeing Markham again filled her with such mortification and dread, her cheeks burned despite her half-frozen state.

With the bridle now as secure as she could make it, Georgie rushed from the stall to search for a saddle. *There.* Along the back wall was an array of neatly arranged tack items. The traitorous head groom had disappeared as soon as she'd requested that her second carriage be readied for her—the one that had conveyed her maid, Jonathon's valet and most of their luggage—but instead of doing her bidding, the man had given her a strange look before informing her the traces were broken and needed repairing. And before Georgie could even draw breath to order him to find her own carriage driver, he'd promptly left—and she was in no doubt he'd summon his employer...which meant she probably only had a few more minutes before Markham appeared to try and stop her.

Surely you can saddle a horse, Georgie. How hard can it be?

She spied a sidesaddle on a rack and attempted to hoist it up. However, her numb fingers and trembling arms clad in wet, slippery silk couldn't manage the hefty leather bulk and she immediately dropped it into the straw at her feet. Cursing, she bent down and somehow dragged it up again then headed back to her horse's stall. Perhaps sensing her anxiety, the beast was restive and moved away from her when she attempted to throw the saddle over his back. It fell again and this time it landed on one of her slipper-shod feet. A sharp stab of pain assailed her and she cried out as another wave of tears scalded her eyes.

This is hopeless. And completely mad. What on earth am I doing? Pulling her foot free, Georgie hobbled into a vacant stall before gingerly lowering herself into the hay to inspect the damage. The light was poor and her stocking was torn, wet and filthy, but as she carefully probed her throbbing flesh, she ascertained her foot was only bruised. *How fitting,* she thought. *It will match my bruised pride just nicely.*

Her whole body quaking with cold and misery, Georgie drew her knees up to her chest and dropped her head forward. Unless the earth suddenly cracked open and swallowed her up, it was time to face the painful truth. She wasn't going anywhere.

"Your Grace?" Rafe pushed his dripping hair out of his eyes and squinted into the gloomy interior of the stables, scanning the shadows for Georgie. There was no immediate sign of her but he was not discouraged. On his headlong dash here, he'd run into the head groom who'd informed him that the duchess was indeed in the stables. And she'd requested a carriage.

Rafe took a few steps farther inside and stopped to listen. Above the insistent tattoo of the rain upon the roof, he could just hear something else—the sound of a woman quietly weeping. *Bloody hell*. His heart clenched at the thought he'd caused Georgiana so much distress. He prayed she wouldn't flatly refuse to speak with him. But he suspected she very well might.

He grabbed a nearby lantern then advanced forward, checking each stall to right and left until midway along, he found her. Huddled in a dark corner, she sat with her head bowed and her arms wrapped around her knees. The sight of her brought so low pierced his heart with another sharp stab of guilt.

He cleared his throat to ease a sudden feeling of constriction. "Your Grace?" he repeated.

Georgie lifted her head slightly and swiped at her eyes. Rafe could barely see her face through the tumble of her sodden brown hair. "Leave me alone, Markham. I'll be all right." Her voice might be husky with tears but there was no mistaking the authority in her tone.

"Perhaps." Rafe placed the lantern on a hook by the entrance before approaching her. "But I am not sure that I will be."

He shrugged off his wool coat—at least it was relatively dry inside—and slid to the hay strewn floor beside her. "You're cold," he said softly as he placed the garment over her quaking body. He was heartened when she pulled it around herself rather than ordering him away again.

"Thank you," she whispered.

"You're welcome." Rafe risked placing his arm around Georgie's shoulders and when she leaned against him, he permitted himself a shaky sigh of relief. "It's the least I can do." Georgie might have hidden behind her cards, her title, her frosty glares and sharp quips and a marriage of convenience for a long, long time, but she couldn't hide from him. He wouldn't let her. "We need to talk."

Georgie shrugged then sighed deeply. "Talking won't make things better."

Her tone was so dejected, Rafe wanted to pull her into his arms and hug her fiercely to his chest, then kiss away all her fears and doubts. But he didn't. He needed to proceed carefully so he simply murmured, "It cannot hurt."

She didn't respond, but Rafe noticed her shivering had started to ease. Taking this as a good sign, he ventured, "I have one question for you, Your Grace. Why did you let me kiss you? The first time we met."

"Are you fishing for compliments now, Markham?"

Rafe smiled. That was better, her spirit wasn't entirely gone. "No, not at all. While I *sense* that you are as deeply attracted to me as I am to you, I just want to make absolutely certain that you feel the same way."

"How I feel hardly matters," she said bleakly.

"Of course it does. I know exactly why I kissed you that night. And why I want you. Despite what you might think, I believe we could be very good together."

Silence. Georgie's head remained bent and Rafe could have sworn she was holding her breath.

"Will you not answer me?" he asked gently.

Georgie's voice when it emerged was the merest whisper. "I hardly know the reason myself. You...you are different to any other man I have ever met."

"How so?"

She raised her head and roughly wiped the tears from her eyes before looking at him. "You aren't intimidated by me, for one thing."

It wasn't an acknowledgement of her attraction to him, but it was a start. And what she'd just admitted was very true —Rafe wasn't intimidated. But while that may be so, he was currently suffering from a bout of gut-churning nervousness when he contemplated how she would react to his next course of action. It was a gamble, but he was going to take it anyway. He drew a fortifying breath. "I know all about your past—"

Georgie gasped and her whole body stiffened as if she'd been doused with a bucket of ice-cold water. "What? Whatever do you mean?" she demanded, pulling herself away from him. "Explain yourself."

Rafe met her furious gaze. "I know your marriage to Darby was in name only. I know how things really were between your husband and your brother... And I know about that bastard Craven."

"Oh, God." Georgie's hand flew to her mouth. "I mean how?—*Jonathon*. Jonathon told you. Last week when you came to Dudley House." She turned her head away. When she spoke again Rafe could barely hear her, but there was an undeniable, heart-rending catch in her voice. "He had no right."

"Duchess..." Rafe ran a hand down his face, trying to assemble his thoughts. He knew Georgie would be upset at his admission but he hadn't been prepared for his own emotional response to seeing her in such pain. He felt like the lowest heel that had ever walked the earth. "Rest assured, I only know the scarcest details. I guessed some of it and Jonathon merely confirmed my suspicions that someone gravely hurt you a long time ago. And that is why you married Darby, a man who could only ever be a friend to you. Your brother only has your best interests at heart."

A bitter laugh escaped Georgie. "*My* best interests. How amusing. Everyone—you, Jonathon, Phillip and Helena—you all seem to presume that you know what they are. Has anyone ever asked me what *I* want?"

Rafe slid closer and gently tilted Georgie's chin up. "Well, what do you want, Your Grace?" he urged, searching her beautiful, tear-streaked face. "Tell me. Because I certainly know what I want."

Her lower lip trembled and her eyes glittered with tears. "We can't always have what we want, Markham."

Dear God, she was making his heart bleed. "But perhaps, if we tried—"

She shook her head and he was forced to release his hold. "You don't understand. Believe me, I wish... I really wish that I *could* be the type of woman you are no doubt accustomed to taking to your bed. A lover who is unafraid. Your equal. But I don't know if I can. And wanting you, well, that may never be enough. What occurred... What Lord Craven did... His deceit and betrayal, and all the rest of it, yes, it has affected me. Profoundly."

Rafe's jaw tightened and his hands clenched into fists. How he'd dearly love to take Craven apart piece by piece or pummel him into dust. Or both. Suddenly aware that Georgie was watching him with a wary expression, he consciously relaxed his muscles. "Duchess"—he caught her hand and pressed it between his—"I want to reassure you that whatever you need from me, I will give to you. In the library, I was overrun with desire and I rushed you. Knowing what I know, my actions were thoughtless and selfish. I didn't take enough care. If you could find it within your heart to forgive me, I promise you that next time—if I am indeed fortunate enough to be granted a next time by you—it will be so much better. I do not want things to end the same way."

"But that's just it. What happened in the library, I fear it will always be like that. And please"—Georgie squeezed his hand—"you do *not* need to ask for my forgiveness when none of this is your fault. It's me. I'm... Because of... because of Craven, I have problems with..."

Georgie closed her eyes momentarily as if gathering her resolve before she met his gaze again. "This is humiliating to admit, but I cannot..." She swallowed and drew a shaky breath. "I cannot achieve satisfaction. Perhaps it's silly or even wrong of me to want more from the sexual act, but I do. I cannot help it. Otherwise the whole business will be nothing but frustrating and ultimately pointless. For me at any rate. It's the reason I've never taken a lover. And it's the reason I will probably never marry again."

Christ, his poor, sweet Georgiana. Rafe had suspected as much, but to have her confirm it, no wonder she avoided any form of intimacy like the plague. "It's not silly or wrong at all to want that. It is one of the best feelings any of us ever experience in life," he said gravely, hoping she would see he was sincere. "And I would be honored if you would grant me another opportunity to show you how wonderful relations between a man and a woman can be. If you will let me."

But would she? Rafe held his breath, waiting.

Georgie studied his face. Her forehead had dipped into a deep frown and his fingers itched to smooth the lines away. "Why? Why bother with me?" she asked eventually. "You could have your pick of any number of beautiful women. Or you could engage a mistress. Women who would be able to share themselves with you in a way that you would want. Who would readily please you and be easily pleased in return without any added complications."

Rafe held her gaze. "But they wouldn't be you."

Time seemed to stop as Georgie considered him, clearly weighing up the merit of his declaration. The sound of drumming rain intensified and Rafe's heart beat hard and fast. God, he wished he knew what she was thinking. He had to get this right.

"I can't easily explain it," he continued softly, "but if I *were* to try and put it quite simply, I would say you fascinate me, Your Grace. There's something between us, an undeniable spark that I cannot ignore. And I know you are aware of it too. No matter how hard you try to deny it."

Georgie's mouth curved into an inexpressibly sad smile. "I'm beginning to think you are just fond of lost causes."

"Why would you say that about yourself?" Rafe asked gently. "I don't see you that way at all."

Georgie dropped her gaze to her lap where she was twisting the ruined, pink silk of her skirts in her other hand. "I've been broken for so long. I know other women don't expect anything at all, that perhaps it is even wrong for a woman to feel this way, to not only want sex but derive enjoyment from it. But to have had those feelings, and to then have lost them..." She raised her head and looked him in the eye. "You make me yearn for what I used to have when I was younger, before Lord Craven took it all away. And that frightens me."

"We are all afraid of being hurt. And you have nothing to fear from me. Do you think you can trust me?"

Georgie pressed her lips together for a moment before replying. "Yes. No... Perhaps a little. I hardly know you. But I want to. Trust you that is."

Rafe hazarded a small smile. "As I've said before, I've never shied away from a challenge. If you could trust me even just a little tonight, I believe we can overcome—"

"Ah, so that's it," Georgie snapped, pulling her hand from his. Even in the gloom he could see her eyes flashing with suspicion. "I knew there must be some other reason behind your interest. I'm a puzzle you need to solve. A mere conquest—"

"Hush." On an impulse, Rafe leaned forward, captured her face between his hands and kissed her. A gentle, fleeting brush of his lips across hers, nothing more. She gasped then relented, pressing her warm mouth against his, the silken caress of her lips as soft as an angel's wing, sweet yet sensual and utterly delicious. When he drew back, he was pleased to see her glare of mistrust had faded. In the light cast from the lantern her eyes now appeared a soft, misty shade of blue.

Holding her gaze, Rafe pushed a damp curl of hair behind her ear. "Make no mistake, you mean much more to me than that. The feelings I have for you, suffice it to say, I've never felt this way before, about anyone. And an attraction, a passion like this should be given a chance don't you think? The question is, will you dare to take that chance, Duchess?"

Georgie searched his eyes so intently, his breath caught in his lungs as he waited for her to respond. *Surely she must see I'm sincere.*

"I want you to call me Georgiana," she whispered at last.

He smiled and he experienced the oddest sensation—like his heart was flipping over in his chest. "Georgiana," he murmured as he cupped her jaw then brushed his thumb along her cheek, wiping away the traces of her tears. "I will take that as a 'yes.'"

She returned his smile. "Please do."

Rafe didn't need any further encouragement to take action. Sliding his hand into the tangle of wet curls at the back of Georgie's head, he gently drew her close and claimed her pliant mouth, reveling in the soft moan she made when he slid his tongue inside her. Despite the relative sweetness of the kiss, his belly tightened and his cock jerked. God, how he wanted her. But they were both cold and wet, and the stables were not at all a suitable setting for what he had in mind. With reluctance, he broke away. "Georgiana, we should go back to the house."

"If you say so," she murmured with such enticing breathlessness, it took every ounce of self-control he possessed not to push her down into the hay and pleasure her right there and then.

Rafe forced himself to stand but as he assisted Georgie to

her feet, she gasped. Frowning with concern, he grasped her by the arms. "What is it? Are you hurt?"

She winced as she tested her weight on her left foot. "I am embarrassed to say I foolishly thought to leave here on horse-back, however I dropped the saddle on myself. I'm sure it's nothing to worry about. I think my foot is only bruised."

Lord, she had really been *that* desperate to avoid him. The thought was indeed sobering. But no more. Rafe would see to that before the night was through. Without giving warning, he scooped Georgiana up into his arms.

"Markham!" she protested. She might be gripping him about the shoulders but judging by her deep frown and the tone of her voice, she was more than a little indignant. Or perhaps it was just apprehension. "There is no need to coddle me."

"Yes. There is." Rafe strode toward the door. "I don't want you slipping over and worsening your injury. Besides"—he smiled—"I like holding you in my arms." He paused on the threshold and looked out into rainy evening before returning his gaze to her face. "Are you ready?"

She'd been biting her lower lip but at his question, she gave him a small smile. "I suppose I am as ready as I will ever be."

Rafe was certain they weren't talking about going out into the rain anymore. "It's too late to turn back now, Duchess. For better or worse, tonight, you're mine."

CHAPTER 13

Georgie sighed deeply as she ran her fingers through her damp hair, lightly tugging out the snarls. After a long, luxurious bath in the biggest tub she'd ever encountered, she'd taken a seat before the roaring fire in her suite's sitting room. She should feel relaxed and contented, perhaps even sleepy. But she did not.

Not when she could still recall the feel of Markham's strong, muscular arms about her as he'd carried her here all the way from the stables. Or his deep voice, low and husky and full of delicious, wanton promise. "I'll arrange for a bath and a supper tray to be sent up," he'd murmured in her ear after he'd finished examining her bruised foot. "And when you are done, it might be a good idea to dismiss your maid for the evening. I will join you around eight."

Eight o'clock couldn't come soon enough as far as Georgie was concerned. Flurries of nervous excitement skittered around inside her belly whenever she glanced at the mantel clock and saw the hour hand creeping toward the appointed time. When she put her hands to her cheeks they were hot and her skin tingled with awareness every time she moved; the lace along the neckline of her chemise scratched the tops of her too sensitive breasts and the cool silk of her pale blue robe slid along her arms as she fanned out her hair, making her shiver. Indeed, her whole body quivered with so much fevered anticipation, it bordered on excruciating.

But amidst all of these acute sensations, Georgie recognized another feeling deep within her heart, a feeling that was almost completely foreign to her—an unfurling sense of hope.

She'd disclosed one of her deepest, most intimate secrets to Markham, a secret she'd never before divulged to any other living soul. And his reaction had been nothing like she'd expected. He hadn't baulked, or even worse, ridiculed her. Neither had he dismissed the impact of her past history nor her deep-seated fears. Somehow, miraculously, he understood.

It was almost as if Markham cared. Indeed, even though he'd only admitted a passion for her, the way he regarded her, kissed her, touched her, *everything* he did, intimated so much more.

Dear God, I pray I'm making the right decision, she thought as she reached for her glass of claret with a trembling hand and took a rather large sip. *I really don't think I can survive another failed attempt to have sex with Markham. It will surely break my heart.*

Her gaze darted to the open doorway of her bedchamber and the magnificent four-poster bed swathed in curtains of sumptuous, rose-pink damask—a bed she would soon be sharing with Markham. Another shiver slid over her skin. Whether it was with trepidation or desire she couldn't have said. Then again, it was probably both. At least she didn't need to worry about an unwanted pregnancy. Markham had already assured her that he would be careful and she was inclined to trust him.

Before Constance had departed, she had turned down the rose-embroidered silk counterpane revealing pristine white sheets and perfectly plumped pillows. Georgie's perpetual blush grew deeper when she contemplated how disheveled the bed would look come morning. But Constance wouldn't remark upon it, just as she wouldn't return until she was summoned. Georgie thanked the Lord yet again for providing her with such a discreet and trustworthy lady's maid. The girl was worth her very weight in gold.

Two minutes to eight. Georgie took another large sip of Markham's very good wine then leaned back against the cream brocade cushions of the settee. She really shouldn't have too much more, considering she'd barely touched her supper. The wine was sure to go straight to her head. Then again, perhaps the alcohol would continue to soften her edginess. Her stomach might still be fluttering crazily, but at least her limbs were now a little looser and heavier, and the mad race of her pulse had begun to slow a fraction. When she glanced at the clock upon the mantel yet again, she could see that it was now only one minute until her would-be lover walked through her door.

Georgie scowled and took yet another unladylike swig of her wine. *Hurry up, Markham. This waiting is almost too much to bear.*

Just at that moment, the door clicked open.

With her heart leaping into the vicinity of her mouth, Georgie turned. And her breath caught.

Clothed only in buff trousers and a loose, cambric shirt, Markham seemed completely at ease with his state of *dishabille* as he padded his way along the plush Aubusson carpet toward her. Never in her life had Georgie seen a man so informally dressed. Barefoot. The sight was absolutely mesmerizing and frighteningly arousing. Her quim began to pulse and her nipples pebbled.

"May I take a seat?" Markham asked, gesturing toward the space beside her when she'd failed to produce a single word of greeting. His mouth lifted into a crooked smile and there was more than a decided glint of mischief in his gray eyes as he regarded her.

Somehow, the arrogant devil knew he had stolen her capacity to speak, and now he was clearly laughing at her. Of all the scenarios Georgie had imagined, this was certainly not how she had anticipated their evening would begin.

Piqued to her bones, she found her breath and her courage. "Out with it," she demanded, deliberately ignoring his request. "What is it that amuses you so?"

"Forgive me, it's just your expression when you saw how I was dressed. It was...it still is, quite priceless." He bit his lip, suppressing a chuckle. His shirt was open at the neck and she could clearly see his Adam's apple bobbing with silent mirth.

Georgie cast him an imperious glare. "I am simply not accustomed to seeing a man—*you*—in such a state of undress. And I am certainly not used to appearing like this before a man"—she gestured at herself—"either."

"I assure you, I will not strip further. Unless you want me to of course."

A vision of Markham wearing absolutely nothing but a wicked smile sprang into her mind and a blush washed over her cheeks. "You are doing it again," she accused with more heat than she intended. She didn't want to feel like this, flustered and exasperated.

Markham raised a dark brow. "What?" he asked with apparent innocence.

"You know exactly what," she retorted. "You are teasing me. You know I don't like it."

His smile softened. "I guarantee that you will love it before the night is through."

Oh... When Georgie didn't reply—simply because she couldn't—his gaze drifted to the glass of claret she still held.

"How is the wine?

Even though her cheeks had grown even hotter in response to his less than subtle double entendre, she was determined to put on a brave face. Lifting her chin, she tried very hard to affect an air of elegant *ennui* as she answered his question. "Very good."

Damn. Her voice sounded breathy. She didn't sound cool or confident at all.

Markham seemed to notice too as his smile broadened. "May I have some?"

She arched an eyebrow. "Well, as it is *your* wine, I can't very well refuse now, can I?" She waved a hand toward the nearby decanter and the additional glass that had been conveniently sent up with her dinner tray. "Help yourself."

"I don't mind if I do." Markham drew close, poured himself a sizeable glass then raised it in a toast. "To you, Georgiana." His eyes met hers and held. "May this evening be everything you hoped it would be."

He watched her over the rim of his glass as he drank, and Georgie's heart began to pound furiously again. "Thank you," she whispered.

"I promise you, the pleasure will be *all* yours," Markham said in a velvet soft voice.

Oh, my goodness. Not able to meet his smoky gaze, Georgie took another hasty sip of her claret. When she raised her eyes, she noticed Markham was still studying her.

"You have the most beautiful hair," he murmured as he placed his glass down then sat beside her. Reaching forward, he wound a damp lock around one long finger, just as he'd done the first night she'd met him. "It is the most glorious color and texture."

Georgie shrugged a shoulder, affecting an indifference she didn't feel. "I have always thought it was a rather ordinary brown."

"Never. It is rich and thick and silky. And the way it

catches the light, it reminds me of toffee or caramel." Markham leaned closer—very close—and pressed his face against her temple, inhaling. "But it smells far sweeter. Like jasmine or honeysuckle. Or orange blossoms. What is the perfume you use?"

"It's from Floris on Jermyn Street in St James's. They make it especially for me." She paused to draw a steadying breath. Heavens, the press of Markham's warm, muscular thigh against hers, the feel of his warm breath and lips at her hairline—it was enough to make her dizzy. "Your powers of observation have quite impressed me, actually. The scent is a blend of jasmine and lily-of-the-Valley."

"Ah, that's it." Markham nuzzled her ear, before pulling back a little. "Your hair is still damp from your bath." He gently slid his fingers through the heavy tumble of curls. "May I brush it?" he asked, nodding toward her silver-backed brush on the nearby side-table.

"I... Ah, yes." Georgie placed her wine down before passing her brush to him. Their fingers brushed and a tingling warmth spread up her arm and bloomed inside her chest.

Markham smiled knowingly. "If it doesn't pain you, can you turn a little, so that your back is to me?"

Pulling her robe securely around herself to ensure that she didn't expose her bare legs when she moved, Georgie did as Markham asked. She knew she was being overly prudish, considering what they would soon be doing, but she couldn't seem to help herself. However, when she felt the brush gliding through her hair, with long, sure, gentle strokes, she closed her eyes and sighed with contentment. "You do that very well. Are you sure you weren't a lady's maid rather than a diplomat?"

Markham's answering chuckle, deep and warm, made her toes curl in her blue satin slippers. "I have been many things, Your Grace, but not that."

Georgie wanted to ask more about his past—for instance,

how he had acquired a broken nose, the slashing scar through his right eyebrow, and why his knuckles were so misshapen— but the moment didn't feel right. She couldn't deny their verbal sparring was exciting. But right now, she was enjoying the companionable silence that had fallen between them.

Apart from the crackle of the fire, the steady patter of the rain against the window and the rhythmic sigh of the brush through her almost dry hair, there were no other sounds. However, when Markham brushed her hair over one of shoulders and then gently kneaded the base of her skull and the tight muscles in her neck with sure fingers, Georgie couldn't suppress an appreciative moan. "Where on earth did you learn to do that?"

"Sweden." His hands moved to her shoulders and began to work out the knots there. "During one of my postings."

"Ah, Jonathon mentioned you had been there. So, where were your other postings, if you don't mind my asking?" He had broached the seemingly forbidden topic so she didn't see the harm in enquiring further.

"Vienna. I had a short tenure in Russia as well."

"You are certainly very well-traveled."

"You could say that."

Georgie suddenly wondered why he never wanted to elaborate. *What is he hiding?* She turned her head a little. "You won't tell me any more about your work, will you?"

She could almost hear the smile in Markham's voice. "Not tonight." He leaned forward and placed a light kiss on the sensitive flesh beneath her ear. "Tonight, I plan to use my mouth for other things besides talking."

Moist heat immediately welled between Georgie's thighs. "Markham," she whispered, leaning back against his wide chest. She arched her neck and he didn't hesitate to respond. He gently pulled on her earlobe with his teeth before skimming his lips along her neck to her shoulder.

"Take off your robe," he urged in a voice suddenly graveled with lust. He slid his hands up and down the fabric covering her upper arms, creating a trail of pleasurable gooseflesh wherever he touched. "And please, call me Rafe." He resumed the sweet assault upon her neck and throat.

Georgie hesitated as a wave of self-consciousness suddenly assailed her. Once she removed her robe, she would only be clad in her chemise. It was the prettiest she owned—a confection of fine lawn and ivory lace—and unlike her chaste flannel night rail, it had seemed entirely appropriate for an evening spent pursuing illicit pleasures of the flesh. But the garment was so flimsy, Markham—*Rafe*—would be able to see straight through it to what lay beneath. He'd seen and kissed her breasts, touched her in her most private place, but to think of his gaze traveling freely over her near-naked body...it was a level of intimacy she wasn't certain she was ready for, just yet.

"Rafe. I..." It was hard to speak whilst he was still feathering hot, soft kisses along her throat and jawline. "Perhaps I'm behaving like a silly, virginal miss, which I'm not, but...but I've never been in a situation quite like this."

Rafe raised his head. "Look at me, Georgiana."

She turned toward him and he cupped her jaw. She couldn't escape his gaze even if she'd wanted to.

When he spoke, his voice was rough with strong emotion. "You are brave and smart and passionate, and so beautiful, you steal my breath away every time I see you. I promised I wouldn't push you for more than you're willing to give, yet a moment ago, I was doing exactly that. My own desire makes me impatient. But, let me reassure you, tonight it is all about you. *Your* pleasure, not mine. All I ask is that you be honest with me. You must tell me what to do. What you like. And if you don't like something, or are unsure about anything, *at all*, you must ask me to stop and I will, without question." He brushed the back of his fingers against her cheek. "I want to fulfill your every desire. Whatever that may be."

Oh my. Georgie worried at her lower lip for a moment considering how to respond. "I hardly know what to say. Where to begin," she eventually said. "I know a little. As I said, I'm not a virgin, but there is also a great deal I don't know about bed sport. And to even speak of such intimate things... to ask you to do certain things..." She shook her head as another wave of anxiety hit. "I'm not sure if I can."

Rafe's wide mouth tilted into a gentle smile. "Perhaps we could begin again with a kiss."

"Yes. I would like that."

Rafe threaded his fingers through the hair at her nape. His eyes then focused on her lips as he slowly, ever so slowly lowered his mouth, stretching out the moment, expertly arousing her anticipation to fever pitch. When his lips finally slanted over hers, she whimpered and curled her hands around his wide shoulders, pulling him closer.

Yes, oh yes. This was exactly what she needed, this deliberate, agonizingly gentle, utterly delicious kiss. Her thoughts scattered as pleasurable sensation overwhelmed her; the hot, wet glide of Rafe's tongue in her mouth as he languidly explored every recess, the tight ache of her sensitized nipples, the growing throb between her thighs. The feel of Rafe's rock-hard body beneath her hands. His heady scent—fresh linen and bergamot cologne and clean male.

As soon as Rafe pushed her down into the cushions, Georgie immediately noticed the insistent press of his aroused member against her belly. Her heart was flooded with immeasurable, bittersweet delight. *He wants me. In spite of everything, my hesitancy, my prickliness, my constant rebuffs, he truly wants me. And everything he is doing, and is going to do, is for me. My pleasure...*

Their kiss soon changed into something wilder, deeper,

purely abandoned. When Rafe nipped at her lower lip then sucked on it, she gasped. Never in her life had she experienced a kiss so decadent. Her desire instantly grew hotter, darker, and she moaned, arching her body against Rafe's, wantonly and deliberately parting her legs. She was so, so wet. And aching, pulsing with urgent need. She suddenly knew she craved more than kisses from Rafe. And this settee was not going to be adequate for what she ultimately wanted.

Georgie dragged her mouth from Rafe's. "Please. If you don't mind, I want to move to the bedroom. It may sound odd, but I've...I've never had sex in a bed before. And I would very much like to."

Rafe smiled, his eyes flashing wickedly. "You have my whole-hearted agreement." He pushed himself up but as Georgie attempted to stand, he swept her into his arms. She let out a squeal of surprise and he laughed.

"I'm sure your foot is still painful," he said as he effort-lessly carried her through to the bedchamber. "I'm surprised you are actually wearing slippers."

"Not anymore." Georgie kicked them off. Her inhibitions seemed to be rapidly dissolving in the steady torrent of unbri-dled lust coursing through her veins.

As Rafe laid her on the enormous bed, then slid alongside her, she tugged at the tie on her robe. "I don't need this either."

"Well, I'm glad there's something else we can both agree on." Rafe helped her to ease off the garment, and in moments, Georgie was clad only in her all but transparent chemise. The awkward shyness that had previously overwhelmed her had vanished at last. When Rafe's avid gaze roamed slowly over her body, she felt adored. *Desired*.

She wanted to see him too. Explore all of his hard, mascu-line body with her hands and mouth. She licked her lips. "Your turn, Rafe. Take off your shirt."

His mouth kicked into a devilish grin. "Certainly, Your Grace." He sat up, raised his arm and snagged the back of his cambric shirt, then in one smooth movement, tugged it up and over his head before flinging it to one side.

Georgie sucked in a sharp breath as Rafe lay down beside her again, his weight propped on one elbow. Just as she'd always imagined, he was lean, his musculature so defined it was as if he had been chiseled from marble. Her gaze wandered over his broad shoulders and bulging upper arms, his wide chest, ridged abdomen and narrow waist. The impressive bulge beneath the fall front of his trousers. Everything about him was perfect.

Feeling strangely bold, and more than a little curious, she reached out and lightly ran her fingertips through the smattering of dark hair covering his pectoral muscles. His nipples tightened and he closed his eyes and groaned. "I'm supposed to be teasing you, sweetheart. Not the other way around."

Georgie smiled, thrilled that she was able to enflame his arousal. And he'd called her *sweetheart*. No one had ever called her that before. "Markham. I mean, Rafe," she said softly and he opened his eyes. Unable to resist touching him, she placed her hand against his strong, square jaw. "Before we go any further, I wanted to tell you that your endless patience, your care, your tenderness, it means so very much to me."

Rafe's mouth tipped into a soft smile. "So much for my reputation of being incorrigible, impossible and wicked. You make me sound as harmless as an innocent choir boy." As if to emphasize he had a disreputable side, he pulled the ribbon at the top of her chemise undone. "However, I think that very soon, you'll be revising your opinion of me."

Georgie's pulse raced faster. Hotter. "I have no doubt that you are most definitely capable of doing very wicked things. In fact, I'm counting on it." If Rafe could fill her senses, overwhelm her thoughts, and in the process, drive away the last remnants of her fears and self-doubt, she was now absolutely certain she would at long last achieve the fulfillment she so desperately craved.

"Good." Rafe ran a fingertip along her exposed collarbone, then lower toward the dip between her breasts, making her shiver. "What wicked thing shall I do to you first? Tell me and I will do it."

Georgie bit her lip. She understood what Rafe was trying to do. He was encouraging her to let go of her inhibitions entirely. But whilst her body vibrated with aching need, voicing her innermost desires with any degree of specificity still seemed like an impossible task. Nevertheless, she would try. "I want... Perhaps you could... I enjoyed what you did to me in the library. At the very beginning."

"You mean when I pleasured your breasts?" Rafe's fingers slid beneath the sagging neckline of her chemise and found one of her nipples. He squeezed gently, then rolled it between thumb and forefinger, coaxing it into a tight point. "Like this?"

"Yes." The word emerged on a pant as wondrous desire flared inside her, setting every nerve alight.

"And what of this?" His lips closed around her other nipple and he suckled it through the lace and lawn.

Georgie gripped his head and shifted restlessly, her body now burning with want. "You are a devil," she managed to gasp. "It's cruel to tease me when you know what I really mean."

"Words can arouse just as much as actions, my beautiful Georgiana. And words have power. I want you to know you are in complete control. What do you want from me? Say it." The whisper of his warm breath across the tops of her breasts was a sweet torment in and of itself.

"I want your mouth...on my bare body."

"All of your body? Kissing you, tasting you, everywhere?"

"Yes," she whispered, frantically pulling at the loosened neckline of her chemise, exposing herself, at last bold and unashamed. Willingly wanton.

Rafe made a low growling sound in his throat as he claimed her naked breast. His hot mouth suckled her. His tongue mercilessly teased her, flicking then curling around the taut, pink tip, making her quiver and whimper. All the while, his fingers tormented her other nipple, rolling it and tugging it, effortlessly building the flames of desire within her to blazing proportions.

When he pulled his mouth away she mewled in protest. "Please, don't stop."

"I promise you, I'm only just beginning, my sweet." He transferred his mouth to her other breast, this time working it with long, pulling sucks that soon had her writhing and gasping. Mindless with pleasure.

"You are coming alive in my arms, Georgiana. I love it. But what do you prefer?" he asked at length, his voice husky with lust. "Light teasing or hard sucking?"

"Sucking. Definitely sucking. But..." Rafe's lavish worship of her breasts was no longer enough. She knew she was ready to take things further.

"But what? Tell me." Rafe's dark whisper against her skin sent a fresh rush of slick heat straight to her pulsing sex.

She couldn't deny him. "I want your fingers between my thighs," she said, reaching for the hem of her chemise. It had already bunched halfway up her legs.

But Rafe was faster. Within seconds, he'd pushed the fabric above her waist. His fingers tiptoed a lazy path across her ribs, her quivering stomach then down toward her hips. He paused, the heel of his hand resting lightly on the curls hiding her mound. "Only my fingers?" he asked, cocking a dark brow.

Georgie's gaze crept along Rafe's body to where his

massive erection strained against the front of his trousers. She gnawed on her lower lip as uneasiness flickered through her belly. "I want you inside me, but I'm not sure if I'm quite ready—"

"Don't be alarmed. You mistake my meaning." He kissed her, his tongue sweeping suggestively over her lower lip. "I want to use more than my fingers. I want to pleasure your sweet, wet quim with my mouth."

What? She'd agreed to Rafe kissing all of her body but surely not *there*. "You cannot be serious," Georgie gasped. His wicked suggestion had immediately triggered a frisson of panic in her belly, but perversely, her curiosity was also piqued. She frowned, horrified yet intrigued. "Why would you want to?"

"I have fantasized about doing this, ever since we first kissed, Georgiana. I'm dying to learn how every single part of you tastes. And I can guarantee that if you allow me to pleasure you this way, you will not leave this room unsatisfied." His burning gray gaze bore into hers. "Trust me."

The thought of his mouth exploring her sex, it was too shocking. Yet Georgie couldn't deny that a small, wicked part of her found the bizarre offer wildly exciting. She certainly knew women pleasured men that way so maybe the idea wasn't *that* outlandish. Perhaps trying something new, outside of her realm of experience was exactly what she needed. "All right," she whispered.

Rafe's wide mouth spread into a slow, thoroughly captivating smile. "I promise you, you won't regret this."

Dear Lord, I pray that I won't either. Georgie forced herself to relax into the pillows as Rafe moved down the bed with studied purpose. Along the way, he slid his mouth down her torso, swirled the tip of his tongue around her navel then traced a line of leisurely, feather-light kisses over her hip and lower belly until he reached the very edge of her light brown curls. Despite her initial trepidation, hot thrills skittered across her sensitive skin wherever he touched.

"Open for me, Georgie."

Her heart crashing against her ribs, Georgie did as Rafe bid. She stole a glance at him as he positioned himself between her trembling thighs and heat immediately scorched her cheeks. *Oh, God*. He was staring at her most private place with an expression that could only be described as rapt. He had the look of a starving man contemplating a feast.

"Rafe," she whispered uncertainly, fighting the urge to close her legs.

"Shhh, sweetheart." He ran a finger through the moisture she could feel drenching her folds and she moaned. How could she be so embarrassed yet so completely aroused all at once?

"How beautifully wet you are for me," he continued hoarsely. "Slick and swollen and flushed with desire." He spread her aching, heavy lips with his thumbs then dipped his head and blew across the throbbing bud at the very apex. "I want you. Tell me you want this too, Georgie."

"Yes." She arched her hips. This suspense was agony. Her need had never been so acute. Unbearable. "I want this."

Her breathless plea was enough to prompt Rafe into taking immediate action. Using his fingers to keep her fully exposed, he closed his lips around her core and delicately suckled. Georgie cried out as a bolt of pleasure streaked through her. She clutched Rafe's head. He was right. This could work. She wouldn't regret it. The sensations he was arousing in her with this outrageous act were utterly divine, unlike anything she'd ever experienced before. Primal yet profoundly intimate. Beyond words.

And Rafe was relentless, unforgiving in his pursuit to drive her to the climax she so desperately needed. Everything he did with his mouth—the hot, wet slide and flicks of his tongue, the tight pull of his lips around the engorged, tender nub of her clitoris—he did with relish. Even the sounds he made—the low growls, his heavy breathing, the lapping and wet sucking noises—sounds that should have shocked her, only served to drive her need higher. As her insides clenched tighter, her pants and moans became increasingly ragged, her thrashing and jerking more frantic. She gripped Rafe's hair—pulling so hard she must have hurt him—but he gave her no quarter, no respite at all from the hot, mad frenzy that he was steadily building inside her.

Suspended on the edge of pleasure, she willed herself to surrender to the pull of release. She was close. So close. She whimpered and brazenly pushed herself against Rafe's mouth. Nothing existed except him and his wicked possession of her sex. "Oh please... Please make me come."

Rafe pressed one finger, then another inside her. Thrusting, pumping. Stroking faster and deeper as he surrounded her clitoris with his lips, increasing the suction, pulling hard. And then suddenly, everything inside her clenched tight. Unbearably tight. Too tight.

Yes. On an exultant scream, she fell. Let go. Spun away into the dazzling ecstasy of a breath-stealing, all-consuming orgasm. As spasms of pleasure racked her womb, wild joy filled her heart. And the warmth of gratitude.

Rafe had truly freed her. Taken her to another place entirely. A place where she was alive and whole again. A beautiful place where hope lived.

She didn't realize she was crying until she felt Rafe brushing his fingers across her wet cheeks.

"Georgie," he whispered hoarsely as he gathered her into his arms. "My gorgeous, passionate Georgie." When she met his gaze, all she could see was tenderness in the smoky gray depths of his eyes. Understanding in his soft smile. There was no self-serving expression of triumph or smugness. He clearly knew she'd been satisfied and he was happy for her.

In that moment, her heart melted just that little bit more. Falling in love with Rafe suddenly didn't seem like such a terrifying prospect after all. She caressed his jaw then kissed him, gently. His lips tasted like sex—his own addictive flavor was overlaid with a hint of her own musk—but she didn't mind.

"Thank you," she whispered, touching his strong, beautiful face again, tracing the line of his lips, his cheekbones, the slightly crooked line of his nose. "You have no idea what you have done for me. I feel like the sleeping beauty in the wood who's just been awakened by the gallant prince."

Although Rafe still smiled, his gaze grew heavier somehow, more focused. It was as if all of her artifice had been stripped away and he could really see her, all of her—her vulnerabilities, the shadows of her emotional scars, her hopes and dreams. Every single piece of her.

"Georgiana," he murmured. "This—what we have started tonight—it's very real, my darling. And I predict it's going to be so much better than anything you've ever read in a fairy tale."

Oh, my goodness. Before she could even think on the implications of what he'd just said, Rafe claimed her mouth in another languid, thoroughly drugging kiss. A kiss that left her in no doubt that their night of shared sensual pleasure was only just beginning. As he covered her body with his, she couldn't fail to notice the hard press of his large, fully erect cock against her bare stomach. She had received a full measure of blissful release, but he had not. *He must be in agony.*

Breaking the kiss, she sought his gaze. "Rafe. You have pleased me so well. I think it's your turn to receive some satisfaction, don't you?" In her wildest dreams, she'd never thought there would be an occasion—or that she would have the confidence—to make such a bold offer. It might have been ten long years since she'd done anything like this, but she was going to try... After all, this was Markham. *Rafe.* The only man she wanted to think about. To pleasure.

I can do this and I'm going to enjoy it just as much as he is.

⁓

Georgie's words provoked an immediate reaction. Rafe's cock jerked and his balls contracted. Painfully. *Christ.* "Georgie. Are you sure, sweetheart? This evening is all about you. What *you* need—"

She smiled and pressed her hips against him; the wicked woman was deliberately teasing him. "What *I* need is for you to experience the amazing pleasure I just felt," she practically purred. She slid her hand between their bodies and gently grasped him through the fabric of his trousers. "I insist."

Fireworks exploded in his head. "Sweet Jesus," he groaned through gritted teeth. He'd vowed to himself that he would ignore his own need, but with the taste of her still on his tongue, and the way she was stroking him, he couldn't take much more. "Georgie..." He stilled her hand and rolled away from her a little to ease the torturous pressure. "How? I mean... I can seek my own release if..." He didn't know what she would feel comfortable doing for him. "Please don't feel you have to—"

"Shhh, I want to." She kissed his throat then ran the tip of her tongue along his clenched jaw. All the while her wicked hand rubbed and squeezed. "And as to your first question..." She drew back slightly and began to unbutton the placket at the front of his trousers with deft fingers. "What would you like me to do?" Her lovely mouth curved into a very feline, very sexually confident smile. "I am open to suggestions."

God, she's a siren. She'll kill me. Rafe hissed as her hand encircled his throbbing shaft. His heart thundered so hard he thought it might explode. "What you are doing is more than fine," he muttered hoarsely. The muscles of his abdomen, his thighs, his arse were bunched so tightly, he shook.

Georgie was stroking him with a steady rhythm, squeezing him with a sure grip whilst she used her other hand to gently roll his aching testicles. "Are you sure?" Her tongue darted out and swiped over her lower lip.

Cheeky wench. The urge to bury himself balls deep in her sweet pussy was suddenly overwhelming. "Yes," he groaned. *No.*

She laughed, a low, musical, tantalizing sound. "Liar."

She pushed him flat onto the bed and worked her way down his naked torso with her mouth, sprinkling light kisses upon his ribs, across his clenched stomach then down to the sharp ridge of one exposed hip. Her hand continued to work his length, sliding up and down, steadily escalating the hot, hungry fire in his veins. By the time her mouth reached the base of his cock, the head was slippery with his leaking seed.

To his frustration, she didn't take him. Instead, she sat up and threw him a coquettish glance; her blue eyes gleamed through the fan of her long, brown lashes. "Tell me what you want," she urged in a throaty whisper, mimicking his earlier teasing as she continued to stroke him.

A cruel wench. She was tormenting him, paying him back. He dropped his head into the pillows and gripped the silk counterpane. The voice he dredged up was little more than a ragged, desperate moan. "For God's sake...your mouth...use it on me. Before you unman me completely."

Another smile. Softer. "Well, we wouldn't want that now."

Bending forward, she licked along his entire shaft from root to head with the soft, moist, flat of her tongue. Then she skimmed the tip over his slit, lapping up his spilled seed. Rafe groaned. Wild lust pounded through his veins, making him dizzy. Making him crave more. He speared his fingers through the tumble of silky hair at the back of Georgie's head, urging her downward. Ravening need was fast consuming him. He couldn't take much more of her teasing. "Georgie...please..."

She relented. *Thank God.* At last her soft lips surrounded his engorged head completely and she sucked. Hard.

Fuck. He bucked, his whole body arching as if he'd been struck by lightning. The sensation was incredible. He'd never dreamed she would...or knew how to...

All further thought fled as she began to work him in earnest. The hot, wet plunge of her mouth up and down, the swirl and quick flicks of her deft tongue were exquisite torture. The gentle rolls and squeezes she administered to his balls were maddening. Everything she did drove him closer to the edge. Built the pressure inside him. When he came, it would be torrential. He glanced at her bowed head, her hand pumping his swelling cock. He should release the tight grip he had on her. He should pull away...

"Georgie. I'm going to—" *Oh God.* She drew hard, her cheeks hollowing with the sharp increase in suction and then he gave in. Lost control. With an almighty, chest-swelling groan, he climaxed, thrusting himself in and out of her hot, greedy mouth as his seed spurted out in an explosive rush. She grasped his shaft tightly with both hands, somehow swallowing everything he poured out. Not letting him go until he was completely spent and gasping as if he'd just sprinted a mile. The pleasure coursing through him was mind-numbing, his satisfaction so complete he could barely move a muscle. But he needed to. He didn't want to fall asleep quite yet.

With an effort, he dragged himself out of the blissful oblivion Georgie had sent him to. Levering his heavy eyelids open, he caught her licking her lips, wiping the corners of her mouth with her fingers. Poignant awe immediately flooded his heart.

Georgie had avoided sex for such a long time. Yet she'd done this. For him.

He had no words. Instead, he lifted a hand and brushed Georgie's hair away from her face, wanting to see her expression. She looked up and he could see that her mouth was curved in a triumphant smile.

Sweet Lord, she is stunning. To see this unabashed sexual side of her flowering before his very eyes stole his breath as surely as the incredible orgasm he'd just had.

"Come here," he urged, holding out his arms. "What you did was amazing... No. *You* are amazing."

Georgie immediately slid into his embrace. "I'm glad you liked it," she murmured against his neck, her breath tickling his skin.

"I think *liked it* is rather an understatement. I loved it." Rafe inhaled deeply, drawing in her unique scent—flowers and the musk of pleasured woman. The tang of his own release. "Thank you."

"You're welcome." She snuggled in closer to his side. Her chemise was still bunched up around her belly, her breasts bare. Unable to help himself, he brushed his fingers against the side of one lush mound, then gently pinched her puckered nipple. As far as he was concerned, any flesh that was exposed was now fair game.

She squirmed and attempted to swat his hand away. "You are insatiable," she admonished but he could detect laughter in her voice.

"When it comes to you, Georgiana, yes I am." He cupped her jaw and kissed her delicious mouth, wanting to show her that he meant every word. When he drew back, she was flushed and breathless, her eyes heavy-lidded with longing. He smiled. "Remember, the night has only just begun, sweetheart. And I'm yet to be convinced that you've been satisfied enough."

She laughed, amusement dancing in her clear blue eyes. "Well, now that you mention it..." She draped her leg over his, unashamedly pressing her sex against him. "What do you have in mind?"

Even through the fabric of his trousers, Rafe could feel how damp and ready she was. He ran his fingers up the inside of her bare thigh and gave her a wolfish smile. "I'm still hungry."

CHAPTER 14

Georgie's eyes flew open. Something had woken her. A cry in the night.

Markham. Disoriented, heart crashing against her ribs, she pushed herself up to a sitting position in the opulent bed in her room at Rivergate. There was enough residual light from the remnants of the fire and the low burning candles to discern Markham lying beside her. Shirtless, the fine cotton sheets tangled around his legs and waist, he would have been a sight to behold—except for the fact that his chest rapidly rose and fell with each shallow, rasping breath he took and his face was contorted into a rictus, as though he was in pain.

A nightmare.

Georgie's heart clenched for him. "Markham... Rafe," she whispered, tentatively touching his shoulder. He was hot, slick with sweat.

He tossed his head on the silk pillows. In the dim light, she could just make out the silver-gray flash of his eyes between slitted lids. His fists gripped the sheets. "Solange," he whispered. "Solange...je suis désolé, mon amour." His French accent was perfect, his voice tinged with despair.

Another woman. Someone he cared about.
How very odd that he spoke in French.

Georgie reached out to him again, wanting to ease his torment as well as satisfy her curiosity about the mysterious Solange, but at the last moment, she drew back her hand. Despite the intimacies they'd shared tonight, there were so many things she didn't know about this man. As she'd kissed him, explored his body, she'd noticed the faded silver of scars upon him—his left hip, along the line of a rib, the shoulder she'd just touched. She hadn't commented, but her interest had deepened. There was violence in his past, that much was clear. For all his charm and rakish smiles, she sensed Rafe wore a mask; that beneath his urbane manner there was steel. A dark edge. Dark secrets he was reluctant to share.

They had more in common than she'd ever realized.

Rafe cried out again. Whimpered. His jaw was clenched so tightly, she feared it might snap.

She couldn't let him suffer so. Drawing in a fortifying breath, she shook him. "Rafe. Please, wake up."

He sat bolt upright. Sucked in one harsh breath after another; he looked as though the very hounds of hell had been chasing him. "Georgie..." His brow knitted into a deep frown when his gaze settled on her. "Are you all right?"

She shook her head, confused. "Y-Yes. Perfectly fine. But you're not. You've been having a nightmare. You don't recall it?" She wanted to touch him again, but he seemed so withdrawn and agitated, she clasped the neckline of her gaping chemise to her chest instead. She could feel her own heart racing, her fingers trembling.

He wiped a hand over his face. "I am sorry to have woken you." He shook his head as if to clear it, then slid from the bed, facing away from her as he stood. The well-defined muscles of his shoulders and back were rigid with tension. His breathing was still effortful, a sharp sawing sound in the almost silent room. "I... I haven't had a dream like that in some time. I apologize if I startled you."

"You did wake me. You called out in your sleep. But I promise you, I am truly all right. But you... Can I get you anything?"

"I have it." Rafe strode toward the door into the sitting room. "I'll get the wine. I think we could both use a drink."

Georgie could not argue with his logic.

Within moments, Rafe returned with their glasses and what remained of the claret. She took her glass and sipped whilst he all but downed his in one gulp before refilling his glass. After depositing the decanter on the side table, he sat back down on the bed. His long, trouser-clad legs stretched out beside her, close but not quite touching. She didn't say anything. Just listened to the ever-present rain and the gentle tick of the clock on the white marble mantel. It was nearly midnight.

"What did I... What did I call out exactly?" he asked at length.

Georgie took a quick sip of her wine before responding. But there really was no point in beating about the bush. "Who is Solange?"

He sighed heavily. "A woman I once cared about. She died. Some time ago."

Georgie didn't want to seem like a jealous lover. Certainly not over a woman who had long since passed, but she had to know. "You loved her?"

Rafe turned toward her and caught her gaze. "I had feelings for her, yes. But I didn't love her. Not like—" He suddenly broke off and took another mouthful of wine before he spoke again. "The way she died..." A muscle twitched in his jaw. "She died well before her time. I've never reconciled myself with what happened. And perhaps I never will."

Georgie didn't quite know what to say. She wanted to ask

him about whom he *had* actually loved, but it was the wrong moment entirely. And she wanted to know more about Solange and the circumstances of her death but the expression on Rafe's face was so grim—the hard set of his mouth, the way the skin drew tightly across his cheekbones—she didn't have the courage to ask him about that either. Instead, she reached for his hand and squeezed it gently. "It seems I'm not the only one haunted by the past."

His mouth twisted into a wry smile. "As I said before, I haven't had that dream for a very long time, Georgiana. I'm sorry to have burdened you with recollections of my misspent youth, shall we say?" He gently scuffed his thumb across the back of her hand. "It cannot have been easy to hear me calling out another woman's name as I lay beside you in your bed. Again, I apologize."

Georgie offered him a smile in return. "There is no need, Rafe. But... Perhaps I shouldn't say this..."

He raised her hand and kissed her fingertips. "Tell me. I want you to feel as though you can share anything with me."

She blew out a breath. "What I found most strange was the fact you spoke French. Very good French. It seems most peculiar."

He quirked an eyebrow and his smile grew wider. The rake had returned. "I pride myself on my linguistic skills. I also speak Russian, German and some Swedish. As well as a smattering of Spanish and Italian."

It was obvious he was attempting to deflect her line of inquiry, however, she decided she wasn't prepared to press the matter. Not in her bed at midnight. Especially when Rafe was clad only in trousers talking about how adept he was with his tongue. He'd effortlessly brought her to orgasm a second time with his mouth before they'd fallen asleep. And she was suddenly dying to know if he could make her climax a third time. There were so many things they could do... So many things he could show her...

"Really? You speak Italian?" she asked absently as her gaze drifted across Rafe's chest, down his taut stomach to the line of dark hair that disappeared into the waistband of his trousers. It appeared he had similar thoughts; she didn't think she imagined the telltale swelling beneath the placket.

"Si, ma bella Georgiana." Rafe replied in a soft, seductive voice that made her belly curl tightly with renewed desire. He set aside his wine glass. "Voglio fare l'amore con te. Togliere la tua camicia."

She'd attended enough performances of the operas *Le Nozze di Figaro* and *Don Giovanni* to know Rafe's Italian accent was also perfect. Given the heaviness of his gaze and the way it traveled over her scantily clad body, it was easy to deduce what he wanted her to do, even though she barely spoke a word of the language herself.

"I will take my chemise off. But only if you undress first," she murmured huskily.

He grinned. "I thought you'd never ask." He rose to his feet, made short work of the fastenings and seconds later, he stood before her, completely naked. And ready for her.

Georgie swallowed. *Dear God above.* Rafe clothed, even semi-clothed, was a wondrous sight, but stripped bare... He was magnificent. And large. She'd pleasured him with her mouth but to see him like this, in a state of full rut with his long, thick cock standing to attention... She'd never seen anything so arousing. Her sex clenched with fresh need. She put her glass down also. She didn't want wine anymore.

"My turn," she whispered. She rose to her knees and grasped the hem of her chemise with trembling fingers. And her belly turned an unexpected somersault. Despite everything she and Rafe had done tonight, this stripping away of her very last layer was proving to be harder than she'd ever imagined. She'd never been fully naked in front of a man before. And Rafe would undoubtedly have seen the bodies of many beautiful women. He might be aroused at the moment, but what would he think of *her* nude body? She was slender, but she was also well-endowed in the areas of hip and bust; at least more so than many of her feminine contemporaries who were considered to be the epitome of elegance and beauty. What if he didn't like what she revealed?

Bury the last of your self-doubt, Georgiana Dudley. A bargain is a bargain. And Rafe is waiting.

She started to inch the garment up. Heat flooded her face, crept down her neck toward her breasts. Rafe's eyes were fixed on her, following her every movement.

"You torture me, sweetheart." His voice was an agonized whisper. He gripped his cock and squeezed; a pearl of semen seeped from the smooth, ruddy head. "Please, let me see you."

Enough hiding. He wants you. Just do it. She sucked in a deep breath and pulled the chemise off completely.

Cool air washed over her skin, raising gooseflesh, tightening her nipples into aching points. She glanced up through her lashes to steal a look at Rafe's face. And she realized how silly she'd been to doubt both him and herself.

He looked like a man enthralled.

"Georgiana," he groaned, his avid gaze tracing over all her curves, and hollows, lingering on the brown curls between her thighs. "You are divine. Exquisite. I'd imagined... If I'd known..." His eyes returned to her face. "God, I really should have convinced you to shed your clothes much, much sooner." He reached out and cupped her swollen breasts, as if testing their weight, exploring the texture of her skin. Ran his thumbs back and forth over the sensitive, furled tips. "If I were fortunate enough to have my way, you would never don another stitch again," he murmured. The heated expression in his eyes suddenly softened, became tender. "You have no need to be shy, sweetheart. You are perfect in every way."

"You read me too well," she murmured, breathless with sharp want. Rafe's adoration was fanning the flames of her desire as surely as the play of his wicked fingers. She pushed her breasts into his hands, at last feeling how she'd always longed to feel with a lover. Brazen and unashamedly wanton.

Deserving of love.

His mouth tilted into a smile laden with sexual promise. "Hmm. Let me guess if I can predict what you would like next." He bent his head and taunted one of her nipples, sucking the tip between his lips before flicking it with his tongue. "Am I right?" he whispered, his breath hot against her flesh, making her shiver.

"Yes. To begin with," she gasped, threading her fingers through his dark silky hair.

He chuckled then one of his hands skated downward; two long fingers pushed gently between her slippery folds and stroked whilst his thumb began to circle the distended nub of her clitoris, setting off more tremors of pleasure. "And what of this?"

Her legs shook. She could barely speak. "Ah...a little better."

Rafe raised his head and kissed her, a sweet, light brush of his lips that was completely at odds with the action of his fingers. "Only a little. I must aim to do *much* better then, Duchess." Before she knew what he was about, he pushed her down onto the bed, hovering over her. He flexed his hips and his erection pressed into her belly, hot and hard and as smooth as an iron rod sheathed in silk. His searing gaze locked with hers. "Do you want me inside you?"

Such a simple question, but the fact he was asking her what she wanted yet again made her heart swell with emotion. "Yes. Please, yes," she whispered, breathless with desire. There wasn't a single doubt in her mind; she wanted Rafe to possess her, pound into her, until nothing existed but him. She parted her legs and slid her hands to his firm buttocks, urging him to take her. "More than anything."

"Thank God." Rafe kissed her, his tongue plundering deeply as he gently pushed her thighs farther apart with one of his muscular legs. She felt the head of his cock pressing against the tender entrance to her passage. Nudging her open. The pressure began to sting. Although she was wet and willing, it had been a decade since she'd had intercourse. And Rafe's member was massive. The pain would get worse before it got better, but she didn't care. The need to feel Rafe inside her bordered on desperation. She dug her fingers into his hard flesh as she waited for the burn that would accompany his entry. It almost felt like her virginity was being taken all over again.

The intensity of the sting increased and despite her best efforts to suppress it, a whimper rose in her throat. Rafe ripped his mouth away from hers. "I'm sorry for hurting you, sweetheart," he gasped against her lips. "But you are so very tight."

She blinked away tears. "I know. Do not worry about it." Even to her own ears her voice sounded thin and shaky. But she wasn't giving up. She slid her hands to Rafe's wide shoulders and gripped tightly, firming her resolve. "Just take me. Do it now."

Rafe bowed his head, touching his forehead to hers. "All right," he gritted out. "Now."

He lunged forward, thrusting hard, filling her completely with his hard, heavy length. A sharp stab of pain tore through her and she bit her lip to stop her cry escaping. But within the space of a few breaths, her inner muscles seemed to adjust to Rafe's intrusion. The discomfort faded and the fullness stretching her sheath was not unpleasant. In fact, she rather thought she liked it. More than liked it.

"I'm fine. It doesn't hurt anymore," she whispered against his throat. He smelled of sweat and spicy cologne and when she kissed the taut tendons of his neck, he tasted of salt.

"Good." He drew back a little and caught her gaze. "Because I want you to enjoy this just as much as I'm going to."

She couldn't fail to notice the tension in his jaw, the burning intensity in his eyes. Entering her with such restraint when he was so engorged was obviously difficult for him too. Tenderness pierced her heart and she pulled him down for a brief, fervent kiss. "I will." She rolled her hips, urging him to move. "Now, show me everything I've been missing."

Rafe closed his eyes and groaned. "If you keep talking and moving like that, this will be over in seconds, my sweet. I don't think either of us wants that." He lowered his head and seized her mouth in a passionate kiss, his tongue lashing against hers as he began to withdraw on a long, slow glide. She moaned, lamenting the loss of him until he thrust back into her.

Oh yes. Her sheath immediately clenched around him. Her womb contracted. "Keep going," she urged on a gasp, wrapping her legs about him, tightening her hold on his shoulders.

"With pleasure," he growled. He loomed over her, his sweat-slickened chest brushing over her sensitized nipples, his eyes never leaving her face as he slid out, then surged back into her, each thrust harder. Deeper. She felt every powerful stroke, every throbbing, rock-hard inch of him. Her memories of sexual congress were hazy but she was sure it had never been like this.

So intense. So intimate.

Raw passion tempered by tenderness, perhaps even affection.

AMY ROSE BENNETT

She dare not think, even for a second, that Rafe was actually making love to her.

Burying her face in his neck, she pushed the thought away —an easy thing to do considering the brilliant, blinding whirlpool of sensation that was rapidly engulfing her. Rafe began to increase the pace of his thrusts, stroking in and out of her with glorious, purposeful precision. And somehow, she met his every demand, lifting her hips again and again to perfectly match his driving tempo. Sounds of their feverish coupling filled her head: the creak of the bed; the slap of Rafe's flesh against hers; her frantic gasps and cries; his harsh groans. Anyone passing by her room would know exactly what they were doing, but she didn't care. Nothing mattered at all except for Rafe and the incredible things he was doing to her body.

Her inner passage began to ripple and a sob of joy escaped her. She was going to climax this way, she was sure of it.

Leaning his weight on one arm, Rafe suddenly grasped one of her legs with his other hand, changing the angle of his penetration. His hips ground harder against her excruciatingly sensitive sex whilst his relentlessly pounding cock abraded some place deep inside her. Her sheath spasmed around him. *Oh God.* She was almost there.

As if attuned to her verging climax, Rafe released her leg and slid his hand between their bodies. His clever fingers stroked her swollen clitoris, pushing her higher. So high. He dipped his head and sucked on her bottom lip. "Come off for me, Georgie," he rasped against her mouth. "Come now."

She couldn't resist him. On a jagged cry of pure elation, she let her orgasm take her. It crashed through her like a tidal wave; the intensity of the pleasure was devastating, overwhelming; the rapture assailing her unlike anything she'd ever known.

As she quaked in Rafe's arms, he continued to slam into her, prolonging her ecstasy even as he sought his own release.

He swelled inside her then on a guttural groan, wrenched himself free of her body. His chest heaving, his whole body shuddering, he came, his hot seed spilling across her lower belly before he collapsed on top of her.

His substantial weight pinned her to the mattress but she didn't mind. Not when she could feel his satisfied gasps warming her ear. The press of his lips against her temple. Her cheek.

She laced her fingers through the sweat-soaked hair at his nape and stroked the strong sinews of his neck. Completely content to bask in the warmth of her own afterglow, she began to surrender to the pull of drowsiness; until Rafe moved a little, reviving her awareness of the telltale stickiness between their bodies.

It wasn't lost on her that Rafe had kept his word. Even in the throes of his own orgasm he had taken care of her, just like he'd said he would. He'd withdrawn from her before he'd expelled his seed. She supposed it was a sexual practice he customarily employed to guard against unwanted conceptions. Regardless of the reason behind his actions, she was grateful.

She'd already learned the hard way that not every man was so solicitous during sex.

Rafe stirred again and she hastily buried her unwanted, bitter memories.

"Forgive me, my sweet." He raised himself onto his forearms and smiled down at her with such affection, her breath caught. "I'm crushing you."

She smiled back and caressed his stubble-clad jaw. "I barely noticed."

"Liar." He gave her a lop-sided grin. "I'm sure I weigh a ton. And I have made a mess of your very beautiful belly. A most unsatisfactory situation that I must rectify." He eased himself off the bed and within a minute, he returned to her side with the basin from her washstand, a washcloth and towel. As he gently sponged her body clean, she closed her eyes, content to enjoy the pleasurable sensations his touch never failed to arouse. Strange how within the space of a few hours she'd also become so completely unselfconscious around him. There was no doubt at all that he'd unequivocally changed her. She'd become the woman she'd longed to be—a woman no longer afraid to take a lover. A woman who took pleasure in sex.

A woman who could fall in love... If she let herself...

"There," he said softly when he'd finished drying her. "Perfect again."

She opened her eyes and caught his hand. "Thank you," she whispered. Her eyes suddenly misted with unexpected tears. "You'll never know how much..." She hesitated, biting her lip, trying to regain a measure of control. "I'm sorry, I'm not usually this emotional. It's just that you wanted to make this evening special for me and you have. I will never forget this night as long as I live."

"Oh, Georgiana." Rafe slid onto the bed and gathered her against his warm chest. "Don't be sorry. I love it that you are sharing so much of yourself with me. And that you've let me show you the pleasure you've been long denied." He raised one hand and cradled her cheek; his gray eyes held a tender light. "It is my fervent hope that you and I will share many more nights like this." His mouth suddenly kicked into a small, wicked smile as his gaze dropped to her lips. "And days."

Oh, sweet Lord. He is insatiable. But then perhaps, so am I. Georgie pressed her mouth to Rafe's, seeking the kiss he clearly offered. Gently, he explored her mouth, his lips sliding over hers with satiny softness, his tongue languidly entwining with hers. Tasting and teasing her. *Loving her.*

Dear God, she wished that were true.

"Stay with me tonight," she whispered when they at last broke apart, both of them breathless.

"Of course." Rafe pulled the sheets and silk counterpane over them then settled back into the pillows. He gathered her close in his arms again and dropped a kiss on her forehead. "Sleep now, sweetheart."

"Good night, Rafe." She snuggled into his beautiful, warm body, her head tucked beneath his chin. The sound of his strongly beating heart and the steady rise and fall of his chest lulled her. The scent of his skin, clean male overlaid with a pleasant muskiness, gently beguiled her. When he stroked her hair away from her face, she wanted to weep. It was so close to the heaven she'd always dreamed of when she was a debutante, it made her heart ache.

She closed her eyes. With all her heart, she wanted to trust Rafe, to believe that everything he'd said to her tonight was sincere. Even though she now believed she was more than a mere tumble for a few days, other concerns had begun to take form in her mind. She had no doubt that Rafe was a man she could fall deeply in love with. But despite the fact they'd been intimate in ways she'd never imagined, and now shared a bed, she still felt she barely knew him.

You know he has secrets that he's keeping from you, Georgiana. Things he doesn't want to talk about. She strongly suspected Rafe had never been just a diplomat, if he'd ever been one at all. He'd led a mysterious life on the Continent. He'd encountered physical violence and was plagued by nightmares from his past. He habitually scoured the shadows for danger. He was adept at both charming and reading people. Uncovering secrets.

He worked for the Crown.

She wasn't naïve. He was most likely a spy. A man accustomed to living by his wits and telling others what they wanted to hear. A pretender of the highest caliber.

He might claim that he wished to establish a home here in England, but could a man with an obviously shadowy, perhaps even dark past, ever truly be free of it? Furthermore, would a man such as he really want to settle into genteel domesticity with a woman like her—a twenty-eight year-old widow with her own, much too complicated history? He'd hinted he had feelings for her more than once tonight. Made love to her; what they'd done, it went beyond sex. But even so, she was the type of woman that men like Rafe typically had affairs with. At best, she'd be his lover for a season. Nothing more.

But, God help me, after tonight, I do want more.

She drew a deep breath and Rafe's addictive scent flooded her senses again. As tempting as it was to throw all caution to the wind, she must be circumspect when contemplating the future direction of any relationship with this enigmatic man. Somehow she must contain her welling hope and guard her heart for a little longer until she knew more about him. And his true intentions.

Because when she gave her heart away, this time, it would be forever.

CHAPTER 15

This is heaven... That was Rafe's first thought when he awoke to find dawn's early light beginning to creep around the edges of the rose velvet curtains in the guest bedchamber. And Georgie's beautiful naked body pressed against his. He'd stayed the entire night in her bed; a highly significant turn of events simply because it was something he'd rarely done—slept with a lover entwined in his arms. And on those few occasions that he had, it hadn't compared to this. Not in the slightest.

His mouth lifted into a smile and his already erect cock grew harder as one of Georgie's long, slender thighs brushed against his shaft. As she moved, her silky brown curls tickled his chest and the intoxicating scent of warm, sleepy female and her floral perfume filled his head. He had to have her again before he left this room.

More importantly, he wanted to show her how much he cared for her.

The fact she'd begun to trust him, combined with the knowledge that he was the first man in a very long time to have brought her satisfaction, was deeply gratifying to say the least.

Warmth bloomed in his chest as he mentally revisited everything they'd done.

The night had been absolutely perfect except for one thing; his nightmare about Solange had been both unexpected and regrettable.

His smile turned to a grimace. What the devil Georgie would make of it all, he wasn't sure. She had seemed to accept his feeble explanation about why he'd had the dream. And he was grateful she hadn't pressed him for further information. God, he'd even spoken in French. He'd had no idea at all he sometimes called out in his sleep. Even more miraculous was the fact Georgie hadn't thrown him out of her bed for calling out another woman's name. One truth he'd been able to share with her was that he honestly hadn't dreamt about his former paramour for years.

Poor, sweet Solange.

Rafe hastily pushed away the guilt and lingering sorrow that always accompanied his recollections of her and their time together. Even though their affair had been eight years ago, the way Solange had died—so unexpectedly and so brutally—it still took his breath away. Yes, it was best that he kept the manner of her passing, and his pain, buried.

He'd never spoken to anyone—not even Phillip—about the horrendous circumstances.

He certainly couldn't disclose the details to Georgie. Indeed, he was loath to share anything at all about his former life with her.

Rafe sighed deeply. He knew Georgie was curious. No, that wasn't the right word—she was suspicious of his diplomatic activities. And rightly so. She was smart. She'd have noticed the scars upon his body. She'd already jested that he was a spy.

The problem was, if he confessed she was correct and told her all about the sorts of nefarious activities he'd really been engaged in over the years, she'd probably run a mile. He was used to redirecting the attention of both men and women alike onto topics other than himself. And for the most part, his strategies worked. But Georgie had seen through him. Her observation that he frequently used his charm to deflect inconvenient interest was quite accurate.

If she knew what he was really like. What he was capable of. The things he'd done...

Would she want anything to do with him?

No, Rafe couldn't take the risk of letting her know everything about himself. Not when he felt like this.

He groaned and took a moment to indulge in the simple pleasure of holding Georgie in his arms. He was on the brink of falling in love. There was no point denying it. It seemed he'd completely lost control of his usually tightly reined-in emotions.

If truth be told, he'd almost let slip how he'd felt in the unguarded moments after his nightmare. But it was too soon to confess such things. He doubted Georgie would believe him. Not yet. It would take time for her to have complete faith in him. To let him into her heart.

But how was he to win her trust and love when he couldn't be totally honest with her?

Rafe's jaw tightened. *Face it, man. Your bloody past will always be a thorn in your side—a filthy, cankerous burr that you must keep hidden.*

Georgie stirred a little, pulling him away from his dark, circuitous and altogether frustrating thoughts. He brushed her tumbling curls away from her face; her cheeks were adorably flushed with sleep and her breath sighed in and out of her slightly parted, oh-so kissable lips. She looked vulnerable and alluring in equal measure.

And he needed her.

He cupped her face with deliberate delicacy and kissed her

gently, rousing her from slumber. When she kissed him back, he smiled against her lips.

Even if he couldn't tell her, he would clearly demonstrate exactly how he felt before she left Rivergate.

When Rafe took a seat in the morning room with a laden breakfast plate an hour and a half later, he caught himself grinning like a besotted boy. Indeed, when he'd returned to his own rooms to attend to his usual morning ablutions, his valet had even had to prompt him to stop smiling during his shave.

Now as Rafe attacked his eggs, bacon, and grilled kidneys with relish, he regretted not inviting Georgie to take breakfast with him. She'd fallen into a light doze after he'd made slow, delicious love to her, and he'd been reluctant to wake her. He assumed she'd probably send for a tray in her room when she did eventually rise. Even though a scant half-hour had passed since he'd left her bed, he realized he already missed her.

He shook his head. *Besotted indeed.*

He'd begun to glance over yesterday's broadsheets for any vaguely interesting stories he might have missed—the rain had eased somewhat, but the roadway was obviously still cut as this morning's deliveries and post hadn't arrived—when the door clicked open and Georgie stepped into the room. Dressed in a simple, lavender blue morning gown, she looked as fresh and lovely as a rain-washed sky in spring.

His blood thrumming with anticipation, he immediately stood and bowed. "Your Grace."

Her answering smile was radiant. "Lord Markham. I am rather hoping that you will not mind some company as you partake breakfast this morning."

"Of course not. I would be honored if you joined me."

After Georgie had selected a simple repast of a roll, butter, and marmalade from the buffet, she chose the seat at the opposite end of the cherrywood dining table. As one of the attendant footmen served her hot chocolate, Rafe rued his decision to staff Rivergate so well. Breakfast rolls and hot chocolate be damned. If they were alone, he would have loved nothing more than to ravish her upon the very table that separated them.

"I hope I am not disturbing you, my lord." Georgie was studying his face, a slight frown of concern creasing her forehead.

Rafe obviously hadn't hidden his scowl of annoyance as well as he'd thought and quickly replaced it with a smile. "Not at all. I apologize for my less than hospitable manner. I was silently lamenting the abysmal state of the weather. I'm afraid our activities will be confined to the indoors." He cocked an eyebrow. "Nevertheless, I dare say we shall be able to entertain ourselves one way or another."

A faint blush stained Georgie's cheeks as she darted furtive glances to the apparently disinterested footmen by the door and buffet respectively before her gaze returned to his. Her eyes gleamed with challenge. "No doubt," she replied smoothly enough. "I would be particularly interested to hear more about your adventures abroad. I'm certain you have many interesting tales of derring-do to share."

Touché. "Indeed I do, Your Grace." Rafe was going to have to regale her with some of his tried-and-true—and largely fabricated—stories in an attempt to quell her persistent curiosity. He didn't want to lie to her, but it appeared that he must.

"So..." She took a sip of her hot chocolate before pinning him with a sharp look. "Given your French is quite impeccable, it would seem that at some point you have spent time in France or its territories. Perhaps the Caribbean or Saint-Domingue? Pardon me, I should say Haiti."

"Nowhere as exotic as Haiti I assure you." Rafe let the silence stretch as he sipped his coffee.

Georgie's keen scrutiny continued. Her head was tilted to the side and her frown had grown deeper. He was evidently still a mystery she was intent on solving.

With a sigh, Rafe placed his cup down and pushed aside a fresh pang of guilt. Perhaps a tale or two about his long-ago *affaire* with the fictitious French émigré, Solange, the Comtesse de Fougères would suffice; he most certainly wouldn't reveal his former lover had really been the wife of a man named Duchamp, one of old Boney's generals. But relating any cock-and-bull story about Solange would have to wait until they were at least out of earshot of the staff. For now, he would tell her something that approximated the truth.

"In actual fact, most of my French was acquired in the schoolroom at Avonmore Park," he offered with one of his most charming smiles. "My father insisted my brother and I receive expert tuition in several languages from quite a young age. Our French tutor, Monsieur Bastien was actually an émigré—"

Over the ever-present patter of the rain against the windows came the distinct sound of carriage wheels crunching upon the gravel drive.

"Jonathon." Georgie discarded her napkin and sprang to her feet before rushing from the room. Rafe followed her out to the terrace and sure enough, the duchess's carriage had halted before the stairs. Two of Rivergate's footmen waited nearby with umbrellas at the ready.

"Hey ho, sis, did you miss me?" called a grinning Jonathon as he alighted and took one of the proffered umbrellas. Lord Farley followed before assisting his aunt, Lady Talbot, and then his sister, Lady Lucinda, to alight also.

Damn. Rafe pushed down an exasperated sigh. *So much for having Georgie all to myself.*

"You know I missed you," replied Georgie when her brother reached the shelter of the portico. She stepped forward and clasped his hand. "If truth be told, I was worried to the point of being quite ill. What if you had been caught in flood waters?"

Discarding his umbrella, Jonathon leaned forward and kissed her cheek. "You are such a peagoose sometimes, Georgie-bean," he said with an affectionate smile. "You had nothing to worry about. I would never have let Benson drive me into harm's way. And I must say, the White Swan Inn where we holed up for the night does a splendid pie. We must stop there on the way home so you can sample one." His gaze shifted past her to Rafe and his smile became impish. "I trust that you have been taking good care of my sister."

Georgie's mouth flattened as a bright red blush stained her cheeks. "Jonathon..." Her voice was tinged with warning.

Impudent sod. I'm sure you'd rather not *know...* Rafe struggled to keep his expression neutral as he inclined his head. "Of course. But I might add, it's very good to see you have arrived safe and sound."

At that moment, Lord Farley, his sister and their aunt all appeared at the top of the stairs. After Rafe welcomed his newly arrived guests to Rivergate, they all moved into the vestibule. Damp coats, hats and gloves were quickly discarded, and then as the housekeeper and butler began to arrange for everyone to be shown to their rooms, Jonathon approached him.

The man's affable expression had disappeared. "A quick word if you wouldn't mind, Markham."

Rafe glanced over Jonathon's shoulder but Georgie didn't seem to have noticed their brief exchange. She was chatting animatedly to Lady Lucinda as they followed Lord Farley and Lady Talbot into the main hall.

"What is it?" he asked. Jonathon's expression had turned

grave and a sensation of foreboding slid over him. "Is it to do with Georgiana?"

Jonathon ran a hand through his damp brown hair. "Look, it could be nothing at all. But..."

"Out with it, man."

Jonathon blew out a sigh. "This morning, just after I'd settled the account at the White Swan, I couldn't help but notice that the next customer who approached the innkeeper was a foreigner. A tall man with dark hair who spoke with a marked accent—very guttural sounding, perhaps Germanic. Not that I'm any great judge. But what caught my interest the most was that he sought directions to Rivergate. After Georgie's incident last week, and your subsequent concern, I just thought it rather peculiar."

Christ. Rafe's blood turned to ice. "Did you catch his name or get a good look at his face? Question him about his interest in Rivergate?"

"Well, no." The expression in Jonathon's eyes suddenly hardened. "Are you meaning to tell me that Georgie is in danger?" He gripped Rafe's arm with surprising force. "Do you know this man? And is there something I should know about him? Or more importantly, about you?"

"Honestly, I have no idea who he is or his agenda," Rafe replied grimly. "But to answer your last question, ask me anything at all and I will do my level best to give you a straight answer."

Jonathon released his arm and snorted. "That's the response of a silver-tongued diplomat if ever I heard one. Phillip and Helena seem to trust you implicitly, but now, I'm not so sure. Georgie was right. You are hiding something."

Rafe inclined his head. "Your concern is duly noted. But please, you can be rest assured that my intentions toward your sister always have been, and continue to be, nothing but honorable. I would never let anything, or *anyone* harm her."

Jonathon scowled. "Well, I should bloody well hope so."
He moved away, heading for the hall. "We will talk later."

Rafe's mouth tightened. "Of course."

When Jonathon had disappeared from view, Rafe ordered
one of the footmen to have his horse readied before he, too,
headed to his own rooms to change into suitable wet weather
riding attire. Enough was enough. It seemed the viper had at
last stuck its head out of the undergrowth.

And if Rafe had to, he would strike it off.

Nearly three hours later Rafe returned to Rivergate, soaking
wet, in a temper as foul as the weather, and essentially none
the wiser. Except for one thing. The stranger had given his
name to the innkeeper, a name that must be false—Herr
Scherzfrage; its literal translation was Mr. Riddle. And of
course, there was no guarantee that his stalker was actually
Prussian, German, Austrian or even Swiss for that matter.

There was no doubt in Rafe's mind that he'd been sent a
message—*I'm watching you, but you don't know who I am.*
Scherzfrage or Riddle was clearly toying with him. And his gut
told him this was for personal reasons. A *vendetta,* as the Italian's would say. *But why?*

One thing was clear to Rafe, this was only an early move in
this man's sinister game. And he didn't like it, not one
little bit.

The White Swan's staff had also revealed that 'Riddle'
hadn't taken a room; he'd dined on simple fare in the main
taproom before swapping his hired mount with another from
the inn's stables. He was reported to be well-dressed, polite,
moderately attractive—according to one of the innkeeper's
daughters, at any rate—with eyes of an unremarkable color,
perhaps light gray or blue...which meant Rafe still hadn't a

clue who he might be. Sadly, his mental list of foreign men, dark-haired or otherwise, who might wish to exact revenge upon him was almost too long to contemplate. But then, Riddle could always be an Englishman who'd adopted a foreign guise. And it was easy enough to use paste in one's hair to mask the color. The fellow could easily be a blond Swede or a red-headed Scotsman for all he knew.

In the murky world of espionage, nothing was too far-fetched to contemplate.

The ostler hadn't noted which way Riddle had gone and the imposter hadn't mentioned his destination either. Once Rafe had established that much, he'd then spent the next hour kicking himself as he conducted surveillance of the road leading to Rivergate and the perimeter of his property. What a fool he'd been not to have brought some of his own men from London to undertake this sort of activity. Instead of being ensconced before the fire with Georgie in his arms, he was soaked through, half-frozen and taut as a *garotte* rope.

When it was evident his scouting exercise was all but useless—he hadn't even spied a single squirrel in the woodland behind Rivergate—Rafe headed for the house. Entering the vestibule, he summoned his butler, Spencer, and issued instructions to the effect that a pair of footmen must be stationed at each of Rivergate's entrances—three in total—at all times, and that no one fitting Herr Scherzfrage's description was to be admitted.

Even though Rafe had regretted having a surfeit of servants earlier in the day, he definitely wasn't regretting the fact now. As an added precaution, he also ordered that the front gate was to be secured, and all visitors had to be vetted by an armed male staff member stationed within the gate-house. And if Scherzfrage did make an appearance, he was to be alerted immediately, no matter the time of day or night.

Satisfied that he'd done all he could feasibly do to keep

Riddle at bay for the moment, Rafe at long last mounted the stairs and headed straight for his rooms. A change into dry clothes and a brandy-laced coffee were definitely in order before he sought out Georgie. And once he found her, he would not leave her side. His instincts still told him Riddle wasn't only stalking him.

"Markham. I mean, Rafe. Is everything all right?"

Georgie.

The duchess rose from the window seat that was directly opposite the door to his suite. Her forehead pleated into a deep frown as her gaze traveled over his sorry appearance. He dared not think that she'd actually missed him or had been concerned for his safety.

"You've been gone for hours," she continued when he didn't immediately respond. "Your butler—Spencer, isn't it? —mentioned you had some sudden business to attend to."

Rafe swiped a rivulet of water from his nose before summoning a grin. "It seems there is no rest for the wicked."

Georgie approached him and grasped his arm. "You jest, but I sense there is something wrong."

Jonathon clearly hadn't told his sister about crossing paths with Riddle. "Mr. Chapel from Lowood House sent word that perhaps the river had broken its banks toward Twickenham," he lied. "Given we are not far away, I wanted to see for myself. But do not be concerned. Everything is well."

"I see..." Her narrow-eyed expression told him she was not convinced. "Well..." She stepped away, suddenly looking uncertain, as if she'd only just noticed they were both standing by the door to his room and he'd been dripping all over her skirts. "I'd best leave so you can change your attire."

"Care to help?"

A deep rosy blush spread over Georgie's cheeks but nevertheless, she smiled. "If my brother and the rest of your guests hadn't arrived, I would be very tempted to oblige. But perhaps there is something else I can do for you? Send up tea?"

Rafe took a step toward her and reached for her hand, drawing her close again. "I don't need tea. I need this." He bent his head and kissed her, his lips and tongue caressing her mouth with such slow, gentle thoroughness it made his own head spin. It was a tender yet calculated kiss bestowed with one sole intention: to make her breathless with a yearning that matched his own.

When he drew back, her eyes fluttered open and he was pleased to see she looked a little dazed. "We have not had an opportunity to talk privately since your brother and the other guests arrived," he murmured, brushing her cheek lightly with the back of his fingers. "Please say you will let me come to your room tonight."

"I would like that," Georgie replied in such a delightfully husky voice, it made him want to make love to her all the more. "I will dismiss my maid again."

He smiled. "Good." He feathered a light kiss over knuckles before reluctantly releasing her hand. "I will meet you in the drawing room in half an hour."

"Yes." She turned to go, but after taking only a few steps away from him, swung back. "Rafe, you *would* tell me if something were wrong, wouldn't you?"

He held her worried gaze and gave her a reassuring smile. "Yes, of course."

She gave a tight smile in return before heading toward the stairs.

Hell. She doesn't believe me.

With a heavy sigh, he entered his suite and rang for his valet. If Jonathon told her about Riddle before he did, she would be as angry as a cat caught in the rain. Even worse than that, her faith in him would be shattered.

Christ, I need a drink. As he poured himself a brandy—

there was always a full decanter in his sitting room—he tried to convince himself that it would be unfair to burden Georgie with insubstantial information about an indistinct threat. Which meant he would continue to lie to her unless and until her brother forced him to reveal what little he did know.

Needs must when the devil drives, eh, Markham? He tossed back a sizeable swig of the brandy and his mouth twisted into a wry grimace.

Sadly, that expression should probably be his epitaph.

"Markham, I thought I'd find you here."

Rafe turned in his seat before the library fire and met Jonathon Winterbourne's hard blue gaze. He raised his whisky glass. "Care for a dram before bed? It's courtesy of Rothsburgh. From his illicit stash." Dinner was long since over and it seemed that everyone bar himself and Jonathon had retired for the night. Rafe had simply been filling in time until he could pay an unobserved visit to Georgie's suite. However, it now appeared he and Jonathon were about to have 'their talk'.

"No." Jonathon flicked out the tails of his evening jacket as he took a seat in the opposite wingback chair. "Care to explain this?" He tossed a calling card onto the mahogany table beside Rafe.

Frowning, Rafe, put down his glass and picked up the card. Ice-cold fear gripped his chest as he took in the print. *Herr Maximilian Scherzfrage* appeared in embossed black letters upon the ivory card. But it was the message scrawled on the back in blood-red ink that chilled him the most.

Please give my regards to the Duchess.
It would be most rude of a gentleman to dash off without having done so.

Fuck. His instincts had been correct. This was a very personal cat and mouse game. The problem was, he still hadn't the slightest idea who his opponent was, or his endgame. And Georgie was in danger.

"Well? Can you please tell me what the hell is going on?"

Rafe met Jonathon's blistering glare. "How did you come by this?"

"My valet found it when he was laundering the greatcoat I wore this morning. That bloody foreign bastard must have slipped it into my pocket when I was settling the account."

Rafe nodded. "Winterbourne..." There was no way around it. He didn't like it, but he was going to have to make a confession about his past occupation. "Not many know this—actually only Phillip and a few others in Lord Castlereagh's office—but up until a year ago, I worked for the Crown. But not as a diplomat."

Jonathon smirked. "So a bloody spy then. I thought as much."

"I know Georgie has her suspicions as well, but I have refrained from disclosing any information to her about my past. As you can well understand, the fewer people who know about my former activities, the better."

"That's all well and good, but it looks like your past," Jonathon glanced meaningfully at the calling card that Rafe still held, "is not dead and buried. And somehow my sister has been dragged into the whole murky business. Who is this devil, Scherzfrage, and what does he want?"

Rafe tossed the card onto the table before running a hand down his face. Frustration clawed at his gut. "Believe me, I wish I knew."

"That's not good enough."

Rafe sighed. "I know."

Jonathon leaned forward and jabbed a finger toward his

chest. "I don't believe you. You strike me as a fellow who has a formidable memory for names and faces."

"He's using a false name," explained Rafe. "Its literal translation is 'greatest riddle'. The bastard is playing some sick game. He probably isn't even Germanic."

"Christ." Jonathon sat back in his chair. His face had grown as pale as the card on the table between them. "I think I *will* have a drink. Whisky as well. A large one."

Rafe fulfilled Jonathon's request then resumed his seat. "Are you sure you don't recall any other distinguishing features or mannerisms about the man? Any detail, however small, may help me work out who he is."

Jonathon rubbed his temple and his gaze became unfocused as he appeared to sift through his memories. "His hair was brown and styled in the current fashion—cropped short at the back but messy and overly long in the front. I think that's why I didn't really notice his eyes. He didn't strike me as handsome, but neither was he unattractive. His coat was well-cut; travel-stained but not worn or cheap looking. He was tall and seemed relatively well-made beneath his clothes. For instance, he didn't stoop. He was neither too thin nor fat. Neither old nor young. Perhaps he was your age, or a little older. Apart from his manner of speaking, he was in fact, rather ordinary."

Except he isn't. Rafe sipped at his whisky, mulling over what to say next. "This cloak and dagger act, it strikes me as unusual. Riddle—that's what I have dubbed him in my mind —is taunting me. It seems very personal. Like an act of revenge. Unfortunately, the list of men who might wish me ill is a long one."

"Why do you think he has involved Georgie in all of this then? She's not a part of your past."

Yes, but she's the woman I care about. The woman I now realize I want to share a future with. Rafe straightened in his seat as a blinding realization struck him. *Maybe... Why haven't I thought of him until now?*

Jonathon's gaze sharpened. "What is it?"

"I think I might have an idea who it is after all."

"Who?"

"A Russian baron and general by the name of Dashkov. Four years ago, when I was in St. Petersburg, I had an affair with his wife."

"Bloody hell, Markham. That's playing it a bit fast and loose, isn't it?"

Rafe shrugged. *You have barely scratched the surface.* "One does what one has to when in the service of king and country."

"What, you mean to say you used the wife of this Baron Dashkov to gather information for the Crown?"

"Yes."

"By Jove, that's a tad ruthless. But I'm confused. Why would he exact revenge for that now? Four years have passed."

"I suppose some scars never heal, Winterbourne."

"I suppose you are right." Jonathon sipped his whisky, his expression pensive. "Well, if this fellow is your Dashkov, we shouldn't have too much to worry about then. I mean, it's not as if Georgie is going to respond to this devil's clumsy attempts to ensnare her. Especially when she finds out he is married. And not when she is so smitten by you."

Rafe wanted to smile at Jonathon's last observation but found himself grimacing instead. "You misunderstand. My explanation of the situation has been inadequate."

Jonathon raised his eyebrows and cold wariness hardened his stare. "Enlighten me then."

"I'll spare you the details. But basically, Dashkov blames me for the death of his wife."

Jonathon's brow plunged into a deep scowl. "*What?*"

Rafe looked him in the eye. "I can assure you I am innocent. I had nothing at all to do with Baroness Dashkovna's demise. It was, quite simply, an unfortunate accident. I would never, *ever*, hurt a woman."

"But..." Jonathon shook his head as if trying to knock his thoughts into order. "Why involve, Georg—" His face grew ashen. "He wants to avenge his wife's death by hurting the woman *you* love."

Rafe inclined his head. "It would seem so. However I would remind you, this is all just speculation at this point." The words printed on the back of Scherzfrage's card suddenly sprang into his mind—the phrase 'dash off' was close to Dashkov. It could be a coincidence, however, Rafe's gut instinct told him the choice of words was deliberate.

Jonathon stood up abruptly and began pacing back and forth on the Turkish hearthrug. "Christ above. Does Phillip know any of this? I can't believe that he would..." He stopped and faced Rafe.

"Support my courtship of your sister?"

Jonathon lifted his chin. "Yes. And I did support you. Now I am not so sure."

Rafe felt a muscle work in his jaw. "Phillip will vouch for me. He knows almost everything. And really, isn't it up to Georgiana to decide if she will accept my suit?"

"She doesn't know the truth about you. What you are." Jonathon's tone was acerbic. Accusatory.

"No. No she doesn't." Rafe's voice was weighted with a guilt heavier than lead. "Please believe me, I want to tell her everything there is to know about me. But men like me..." He dragged a hand down his face as he struggled to find a way to explain. "Sometimes it's best that those around us are kept in the dark. Knowledge—and by that I mean having too much of the wrong type of knowledge—can be dangerous also. Aside from that, I'm loath to burden Georgie with something so worrisome. Particularly if my current assumptions are incorrect."

The scorn in Jonathon's eyes was clear as he scrutinized Rafe over the rim of his whisky glass for one long moment. He threw back the last mouthful then placed his glass on the marble mantel with a decided click. "What measures will you take to keep my sister safe?" he asked in a flinty tone. "God knows she's already been through enough with Craven. I won't see her hurt again."

Rafe breathed an inward sigh of relief. Jonathon wasn't going to drag Georgie off into the night and forbid her from seeing him again. Not that he could imagine Georgie letting her brother dictate how she should live her life.

He turned his attention back to Jonathon and outlined the additional security measures he'd put in place around Rivergate. "Actually, I don't know if you noticed anything during the week, but since the incident outside Latimer House last Friday, I've had a team of my men—all former Bow Street Runners or soldiers with impeccable records—conducting continuous surveillance around Dudley House, monitoring Georgiana's movements. I'd started to think I was being overly vigilante as no one reported seeing a man fitting Riddle's description. But now I am relieved that I did."

Jonathon snorted. "Egads, you're a crafty bastard. I had no idea you had put any type of surveillance in place." His eyes narrowed to slits. "So you have been seriously worried about Georgie's well-being for that long?"

"One can never be too careful. I promise that I will double my team's efforts in keeping an eye on Georgie. And of course, if you are still in agreeance, I will continue to see your sister on a daily basis. Not a single hair on her head will be harmed whilst she is under my protection."

Jonathon dropped his gaze to the fire; he was clearly considering the situation and everything they'd discussed. At length, he sighed heavily and skewered Rafe with a gimlet stare. "If anything happens to Georgie, I will hold you personally accountable."

"Understood."

"And I agree that we should both stay silent about the matter until more information comes to hand. I probably shouldn't be telling you this but," Jonathon's expression softened a little, "I have never seen Georgie so uplifted. Brimming with life. I do not want to see her happiness crushed."

"Nor do I." Rafe's heart swelled with quiet joy but he kept his expression suitably grave to mollify Jonathon. "And thank you. Again, I promise you that Georgiana will not be hurt. I care deeply for her."

Jonathon gave a curt nod. "Good. She deserves nothing less." He marched toward the library door, but then paused on the threshold. "Keep in mind, my warning stands. If anything untoward should befall my sister, it won't be Riddle—or Dashkov, or whatever his name is—you have to worry about. It will be me."

As the door clicked shut, Rafe sighed, his heart heavy with remorse and untold regret. *And I will not blame you for that, my friend,* he thought to himself as he tossed back the last of his whisky. *If the worst should happen, there is no doubt at all that the fault will be mine.*

And for that, I will never be able to forgive myself.

CHAPTER 16

Dudley House, Hanover Square, London
A week later...

"Your Grace, would you like to wear the silk bonnet with the tea roses and ivory ribbons or the wine velvet cap? Either would go well with your raspberry, pink and ivory striped walking gown... Your Grace?"

Georgie shook herself from her delicious daydream about Rafe, and what they'd done in this very bedroom at Dudley House last night. She blinked and met her maid's expectant gaze. "My apologies for wool gathering, Constance. I'm afraid I haven't been sleeping too well of late." She blushed when Constance pursed her lips a little; the girl must have a fair idea why her mistress was sleep deprived; not only had Lord Markham dined at Dudley House every single night of the week since they'd returned to London, Georgie had also dismissed Constance early every single night. But as usual, it seemed her ever discreet and patient maid would hold her tongue.

"That's quite all right, ma'am," she replied in a neutral

tone. "I just wanted to make sure that your ensemble would be ready in time for your...'er outing with Sir Jonathon and..." She bit her lip. *And Lord Markham* were the words she'd obviously left unsaid.

"Yes. Of course." Georgie focused her wandering attention back on hats Constance still held. Rafe had insisted she accompany him on a shopping expedition in and around nearby Bond Street today. To what end, she had no idea, but it seemed she was powerless to resist any of his requests of late. His company—and his love-making—were as addictive as laudanum. "The silk with the tea roses, I think."

"Very good, ma'am." As Constance helped her to put the bonnet in place without destroying the arrangement of curls around her face, Georgie suddenly noticed shadows of fatigue beneath the young woman's eyes that were even worse than her own. Despite the reduction in her evening duties, Constance didn't appear to be getting enough sleep either.

"Constance, are *you* well?" she asked gently. "You seem a little out of sorts also."

Her maid blushed hotly as she finished adjusting the bow beneath Georgie's chin. "Why, yes, Your Grace. I am perfectly well." She gave Georgie a small smile then stepped away from the mahogany dressing table. "Shall I fetch the matching spencer and your ivory kid gloves? Or do you think you will need your burgundy wool pelisse?"

Georgie glanced toward the windows. It was overcast, but the clouds were high and the threat of rain slight for once. "My spencer will suffice I should think."

Once she was ready, Georgie descended to the vestibule to find Jonathon pulling on his own gloves. "Hey-ho, sis." He threw her an irreverent smile and winked. "Ready to spend a bit of Markham's blunt?"

"Jonathon," she admonished under her breath as their footmen—Perkins and the very well-proportioned and very recently employed, Lumsden—stood on duty by the front door. "Please, watch your tongue. That is not what this morning is about."

Jonathon quirked an eyebrow. "Oh really? Don't tell me you're not anticipating getting a little spoiled this morning. Lord knows, you deserve it."

"And what is that supposed to mean exactly?" Georgie demanded, her whisper harsh, her glare fierce. Jonathon must have guessed by now that Rafe shared her bed, but to suggest she deserved some type of reward or worse still, payment like a common harlot... Well, that sort of thinking was beyond the pale.

Jonathon blushed a little. "Nothing at all," he muttered, suddenly interested in the fit of his gloves until a sudden and decisive knock on the door drew his glance. "Ah, saved by the devil himself, I suspect."

Sure enough, Rafe was at the door. As usual, his wide smile and the drift of his gaze over her body sent Georgie's pulse racing and her heart flipping. "Your Grace," he murmured, bowing over her hand. "You are looking more than splendid this morning." He straightened and inclined his head toward a still flushed Jonathon. "Sir Jonathon."

Jonathon gave him an overly bright smile and rubbed his hands together. "Well, let's sally-forth you two, and make the most of this morning. I think a luncheon at Gunter's could well be on the cards, if we don't dillydally over this shopping business."

Rafe raised a quizzical brow at Georgie as she took his offered arm. "Is everything all right?"

"It's nothing out of the ordinary. Jonathon is simply being an ass," she whispered as they exited Dudley House. Rafe chuckled low in her ear and she shivered with warm delight. It was moments like these that it struck her how close she and Rafe had grown within the last week. Only a fortnight ago, she would have been loath to acknowledge a connection with him. But now, as they strolled across Hanover Square in the direction of New Bond Street, she realized she didn't give a fig what the gossipmongers within the *ton* thought.

The only cloud shadowing the horizon was Rafe's constant evasion when it came to discussing his past. Despite the growing intimacy between them, Georgie could not coax him into revealing anything more than amusing anecdotes about his time abroad. He never again brought up the topic of Solange, and truth be told, she didn't have the heart to quiz him about his former lover. At the back of her mind, she was also concerned that if he did share details about his affair with Solange, he might expect her to reciprocate and confide in him about her disastrous liaison with Lord Craven. And that was something she could never do.

She'd never related the entire account to a single soul—not even Jonathon or Teddy. She sighed heavily; some things were just too painful to revisit.

"Penny for your thoughts, sweetheart. I swear you haven't heard a single word I've said since we left Dudley House."

Georgie felt a blush heat her cheeks and she offered Rafe an embarrassed smile. "My apologies, Rafe. I... I'm afraid I've been a little absent minded this morning."

"I'm sure that's my fault," he murmured. "I'm interfering with your rest."

"Yes... Well..." Georgie broke away from his gaze, scrabbling for a vaguely suitable response that she could safely articulate in public. They were ambling their way southward down New Bond Street and even though it was early in the day, there was a steady flow of pedestrian traffic along the pavement, including a fair few familiar faces with decidedly inquisitive expressions directed their way.

Georgie chose to ignore them. "Where are we headed, if you don't mind my asking?" Jonathon had wandered off and she could barely see his top hat above the bobbing bonnets and hats of the other pedestrians up ahead. He was no doubt making his way toward his favorite snuff shop or Hoby's in St James's Street to pick up the pair of Hessians he'd ordered last week.

Rafe smiled. "Nowhere in particular, but..." He suddenly paused outside a gleaming shop window. Georgie gasped when she read the sign: Stedman and Vardon, Goldsmiths and Jewelers.

"I would very much value your opinion on a few items of jewelry I have had my eye on. Pieces that are purely for investment purposes," he continued, his voice low and warm and his gray eyes shining with an emotion Georgie dare not put a name to. "Do you see anything you like?"

Georgie swallowed. Somehow she tore her gaze from Rafe's and peered in the window. "Everything on display is beautiful. Are you after anything in particular? There's quite a lovely golden fob watch up the back. And that gold and onyx signet ring to its right is very eye-catching as well."

Georgie glanced at Rafe's reflection and noticed he was smiling at her rather than looking in the window. "I'm not looking to purchase anything for myself, Duchess," he said softly.

"Oh..." Teddy had given her many pieces of jewelry during their marriage—some of them were family heirlooms and many were unique pieces he'd had his favorite jeweler, Rundell, Bridge and Rundell, create for her. But never in her life had she been asked to choose a piece of jewelry based on her own taste. Because surely that was what Rafe was doing.

Georgie blinked away tears as a strange warmth flooded her heart. "I rather like the look of the sapphire and diamond earrings over there." Set in silver and edged by a row of delicate white diamonds, the teardrop shaped sapphires were an unusual yet beautiful shade of pale blue.

"You have excellent taste, Your Grace," Rafe murmured. "But what of the matching brooch, ring, bracelet and necklace? Don't you think they make a remarkable parure?"

"Yes..." Georgie had to silently concede the whole ensemble was truly exquisite. "But a set such as this would be worth a king's ransom. It is too extravagant for words." She placed her free hand to her throat, determined to still her wildly beating pulse, not sure if she was terrified or thrilled by the implications of Rafe's actions. *We've only been lovers for a week. Why is he doing this? Sending roses is one thing but this—buying me jewelry—is too much, too soon. Isn't it?*

"There's nothing wrong with being extravagant on occasion." Rafe ran his leather-clad thumb over the sliver of bare skin between her glove and the woolen sleeve of her spencer, making her breath catch. "However, we have only just begun to browse. Would you like to step inside and view something else? I believe there is an exceptional strand of pale pink pearls, and an exotic black pearl from the South Pacific, at least the size of a quail's egg. And then we could always stroll by another excellent jewelry store I know of in Old Bond Street. I hear they have a superb gold necklace featuring the rarest of rubies. I've been told the stones are from Burma and are a most extraordinary hue. Pigeon blood red."

"I don't know what to say. Perhaps we could pass by my favorite milliner's shop first, just a little farther along on the corner of Grafton Street. Mrs. Millburn has the most delightful velvet and satin covered poke bonnets in the window. I've been meaning to purchase one to match my new carriage dress."

Laughter danced in Rafe's eyes. "As you wish. Wherever you lead, I will follow."

Breathing a sigh of relief, Georgie turned and then froze, riveted to the spot. Her lungs seized up as if she'd been slammed into by one of the hackney cabs rolling by. Clutching at Rafe's sleeve, she dipped her head to hide her face, and willed herself not to throw up or pass out or both.

"Georgie?" Rafe's voice was at her ear, his tone urgent as he gripped her about the shoulders to keep her upright. "Christ. What's wrong?"

"Help me inside...please," she whispered, her voice a ragged thread of sound. "I need to sit down."

Without a word, Rafe helped her into the cool and dimly lit interior of the jewelers and guided her to a satin-lined chair beside one of the counters. Bending her head, she wrapped her arm about her waist and closed her eyes, trying to control her roiling nausea and the frantic pace of her shallow breathing. All the while Rafe held her other hand, offering silent support and comfort.

When her panic at last began to ebb away, she opened her eyes to find Rafe kneeling beside her, his eyes shadowed with concern. "Would you like some water?" he asked gently. "I'm afraid the staff at Stedman and Vardon don't have anything stronger at hand."

She nodded and gratefully accepted a glass from a nearby employee. "I'm so sorry I've caused such a fuss," she murmured after the man had retreated a discreet distance.

Rafe frowned. "You have nothing to apologize for, Georgiana. However, I want to know what happened."

"I—" Georgie swallowed past her tight throat trying to think of something, anything to say that would sound plausible. Anything but the truth. She attempted to take a sip of water but was mortified to see that her hand trembled when she raised the glass.

"You saw someone across the street. In front of the tobacconist's shop." The gentle tone of Rafe's voice belied the hard look of determination in his eyes. "Who was it? You must tell me."

Georgie drew a shuddering breath and somehow forced

her lips and tongue to produce the name of the man she would always dread and despise in equal measure. "It was Lord Craven."

Rafe cursed inwardly as hot, hard anger spiked his gut. He'd suspected it was Craven that Georgie had spied rather than Riddle—Cowan and one of his other men had been shadowing the duchess, Winterbourne and himself since they'd struck out from Dudley House. If Riddle had been following, his men would have spotted him and intervened much earlier. And he doubted Georgie would have reacted so violently if she'd merely caught sight of the man who'd bumped into her outside Latimer House. She still didn't know about the incident at the White Swan Inn.

He watched Georgie as she sipped her water. Her face was deathly pale and her hand still shook. The passing of a decade clearly hadn't reduced her emotional scars. He suspected they ran as deep as some of his own.

His desire to reduce Craven to a bloody pulp was stronger than ever.

"Rafe, you're hurting my hand."

Rafe immediately loosened his grip. "My apologies, Duchess." Ignoring the presence of the curious Stedman and Vardon employees, Rafe pushed a curl back from Georgie's ashen cheek. "Even though Dudley House is not too far away, I think it would be best if we hailed a hackney cab, don't you?"

Georgie nodded and offered a weak smile. "Yes. I suspect you may be right." Her expression changed, her forehead creasing into a slight frown. "But what of Jonathon? I don't wish to worry him."

Bugger Jonathon. Rafe bit back what he really wanted to say and instead replied, "I am sure your brother will work out we have returned to Dudley House before too long. And we can always send one of your footmen to find him." *Or one of my men.*

Georgie acquiesced and within the space of ten minutes, Rafe was escorting her into the drawing room of Dudley House. Despite his grim mood, he smiled when he saw the arrangement of pale pink roses he'd sent this morning taking pride of place on the mahogany table near the window. He fervently hoped Georgie would accept the other gift he'd planned when the right moment came. Unfortunately, that wasn't going to be today, no thanks to bloody Craven.

After Georgie had taken a seat before the fire, Rafe poured them both a rather sizeable brandy.

"Brandy? At this hour?" Georgie's nose wrinkled with displeasure. "I'd much prefer tea."

Rafe smiled as she took the glass from him anyway. It was reassuring to see her spirit returning. "You've had a rather large shock and I'd prefer to see some color restored to your cheeks before we order tea."

Georgie scowled at him, but he knew it was only a half-hearted attempt at indignation. "You are so—"

"Attentive?" Rafe suggested with a smile as he took the bergère armchair beside hers.

She laughed a little. "I was going to say domineering, but for once I will concede that yes, you are without a doubt attentive," the expression in her blue eyes softened imperceptibly as she regarded him, "and understanding."

Even though a hard knot of anger still tightened his gut, Rafe felt his heart swell at the compliment. "I would do anything for you, you know that, don't you, Georgiana?"

A blush crept over her cheeks. "I... I know you care for me," she whispered.

"If I could ease your pain..." Rafe barely resisted the urge to pull Georgie into his arms. The words he longed to say to her were on the tip of his tongue, but he swallowed them back. Even though he risked upsetting Georgie all over again, he had to find out more about Craven. "I know it is probably none of my business, but to see you so affected by the mere sight of that man, I can't help but wonder what happened—"

Rafe clamped his jaw shut at the moment Georgie's gaze slipped from his. When he saw how tightly her slender fingers gripped her brandy glass and the arm of her chair, he inwardly cursed himself.

He took a deep breath. "Forgive me. I shouldn't pry."

Georgie shook her head and to his relief, met his gaze again. "No. It's all right. You aren't prying. It's completely understandable that you would have questions about him. About what happened. As you know, I've always found it difficult to talk about. Indeed, most of the time I try very hard to forget the whole sorry, sordid mess. But I trust you, Rafe."

"It must be very hard moving in the same circles, knowing that you may encounter him from time to time."

Georgie gave him a small, sad smile. "That's what Teddy was adept at—helping me to avoid him. He had a very tight-knit group of friends and Craven was never on the guest list at any of the London functions we attended. Jonathon used to joke that Teddy was my self-appointed champion. I don't know how well you recall him, but he had a rapier-sharp wit, and a formidable glare. It was an unspoken rule that if you were given the cut direct by Teddy, it was tantamount to being socially ruined for all eternity. I suspect Craven probably avoided the functions we attended for that reason alone. And both Teddy and Jonathon didn't mind if I hid myself away in the country at Harrow Hall whenever I felt like it. So you see, accidental encounters with Craven have been quite rare."

Rafe sipped his drink, weighing up all that she had said or rather, left unsaid. "Yet there was a time, before your marriage to Darby, that you and Craven crossed paths."

"Yes..." Georgie took a hasty sip of her own brandy, perhaps to bolster her courage before continuing with her story. "Yes. I met Lord Craven—Oliver—when I was eighteen during my debut Season. Jonathon had gone up to Cambridge the year before to commence his bachelorship of arts. That's when he met Teddy of course—he was actually two years ahead of Jonathon, and almost finished with his studies. But I digress." Georgie sighed and plucked at her skirts with restive fingers. "I don't know if you have heard any of our family history from Jonathon, or Phillip and Helena—"

"Nothing at all." He wanted to reassure her that he hadn't been delving into the private details of her life. "As I mentioned last week, they only shared the barest of details about your marriage and your...involvement with Lord Craven."

Georgie nodded and sighed again. "Well, perhaps I should start at the beginning. Sadly, Jonathon and I never knew our mother; she passed away soon after our entry into this world. And our father, Sir Edmund Winterbourne, never remarried."

"I'm sorry to hear that."

Georgie inclined her head. "Thank you. As tragic as that sounds however, we really wanted for nothing as children. Father had a very lucrative ship building business in Plymouth, and we had a lovely home by the seaside, Periwinkle House. My father's older sister, Louisa took care of us along with a nurse and governess."

She swirled her brandy about in her glass and stared into the fire, her gaze unfocused as she appeared to sort through her memories. "My father was an older man—fifty when he wed my mother—so by the time Jonathon and I were fifteen, he was beginning to suffer from the ill health that comes with advancing age," she said at length. "Not long after our sixteenth birthday, he passed away and we were left solely in the care of our elderly aunt Louisa."

Georgie threw him another sad smile. "Our aunt meant well, but her memory was beginning to fade a little and she would tire very easily by the time I made my London debut."

Rafe raised an eyebrow. "I imagine she wasn't the most vigilante of chaperones then."

"You would be correct." Georgie set her brandy aside. "Father had been well connected enough that Aunt Louisa was able to procure vouchers for Almack's and from there, we were invited to any number of balls, assemblies and soirées. Jonathon and I had each been bequeathed a substantial trust fund so my aunt was able to rent a respectable townhouse in Brook Street. I was so thrilled, you have no idea." Another heartbreaking smile lit her face. "I had a beautiful new wardrobe and like every other young woman making a come-out, I had the highest of hopes of meeting my husband-to-be. A man I could love and who would love me in return. Someone to have a family with." She folded her hands in her lap and shook her head. "I was such a fool to believe that Oliver Cantwell, the Earl of Craven, was that man."

Anger slashed through Rafe's heart at the thought of a sweet, innocent eighteen-year-old Georgie making her debut without adequate chaperonage. *Bloody Winterbourne should have known better.* A muscle twitched in his jaw. "What happened, Georgiana?" he asked gently.

Her blue eyes were unusually bright. Her smile too brittle. "I fell hopelessly in love with Lord Craven the moment I saw him at Almack's. He was young—only twenty—handsome and dashing. He made me laugh. Aunt Louisa fell for his charms as well. He courted me by the book. At first." She bent her head for a moment as if regrouping. "I was so, so certain that Oliver truly loved me. His tongue dripped with honeyed words and beguiling promises. Promises I was all too ready to believe."

"He promised you marriage?" It was more of a statement than a question as Rafe already knew the answer.

"Yes. And so I..." Georgie's nervous swallow was audible and a blush stained her cheeks. "We became lovers. For a month, regardless of the function—be it a ball, a trip to the theatre, a garden party, a musicale—we found a way to be together. Aunt Louisa did not suspect a thing. But after a while"—Georgie took a deep breath clearly mustering her resolve to continue—"after a while, when Oliver had not approached my aunt to seek her permission for us to wed, when he continually evaded my questions about when we would formally announce our betrothal, I naturally began to suspect that I was being played for a fool."

"At some point I imagine you confronted him about your suspicions."

"Yes. And he hastily convinced me that we needed to elope to Scotland because his family—namely his mother, and his uncle who was his guardian—would never agree to our match. You see, he had not yet reached his majority and needed permission to wed. Accomplished liar that he was, he also made me believe that at a young age, he'd been forced into a betrothal with the daughter of another *ton* family, hence the added need for subterfuge. Of course, he never told me the girl's name." Her mouth twisted into a cynical smile. "But I was as gullible as a babe, willing to accept anything he told me if it meant I could preserve my dignity and be saved from ruin."

"But something went wrong."

Georgie pressed her lips together and nodded. Before his eyes, the color leached from her face and he noticed that she was clasping her hands so tightly, her knuckles had turned stark white. When she spoke, her voice trembled as if she were close to tears. "Forgive me, I cannot speak about what happened next... Suffice it to say, Lord Craven and I did not elope."

Rafe frowned, torn between his driving need to know everything about Georgie and concern that he was hurting her. "Georgiana, I understand completely that it can be too painful to speak about certain things."

She nodded and dashed a tear from her cheek. "Once I knew the truth of the matter, that I'd been well and truly duped and betrayed, I was so desperate, I traveled to Cambridge to seek out Jonathon."

"On your own? That is a long way for a young woman to travel by herself."

Georgie shrugged. "I had little choice. Aunt Louisa was unwell. And my business was most urgent."

"You were with child," Rafe whispered as the truth slammed into him. *God, my poor, sweet Georgiana.*

"Yes." She wiped away another spilled tear. "Jonathon had no idea what I had been up to. Not only was he about to commence his end of term examinations, he was head-over-heels in love with Teddy. To say Jonathon was surprised when I arrived on the doorstep of his lodgings would be an understatement indeed."

"You told him everything?"

Georgie bit her lip as if hesitant to continue. "Almost everything," she clarified. Her voice was low, little more than a whisper. With an abruptness that surprised him, she stood and paced over to the fireplace. There was tension in every line of her body—her ramrod straight spine, her shoulders—yet her every movement was agitated. *Christ, she was wringing her hands.*

Guilt sliced through Rafe again at the thought he was making her relive so many painful memories. "You don't have to say any more—"

"I know." She lifted her gaze from the fire. "But you deserve to know at least as much as my brother."

Rafe stood and approached her carefully. "I'm listening," he murmured softly.

She sucked in a shaky breath before going on. "When I told Jonathon about my affair with Craven and that I was pregnant, of course he was livid. Literally gripped by murderous rage. He wanted to avenge my honor by calling Oliver out, but I begged him not to. I didn't want there to be a scandal. I didn't want to be ruined. So then Jonathon came up with a plan to make it all go away."

"He suggested you wed Teddy."

"Yes. A marriage of convenience suited both my needs and Teddy's perfectly. You see, Teddy was the duke's only child and the heir apparent. But Teddy's father had grown suspicious that his son preferred the company of men. Indeed, the duke had threatened to cut off all of Teddy's allowances and dispose of his unentailed properties unless he took a wife before the end of that year. He was adamant that he didn't want the dukedom to go to a distant, quite possibly unsuitable relative if Teddy died without issue."

Rafe had to concede that it was a clever plan, up to a point. "Your brother and Teddy would be able to reside within the same household without arousing undue suspicion if you and Teddy wed. And Teddy had a very good chance of gaining an heir." He gentled his voice. "But it seems, he did not."

Georgie's arms slipped about her waist. "No..." More shadows clouded her eyes. "I lost the baby, shortly after Teddy and I were married. As terrible as it sounds, part of me is relieved that I didn't bear Craven's child."

Rafe wanted to reach for her and gather her into his arms, but Georgie seemed so on edge, he didn't want to overwhelm her with his own need to offer comfort. "Your reaction is natural, not terrible at all, my love. And I can't begin to imagine the frustration you must have felt knowing that you had needlessly tied yourself to a man who could never be a real husband to you. That you could never have children."

Georgie shook her head. "I don't see it that way at all. I grew to love Teddy as a friend and after having suffered so much, well, I certainly didn't think I would ever want to marry again."

Rafe drew a steadying breath. "And what do you think now?" he asked, searching her eyes.

"I..." Georgie blushed but didn't look away. "I am beginning to revise my opinion. Perhaps, in time... It is not easy to trust someone with your heart when it has been broken so very badly. And I won't marry again unless it is for love. The sort of love that will last a lifetime."

Rafe reached for one of Georgie's hands, drawing her closer. "I understand," he murmured. His other hand gently cradled her jaw and he stroked her flushed cheek with his thumb. "And I agree with you completely about marriage. An enduring love is what I desire as well."

Georgie's breath caught and her gaze dropped to his mouth. Leaning into him, she slid her hands to his shoulders and whispered his name, "Rafe."

He couldn't resist her plea. Slanting his mouth over hers, he kissed her tenderly, languidly worshipping her with lips and tongue until she was gripping his hair and roughly tugging at his cravat and morning coat. Demanding more.

With a groan of reluctance, he pulled away. "I should go," he whispered against her lips, somehow crushing down the urge to ravish her mouth all over again; to push her down onto the hearthrug, push up her skirts and take her right here, right now. "You need to rest."

"No, stay." Georgie's voice was husky with need. "If you go, I'll be left to dwell on things I'd rather not. And I want to think of you. Only you." She speared her fingers into his hair and drew him closer, nipping at his jaw. His ear lobe. "Nothing and no one else." Her lips moved to his throat as she fumbled with the buttons of his satin waistcoat. "Take me. Make me yours."

God help me. How can I refuse?

Lust surged hot and heavy through Rafe's veins, straight to his groin. He backed Georgie toward the settee, licking and sucking at her neck as she continued to frantically tug at his waistcoat and pull his shirt from his breeches. Breathing heavily, he all but tore off his coat as Georgie flicked open the buttons securing the fall front of his breeches, freeing his rock-hard erection. Pushing him down onto the chair, she then lifted her skirts with one hand and swiftly straddled his lap; with unerring accuracy, her other hand guided his pulsating shaft to her slick entrance. Moist heat immediately engulfed the crown of his cock and then without the slightest hesitation Georgie slid downward until he was buried to the hilt.

Fuck. A low growl rumbled in his throat as he gathered her close and pressed his face into her sweetly scented neck. Her passage was as sleek as a satin and gloriously wet and tight. If he could stay in control for a longer than a minute, it would be a miracle.

"Ride me," he groaned, holding her waist and thrusting his hips upward, encouraging Georgie to set the pace of their lovemaking.

Gripping his shoulders for purchase, Georgie immediately responded to his crude demand and began to plunge up and down with almost desperate abandon. Panting, her eyes dark with raw desire, Rafe had never seen her look so beautiful. He wanted to bare her breasts, but her woolen spencer and all her other layers were too difficult to deal with as the tempo of their rough coupling increased. Instead, he pushed his fingers into her hair and pulled her head down so he could ruthlessly plunder her hot, sweet mouth. When he pressed his teeth into the sensitive spot between her neck and shoulder, she ground herself against him and released a hoarse cry of pleasure, "Rafe. Oh, God."

Her sheath convulsed around his length with such force, he had no choice but to follow her over the edge as well. With a deep, shuddering groan, he let go and pumped into her, too far gone to pull out.

Gasping, Georgie touched her forehead to his and a warm wave of tenderness washed through him, mingling with the pulsating aftershocks of pleasure.

Georgie was undeniably his, and even though he hadn't taken care this time and had spent his seed inside her, he had no regrets. Indeed, as Georgie feathered kisses across his forehead and cheeks and jaw, he silently rejoiced at the idea that one day she might bear him a child.

He prayed that she would feel that way too.

He raised his head and caught her flushed face between his hands. "Don't ever doubt me, or us, Georgie. This—what you and I share—it is honest and real." He wanted to tell her that he loved her, but after such a fast and furious coupling, now didn't seem like quite the right moment.

"I know," she whispered, a soft smile curving mouth. She pressed her palms against his chest. "Rafe, I want to tell you—"

A sharp knock at the door had Rafe cursing beneath his breath.

"Georgie? Are you in there?"

It was bloody Winterbourne.

"Yes, but I'm rather busy right at this moment, Jonathon," she called back. "Lord Markham and I are having...an in-depth discussion."

"Oh... Right... I'll be in the library if you would care to join me when you're done."

Georgie bit her lip and her shoulders shook as she tried to stifle a fit of laughter.

Rafe grinned too. "Do you know how beautiful you are when you smile?"

Georgie's smile grew impudent and she wriggled a little. "Well, I would be more inclined to believe you if I wasn't still sitting in such a wicked position."

"Wench," he groaned, grasping her about the hips to still her movements. "You'd best stop or you won't be leaving this room for quite some time."

"Hmm, I will need to go up to my room to rectify my appearance before I speak with Jonathon." A slight frown creased her forehead. "How do I look?"

Rafe took in her crumpled gown, her tumble-down curls that barely concealed the bruises from his brutish assault on her neck, and her red, slightly swollen lips. "Thoroughly swived."

"Well, I suppose it will be more of a dash upstairs then—"

He brushed a kiss across her lips. "I will distract your brother."

"Thank you."

Once Rafe had assisted Georgie to her feet, and after she'd shaken out her skirts, he caught her hand between his, preventing her retreat. The guilt for not withdrawing from her in time—and the fact that they hadn't yet discussed it—still pricked at his conscience. "Georgiana, I'm sorry I did not take more care with you. If there should be a child—"

Georgie put a finger to his lips. "Hush. Do not worry. Everything will be fine. I trust you, Rafe." Reaching up, she gave him a quick kiss and slipped from the room before he could say another word.

Everything will be fine. As Rafe restored his own appearance, he fervently prayed that Georgie's assertion was right. A baby would be a joy. And Craven could be easily dealt with.

But Riddle...now he was another problem entirely.

Rafe downed the last of his brandy, hardening his resolve. He'd had enough of this waiting game. He'd double the men he had scouring the streets. The sooner he disposed of the cur, the better.

CHAPTER 17

14th November 1816

"Bloody hell, Markham. Steady on. There's no need to knock a man's daylights out."

Rafe lowered his fists and grinned. "It seems you've grown soft in your old age, Phillip." His friend had agreed to be his sparring partner for a round or two of boxing at Gentleman Jackson's Salon, but it seemed he was sadly out of practice. "I didn't hit you that hard."

"You bloody well did," accused Phillip, rubbing his jaw. "Helena will have your guts for garters if you rough me up too much. I can't very well attend Lord Derwent's ball tonight if I'm sporting a black eye or a split lip."

Rafe used his forearm to wipe away the sweat trickling off his brow. "It's a masquerade ball. No one will notice." He and Georgie were attending also—he'd have preferred not to. In the last week, he'd been caught up with matters related to organizing protection for the Prince Regent and his family, and he hadn't spent nearly as much time at Dudley House as he would have liked. If he could have his

way, he'd spend the entire evening alone with Georgie
—in bed.

Phillip's mouth twisted into a wry smile. "You're a braver
man than I then, Markham. Do you really want to put my
wife in a state of high dudgeon?"

Rafe couldn't contain his huff of laughter. "All right then,
my featherweight friend. Would you like to throw in the
sponge?"

"God, yes." Phillip waved over one of the attendants to
help him remove the mufflers from his hands. "And perhaps
you could save me from further bruising and humiliation by
asking your old mentor himself to be your sparring partner
from now on." He nodded toward one of the wooden benches
by the windows facing Bond Street. "Your man Cowan is chatting to him now."

Sure enough, Cowan was deep in conversation with
Gentleman Jackson. Rafe had asked him to find out if anyone
fitting Riddle's description had been seen at the salon of late.
Even though Rafe had his men watching Georgie's and his
own movements at all times of the day and night, it would be
foolish not to continue making discreet enquiries. Cowan had
once been a former employee of Jackson's—in fact at one
stage, Cowan had apparently contemplated becoming a prize
fighter, but had then opted for a career as a Bow Street
Runner. In any case, Rafe knew Jackson would readily disclose
what he knew to Cowan. At that moment, his mentor looked
up and on spotting Rafe, beckoned him over.

As Rafe approached, Jackson rose and then greeted him
with a warm smile and clap on the back. Although the former
prize-fighting boxer's dark hair was now streaked with silver,
anyone could see he was still fighting-fit beneath his white silk
shirt, and magenta and violet striped satin waistcoat.

"Markham, our mutual friend was just asking me when
the next prize fight is scheduled," he said with a conspiratorial

gleam in his dark eyes. "I have not been able to convince Tom Cribb to come back to the ring, but up-and-coming Jem Ward has taken the bait. At any rate, there's sure to be a big purse on the night." Jackson lowered his voice. "I hear even Prinny is keen to attend. It will be out of town in a week. In Surrey, if you are at all interested."

Rafe grinned as he pulled at the ties on one of his mufflers with his teeth. "It sounds like it will be quite an event." He already knew all of the details because he'd been planning which of his men would accompany the Prince Regent on his foray.

"I certainly hope so." Jackson clasped his shoulder. "You know, I might have actually considered asking you to step into the ring, only we both know the night would most likely turn into a riot after you knocked out your opponent within half a minute."

Rafe chuckled. "You taught me everything I know so you only have yourself to blame."

John Jackson had been his first boxing tutor when he took up the sport at the age of fourteen. Even though the boxing legend was renowned for promoting fair play within the sport, as soon as Rafe knew that he was bound for a career in espionage, he had asked his mentor to teach him how to fight outside the rules—how to incapacitate or even kill a man with only a few blows. Jackson had been an excellent teacher; Rafe's singular knowledge had saved his life on more occasions than he cared to count over the years.

Jackson's smile slipped away to be replaced with a frown. "Now, Cowan here tells me you are still on the lookout for a particular man—a foreigner with a German or Russian accent. But I'm sorry to say, I haven't seen anyone fitting his description. And as far as I know, none of my staff have either."

Rafe blew out an exasperated sigh; catching Riddle was proving to be about as easy as catching an eel with one's hands tied behind one's back, whilst blindfolded. Another thought suddenly occurred to him. "You haven't by any chance seen the Earl of Craven in here, have you?"

Rafe visited Gentleman Jackson's several times a week to maintain his self-defense skills and strength. He'd never seen Craven in the salon, but because he knew the man was an inveterate gambler and was currently up to his eyeballs in debt at most of the respectable gambling clubs, he wondered if the scum-dweller might be hunting for other opportunities to recover his losses, such as laying bets on boxing matches or even worse, cockfights. He didn't know why he hadn't thought of it sooner.

Jackson's brow lowered into a thoughtful frown. "You know, I have seen him once or twice in the past fortnight. He's been in the company of Lord Bolton—a keen boxer. Comes in once a week. But all Lord Craven does is take snuff while he watches his friend."

Rafe's interest sharpened. He'd dearly love to know how much farther the bastard had fallen into debt over the past few weeks. He couldn't imagine that it would take much to push him over the edge into complete ruin. He lowered his voice. "Do you know if he's been making discreet enquiries about any backstreet fights by any chance?" Bare-knuckle prize fighting was illegal, despite the fact that it was popular amongst members of the *ton*, and Prinny himself was an enthusiastic patron. However, it wasn't too difficult to find an 'at home' match to lay a wager on if one knew who to ask at Gentleman Jackson's or at Limmer's, a hotel not far from Dudley House where many Corinthians and boxing enthusiasts congregated.

"I'm not certain, but I'll question my staff at the end of—"

Cowan gave a low whistle. "Well, well, speak o' the devil himself," he muttered under his breath.

Rafe followed his man's gaze. Sure enough, Lord Craven had just sauntered into the room in the company of another young aristocrat—Jackson confirmed it was Bolton. Head held high, Craven's cool, arrogant gaze slid over the other patrons as he crossed the room as if he were taking stock of who was about—and who might be worthy of his attention. Attired in a burgundy tailcoat, a chocolate brown satin waist-coat and fawn breeches, at first glance, he appeared to be a moneyed buck. But as he drew closer, Rafe noted obvious signs of dissipation and his slide toward penury—Craven's brown eyes were blood-shot, his overly long, brown hair curled around a graying shirt collar, his Hessians scuffed, and the shiny patches at his elbows suggested his coat had seen better days.

What a pathetic peacock. Rafe's jaw tightened and he clenched his muffler clad fists tight as he imagined splitting Craven's patrician nose with a well-aimed left cross. And worse. Much, much worse. Seemingly oblivious to his dark thoughts and hard stare, Craven continued to follow Bolton, heading toward the hall that led to the change rooms.

"Keep an eye on him, Cowan," Rafe gritted out. Although he'd dearly love to stay and engage with Craven himself—assess his weaknesses first-hand—he had other places to be and other things to do. There was a masquerade ball to attend. And a beautiful duchess to pay homage to. "See if you can find out his preferred gambling haunts. And what he currently owes his money-lenders."

His movements rough, almost clumsy, Rafe pulled off his other muffler and flexed his stiff fingers. His knuckles cracked. Yes, one way or another, Lord Craven would be paying his dues before the week was out.

~

"Mind your step, sis," Jonathon cautioned as he escorted Georgie along the wet, leaf strewn cobblestones of Berkeley Square toward the end of the long receiving line of masked noblemen and women all waiting to be admitted to Lord and Lady Derwent's masquerade ball. "I'm afraid Markham was right. With close to two hundred guests, it's going to be a dreadful press inside. We really should have arrived fashionably late."

Georgie ignored Jonathon's grumbling. Nothing could spoil her mood—not even a long wait outside on such a damp, blustery and icy evening. Her free hand slid to her throat where her new sapphire and diamond necklace was hidden beneath her midnight blue velvet domino. Rafe had bestowed the extravagant gift upon her at Dudley House late this afternoon, as she was beginning her preparations for the ball. She could still scarcely believe he'd made such an outrageous purchase at Stedman and Vardon's; not just the necklace, but the entire parure—the bracelet, earrings, matching ring and even a brooch. And the light in Rafe's eyes when he'd watched her admiring how the necklace looked against her throat in her dressing table mirror, she'd never seen such an expression. Heated and adoring. Possessive yet tender.

Every time Georgie recalled that moment, her whole body tingled with warmth and a thrill that went beyond mere happiness. It was joy. She now wasn't afraid to admit to herself that she loved Rafe and she instinctively knew he felt the same way. Even if he hadn't made a declaration yet. Or revealed all of his secrets.

Georgie smiled to herself as she slipped her fingers beneath the velvet of her cloak and touched the delicate, teardrop shaped gemstones resting just below her collarbone. Secrets—his and her own—didn't matter to her anymore. Not when she felt like this. Before this night was through, she would confess her feelings to Rafe. And she had no doubt he would reciprocate.

She closed her eyes as another rush of excitement warmed her from the top of her head to the very tips of her toes. The thought of Rafe telling her that he loved her made her pulse race and her heart soar. She suddenly couldn't wait to meet him inside. To feel the caress of his hot gaze and the press of his hard body against hers as they waltzed. To hear him whispering wicked, yet wholly welcome suggestions in her ear. He'd planned to arrive with Phillip and Helena, for appearance's sake.

After tonight, she knew she would not care about maintaining appearances any longer.

"Georgie? I swear being in love has turned you into an addlepate."

Georgie turned her head to look up at her brother. Even though Jonathon's expression was somewhat obscured by a black, crimson and gold Harlequin style mask, a nearby gas lamp cast sufficient light for her to catch the twinkle of fond amusement in his eyes. "My apologies," she said, offering him a smile. His teasing didn't bother her in the slightest. And it wasn't as if she could deny what he'd just said. "Ask me again."

"Do you, by any chance, have our invitation?" He patted the pockets within his evening jacket and black wool cloak. "I could have sworn I had it with me."

Georgie checked inside her ivory silk and crystal beaded reticule. "No, I'm afraid I do not. Did you leave it in the carriage?"

Jonathon swore under his breath. "Yes. I left it on the seat. It seems I'm an addlepate as well." He clasped her gloved hand between his. "Georgie, I'm so sorry, but we're going to have to relinquish our place in the queue so I can retrieve our invitation. I don't know Derwent or his wife that well, and with so many guests, I doubt the attending footmen will admit us without it."

"Don't be silly," she replied. "I will stay here and mind our place. I am sure you will only be gone a minute or two at most." She peered around the broad-shouldered bulk of the tall gentleman in front of her to better view the receiving line. "It will take at least another five minutes for us to reach the bottom of the stairs in front of Derwent House."

Jonathon's mouth flattened with concern. "Hmm. I really don't think this is a good ide—"

"Just go." Georgie gave him a gentle prod in the ribs. "We are in Berkeley Square and I am surrounded by members of the *ton*. I will be fine."

"All right, then." He shook a finger at her. "But do not, under any circumstances, talk to strangers. And do *not* tell Markham. You know he will kill me."

Georgie laughed softly. "I am not a babe in the woods. And you're wasting time. Hurry up."

Jonathon disappeared into the milling crowd behind them; she suspected he'd head toward the adjacent mews or one of the other nearby thoroughfares in an attempt to locate their carriage. Hopefully, he would return *before* she reached the front door.

A sudden gust of chill wind tore at her hair, cloak and ivory silk skirts, and the black satin domino of the man in front of her whipped dangerously close to her face. Pulling her own cloak tightly about herself, she attempted to step back a pace, but was hindered by the close proximity of the elderly couple directly behind her. Deep in conversation with another party of three—a pretty young woman in a pink muslin gown and matching mask and a middle-aged couple, her parents perhaps—they all seemed oblivious to her plight. And then before she could even draw a breath to politely ask them to move a little, the man before her stepped back, the heel of his black leather shoe crushing the toes of her right foot. Georgie's cry was little more than a strangled gasp as white-hot agony knifed through her foot. Breathless with the pain, she clutched at the man's arm, frantically trying to push him forward. Away from her.

Without warning, he swung around and seized her by the shoulders. "You should be more careful, Your Grace." His voice was a low growl, his speech heavily accented. His leering Pulcinella half-mask in no way obscured the malice glittering in his pale eyes or the hard sneer contorting the line of his mouth. She knew who he was even if she didn't know his name.

Oh, God. Georgie sucked in a breath to scream but he clamped a hand over her mouth then crushed her face into his chest, effectively smothering her and cutting off her sight. *Why hasn't anyone noticed what he's doing? And what in God's name does he want with me?*

The press of something hard and sharp beneath her left breast made her blood freeze. Her heart stuttered. *A blade.*

"Do not utter a sound and do not move unless I tell you to," he hissed into her ear.

Despite the almost paralyzing fear gripping her body, blistering anger suddenly seared through Georgie's veins. *No. I will not let this happen. Never again.*

Drawing in another shallow breath, she jerked her head and sank her teeth into the gloved fingers that cruelly covered her mouth. As hard as she could.

"*Blyad!*" The foreigner released his hold on her face and she screamed.

Chaos erupted around them.

Heads turned and other women shrieked as Georgie poured every bit of air from her lungs into the longest and loudest ear-splitting scream she could manage. With a grunt, her assailant shoved her to the ground, knocking the wind out of her. Although dark spots peppered her vision and a strange squeezing pain gripped her chest, she caught a glimpse of her attacker dashing toward the park in the center of the square. The dark shadows of the plane trees swallowed him up within seconds. The elderly couple, now white-faced, had backed away, but the young woman in the pink gown and her parents knelt down beside her.

"Are you injured?"

"What's wrong?"

"Did that man hurt you?"

"Someone summon the Bow Street Runners."

Georgie, shaking and still gasping for air like a fish out of water, ignored the barrage of questions from the gathering crowd of onlookers as she attempted to sit up a little straighter. She'd landed on her bottom, her arms outstretched behind her. She supposed it was fortunate that she'd decided not to care about appearances.

Then a vaguely familiar face materialized in front of her. She shook her head and then blinked, attempting to clear her hazy vision. Then she realized her silver filigree mask had slipped over her eyes. She tugged it off. "Lumsden?" she wheezed, still short of breath. Dudley House's new footman, clothed in a greatcoat, and an ordinary shirt, waistcoat, and breeches instead of his livery, squatted beside her. "I almost... didn't recognize you...without your wig. What...are you doing here?" Perkins had accompanied them tonight. It was Lumsden's evening off.

"Yes, it is me, Your Grace," he confirmed, ignoring her other questions. "Are you hurt?"

Georgie shook her head. "No... I don't think so." Apart from being winded, having crushed toes, a wet and bruised backside and a ruined gown, no other damage had been done.

The young man smiled reassuringly. "Good to hear.

Would you like me to help you up? I'm sure your brother is somewhere hereabouts."

She swallowed and grimaced. Her throat was dry and raw from screaming. "Yes. Thank you."

No sooner had she regained her feet, Jonathon appeared at her side, puffing as if he'd run a mile. "Good God! Georgiana," he gasped as he took her arm. "Was that you...? Screaming? What happened?"

"The man in front of us—me—it was the same man who ran into me at Latimer House." Georgie began. "He tried to—"

"Georgiana?"

Rafe. Georgie didn't resist as he pulled her into his arms. She sagged against him, winding her fingers into the lapels of his evening jacket, breathing in his familiar scent. His chest was heaving as if he'd been running also. Tears of pure relief pricked the back of her eyelids.

"Thank God, you're all right," he whispered against her temple, hugging her even closer.

Georgie only rested against him for a moment longer. Too many unanswered questions and troublesome doubts twisted and tumbled about her mind. Wanting to see Rafe's face, she drew back a little. He wasn't wearing a mask and she was nothing but relieved. If she never saw a masked man again, it would be too soon. "How...how did you know something had h-happened?" she asked, her voice fragile and trembling. "That I was in danger?"

Rafe pushed a snarled curl away from her cheek and tucked it behind her ear. "As Phillip's carriage entered the square, I heard you scream and then I saw a man bolt for the trees. I gave chase but he jumped into a waiting hackney cab on the other side of the square, on the corner of Bruton Street." He lowered his voice and his gaze hardened. "It was the foreigner, wasn't it?"

Georgie nodded. "Yes. He knows who I am. He called me, Your Grace, before he tried to force me to go somewhere with him. I don't understand what's going on." She searched Rafe's face. She read concern, caring, and something else... She could have sworn it was guilt. Swallowing past the obstinate lump in her throat, she firmed her voice and said, "But you know what this is all about, don't you?"

Rafe released a shaky breath. "Yes." The haunted look in his eyes frightened her almost as much as the memory of the stranger's blade pressing against her breast. "Let me take you home. Then I will tell you everything."

CHAPTER 18

Dudley House, Hanover Square

R afe tossed back his brandy in one gulp. His reliance on alcohol to quell the tempest of dark emotions rampaging inside him had become an ingrained habit over the years. While the rational part of his brain knew it was far from healthy, perhaps even destructive, tonight was not the night to wrestle with overcoming his uncontrollable need for the demon drink in times such as these—those particular moments when his inner turmoil threatened to overwhelm him. Pull him asunder.

No, he had other, more important demons to deal with. Actually, there was one in particular...

Scherzfrage. Riddle.

Dashkov.

It had to be him. From Georgie's succinct recount of the events outside Derwent House, it sounded like the viper had cursed her in Russian. *Blyad*. *Whore*. But no matter his name or his agenda. The devil had gone too far tonight. And Rafe would crush him.

He had to. If Georgie hadn't had the wherewithal and the guts to retaliate and scream for help... He inwardly shuddered as razor-sharp guilt sliced into his heart all over again. *I should have been with her. She should not suffer because of my past mistakes.*

"Rafe?"

The sound of Georgie's voice pulled him out of the wild tumult of his thoughts. With an effort, he loosened the white-knuckle grip on his now empty brandy glass—he was surprised he hadn't shattered the vessel—and placed it with deliberate care upon the mantel in Georgie's sitting room. His drinking might be a vice, but at least it was having the desired effect; the excruciating tension within his body had begun to ease. The ferocious, red haze that had clouded his vision and played havoc with his thoughts had begun to fade.

But no, it wasn't just the brandy that had succeeded in calming him. If he were honest with himself, he would acknowledge that it was Georgie who soothed his tormented soul. Breathed life into his dark heart.

Rafe ran a rough hand through his hair as he turned to look at her. They were alone; after he'd listened to both Georgie's and her brother's accounts in the carriage on the way back to Dudley House, he'd told Jonathon he wanted to speak with his sister in private. Jonathon hadn't looked pleased, but Rafe had been so incensed with him for leaving Georgie alone, he didn't give a fuck. As for his own lack of care and foresight —he should have escorted Georgie to the masquerade ball, not her brother—he doubted he'd ever be able to forgive himself.

The woman he loved had been placed in mortal danger, and it was his fault entirely. And now he had to tell her. Cold dread chilled his blood at the mere thought of her reaction.

Still dressed in her ruined ivory silk evening gown, Georgie perched on the edge of a brocade-covered settee, watching him with worried eyes. Yet the firm line of her mouth and her ruler straight posture suggested that beneath her apprehension, there was also a good deal of steely determination. She might be shaken, but she wouldn't be put off in her quest to unearth the truth about him. Not this time.

I don't deserve her.

"Rafe," she prompted again. "I've told you everything I know about the attack. Now I want you to tell me about that man." She lifted her chin as if daring him to deny her request. "He's someone you know from your past, isn't he?"

"Yes." Shedding his evening jacket, Rafe approached the settee and took a seat on the ottoman directly before her. Now that he was going to confess all to her—his dark past, his culpability for placing her in harm's way—he wasn't going to hide, come what may.

"So all the years you spent abroad," she continued with a quiet strength that he couldn't help but admire, "you were never just a diplomat, were you?"

"No," he replied steadily, holding her gaze. "I was mostly involved in intelligence gathering for the Crown."

"In other words, you were a spy."

Rafe suspected Georgie wouldn't be at all surprised by his disclosure, given she had often quizzed him about the exact nature of his work over the past few weeks. "Yes," he confirmed. "But I think you already knew that."

She swallowed then nodded. "Are you...are you still a spy?"

"No. I mean to say, I'm not actively involved in that line of work any longer. I was decommissioned, for want of a better way to put it, a little over a year ago. As you know, my brother passed away in September last year, and as the threat posed by Bonaparte and his army had been effectively neutralized, I returned home. There was much less of a need for the sort of investigations I conducted. But men like me..." He felt a muscle tic in his jaw. How could he put this so she'd under-stand? "I may have resigned, but it can be difficult for someone like me to leave the past behind. And I'm afraid that is currently the case."

Georgie tilted her head and her expression grew pensive. "You have enemies. Like the man who attacked me. Who is he?"

"I have little to go on, but I believe he is Baron Viktor Ivanovich Dashkov. A Russian general and former French sympathizer. He and I crossed paths in St. Petersburg in early 1812."

Georgie's eyebrows rose in surprise. "But that was over four years ago."

"Yes."

"So why has he come to London? And why am I his quarry rather than you?" Her forehead arrowed into a deep frown and her blue eyes glinted with suspicion. "What happened between you two? Is this man plotting some bizarre kind of revenge?"

"If it is Dashkov, then yes. Revenge is most certainly on his agenda. I suspect he wants to hurt me...by hurting you."

"Because he thinks you care about me." Georgie's voice might have grown soft but her gaze didn't waver.

Neither did Rafe's. "Yes."

"Because you hurt him or someone he cared about."

"His wife."

"Oh." Georgie dropped her gaze to her tightly clasped hands in her lap. "You had an affair with her." It was more of a statement than a question.

"Yes. But it's more complicated than that."

"I don't doubt that for a minute." Georgie's tone had a bitter edge to it and Rafe didn't blame her in the least for feeling resentful toward him.

He blew out a sigh. Speaking about his past liaisons— which for the most part had been contrived affairs simply because they had helped him gain some type of ground during a mission—was going to be harder than he'd initially anticipated. Exposing his flaws—and sins—to the woman he loved felt like one of the biggest risks he had ever taken. If she rejected him...

Ignoring the apprehension tightening his gut, he drew in a steadying breath. "You understand that what I am about to tell you is very sensitive information. Information that has always been kept under lock and key. Indeed, only a handful of men in the Foreign Secretary's Office have been privy to it."

Georgie's mouth lifted into a wry smile. "So after you've told me, you will have to kill me?"

Rafe's answering smile was fleeting. "No. But please understand, the more you know about what I've done and who I've pretended to be, the greater the danger for you."

"Wouldn't you say that leaving me in the dark has also put me in danger?" she demanded. "If Jonathon and I had known that this Dashkov was following me, intending me harm—"

"Jonathon knew."

"*What?*" Georgie bolted to her feet before stalking toward the fireplace. Away from him. When she turned around to regard him, her eyes practically darted blue fire. "Jonathon knew I was being hunted by a mad Russian baron, but he didn't say anything? Or stay with me tonight? *I* will kill him."

Rafe barely resisted the urge to haul Georgie into his arms. To try and douse her understandable anger with kisses. "While I agree that he shouldn't have left you alone outside Derwent House, I shouldn't have done so either."

Georgie's voice vibrated with anger. "He... You... Both of you should have told me I was in danger."

"I swore your brother to secrecy, Georgie. Without any credible evidence to hand, we both decided that we didn't want to worry you unnecessarily."

Georgie's eyes narrowed. "I *knew* there was something

going on. Ever since that man—Dashkov—ran into me outside Latimer House. Is that how long you've known?"

Rafe grimaced. "I can't be sure, but I've long suspected that someone watched us the night we first met. At Phillip and Helena's townhouse, when we were on the terrace. But that's just it, Georgie. It was only a suspicion. It wasn't until the house party at Rivergate that I knew for certain that the man following you and me was probably Dashkov. That's when Jonathon found out too. As he was arranging his departure from the White Swan Inn, he observed a foreign man making enquiries about Rivergate. He thought it odd and confided in me."

"But not me." Georgie drummed her fingers in an angry tattoo on the white marble mantelpiece.

"I don't know if this will make you feel any better about all of this, but I've had a small team of men in my employ— men whom I trust implicitly—keeping watch over you ever since the incident at Latimer House. Of course, they've also been looking out for Dashkov. Your new footman, Lumsden, is one of them."

Georgie's expression softened a little. "I wondered why he was in Berkeley Square tonight. It was his night off. Only I suppose it wasn't."

"No. It is a shame he wasn't closer to you after Jonathon left. He told me he'd been scouting around the other side of the park in the square when you screamed."

Georgie shivered. "Tell me about him. Dashkov. What happened in St. Petersburg?"

Rafe rose from the ottoman and approached the other side of the hearth. Rubbing his chin, he contemplated the best way to begin his story. And how best to edit it. "I suspect you may have heard of the Treaty of Tilsit?"

Georgie's brows drew together in apparent recollection.

"While I admit I have heard of it, I must confess that I know little about the exact nature of the Treaty."

"It was an alliance formed between France, Russia and Prussia nine years ago," explained Rafe. "At the time, it was not a popular decision with most of the Russian court as it meant Anglo-Russian trade ceased. Profits were lost on both sides. However, by all accounts, Tsar Alexander became disenchanted with Old Boney—for various reasons—and so he began to turn a blind eye toward the resumption of trade with our fair land. Indeed, by the end of 1811, our intelligence indicated that the Tsar was more than a little interested in negotiating a new alliance, but this time with England and Sweden. One of our—shall we say—*friends* within the Russian court had also heard that someone within the highest levels of the Russian military was still very much an ally of Bonaparte; it was believed this particular person was actively attempting to undermine the process of forging the new alliance. All sorts of classified information was making its way into the hands of the French ambassador, Caulaincourt."

Georgie nodded. "I know the name but little else. I'm assuming this was about the time you were 'posted' to Russia?"

"Yes. I was tasked by the Foreign Secretary to travel to St. Petersburg. You may recall our last ambassador to Russia, Lord Grenville, had returned home after the Treaty of Tilsit was signed. Whilst I posed as a wealthy British arms trader, Sir Richard Mallory, the rumor was also cast about by our ally within the court that I was really a British diplomat, on a mission to secretly shore up the new treaty. There was also a good dose of speculation that I might be a candidate for the post of British ambassador, once Anglo-Russian relations were restored."

"So what you are saying is the traitor would see you as a target and attempt to steal information from you about any armament deals or perhaps even the treaty negotiations," Georgie observed.

Rafe was impressed by her quick and entirely accurate assessment. "Exactly. I was ostensibly the bait that would lure out the weasel."

"I take it the traitor was Dashkov."

"Yes, but it turned out that he wasn't working alone. His wife, Baroness Anna Petrovina Dashkovna was involved."

Georgie was frowning again. "How so?"

"When I arrived in St. Petersburg—this was in January 1812—my favor was secretly courted by certain members of the Imperial Russian Army, including the Minister of War. Aside from attending numerous closed-door meetings about security matters, invitations to any number of balls, soirées, and dinner parties ensued. At one of the very first balls I attended, the baroness approached me. Needless to say, her very forward approach to cultivating a closer relationship between England and Russia, had me—" He'd been about to say intrigued but decided to amend his choice of words. "I was suspicious of her motives."

"Surely not." Georgie raised a cynical brow. "You are a very attractive man. I'm certain Baroness Dashkovna isn't the first married woman to have ever taken an interest in you."

Rafe winced. "True, however Dashkov had an imposing presence. In all of our negotiations regarding armament contracts, he came across as a man not to be crossed. So I thought it more than passing strange that he tolerated his wife's very blatant and very public cuckolding."

"Yet it sounds as if you encouraged her interest, despite the fact she was married and her husband was aware of what she was doing." Georgie's mouth tightened into a disapproving line. "How very...odd. And dangerous. I imagine it felt like you were playing with fire."

"Yes." Rafe wasn't about to admit that he'd actually been

deeply attracted in a physical sense to the beautiful, blonde baroness. Perhaps he'd even been a little infatuated with her, despite the fact he'd suspected she was attempting to use him. The element of danger had definitely heightened the thrill of their encounters. "However, it was my duty to discover who the traitor in the Russian court was," he added, feeling compelled to explain why he'd engaged in such an unsavory affair. "I had to play along so to speak."

"So you really suspected that Dashkov *and* his wife were the spies selling information to the French."

Rafe permitted himself a small sigh, relieved Georgie hadn't roundly condemned him. At least not at this stage. "Yes. Our supposed clandestine affair continued for a few weeks until I confided in Anna—well, pretended to anyway. During one of the Tsar's private dinners at the Winter Palace, I told her I was really a diplomat and I couldn't afford to incur the wrath of her husband, given his position within the Imperial Army and the court. When I suggested we end our affair, she implored me not to. In fact, she begged me to meet with her after the dinner at my rented townhouse on the Nevsky Prospect, not far from the Palace. Curious that she seemed so upset and desperate—she did not strike me as the sort of woman who would easily fall in love—I agreed as I suspected she had an ulterior motive. You see, we'd never met in my rooms before. Hitherto, our assignations had always been furtive, stolen moments at whatever function we both happened to be at."

Georgie fiddled with one of her new sapphire and diamond earrings as if it bothered her, then slid it off; the other quickly followed. She placed them both with deliberate care upon the mantel, avoiding his gaze. "I take it the baroness did have an ulterior motive."

Rafe swallowed, a prickle of uneasiness making him hesitant to respond. He would need to choose his next words carefully. If Georgie didn't believe him, if she thought he was playing fast and loose with the truth. Lying...

How much does she trust me? Will she take me at my word about what happened? Rafe searched her face and a chill touched his heart. Her expression was shuttered. Wary. But there was no going back. He had to tell her everything. "We met...and afterward, I pretended to fall into a light doze. Anna rose from the bed, found her clothes, then slipped from the room with a branch of candles. Suspicious, I threw on whatever clothes came to hand and followed a minute or two later. I found her..." Rafe clenched the marble mantel for support, forcing himself to continue. "She was in my study, rifling through all of my papers. False papers mind you, but she was doggedly looking for something of import all the same."

A vision of a half-dressed Anna, her silver blonde hair tumbling round her slender shoulders like a moonlit waterfall, sprang into his mind. When she'd seen him, her pale blue eyes had widened at first, then narrowed, their expression growing as hard and deathly cold as an arctic wasteland. Strange how the lack of fear in her eyes had stunned him the most. "It was stupid of me to be shocked. It wasn't as if I hadn't known what she was really after all along. But nevertheless, I froze when I should have acted."

"What happened?" Georgie whispered.

"She trained a pistol on me. A tiny weapon—it was small enough to be secreted in a muff or a reticule—but deadly all the same, considering her hand was so steady. She aimed it straight at my chest, cocked it." Rafe closed his eyes as the memory came flooding back. "I lunged sideways, but not fast enough. The shot grazed my side."

"The scar, along your rib cage. She did that?"

Rafe opened his eyes. He could see that Georgie's face had grown as pale as the white marble beneath his hand.

"She could have killed you."

Rafe shrugged a shoulder. "The caliber of her weapon was small, thank God, so the damage wasn't too bad. But by the time I'd regained my footing, she'd bolted. I followed, of course. I had to see if her husband—or anyone else—was waiting for her. When I gained the street, it was dark and bitterly cold. Snowing. I could barely see. Then I heard a brief cry. As if someone had been startled. And a sharp crack. Another shot. I headed toward the sound... And then I saw her..." Rafe paused and swallowed. His voice was a mere rasp when he managed to speak again. "Even though snow flurries hampered my vision, there was enough light cast by a nearby streetlamp to see that Anna... She was lying prone on the icy pavement. I think in her haste to escape, she'd slipped and fallen, and her pistol had accidently discharged."

"She was dead?" Georgie asked softly.

"I believe so. Or very nearly so." He couldn't bear to think of the horrific damage to Anna's beautiful face, the wet, ragged sound of her very last breaths. The dark stain in the snow beneath her head...

Rafe raised a shaking hand to his forehead and massaged his temple. *Christ, I need another drink.*

"What...what did you do?"

Rafe dropped his hand and met Georgie's worried gaze. "I heard a carriage approaching and then a shout. A man's voice. This may seem callous to you, but the only sensible course of action I could take was to get the hell out of there. I knew it must have been Dashkov and he would be out for my blood, despite the fact he and his wife were undoubtedly spying for the French. So I ducked down a nearby side street. After I had sighted Dashkov..." Rafe stumbled to a halt. He may have learned to harden his heart against most of the distressing recollections from his past, but whenever he recalled Dashkov's agonized cry, whenever he pictured the baron gathering Anna's limp form into his arms, a strange pain that he didn't want to examine burned deep inside him. "There was nothing I could do. And so I left. I had another set of rented rooms nearby with items I would need in case of an emergency. When I ascertained that I hadn't been followed, I quit St. Petersburg altogether."

Rafe had patched himself up, then after penning a coded letter for their agent within the court about his findings, he'd stolen away like a thief in the night. Even though Dashkov had somehow managed to escape arrest for treason, Castlereagh had been pleased with the result; Rafe's mission had been declared a success. Negotiations with the Russians resumed and a new treaty with Britain and Sweden had been signed in the Spring of 1812.

But Anna had been killed. Even though her death had been accidental, her husband didn't know that. One way or another, it seemed Dashkov was after his pound of flesh.

Georgie's. Rafe's heart squeezed tight, as tight as his clenched fist. He could never let that happen.

He raised his gaze to Georgie's face. She was watching him, a deep furrow between her brows as her fingers absently played with the sapphire and diamond necklace at her throat. He wished he knew what she thought of him. Did she think he was a monster? A man who would do anything—lie, commit adultery and yes, kill. A man who was unworthy of trust. And love.

Georgie knew that his former lover Solange had died under suspicious circumstances and now she'd learned another of his lovers had met a premature and violent end. Whether she blamed him or not for what had happened to Solange and Anna, one thing was certain—she knew the women he cared about, died.

Rafe wouldn't blame Georgie in the least if she decided to cut all ties with him.

And perhaps it was best if she did. Then at least Dashkov would leave her alone.

~

Georgie could clearly see that Rafe's past was an albatross about his neck. Disclosing the details of his affair with Dashkov's wife and her dreadful demise had cost him dear; his gray eyes were as dark as brooding storm clouds and deep ridges bracketed his tightly compressed mouth. Indeed his whole body was as rigid as marble.

He feels guilty about Anna's death. And Dashkov's apparent plan for revenge.

I am in danger...

Georgie laid a trembling hand against her throat where her pulse fluttered as wildly as a trapped bird. God, this couldn't be happening, could it? That she was truly the target of one Rafe's old enemies? The muddy stains on her gown and her bruised body told a different story. She shivered, suddenly filled with the unexpected craving to imbibe alcohol in an attempt to soothe her jangled nerves.

As if reading her mind, Rafe spoke in a low voice almost as ragged as his expression. "I think another drink is in order. For myself and for you, my love." His own glass in hand, he pushed away from the fireplace then poured them both a brandy; Georgie always kept a decanter on the sideboard in her sitting room for those occasions when Jonathon wanted a tipple. Crossing the room, she accepted the glass from him with a less than steady hand and took a small sip. But even the fiery alcohol couldn't loosen her tongue or alleviate the dread constricting her throat.

Georgie hadn't been surprised in the least to learn Rafe was a spy. She glanced at him over the rim of her glass as she took another, larger sip. What he'd shared tonight about

Dashkov's wife was probably only one of many violent incidents that he'd witnessed. Or instigated.

She'd be naïve to think it otherwise. She studied Rafe's imperfect yet still ridiculously handsome face as he swirled his brandy about in his glass; his expression was withdrawn. She sensed he struggled to control a deep, inner turmoil she couldn't even begin to understand. She'd love to know what he was thinking right now. What was he planning with regards to Dashkov? And herself?

She realized that in many respects, Rafe was still unfathomable, and that perhaps he always would be. She thought they had grown close over these past weeks—closer than she'd ever thought possible, but there was so much she didn't know. One thing she was certain of, Rafe wasn't an ordinary nobleman with only the usual scandals to hide—too many nights of wild carousing that he'd rather she didn't know about; the occasional duel over a woman or some other matter related to slighted honor; a profligate brother or uncle who'd brought the family name into disrepute, or had almost bankrupted the estate.

He has worse secrets. Dark, dark secrets, too many to count. Secrets he will never share. And enemies. Those who hate him and would do him and his loved ones, harm.

Could she live with that?

What Georgie *did* know about Rafe, all the finer qualities she'd seen so far, the things she loved—his wit, his intelligence, his honor, his strength and the care and respect he showed her, his passion—would they be enough to compensate for the darkness surrounding him? The shadows plaguing his soul?

Her gaze traveled over his face again. He looked so harrowed, worn down by guilt and the horrors from his past that her heart ached for him. *He is so alone.*

"No one truly knows you, do they?" she asked in a soft, shaky voice.

Rafe put his brandy down on the mahogany sideboard and his mouth slanted into an approximation of a smile, although perhaps it was more of a grimace. "Not really. I've never had the opportunity..." He took a step closer and his turbulent gray gaze bore into hers. "I've never been particularly close to anyone before... Until now."

Georgie's heart began to race and her breath hitched. Anticipation swirled through her, making her breathless, almost giddy. She was suddenly so very tired of dancing around the truth. And of being afraid. The past didn't matter. Neither his nor her own. What mattered was how she felt right at this very moment.

Discarding her brandy, she stepped forward and touched Rafe's smooth, strong jaw with gentle reverence. "Rafe, the man I see before me... The man I know..." She drew in a deep breath and at last allowed herself to utter the confession she'd been longing to make for weeks. "I love you."

"God, Georgie." Rafe captured her face between his hands and brushed his thumbs back and forth over her cheeks as if reassuring himself she were real. That what she'd told him was real. His eyes searched hers. "You have no idea how much I've wanted to hear—" He paused then swallowed, clearly lost for words. But the moment quickly passed and when he spoke again, his voice was rough with emotion. "My brave, sweet, beautiful Georgie. I'm in love with you too. Utterly and completely."

Georgie couldn't stem the rise of joyful tears in her eyes as Rafe pushed a hand into the tangled curls at her nape, drawing her closer. His kiss was gentle at first, a soft, satiny brush of warm lips against hers, the sweep of his tongue against the seam of her mouth no more than a beguiling flicker. Yet whilst Rafe's kiss clearly demonstrated his tender regard for her, it was also a teasing caress. Georgie didn't doubt for a moment that he was ruthlessly holding himself back. She was fleetingly reminded of their very first kiss on the terrace of Latimer House. Just like then, Rafe was deliberately building her anticipation, making her want more. But this time, there was no doubt in her heart or her mind. She did indeed want more.

She wanted everything.

With a moan, she slid her hands into Rafe's silky dark hair and pressed herself closer, her mouth moving urgently against his, demanding him to let go, beckoning him to take everything she offered. Her body, her heart, her soul, forever.

Rafe responded to her unspoken plea with a deep groan and an equally ravenous and wholly welcome assault. Fiery need unfurled between them as he backed her toward the settee, his mouth devouring hers whilst his hands made short work of all her buttons and ribbons and laces. When her gown and stays slipped to the floor, he slid his hot mouth to her neck, nipping and laving all of the tender spots that always made her tingle and shiver and writhe in ecstasy. He palmed her breasts through the thin silk of her shift and her nipples hardened; sparks of pure lust shot straight to her pulsing, already wet sex.

Aflame with want, impatient to touch his hard, bare flesh, Georgie wrenched his silk shirt from the waistband of his black satin breeches. Sliding a hand beneath the fabric, her eager fingertips found the sleek, taut muscles of his abdomen, the sharp ridge of a lean hipbone. The insistent jut of his long, rock-hard cock. Her mouth watered.

She turned and pushed him onto the settee before falling to her knees between his legs. As she began to attack the buttons at the fall front of his breeches he stilled the feverish movement of her fingers. "Georgie—"

"Shhh." She pressed her fingers to his kiss-slickened lips. "I want to do this. So very much." She would do anything for Rafe. This man, like no other, who'd taught her how to truly love—and be loved.

He chuckled, a low, rich sound that ignited a fresh burst of need deep inside her. "Go on, have your wicked way with me then, my love," he said, in a voice graveled with lust. "Who am I to deny anything you desire?"

"I'm glad you see it my way." Georgie freed his engorged member and began stroking him with her fisted hand, reveling in the sight of his surrender. His head fell against the back of the settee and he bit his bottom lip as if stifling a groan. Even though a shining bead of semen appeared at the tip of his cock, he wasn't far gone enough yet, not by any means—she wanted him writhing, out of control. Completely lost to pleasure.

Georgie licked her lips and bent to her task with joyful yet determined abandon. Loving his rigid length with her fingers, lips and tongue, it wasn't long before Rafe began shuddering and bucking his hips in time with her rhythmic sucking. The taste of his spilled seed and his deep growls of pleasure only fueled her own desire all the more; the throbbing in her lower belly was almost unbearable and she squeezed her thighs together in a feeble attempt to ease the building pressure.

She rolled his tight, swollen bollocks between her fingers and felt them draw up; at the very same moment Rafe speared his fingers into her hair, pressing himself even deeper. Sensing he was about to climax, Georgie gleefully renewed her efforts, hollowing her cheeks to increase the suction, taking his hot pulsing length as far back into her throat as she possibly could. Her strategy worked—with a guttural cry, Rafe exploded, his seed a hot, salty jet momentarily flooding her mouth before she eagerly swallowed it down, taking everything he gave her.

Elation suffused her heart. Rafe loved her. He was undeniably hers. She brought him immense satisfaction—not just physically, but emotionally as well. She could see it in his eyes as he pushed the tangled hair from her eyes and stroked her flushed cheek. In the way he kissed the top of her head as he carried her through to her bedroom and laid her gently across the end of her four-poster bed. When he stripped the remaining garments from her body, worshipping her fevered flesh with his hot gaze and ardent kisses, her heart sang with the certain knowledge over and over again, *he loves me, he loves me.*

"Will you help me remove my necklace?" Georgie sat up a little and pushed her hair over one shoulder, reaching for the clasp when Rafe began to shed his own clothing.

"Oh no, my sweet." Rafe tugged his shirt over his head in one swift movement revealing the muscled chest and abdomen she loved so well. "I want you to wear it exactly like that." His mouth lifted into a wolfish grin as he toed off his evening shoes. "It's the way I've always wanted you to wear it, ever since I first laid eyes on it in the jewelry shop window."

Oh. Georgie's nipples tightened and her cheeks grew hot—not with shame or self-consciousness, but with desire. Naked but for her necklace, she sank back against the silk counterpane again, watching Rafe divest his breeches. All the while he raked her with his hot, hungry gaze, and not for one moment did she think to cover herself. Strange to think how much she'd changed... How much Rafe had helped her to change.

She smiled as he joined her on the bed and covered her body with his. Looking into Rafe's deep gray eyes, she had one last coherent thought before he once again overwhelmed her with the head-spinning pleasure of his kisses.

Love was truly a miraculous thing.

In spite of everything, she loves me. His heart thrumming with profound joy at Georgie's unexpected admission, Rafe silently vowed that he would show this wonderful woman just how deeply he adored her. How much he worshipped her.

He kissed her thoroughly, not only her delicious mouth but her sweetly scented neck, her full breasts with their tightly furled, rose pink nipples, her smooth belly. When she began to writhe and gasp beneath his deliberate and tauntingly slow ministrations—his hands and mouth swept close, but not quite close enough to the light brown curls hiding her sex—he chuckled against her alabaster skin, raising gooseflesh.

"Rafe, please," she begged, her voice hoarse with need.

How could he deny her, the woman he loved? Taking up a position between her slender thighs, he gently parted the deeply flushed folds of her sex with his fingers. The heady, musky scent of her arousal greeted him, and he smiled, relishing the fact Georgie's entrance glistened with moisture, how very ready she was for this most intimate possession.

Dipping his head, he set about teasing her clitoris with the tip of his tongue, rapidly flicking and circling the tight, swollen nub in the way he knew would drive her wild. As he continued to suckle and lick, savoring her juices, he pushed two of his fingers deep inside her tight, slick passage and mercilessly stroked her, over and over again, steadily driving her toward the precipice of release. When her orgasm claimed her, she cried out his name and clutched at his head, her hips arching upward, her sheath clenching around his fingers. A fresh surge of moisture welled and he eagerly lapped at her until she pulled at his hair and begged him for mercy. Rafe raised his head and on seeing Georgie's flushed face, her contented smile, a feeling of deep satisfaction flooded his heart at the thought that he alone could arouse her and ultimately bring her such untold pleasure.

He slid up beside her and pulled her into his arms before kissing her mouth. The press of her smooth, warm flesh against his body made his already hard cock stand to attention all the more. "Do you trust me?" He drew back a little and brushed the tumble of curls from her eyes so he could study her face. "I want this to be a night of firsts, of special memories, for all the very best reasons."

"Yes," Georgie whispered. "With all my heart I trust you."

"Good. I want us to lie across the end of your bed so we can both see each other in the mirror above the fireplace. I want you to watch as we love each other. Will you do that for me?"

An expression of uncertainty clouded Georgie's eyes before she gifted him with a small smile and a nod. "You are turning me into a wanton, Rafe, but all right."

"I love it that you are wanton. And may you always be so with me," he returned with an answering smile that he hoped would reassure her.

At the gentle urging of his hands Georgie rolled onto her side, her weight resting on her elbow, her back flush against his front. She parted her legs for him and he guided his throbbing shaft toward her entrance. As he pushed in, her lush, greedy quim immediately sucked at him, engulfing the head of his cock, and a deep, appreciative growl escaped him. Sweet Jesus, he wanted her so badly, he prayed he could maintain his control long enough to bring her to orgasm a second time.

Reaching forward, he found Georgie's breast and rolled the distended nipple between his thumb and fingers as he thrust deeper into her. The tightness, the wetness, the friction were so incredible, his aching balls were already contracting. Gritting his teeth, he focused on pleasuring Georgie. In the mirror, he could see that her eyes were closed tight and she was biting her lip.

"Open your eyes. Look at us," he demanded in a voice rough with lust, but nevertheless, she did as he bid without pause or question. He began to stroke in and out of her, with long, slow slides. Their reflection revealed that she'd fixed her gaze on the place of their joining. Panting, her eyes glazed with desire, Georgie began to push back, meeting him thrust for thrust even when he began to pick up the pace. Above her perfect breasts, the diamond and sapphire necklace glinted as she moved with him. He'd never seen anything so erotic in his life.

"God, Georgie, look at you," he rasped and skimmed his hand down her body until his fingers found her slick folds. "You're a goddess in my arms. So wild and beautiful. We were made for each other, you and I. See how well we fit together. Move together... Tell me you see it too."

"Yes," she whispered hoarsely. "Yes I do." Her hand slid to one of her breasts and she plucked at the rosy nipple with her fingertips. "Love me, Rafe."

"Oh God, yes. Forever." He pressed his teeth into the sensitive curve of her neck, tasting her fragrant skin. His fingertips circled over and around the hard bud of her clitoris, and he plunged harder, faster, determined to push her over the brink into sweet oblivion again.

Within moments Georgie came on a sharp cry, her whole body shuddering, her inner passage gripping him so tightly, he had no choice but to dive headlong into ecstasy with her. Groaning, he continued pumping into her even as the intense waves of pleasure began to ebb away, until he lay sprawled over her, spent and gasping, the happiest he'd ever been in his life.

Rafe smoothed the tangle of curls away from the side of Georgie's face and kissed her cheek, her temple, the corner of her mouth. Even in his blissfully drowsy state, one thing above all others was clear—he could never let Georgie go. She was perfect. She was his. And against all odds, she loved him.

What more could he ask for?

"I love you, Georgie," he whispered, and when she turned her head and smiled back at him, Rafe knew he would love and protect this woman until his dying day.

As soon as he'd disposed of Dashkov and Craven, there would be nothing to stop him from proposing.

A harsh cry rent the night.

Rafe...

Georgie bolted upright in her bed to find Rafe sitting with his back against the mahogany headboard, panting, his naked chest and torso slick with sweat. His eyes were screwed shut and he gripped the sheets so tightly, the knuckles of his fists stood out stark white even in the insubstantial light cast by the low burning fire. He was clearly in the grip of another nightmare and her heart cried for him.

"Rafe." She reached out and gently touched his hand. His eyes flew open.

"Georgie? Christ..." He shook his head and scrubbed his face with his hands. At length he murmured, "I'm so, so sorry, my love. I don't know what's come over me. And tonight, of all nights."

"Shhh. It's all right." Whether Rafe had dreamed of the cold-hearted Anna, the mysterious Solange, or someone or something else entirely, it didn't matter one whit to Georgie. She slipped from the bed and after wrapping a silk robe about herself, retrieved the brandy decanter and a glass from her sitting room. She handed him a rather large measure of the amber-hued spirit then crossed the room and found a taper to light a pair of candles on the mantel.

"You are too good to me, Georgie," Rafe said softly when she climbed back into the bed.

"Nonsense," she returned. She laid her head upon his wide shoulder. "I'm not so unlike you. I would do anything to ease your pain. I wish I could do more."

"You are helping, believe me," he murmured, his tone gentle. He threaded his fingers through hers and raised her hand to his lips. "I wish I could do the same for you, you know. The other day, when you saw Craven in the street... To see you so upset..." Rafe's grip tightened on her hand. "Well, suffice it to say, I do not like to see you so. I hope you know that if you ever feel the need to talk about what happened, I'm here for you, my love."

Georgie closed her eyes as all the disturbing memories from a decade ago invaded her mind. She shivered and Rafe wrapped one strong arm about her, pulling her close. For so long she'd tried so hard to forget everything that had befallen her, especially the night of her supposed elopement. Of course, she realized now she never would. Part of the reason for her never having spoken about that night was simply due to the fact she'd never felt close enough to anyone who would truly understand. But Rafe would.

Perhaps if Georgie confided in him as he'd suggested, it would ease her burden a little bit. And didn't he deserve to know the truth?

If only her stomach wasn't so completely tied up in such intolerable, tortuous knots.

She sat up straighter and eyed Rafe's brandy. "May I?" she asked.

Rafe's lips twitched. "Be my guest."

She took a large, fortifying sip, then another before handing the glass back to him. "I want to tell you everything about Lord Craven and what he did... If that's all right with you."

All levity fled Rafe's expression and a frown of concern creased his forehead. "Of course it is. I am honored that you feel you can confide in me."

Georgie nodded and swallowed hard in a feeble attempt to moisten her suddenly very dry mouth. "You may recall he made a promise to me that we would elope."

"Yes, but then you did not."

"No." Georgie's mouth twisted into a bitter smile. "We most certainly didn't."

Rafe squeezed her hand, lending her support. "What went wrong?"

"It all sounded so romantic to a naïve debutante. A midnight elopement. Lord Craven sent me a note, asking me to wait for him near the servants' entrance of the Brook Street townhouse I shared with my Aunt Louisa. It was a bitterly cold Sunday night, foggy and quiet as the grave. A night made for conducting secret liaisons, I told myself. My aunt had retired early as she was wont to do when her rheumatism was acting up. I was convinced that everything would work out perfectly."

Rafe's mouth was a hard, grim line. "Did Craven show?"

"Yes, he did. In hindsight, I really wished he hadn't." Now was the time for Georgie to put on her brave face, but it was taking everything she had just to keep her already tight throat from closing up completely and to keep her bottom lip from trembling. "As planned, Oliver arrived at the appointed hour, but when he dismissed my request to have one of his footmen load my small traveling trunk onto the back of the carriage, I should have known something wasn't quite right." A brittle laugh escaped her. "Of course I knew something was very wrong as soon as I entered the carriage."

Rafe's frown deepened. "What do you mean?"

Georgie forced her stiff lips and tongue to formulate her next words. "There was another man in the carriage. I...I paused in the doorway but Craven pushed me in and forced me to take a seat. Then he slammed the door shut and we moved on."

"Go on," Rafe said softly, his voice nothing but kindness. But Georgie could see a muscle ticking in his lean jaw.

She swallowed again and cast her gaze downward to where she twisted her silk robe in her fingers. Tears burned at the back of her eyes and she blinked rapidly to clear them. Making this disclosure was going to be harder than she'd ever anticipated, but she wasn't going to stop now. Somehow, Rafe's quiet presence gave her strength. "I asked Lord Craven, 'Is this gentleman to be a witness at our wedding?' but he merely smirked and then addressed his friend, 'What say you then, Lord Blaire?' and then the other man, Blaire, laughed and he said..." Georgie made herself say the words. "He said that he thought he was supposed to be a participant, not a witness. Dolt that I was, I asked, 'Participant in what?' and Lord Craven stroked my cheek and said, 'Come now, my dear, surely you cannot be that naïve as to think that I ever really intended to wed someone like you, the trumped up, sluttish daughter of a mere tradesman. Your father may have been a baronet but he was only a ship builder after all. Countess material, you are not.'"

Georgie's voice had faded to a husky whisper at these last words. Burning anger and shame tangled inside her, an ugly mess of emotions that threatened to rise up and choke her all over again. Ten years had gone by, but the passing of time had done nothing to ease the pain of being so put down. Dismissed and abused.

She cleared her throat. She'd started her story and she was going to finish it. "Before I could even think to protest, Lord Blaire reached forward and grasped my leg, but he addressed Lord Craven, 'You said she'd do anything, Oliver. Come now, Miss Winterbourne, don't be shy. I've heard all about what you are particularly good at.'"

"Oh Georgie," Rafe squeezed her hand again. "Unfortunately, I've come across Blaire before, and I know exactly what he's capable of. I can well imagine—" He broke off and swallowed hard; he was clearly struggling to contain his emotions as well. "I can see how difficult this is for you. You don't have to tell me any more."

Georgie shook her head. "No, no it's all right. Thankfully, I actually can't recall much after that. When I...when I refused to comply, Craven forced me to drink a foul, bitter concoction from a flask—I suspect it was cognac, something very strong at any rate, laced with laudanum. I lost consciousness and have no clear memory of what happened to me save for a few disjointed, hazy impressions, like a nightmare I can't quite remember. So perhaps the fact I was drugged was a blessing in disguise. The next thing I *do* clearly remember is waking up on the doorstep at the servants' entrance of the Brook Street townhouse. I had no idea of the time, but I suspected it was close to dawn."

Georgie shuddered at the horrific memory. Quaking with cold, disorientated and nauseated to the very bone, both from the laudanum and the knowledge she'd been abused so foully by not one, but two men, she'd promptly vomited on the cobblestones before dragging her aching, shaking body upright, and letting herself inside. Too ashamed to call her maid once she'd reached her room, she'd washed herself as best she could, and had then burnt all her soiled clothes on the fire before collapsing into bed.

Pushing aside the painful recollections of that night, she continued, "The next day, I claimed I had taken ill with a terrible stomach affliction and no one, not my aunt, my maid, or any of the other servants suspected a thing. My traveling trunk—*my trousseau*"—she laughed briefly with undisguised bitterness—"which had been left by the servants' door, I explained away easily enough by claiming the items were things I no longer needed and were to be donated to the poor."

"Christ, Georgie." Rafe wrapped his arms about her and hugged her close. "My brave, brave girl. What those heels did to you, it is unforgiveable."

At his words and the sound of grave compassion in his voice, Georgie at last gave herself up to the tears that had been threatening to fall since she'd begun this conversation. Rafe rubbed her back and kissed her hair, offering silent comfort until she was spent and quiet in his arms.

"Thank you for listening," she whispered huskily against his chest.

"I wish I could do more than listen, my love." Rafe's muscles tensed beneath her hands. "Craven and Blaire are both lucky they can still draw breath."

A cold tremor of fear slid down Georgie's spine as an altogether horrible thought occurred to her. She sat up and met Rafe's icy gray gaze. Without thinking, she'd confessed her deepest, darkest secret to a man who was dangerous in his own way. "Rafe, please do not think you need to somehow avenge my honor. What happened to me, it was such a long time ago. I will not have you do anything rash. Promise me."

Rafe gently cupped her jaw. "Georgie, I promise you I won't do anything reckless or foolish. Not that I want to ever articulate the man's name, but I wonder if you had heard that Fate has already meted out a form of justice to Blaire."

Georgie frowned. "No. Whatever do you mean?"

Rafe's jaw hardened. "I have it from a reliable source that Blaire is in a very bad way—feeble in both mind and body—after he ingested too much cognac and opium in the form of laudanum, a few months ago. He ran with pack of noblemen that included Lord Beauchamp, the first husband of Beth, the new Lady Rothsburgh. Blaire and Beauchamp were both so low, even the word degenerate isn't strong enough to describe them. In my opinion they've received everything they deserved."

But not Craven.

The words were not spoken but Georgie knew that's exactly what Rafe was thinking. Only he'd promised he wouldn't do anything rash. And she trusted him to keep his word.

Besides, in the coming days, she suspected he would be

devoting most of his energy to locating the Russian general, Dashkov.

As she and Rafe settled beneath the covers once more, she couldn't help but wonder how much danger she was really in. The idea that someone she didn't even know would want to inflict harm upon her to punish the man she loved was sobering indeed. Even though she knew Rafe would do his utmost to keep her safe, unease pricked at her like a burr until the gray light of early morning began to creep around the edges of the curtains of her bedchamber window, dispelling the darkness in her room.

Her last coherent thought before exhaustion claimed her was a wistful prayer: if only all the other shadows in her life, and Rafe's, could be chased away so easily.

CHAPTER 19

The Hound and Hellion Club, Soho
One night later...

"Craven's definitely 'ere," murmured Cowan. "Far left corner. Been playin' an' losing at Hazard for the last 'our. An' afore tha', Lumsden says 'e lost a 'uge sum at the cockfights at the Birdcage Walk. The way the money lenders 'ave been tailing 'im, all day an' night, I'd wager my own soul tha' e's not far from losin' everythin'. The word 'desperate' springs to mind."

Perfect. Rafe took a sip of rum to help mask the wolfish grin he could feel tugging at the corners of his mouth. The cur was making this too easy for him. "Thank you, Cowan. You and Lumsden have done a sterling job. If you'd be so kind as to make yourselves scarce, I'll take care of things from here."

Cowan gave a curt nod and slipped away into the shadows. He knew better than to use any form of address that might draw attention to the fact that he was in the employ of a toff.

Peering through the smoky gloom and over the heads of the other unsavory characters crowding this stinking den of iniquity—an assortment of well-heeled and not so well-heeled patrons, at least a dozen burly ruffians in shabby livery who appeared to be employed as "doormen" or bankers, and perhaps the same number of scantily clad barmaids who were obviously demireps—Rafe spied his quarry. Ever since Georgie had confided in him the night before, he'd been champing at the bit to finish the bastard off.

Ruining Craven financially now seemed too light a punishment given the severity of his crimes against Georgie, but he'd promised her that he wouldn't do anything reckless.

Although technically, his pursuit of Craven was anything but reckless. Cold and calculated destruction was what he had in mind.

As Rafe neared the far left corner Cowan had indicated, he had to suppress another grin when he noted Lord Craven was attired in practically the same set of clothes he'd been wearing in Gentleman Jackson's the day before. The light of a nearby wall sconce revealed the less than noble, nobleman's hair was greasy, his cravat was in hopeless disarray and his satin waistcoat and linen cuffs were spotted with various stains. Staring blearily at the nearby crowd around the Hazard table, an empty glass at his elbow, he did indeed appear desperate.

Rafe leaned heavily against the water-stained, blue silk wallpaper above the chipped chair-rail and plastered a foolish smile on his face, affecting the demeanor of a man who was well into his cups. "Rumor has it you're quite the punter, Lord Craven," he slurred, gesturing toward the earl with his half empty glass. Rum sloshed onto the sleeve of his fine woolen tailcoat. "Up for a game? You name it, I'll play it."

Craven's blood-shot eyes narrowed with suspicion as he looked him up and down. "And you are?"

Rafe took the empty seat in front of him. "Lord Rafe Landsbury," he whispered theatrically. He used his former, lesser-known title.

"Never seen you in here before, nor heard of you," sneered Craven, his lip curling like a dog that had been kicked too many times.

Rafe shrugged and yawned. "Not many have. Been on the Continent and in the East for quite some time. And I must say, now that I've returned to *Polite Society*, White's is just too damned stuffy for words." He waved over one of the barmaids-cum-prostitutes and pulled a wad of pound notes and coins from his coat pocket. "Two shots of rum, thank you, my sweet," he said with an exaggerated wink and pressed several crowns into the smiling girl's hand before patting her behind. "And keep the change for your own pocket."

His actions had the desired effect. Craven's eyes fairly gleamed with a lascivious light at the sight of Rafe's money. "Landsbury, you say."

Rafe affected a clumsy, lop-sided smile. "At your service."

"Join me in a game of piquet then." Craven jerked his chin pugnaciously toward a heavily populated connecting room where the card tables lay. He cocked an arrogant eyebrow. "If you think you can keep up."

So the earl clearly thought an inebriated opponent wasn't up to concentrating during a lengthy, convoluted bout of piquet. And he obviously wanted a private game, just between the two of them with no banker involved as there would be if they sat down to Baccarat, Faro, or *Vingt-et-un*. Rafe couldn't suppress his smile as he stood and gestured expansively. "I concur. Lead the way, sir."

They quickly found a vacant table, ridiculously high stakes were agreed upon—fifty pounds per point gained, plus a bonus five hundred pounds for whoever reached one hundred points first, the usual vowels were acceptable—and play began.

Rafe deliberately lost the first hand in the *partie*—he made a series of bad calls, consistently lost track of the play during tricks, and at the end of the sixth hand, he found himself writing an IOU for four thousand five hundred pounds for a widely grinning Craven.

Given the nature of the stakes, a considerable crowd had gathered around their table by the end of the game. One of the gaudily painted demireps—who wore nothing more than a scandalously low-cut gown of sheer violet gauze—draped herself around Craven's shoulders as soon as he tucked the signed vowels into his coat pocket. When Craven whispered something in her ear and squeezed her all-but bared breast, it took every ounce of control Rafe had to adopt an appreciative leer, considering all he really wanted to do was grab the back of the man's head and slam it into the table to break his nose.

The demirep giggled and straightened. "Would you like another rum too, milord?" she asked Rafe, thrusting her breasts in his direction.

"The drinks will be on my chit this time, Landsbury," added Craven, his expression smug now he'd won.

"Thank you." Rafe sighed heavily and drummed his fingers on the sticky tabletop as though he was unsettled. "Care to go another round?" he asked, feigning a pained expression that fell somewhere between troubled and hopeful.

Craven rubbed his stubble-shadowed jaw. "Well, I don't know…"

"What's life without a little risk? What say we double the stakes?" suggested Rafe. He'd lowered his voice, aiming for a persuasive note with a hint of desperation. "One hundred pounds per point gained, and a thousand-pound bonus for the first one to cross the Rubicon."

Craven's eyebrows shot up. "You can't be serious?"

Rafe shrugged. "Call me mad if you will. But the offer still stands."

At that moment, the demirep returned with their drinks and Rafe bolted his in one gulp before immediately ordering another.

Craven's mouth twisted into a malicious smile as he extended his hand. It was clearly a gesture of condescension rather than a way to formally mark the closure of their deal. "All right. Done."

Forcing himself to shake the bastard's hand, not break it, Rafe then shuffled and cut the pack to reveal the ace of clubs. Craven's smile became decidedly stiff when he turned over a jack of spades.

Rafe blew out a low whistle between his teeth. "I'll claim the younger hand, if you don't mind?" he said as he began to shuffle the pack again. Craven would have the advantage during this round given that he'd get to choose from the talon first, but in the final, most important round of the *partie*, the advantage would be entirely with Rafe. If they made it that far...

Craven inclined his head, his dark eyes cold. "Naturally."

Rafe again played the foxed fool and deliberately lost the first two rounds. Craven was twenty-six points ahead and judging by his self-satisfied smirk, he believed he was well on the way to claiming a second lot of sizeable winnings for the night.

As Rafe dealt the third hand, he decided it was high time his gloves came off. It was with considerable satisfaction that he declared a point of five, a septiéme followed by a trio of kings, and then watched Craven's face blanch to the color of whey when he won every trick gaining a *capot*, an additional forty points, and the lead.

During the fourth hand when he declared a quatorze of knaves, Craven sneered, "I demand proof, *Captain*."

"I assure you, my name is not Sharp," returned Rafe coolly, refuting the accusation he was cheating at once by showing him the sequence in question.

Craven ground his teeth, but nevertheless play continued until Rafe claimed victory again.

By the time Rafe dealt the fifth hand—he was a clear fifty-seven points ahead, and only fourteen points from one hundred—Craven's hands were shaking so much he dropped several of his cards on the table as he made his selection from the talon, and judging by the sheen of sweat on his very pale face, he had the look of a man about to cast up his accounts in the moment before he stepped up to the gallows.

Declarations commenced, but when Rafe easily scored a *repique*, thus gaining an additional sixty-point bonus, it was clearly the last straw for Craven.

With a disgusted growl, he threw his cards on the table and jabbed a finger toward Rafe's face. His voice shook with barely contained fury, and probably a good dose of fear. "I refuse to continue this...this farce. You *must* be cheating. *Sir.*" With this last word, he poked Rafe in the chest.

Rafe cocked his brow. "I assure you, I am not, *my lord*," he returned in a deadly quiet voice. All traces of the affable drunkard cast aside, he grabbed Craven's wrist in an uncompromising grip and slammed his arm with bone crushing force down onto the table.

A pitiful whimper escaped Craven. "Fuck you," he hissed as he attempted but failed to wrest his arm back. "Let go. You have gone too far. I demand satisfaction."

"So do I." Rafe bared his teeth in a predatory grin as he ground the bones of Craven's wrist together even harder. "You lost because you are a mediocre player at best, yet you accuse me of cheating. Name your terms. I will meet them."

"Pistols at dawn. Battersea-fields. The common behind The Red House Inn. You know it?"

"Yes, I know it."

"And as far as I'm concerned, your debt still stands."

"Really?" Rafe raised his eyebrows to indicate his incredulity. "My, my we are confident aren't we? Might I suggest we wait and see who is left standing at the end of our next *tête-a-tête* before any debt is settled?"

"Fuck you." Craven at last managed to twist out of Rafe's grip.

"Tut, tut," Rafe chided as he stood and looked down his nose at a puce-faced Craven. "It seems you are not one to live by the expression, 'manners maketh the man', are you?"

With a roar, Craven leapt to his feet and attempted to hurl himself at Rafe's throat, but Rafe, anticipating his move, neatly stepped to the side and watched Craven plough head-long into the filthy, threadbare Turkish rug on the floor.

Turning on his heel, Rafe pushed through the crowd of laughing on-lookers, making his way for the stairs and the nearest door.

Lumsden and Cowan gave up their posts at the bar and followed him outside into the narrow, littered laneway.

"Well done, my friend."

Rafe spun around to find Georgie's brother also emerging from the gaming hell. The dim lighting that slipped into the lane before the door slammed shut revealed that Jonathon wore a redingote of dubious quality and a somewhat dented top hat. The guise of a gentleman down on his luck.

"What the hell are you doing here?" Rafe demanded, his voice a low growl.

Jonathon's brows shot up in surprise. "Steady on. As soon as I heard you wouldn't be dancing attendance on Georgie tonight as you usually do, I had you followed. You are not the only one with resources, old man. And I must say the show has been well worth any effort expended on my part. I wouldn't have missed witnessing the Lord of Cowards getting his comeuppance for the world. Bravo!"

And you don't even know the half of what your sister has suffered. Nevertheless, Rafe inclined his head. "Thank you."

As they negotiated the filth-strewn cobblestones of the

laneway, making their way toward the gas lamp lit thoroughfare beyond, Jonathon added in a grave voice, "I would be honored if you would consider me for your second."

"Duly noted," Rafe replied in an equally solemn tone. "However, even though I have men guarding Dudley House, I would prefer it if you remained with your sister. As you well know, I haven't yet located Dashkov."

A muscle worked in Jonathon's jaw for a moment before he gave a curt nod. "Understood. I suppose you will ask Phillip to stand in as second then."

"Yes." Rafe hailed a hackney cab. "That is the plan. I am on my way to Latimer House now."

Jonathon grasped his shoulder, catching his eye. "I know I shouldn't have to wish you good luck, given the outcome is obvious," he said with quiet sincerity, "but I will do so at any rate." His mouth suddenly curved into a wicked grin. "And the more blood you can draw, the better."

Rafe grinned back before he swung himself into the cab. "Naturally," he replied.

"I look forward to hearing all of the details tomorrow." Jonathon slammed the door and the cab rolled on.

Sinking back against the cracked leather squabs, Rafe closed his eyes and sighed. Justice would be meted out to Craven easily enough. And then he could focus all of his energies on dealing with Dashkov, once and for all.

He could hardly wait until morning.

CHAPTER 20

Dudley House, Hanover Square

Georgie tossed *Emma* onto the floral chintz cushion of the shepherdess chair beside her then scowled at the gilt carriage clock on the mantelpiece in her sitting room. After her sixth game of Patience, she'd taken up her favorite novel to while away the long hours of an evening spent alone. But the lively and amusing tale of Miss Woodhouse and Mr. Knightley could only hold her attention for so long, and sadly, not at all after midnight. Especially since Rafe was not with her, and Jonathon hadn't returned home yet.

Not that it was all that unusual for her brother to stay out until the early hours of the morning at his club—or more lately, at Lord Farley's residence—but as Rafe had indicated he had unexpected "Crown business" to attend to this evening, Jonathon had promised to keep her company. That state of affairs had only lasted until nine o'clock, when Reed had apologetically invaded the drawing room and had presented her brother with a mysterious missive.

Of course, Jonathon would not be drawn on the content

of the message or its sender, although on noting the wicked twinkle in his eye, Georgie had at once suspected Farley had invited him on some kind of jaunt, something that Jonathon did not want her to know about. She definitely knew he was up to some sort of underhand activity when she'd spied him all but sneaking out of the front door dressed in the oddest attire—a shabby redingote and a sorry excuse for a top hat; garments that would ordinarily make her brother shudder with revulsion.

Georgie had at once determined that she would stay awake until he returned, even if she had to wait until dawn. A wistful part of her more than half wished Rafe would surprise her with a visit, although he had been quite adamant his business would keep him busy until the following day. It had been the first night since the house party at Rivergate that Georgie had spent without him, and she missed him dreadfully. How quickly she had become entirely addicted to his company—his clever conversation, his teasing, his smiles, his kisses and of course, his lovemaking.

After Jonathon had departed, she'd once again determinedly shrugged off the altogether silly and self-indulgent shroud of loneliness that had been threatening to overwhelm her all evening. But it wasn't so easy to ignore the persistent gnaw of anxiety whenever she contemplated Rafe's safety. He might have said he was on Crown business, but what did that really entail? Dashkov was still out there, somewhere, wishing them both harm. She shivered and crossed over to the fireplace to shift the logs and stir the coals. Sparks flew and the fire sprang back to life, but the bright flames failed to warm her. The thought of Rafe in danger—it made her blood run colder than the Thames this time of year.

Best not to think about it.

Georgie wrapped her arms about herself and sighed. Despite the late hour, the thought of ringing for tea suddenly had great appeal. What she wouldn't do for a cup of her remarkably calming herbal tisane right now to help soothe her jangled nerves...

She'd have to summon one of the chambermaids for hot water, a tea tray, and her tea caddy as she was reluctant to disturb Constance. The young woman had looked so terribly fatigued tonight. Georgie had dismissed her shortly after Jonathon had departed. Indeed, as she'd helped Georgie change into her nightgown and robe, the dark circles under her eyes and her wan complexion were so noticeable, Georgie had been quite alarmed. Not only had she urged Constance to have a cup of her own herbal tea, but she'd also offered to send for a physician. But Constance had denied she needed more than a good night's rest, and so in the end, Georgie had simply insisted the girl retire early.

The clock struck a quarter past the hour and Georgie decided that even though tea would be welcome, the wiser course of action would be to go to bed. Yawning, she began to snuff out the candles on the mantel, but the sound of a footstep in the hallway right outside her sitting room gave her pause. Jonathon perhaps? She dare not think it was Rafe.

She opened her door in time to catch a glimpse of her brother as he disappeared into his own suite of rooms. "Jonathon," she called, throwing decorum to the wind and hurrying after him. She never usually quizzed him about his comings and goings, but she was too on edge with restless curiosity.

"Georgie! Why in God's name are you still awake?" Jonathon demanded as she shut the door behind her. "Do you know what time it is?"

"Of course I do." Georgie crossed her arms and pinned her brother with a narrow-eyed look. "I've been waiting for you. Aside from the fact you are the most pernickety person I know when it comes to clothes, your valet would never have let you leave the house looking like that," she gestured at his shoddy apparel, "unless you had a very good reason. Something very odd is going on, and I want to know exactly what it is."

Jonathon sighed heavily as he removed his misshapen top hat and tossed it onto a nearby chair. "You've been spying on me, haven't you? You watched me as I left."

Georgie lifted her chin. "I may have. But that matters little. You've been up to some sort of mischief, and considering there is a dangerous, vengeful man at large, I demand you give me a full account."

Jonathon's expression softened a little. "You're worried about Markham, aren't you? He'll be fine, you know." He clamped his jaw shut as if he'd said too much and turned away, shrugging off his coat.

"What do you mean, he will be fine?" Georgie took a step closer to her brother as icy dread suddenly began to tiptoe down her spine. Another altogether too horrible thought occurred to her. "Were you with him tonight? Have you been helping him look for Dashkov?"

"No." Jonathon avoided her gaze.

Fear fueled Georgie's temper. "Do not dissemble," she demanded hotly. "Tell me. Do you mean no, you haven't been with him, or no, you were not helping him to search?"

"Georgie…" The note of warning in Jonathon's voice was only half-hearted, but nevertheless, he still wouldn't look at her. He crossed to the walnut cabinet on the other side of his sitting room and poured himself a brandy. "It's late. As I said, Markham is well. That is all you need to know."

"No, that's not good enough, Jonathon. I've been worrying for hours about you. And Rafe. If he has dragged you into some dangerous scheme…" Georgie's voice cracked and tears clouded her vision. "I couldn't bear it if something happened to either of you."

"Oh, Georgie-bean." Jonathon crossed the room and

hugged her close. "I haven't been taking any unnecessary risks. I would never do such a thing."

Georgie pulled away and prodded her brother in the chest. "I won't be satisfied until you confess what is going on."

Jonathon closed his eyes and groaned. "Markham really will kill me this time if I tell you, you know. That's the real danger."

"No, he won't. Not when he has me to answer to." She poked him again. "Now confess."

Jonathon's shoulders heaved with a weary sigh. "I suppose you will hear all about it soon enough. And when all is said and done, you have every right to know, because in a way, this is all about you."

Perplexed, Georgie's brows snapped into a deep frown. "Whatever do you mean?"

"Markham's been playing the knight-errant again." Jonathon held her gaze and his expression was so serious, another frisson of unease slid over Georgie's skin. "He's utterly ruined Craven. Aside from his entailed property, I suspect the dog has nothing more than a few farthings left to his name."

"*What?*" Georgie gripped her brother's arm. Had she fallen asleep after all? Surely what Jonathon had just stated couldn't be true. "How?"

She didn't need to ask *why*. She'd heard the steel in Rafe's voice whenever they'd discussed Craven; it wasn't as if she hadn't suspected that he would want to avenge the wrong that had been done to her.

But to actually hear Rafe had taken such deliberate action, it was more than a little terrifying. Whilst she felt not one whit of compassion for Lord Craven, surely she should be pleased that he was at last being made to pay for his past transgressions. But perversely, she wasn't. Indeed, she felt strangely numb and not herself at all; it seemed like she was watching herself and Jonathon from the other side of the room.

"Georgie, you're shaking like a leaf. I've shocked you. Here"—Jonathon retrieved his discarded brandy and passed the tumbler to her—"sit down and take a sip or two."

She did as he asked, taking a seat in a wingback chair before the fire. Jonathon poured himself another brandy and took the seat opposite her.

"You haven't told me how Rafe accomplished any of this," she said at length when her trembling had begun to ease.

Jonathon grinned, his glee at Craven's misfortune blatantly obvious. "Apparently Craven has had debt collectors dogging his heels for some time, and he's been desperately trying to win back some of his fortune through gaming. Markham suspected it wouldn't take much to push him into penury. He tracked Craven to a less than reputable gaming hell he's been known to haunt of late and trounced him at the card table. Piquet." Her brother's grinned widened. "Such a beautiful thing to witness."

"From what you've told me, it would seem Rafe has been gathering intelligence on Craven and his situation for a good while." Had it been since she'd seen him outside the jewelry shop in Bond Street? Or longer? Jonathon had told Rafe about Craven even before the house party at Rivergate, before she barely knew him.

Jonathon shrugged. "I would say so. The man is determined if nothing else."

Determined was an understatement. Ruthless seemed more apt. Georgie sipped at her brandy, unsure what to think, or how to feel. Last night, Rafe had promised her he wouldn't do anything rash when it came to dealing with Craven. However, it was evident he'd been plotting the man's demise for some time.

She was only now beginning to fully understand that Rafe

had his own interpretation of morality and what constituted just retribution.

What lengths would he go to for someone he loved? Perhaps he had more in common with Dashkov than he realized. The thought chilled her to the very bone and she shivered.

However, when she caught Jonathon's next softly uttered words, her heart froze altogether. "I certainly wouldn't like to be in Markham's line of fire come morning."

Her gaze snapped to her brother. "What did you say?" she gasped.

"I... er... I meant I would not like to be in Craven's shoes when the creditors come looking for him on the morrow."

"No. No, you did not mean that. You said you would not like to be in Markham's firing line." And then she knew and her heart started again, racing at such an unsteady gallop she could barely summon enough breath to speak. "Rafe has challenged Craven to a duel, hasn't he? He means to kill him."

Jonathon squirmed in his seat. "No. That's not what happened. Without a word of a lie, Rafe did not do that."

But Craven was a vindictive monster. Years might have passed, but Georgie doubted he would have changed. "So it was the other way round then. Craven threw down the gauntlet. Rafe pushed him too far and he bit back."

Her brother wouldn't meet her eyes, and she knew she was correct even before he confirmed her suspicions with his next words. "Yes. All right," he said with a deep sigh. "Craven challenged Markham. Not that it matters." He shrugged. "The result will be the same. Craven will be erased from this earth. And good riddance to the bastard, I say."

"But... How can you be so sure of the outcome? I know Rafe is very much a man of action but Craven used to be quite the Corinthian as well."

Jonathon snorted. "That was years ago, dear sis, and does

not signify in the least. You know who is the better man in every sense."

"On the other hand, if Rafe kills Craven..." Too agitated to sit still a moment longer, Georgie rose and began pacing back and forth across the hearthrug. Her mind reeled from all of the implications. Dueling was forbidden—illegal in fact—even amongst noblemen. Rafe could be arrested and held to account by a jury of his peers if Craven died by his hand. Unless he fled the country and lived in exile...

She couldn't let him risk so much for her. "I can't let him do this. Craven is just not worth it." She stopped in front of Jonathon. "When and where is this happening? We must stop Rafe."

"Now *that*, I will not tell you. I'm not that much of a nincompoop. Can you imagine Markham's reaction if you try to meddle?" Jonathon rose and crossed to her. Grasping her shoulders, his gaze bore into hers. "You've got that stubborn look in your eye, Georgie. Do not fight me on this. I promised Markham I would take care of you. Do not make me lock you in your room."

"But Jonathon"—hot tears scalded Georgie's eyes—"I love him. The thought of losing him... I'm sorry." She bit her lip and turned away, blinking rapidly, willing herself not to cry. She was not one to weep and wail to get her own way, but right at this moment, she couldn't seem to control the wild emotions careening around inside her.

"Oh, God, Georgie, don't cry. Please don't cry." Jonathon pulled her in for a hug. "I understand. Trust me, I do." He stroked her back and dropped a kiss on the top of her head. "If there had been anything at all I could have done to save Teddy, I would have."

Georgie drew back and searched Jonathon's face. "So you'll help me?" she asked, barely able to believe he had capitulated so readily.

He offered her his silk handkerchief with a sad, knowing smile. "How could I not? He makes you happy. I would risk anything to ensure you remain so. Even Markham's wrath."

"Thank you." She dabbed at her eyes and dragged in a steadying breath. "Now pour me another brandy. We have plans to make."

The clock was striking a quarter to one when Georgie at last bid her brother goodnight. To her surprise she found Constance sitting in a chair outside her suite, still wearing her maid's attire, her posture as rigid as a poker and her face as pale as the ornate plasterwork on the ceiling above her head.

"What is it, Constance?" Georgie asked more sharply than was usual, but she truly was alarmed. "Has something happened?"

Constance sprang to her feet and bobbed a curtsy. "Please forgive me, Your Grace. I find...I find I have not been able to sleep a wink. And the more I try, the worse it is. You had offered me some of your special tea earlier, and when I saw the lamps were still lit, and I heard voices coming from Sir Jonathon's chambers... Please believe me, I was not eavesdropping, Your Grace. I would never do that. But I wondered if I might try some of your tea after all. I hope you'll forgive me for taking the liberty of bringing up the caddy from the kitchen." Her fingers fluttered nervously in the direction of a nearby occasional table where the small, locked wooden box now sat.

Ordinarily, Georgie would have a rebuked a servant for such presumption, but she *had* offered Constance the tisane earlier. And she was genuinely concerned about the girl's health. "It's quite all right," she said gently. She examined her maid's face; her hazel eyes were glassy with exhaustion, the shadows beneath her lower lids darker still, and she was pale rather than flushed, so at least she didn't have a fever.

Beckoning Constance to follow her, Georgie entered her

sitting room and retrieved her keys from a drawer in her cherrywood writing desk. Constance placed the octagonal shaped box of mahogany, inlaid with satinwood roses, on the leather blotter. After unlocking the box, Georgie measured out a small amount of the fragrant dried herbs and flowers, and deposited them carefully in a clean, dry tumbler. "Infuse the mixture in hot water for a few minutes only," she said, as Constance took the glass from her, "otherwise it will be bitter."

"Yes, Your Grace." Her maid curtsied deeply, her head bowed. "Thank you, Your Grace."

"Think nothing of it, Constance," replied Georgie. "And if there is anything else I can assist you with, anything at all, please let me know. As I mentioned earlier, I am quite happy to send for my physician."

Constance curtsied again. "You are much too kind, ma'am. But I think the tisane will help immensely."

Georgie inclined her head. "I'm sure it will too."

Constance took her leave and Georgie retired to her bedchamber. Leaning against the doorframe, she eyed her bed without a single ounce of enthusiasm. Her head ached and her eyes felt gritty. She might be weary beyond measure, but she doubted she would be able to sleep at all between now and the pre-dawn hour. Not when her heart clenched and her stomach twisted into tight, painful knots every time she imagined Rafe and Craven on the dueling field, pistols aimed straight at each other's chests.

She shuddered and retired to the fireside to try and find some solace in the pages of *Emma* until it was time to dress.

CHAPTER 21

Battersea-fields, South Bank of the Thames
16ᵗʰ November 1816

"Do you think he will put in an appearance?"

Rafe glanced at Phillip. In the weak, gray light of early morning he could scarcely make out his friend's features. "I would say so," he answered in a low voice, his breath a white cloud in the frigid air. "He was certainly baying for blood last night. And he doesn't seem the type who would let go of an opportunity to exact revenge. Aside from that, he's desperate to collect on what he thinks he's owed. For a man with no coin and no honor, that is a powerful incentive indeed."

"How good a shot do you suppose he is?"

Rafe shrugged as he threw his friend a wolfish grin. "We'll soon find out. At any rate, I rather doubt I will require the services of your surgeon, Mr. Emerson." He nodded toward the dour-faced man waiting with Cowan by a nearby copse of plane trees before adding, "I can't say the same for Craven."

His flippant response was at odds with how he truly felt. His muscles were tense, his senses were sharpened, his entire body was primed for action. He certainly wasn't nervous. His resolve and control were as hard and cold as the frost-bitten ground beneath his feet. At long last, Craven would pay for what he had done to Georgie. When the moment came to fire his pistol, Rafe's hand would be steady and his aim true.

Phillip shook his head. "Your sang-froid always amazes me, my friend. Do you think Craven will be content to agree to your preferred terms?"

"Perhaps," Rafe replied with another shrug. "Craven's destruction at the hand of his creditors is imminent so whether we duel until first-blood, or until one of us can no longer stand, it matters little to me. And as terrible as it sounds, I must say, the idea of him being wounded appeals to me no end. The more pain he suffers, the better."

They had discussed each of the options last night at Latimer House. Whilst Rafe would like nothing more than to put a bullet in the blackguard's heart, he also wasn't willing to forfeit his home in England when he'd only just returned. His dream of sharing a full, happy life with Georgie until they were both old and gray with a surfeit of children and grand-children was far too beguiling a prospect to abandon. Especially for a scum-dweller like Craven.

"If you've pushed him too far though..." Phillip's tone was grim. "Now that I think on it, he might very well be suicidal —" He broke off at the sound of a carriage door slamming in the distance.

Within a few minutes, the bulky forms of two men in greatcoats emerged from the shadows and rising mist. Craven and his second. As they drew closer, Rafe noted the other man was Lord Bolton, the nobleman he'd seen with Craven in Gentleman Jackson's two days ago. A third man—plainly dressed, but clearly a manservant of some kind—trailed behind.

Phillip approached Bolton, and whilst the two went about

the usual business of discussing terms, inspecting and loading the dueling pistols, and marking out the ground, Rafe took the opportunity to observe Craven; there was now sufficient light to see that other man's complexion was pallid beneath his arrogant manner. He might pretend indifference, but he was clearly nervous. His hands shook ever so slightly when he removed his gloves and his movements were clumsy as he shrugged off his coat and handed it to the manservant.

Unshaven and clothed in the same stained and rumpled garments he had worn last night, he was a pathetic mess. Rafe strongly suspected that he was still a little bit drunk.

A better man would have called a halt to the duel for that reason alone, but Rafe wasn't that man. In fact, he had to turn away in order to hide his smile.

Phillip's voice carried clearly across the field. "In the absence of any apology being issued by either party, Bolton and I have settled the terms. The duel will conclude when one of you can no longer stand. Are you in agreeance, gentlemen?"

Craven's upper lip curled into a snarl. "So be it."

Rafe inclined his head. "Agreed."

Cowan proffered the polished walnut dueling box and Craven and Rafe approached to select their weapons. Light and perfectly balanced, fashioned from steel and walnut, the highly prized brace of Manton pistols were in fact, Rafe's. Neither Craven nor Bolton had brought a set. It wouldn't have surprised Rafe in the least if Craven had needed to pawn his at some stage.

Their choices made, Craven and Rafe stepped away with pistols in hand and crossed the frozen ground to their appointed positions.

Rafe couldn't suppress another predatory smile as he turned to salute his gray-faced opponent. With only fourteen yards separating them, felling Craven would be like child's play.

Georgie clutched at the leather strap above her head, trying to maintain her balance as their carriage clattered at breakneck speed over the rickety wooden boards of the Battersea Bridge. Peering out the window, she could barely make out the dull, pewter surface of the Thames through the drifting shroud of mist. Dawn wasn't far off. A brooding bank of low clouds along the eastern horizon would obscure the moment the sun actually rose, but the bruised-purple sky above was already growing lighter by the second.

Just as Georgie's panic was rising by the second. Her heart raced faster than the matched team of bays pulling their carriage.

"How much farther?" she asked Jonathon once they'd cleared the bridge. To her chagrin, he'd fallen asleep during the early hours, and she'd had difficulty rousing him so now they were running late. "If we don't reach Rafe in time..." She bit her lip hard, unable to continue. She wouldn't cry. There was no time for tears. Of course, she couldn't care less about Lord Craven, but if Rafe was wounded or worse... No, she refused to contemplate her worst fear, that Rafe might actually be killed. The thought of living without him was, quite simply, unbearable.

Jonathon leaned forward and patted her knee. "Try not to lose heart, Georgie-bean. I estimate we'll be there in five minutes at this rate. Just in time. We should be passing the village very soon, and a mile on is an inn, The Red House. The duel will take place in a field not far from there."

Georgie nodded, not trusting herself to speak. She dare not ask Jonathon how he knew the precise location of the relatively remote dueling site. There were some things she'd rather not know about her brother. She pushed her tumbledown curls out of her eyes—she'd dressed without Constance's assistance and hadn't bothered to do all that much with her hair other than shove it beneath a velvet cap—before returning her gaze to the landscape outside. Sure enough, up ahead was the village of Battersea. It passed by in a flash and then they were hurtling along a frozen, rutted causeway with the Thames on one side and a haphazard network of ditches, marshy fields, and reed-beds on the other.

If Georgie wasn't so frightened for Rafe, she might have been frightened for herself and Jonathon.

"There's the inn." Jonathon rapped on the wall of the carriage with his silver topped cane and Benson, their driver, immediately slowed the horses. They entered an overgrown field and followed a rough, muddy path before finally drawing to a halt beside an unkept hawthorn hedge. Four other carriages—all unmarked—were also lined up at various intervals bedside the path. As Jonathon alighted, Georgie gathered up the woolen skirts of her cobalt blue carriage gown and then jumped down after him. She didn't have time to wait for the stairs.

Heart in her mouth, she raced after Jonathon toward a wooden stile in the hedgerow. He helped her to clamber over, and then they dashed headlong across another short expanse of mist-shrouded grass into a dense copse of golden leaved plane trees.

Panting, her blood thundering in her ears, Georgie stumbled to a halt when Jonathon bade her to.

He put a finger to his lips and pointed through the trees to the field beyond. "Best not to startle anyone," he whispered against her ear.

Georgie nodded and desperately tried to calm her breathing. A breeze stirred the yellowing leaves in the branches above them and carried snatches of conversation to her. Male voices.

Her heart drummed a wild tattoo inside her chest as she began to edge her way forward. Thankfully, the damp carpet of leaves beneath her booted feet deadened the sound of her footfalls.

"In the absence of any apology being issued by either party, Bolton and I have settled the terms. The duel will conclude when one of you can no longer stand. Are you in agreeance, gentlemen?"

Phillip. She recognized his voice immediately. Then she heard another man—it had to be Craven—and then Rafe, respond.

"So be it."

"Agreed."

Thank God they are not going to fight to the death. But what, in Heaven's name, could she say or do to stay both their hands completely?

"We're not too late," Georgie whispered over her shoulder to Jonathon. When he didn't respond, she turned around...and discovered he was lying face down in the leaves a few feet away.

What on earth? Fear spiked through her as she sucked in a breath. "Jo—"

An arm—a man's arm—snaked around her throat and her head was pushed roughly forward. His grip as unrelenting as a hangman's noose, the man choked her. Cut off all her air. Her vision blurred and her head swam.

Dashkov? Oh, please no. No.

White-hot anger and terror burst to life inside Georgie, lending her momentary strength. She tried to scream. Clawed and kicked and thrashed with all her might, but it was to no avail.

As dark oblivion engulfed her, her last thought was of Rafe.

"Gentlemen. Take up your positions," instructed Phillip from the edge of the copse. "When the handkerchief falls," he indicated Cowan, "you may fire your first shot."

Rafe angled his body in a side-on stance and raised his pistol. His pulse remained steady, his breathing even as he cocked his weapon and adjusted his aim a fraction.

There was no doubt in his heart or mind that what he was about to do was just, in every sense of the word.

This was for Georgie.

Even though Rafe focused on Craven, he kept Cowan and the white kerchief within the corner of his vision. Craven also stood side-on; his eyes were narrowed in concentration, his arm shook ever so slightly.

Phillip, Bolton and the manservant retreated to a safe distance with Mr. Emerson. As expected, the surgeon turned his back.

The handkerchief fell.

Rafe fired and straightaway, Craven dropped to the ground, screaming and clutching his thigh.

Bolton rushed over. Emerson followed, the manservant at his heels.

Ignoring the commotion surrounding Craven, Phillip crossed the field toward him. "Nicely done," he murmured when he reached Rafe's side. He glanced at his pocket watch. "His two minutes will be up soon enough. It doesn't look like he will be taking his shot after all."

Rafe shrugged. "That was the plan. I don't think I've hit anything of vital importance. Although it will still hurt like the very devil."

Phillip's mouth kicked into a smile. "Good."

"Yes." Glancing back over to Craven, who still groaned and writhed in agony, Rafe felt not one iota of remorse. But there was definitely satisfaction. "My work here is done."

He tucked his pistol into an inner pocket of his black,

woolen redingote and turned to leave the field, heading for the copse and his carriage.

Then Cowan shouted, "Milords! Look out!"

Instinct and experience triggered an immediate response. As Rafe dove into the grass, dragging Phillip down with him, there was a crack beside his right ear.

Bloody fucking hell. He couldn't believe it! Did Craven actually just attempt to shoot him when his back was turned?

A blistering wave of anger surged and he shot to his feet. Of all the low, cowardly, dishonorable acts he had ever encountered, this had to be one of the worst.

Rafe charged toward Craven. Bolton put up his hands to ward him off, but Rafe simply thrust him aside.

"You utter, sniveling, bastard," he growled, yanking the smoking pistol out of Craven's grasp.

Emerson raised his blood-covered hands in a gesture of appeal. "Please my lord, I must protest!"

"In a minute. I desire a word with Lord Craven."

Craven closed his eyes and rolled his head away. "I'm down for Christ's sake," he rasped. His breathing was erratic, his face ashen with pain. "You can't do this."

"I think you and I both know that we're well past playing by the rules, Craven."

Craven spat into the grass at Rafe's feet. "Fuck off. Leave...me be."

"Not a chance." Rafe gripped the earl by the hair and forced his head around to face him. "I should have shot you dead. Do you know why?"

Craven's pale, bloodless lips twisted into a rictus of a smile. "Why...the fuck...would I care?"

Rafe tightened his grip a little more. "What you want or care about doesn't matter to me. At all. But I *do* want you to know this. This—all of this—this duel, your failure at the gaming table last night, and your ultimate ruin—it is retribution, pure and simple. Retribution I'm exacting on behalf of another for a crime you committed a decade ago."

Craven's chest shook as if he was attempting to laugh, but he couldn't harness enough breath to produce any sound. "Which one?" he eventually gasped. "And to whom?"

Georgie's name hovered on Rafe's lips, but as he stared into Craven's pain-glazed eyes, he decided he did not want to say it.

Craven didn't deserve to know.

But most of all, he didn't want the worthless swine thinking about the woman he loved.

Rafe released his hold and stepped away. "As you were, Mr. Emerson," he said quietly, his iron-hard control back in place.

He turned on his heel and strode away.

It was time to go back to Georgie.

He smiled to himself, wondering if she was still abed, and if she was, how he would go about pleasuring her. And how her smile would reach her beautiful blue eyes when he told her he loved her.

However, all thoughts of making love to Georgie fled the moment Rafe entered the copse. Cowan called out to him again, his tone urgent. "Milord. Over 'ere."

Rafe located him in the gloom a few yards away, kneeling beside Jonathon, who sat with his back against the trunk of a plane tree, his head between his legs.

"What the hell are you doing here? What's happened?" Rafe demanded. Something was wrong. Very wrong.

Cowan ran a hand down his face, and the cold foreboding in the pit of Rafe's stomach increased ten-fold.

"Looks like someone's given Sir Jonathon a nasty whack on the skull wiv that." Cowan nodded toward a sizeable rock lying in a nearby pile of leaves. It was streaked with red. "He's only just come to."

Sure enough, Rafe could see a bloody gash on the back of

Jonathon's head. His gut told him this wasn't the work of common footpads. He dropped to his knees and squeezed Jonathon's shoulder. "Winterbourne. What's going on? Who did this?"

Jonathon winced as he lifted his head. He was as pale as the linen of his cravat. "I don't know... I didn't see. Where's Georgie?"

Panic seared through Rafe's chest. "Georgie's here?"

Cowan spoke. "I 'aven't seen 'er Grace, milord."

Jonathon swallowed, his face a sickly shade of green. "She came with me... She found out about the duel and insisted we follow you...to stop you." He grabbed Rafe's sleeve. "Are you saying she's not here? Oh, sweet Jesus... Don't tell me Dashkov's taken her."

"I pray to God he hasn't." Tamping down the urge to rail at Jonathon for both his loose tongue and rampant stupidity, Rafe sprang to his feet. "Cowan. Call Lord Maxwell. Start looking for any signs of the duchess and Dashkov." He addressed Jonathon again even though it looked like he was about to lose the contents of his stomach. "When did you get here? Were you followed?"

"God," Jonathon clutched his head. "I'm not sure. I'm sorry. I'm having trouble recalling—" He leaned sideways and vomited into the leaves.

Leaving him to it—he obviously wasn't going to be much use in his present state—Rafe ran his eyes over the surrounding ground carpeted in damp, browning leaves. Several yards away, something blue caught his eye.

He sprinted over and scooped it up. A blue velvet cap. *Georgie's.* It had to be.

His blood froze when he saw a white card tucked inside. Herr Maximilian Scherzfrage's card.

Something was scrawled on the back in red ink. A taunt.

A threat.

Have you pieced the puzzle together yet?
Must dash.

Fuck. This was Rafe's worst nightmare coming to life. But he didn't have time for fear. Or guilt. Not when Georgie's life hung in the balance. Rafe closed his eyes for a moment and let black, murderous rage take over. It pounded through his veins, washing away all traces of terror, clearing his mind, hardening his resolve.

Dashkov would die for this.

But first, he had to find Georgie.

Before it was too late.

CHAPTER 22

Somewhere in London...

Her head throbbed. Pounded.

Her jaw ached and it hurt to swallow. There was something—a rag—jammed in her mouth and she couldn't speak. Couldn't move, couldn't breathe...

Oh, God!

Georgie jerked, her head bobbing like a puppet's when the strings were cut. Fear burned through her veins and acrid nausea swelled as full consciousness returned and her memory came flooding back.

Dashkov has me.

She prized her heavy eyelids open and the room swam before her eyes. She recognized this hideous feeling. Knew it well. She'd been drugged.

But worse than that, she'd been kidnapped. Gagged, bound and tied to a chair in a strange, shabby room that could be anywhere.

Panic flared again. The pace of her breathing increased, grew frantic as she tried to suck in enough air through her nose. The gag tasted foul and another wave of nausea hit. *Oh, dear Lord.* She was going to be sick. But she would choke. *No, no, no.*

Georgie closed her eyes and focused on trying to control her breathing, to swallow down her terror and to concentrate on thoughts that would help. *Rafe will find me. I will be all right. I am strong. If I keep calm and I use my wits, I can survive this.*

As her breathing slowed, and her nausea abated a little, she opened her eyes again and tried to make her foggy brain work, to take in her surroundings, to assess where she might be, and what, if anything, she could do to escape. Straining against her painfully tight bonds of coarse rope proved futile. Bound at the wrists, ankles and around her torso to a heavy oak, Jacobean style chair, she could barely move anything except her head.

She was alone as far as she could tell; positioned in the middle of the room, she couldn't see behind her. Disconcerting to think someone might be watching her... She couldn't hear anyone else, only her own shallow breathing, but still...

She shivered and directed her attention elsewhere.

Her first impression that the room was shabby had been correct. It appeared to be a small parlor of some kind that had clearly seen better days. She faced an empty, filthy fireplace, a horsehair sofa with torn upholstery, and a scratched and chipped occasional table. Moth-eaten, rust colored curtains hung drunkenly from a window to her left. Only partly drawn, weak, gray light filtered through the grimy panes onto the bare, dusty floorboards. The only view afforded to her was a grubby, brown brick wall. She sensed the room was a few stories up and adjacent to an alley. Noises—voices calling and the insistent clatter of hooves and cartwheels—reached her easily. *A London alley?*

Dear, God, Georgie hoped so.

It was difficult to tell how much time had passed between when Dashkov had taken her and now, but she guessed it had only been a few hours. Beneath her nausea, her stomach grumbled and she was conscious of the call of nature, but the feeling wasn't too strong. Yet.

Georgie grimaced. It wouldn't do to dwell on that.

A hazy recollection of waking up in an unfamiliar carriage, trussed up like a Christmas goose, suddenly surfaced in her mind. She'd tried to scream but the baron—if that's who it was—had forced her to drink a bitter tasting concoction of laudanum and heaven knew what else. She also vaguely recalled they'd clattered over the Battersea Bridge before she'd passed out again. So perhaps they were in London. Which meant Rafe and Jonathon would find her.

Then she remembered. Jonathon lying face down in a pile of leaves. Her breath caught. *Please God, let him be all right. If Jonathon were dead...* Tears scalded her eyes and she snuffled awkwardly around the gag. Even crying was impossibly difficult.

And what of Rafe?

What if he'd been injured or killed as she had feared from the very start?

And if Rafe and Jonathon were both dead, who would come for her?

A muffled sob escaped Georgie as wave after wave of painful despair coursed through her heart. This couldn't be the end. For her, or those dearest to her.

Offering up a silent prayer to heaven, she vowed she would do whatever it took to save herself.

Time dragged on and despite her distress and physical discomfort, she eventually succumbed to the lingering effects of the laudanum and slid into a fitful doze.

Then something roused her. A metallic rattle and scrape. A key turning in a lock.

Her heart crashing against her ribs, Georgie raised her head and turned toward the sound, ears straining. The door was somewhere behind her, out of her line of sight.

Who was on the other side?

And if it was the man she thought of as Baron Dashkov, what in God's name did he want?

The door opened, clicked shut, and the key scraped in the lock again. Heavy footsteps sounded on the wooden floor and her heart leapt into a full gallop.

Dashkov, then.

Georgie tried but failed to stifle a whimper when her captor stroked a hand lightly down the back of her hair. Threading his fingers through the tangled locks at her nape, he then caressed the sensitive skin beneath, raising gooseflesh.

"Shhh, *moya dorogaya*," he crooned beside her ear. She recognized the deep, guttural tones of the man who'd crashed into her outside Latimer House and had then tried to abduct her at knife point in Berkeley Square. The man who'd called her *whore*. "This part will not hurt."

Terror snaked its way down Georgie's spine, making her shiver uncontrollably. *What is he going to do to me?* She didn't understand. She didn't even know the man, had never done anything to deserve this cruel treatment.

He was clearly mad.

She closed her eyes and bit down on the gag to stop herself from making another sound. She wouldn't give the monster the satisfaction of seeing her cry, whatever happened next.

The man suddenly gripped and twisted her hair, giving it such a vicious tug, her eyes watered. And then something cold and metallic touched the back of Georgie's neck. A blade.

Oh, no. Please, God, no!

There was a snipping sound, the sound of scissors, and a

lock of her hair fell onto her shoulder and then into her lap. He was cutting off her hair! All of the long curls that Rafe loved so much.

Despite Georgie's resolution not to cry, a tear escaped. Whether she wept with relief or sorrow she really had no idea. Why? Why would Dashkov do such a horrible thing? An act meant to disfigure and debase her?

She'd been callously abused and humiliated a decade ago, and she really didn't want to go through anything like that again.

But there was nothing she could do. Nothing at all.

Another tear slid down her check, then another. *It's only your hair, Georgie* she told herself. *It will grow back.*

But then Dashkov had said '*this* part will not hurt', which begged the question, what about the other parts? What else was he going to do?

Georgie thrust the thought aside. She didn't want to think about it. If she did, *she* might go mad.

The cutting ceased. Cold air drifted over the back of her neck. Her hair had been completely hacked off at the nape.

Then another whisper gusted over her ear. "Do you know who I am, Your Grace?" the man asked. His breath smelled sour—like stale cabbages and onions. Small beer. Georgie tried not to shudder. "Did your lover solve the puzzle?"

She hesitated, not sure how to respond until Dashkov squeezed the back of her neck in a vice-like grip. "Answer me, *blyad*. Do you know my name?"

Georgie nodded and the pressure on her neck eased. Became a caress again.

"Then you know why I do this. He told you about our history, did he not? What he did to my poor Anna."

It *was* Baron Dashkov. Rafe had been right.

Georgie nodded again. The baron might be insane, but the

317

motivation behind her kidnapping was as clear as crystal. Revenge. An eye for an eye. Just as Rafe had suspected.

But how far would Dashkov go?

Will he actually kill me to punish Rafe?

Dashkov suddenly stepped in front of her, and she jumped in her seat, her startled gasp muffled by the gag.

She'd never seen him properly before, up so close with his face fully exposed by the light of day. He might be tall and well-made beneath his brown woolen frock coat, but his cheeks were gaunt and his jaw was covered in dark stubble. His dark hair was unruly, in need of a cut. He appeared to be older than Rafe—perhaps about forty—and he would have been attractive but for his unkept appearance and the wild look in his pale gray eyes, the dark shadows beneath. And the sneering smile.

"I've made you cry, *moya dorogaya*," he said softly, bending down and stroking her cheek. A mocking caress. "Do not worry. I will send this," he held up her lopped off curls, "to your Lord Markham."

If he is alive... No, don't think that way, Georgiana Dudley. She swallowed past her tight, aching throat. Then nodded.

Dashkov seemed to like that as his smile widened. "Very good. I will leave you now. But never fear, I shall be back before too long. For the next part."

The next part? Did he mean to take something else away from her? Her clothing? Surely he couldn't mean anything else. It didn't bear thinking about.

The door shut, the key turned in the lock, and Georgie let the tears flow unheeded as she struggled to loosen her bonds again.

And she prayed.

∽

Dudley House, Hanover Square
Eleven o'clock in the morning...

Rafe knew the news wasn't what he wanted to hear as soon as Cowan entered the library at Dudley House.

"I'm sorry, milord," he said, cap in hand, his tone as grave as an undertaker's. "Your men and I 'ave not been able to dredge up a single clue these last few 'ours."

"Any word from Lord Maxwell?" Phillip was working with John Townsend, the former head of the Bow Street Runners, helping him to coordinate the London based search. A peeress of the realm had been abducted and every effort would be expended, no expense spared.

Cowan shook his head. "No, milord. It seems there ain't a trace to be found of Baron Dashkov or the duchess. But we will keep lookin'. No stone left unturned 'an all tha'."

Rafe ground his teeth together with frustration. Nevertheless, he gave Cowan a curt nod of thanks. It wasn't his fault that nothing helpful had come to light.

No, the blame for this entire nightmarish debacle lay squarely at his own feet. "Is Lumsden still questioning the servants?"

"Yes, milord. Reed is 'elping out too. There ain't many to go, so I might lend a 'and, if that's all right wif you. An' you never know..."

"Yes, of course." Rafe replied. "One must never give up hope."

But as the door shut behind Cowan, he did indeed feel there was precious little hope.

He closed his eyes as insidious despair suddenly broke through his carefully constructed armor of icy composure. *Shit.* The thought of Georgie in pain...of being tortured... He clenched his fists so hard his knuckles cracked.

Stop it, Markham. Buck up. Keep calm and think.

Georgie's fate wouldn't be the same as Solange's, not if he could help it.

Somehow he would find a way to save her. His duchess.

He crossed over to Jonathon's desk and poured himself a cognac, his chosen remedy to keep his head clear. Jonathon was currently indisposed with an abominable headache and had quite rightly taken to his bed. Although it was fortunate indeed that he hadn't actually been killed, now wasn't the time to worry about Georgie's brother.

Taking a large swig of his drink, Rafe began to sift through the scraps of information they *did* have, which at this stage, was nothing substantial at all.

Dashkov was proving to be far too clever—not new intelligence by any means; the man had been alternately taunting and evading Rafe and all of his men for weeks now. This morning he'd struck hard and fast like the true snake he was, before disappearing without a trace.

The most disconcerting part was, Rafe sensed Dashkov would only rear his ugly head again when he wanted to share what he had done to Georgie. To torment and to gloat. The message on his calling card was *very* clear in that regard. The sick bastard might be torturing Georgie right at this very moment and there was nothing on earth that he could do about it.

Rafe closed his eyes and pinched the bridge of his nose. *Think, man.* There was something he was missing, some link, a puzzle piece.

Dashkov had always been one step ahead. He always seemed to anticipate both his and Georgie's movements.

This morning was a case in point. Barely anyone knew about the duel, and that it would be in a location as remote as Battersea-fields.

But by all accounts Dashkov had been there, lying in wait for

Georgie and Jonathon. Benson, Dudley House's coachman, had reported that there were four other carriages in the field adjacent to the dueling ground when they arrived. Rafe had traveled with Phillip in his carriage; the surgeon, Mr. Emerson had arrived in his own conveyance; and Craven had traveled with Bolton.

So who had taken the fourth carriage to Battersea-fields?

It must have been Dashkov.

Benson had also reported that after Georgie and Jonathon had disappeared behind the hedgerow, he'd left Perkins, the footman, to mind the carriage whilst he'd walked back to The Red House Inn to purchase a pint of small beer and a crumpet. When he'd returned, the fourth mystery carriage had gone. He hadn't thought anything of it at the time. Not until the alarm was raised that Sir Jonathon had been attacked and the duchess had been kidnapped.

Perkins, at one point during Benson's absence, had gone into the bushes to relieve himself and had not noticed anything untoward either.

The other coach drivers had been as equally unhelpful. Lord Bolton's man had fallen asleep in his seat, and Mr. Emerson's man had been attending to the traces and back straps on one of the horses when the other coach had driven off. The only other attendant footman was Lord Bolton's, and he had been assisting his master on the dueling field.

As expected, Jonathon didn't recall a single damn thing.

Which meant Georgie could be anywhere in, or outside of London. It was like looking for the proverbial needle in a haystack.

Rafe was just reloading his dueling pistol and another barreled flintlock—it paid to be prepared for any circumstance —when there came another knock at the door.

At his bidding, Cowan entered and his expression was so grave, Rafe was immediately filled with a sense of foreboding all over again. Especially when he noticed that Cowan was holding a parcel.

"It's addressed to you and Sir Jonathon, milord." He placed the package very carefully on the oak desk then stepped back. "An urchin delivered it to Perkins, not one minute ago. Lumsden is questionin' the lad, but I don't think he'll get much out of 'im."

Rafe took a deep breath and stepped forward. As he'd expected, red ink had been used. The handwriting was undoubtedly Dashkov's.

He found a letter opener and sliced through the wrappings. Beneath the brown paper and string was a plain wooden box. A plain sheet of folded parchment lay on top.

Rafe snatched it up.

The first piece.

His heart hammering, he lifted the lid and didn't know whether to sigh with relief or curse the heavens.

A large cluster of long, soft brown curls lay inside. Georgie's hair.

Sweet Jesus. Dashkov was clearly insane.

Cowan cleared his throat. "What is it, milord, if you don't mind me askin'?"

Rafe pushed the box toward him and Cowan paled.

"We need to act quickly," Rafe said; somehow his voice held steady. "If we don't, there will be more parcels."

Cowan nodded. "Yes, milord. I'll make sure the men—"

Another knock sounded and Lumsden entered without waiting for a summons. "My lord, a word if you would." His expression was sober but Rafe detected a decided glint of excitement in the young man's eyes.

"Go on," he prompted, not daring to hope that this might be the missing piece.

Lumsden closed the door and took a few steps closer. "Her Grace's lady's maid, Miss Constance Lovedale, might be able to shed some light on the situation at hand. At two o'clock this morning, the night footman witnessed Miss Lovedale leaving via the servants' entrance, and she didn't return home until an hour and a half later. I've attempted to question her, but she became very agitated and teary. She says she won't speak to anyone but you, my lord."

Whatever Miss Lovedale had to say, Rafe would listen. "Bring her in."

The young woman was indeed tearful and trembling like a leaf when she entered the room and took a seat at Rafe's direction. He was familiar with her; had passed her in the hallways of Dudley House many times.

Georgie had always spoken highly of her.

He leaned his hip against Jonathon's desk and folded his arms. "I believe you wanted to speak with me, Miss Lovedale," he said as gently as he could. "That you may have some information regarding Her Grace's kidnapping."

The maid dabbed at her red-rimmed eyes with a wrinkled kerchief. "Yes... Yes, I might have." She bit her lip then took a shuddering breath. "It's all my fault, my lord. And I've been so, so frightened. For...for weeks if truth be told." She twisted the kerchief in her hands and her words began to tumble out so quickly, Rafe could barely keep up. "I... I had no idea that what I was doing would lead to this. I knew it was wrong, but I kept telling myself it couldn't do any harm, not really. But then, what else could I do?" She looked at him beseechingly, her large hazel eyes glazed with tears and her bottom lip wobbling.

Rafe tried not to lose his patience. A gentle, sympathetic approach was clearly required. "Miss Lovedale, I am grateful you feel you can confide in me, but I'm afraid you are going to have to speak more plainly."

"I'm sorry." A tear dripped onto the girl's cheek and she sniffed. "I hardly know where to begin..."

Rafe prompted her. "You said this all began some weeks ago. That you've been frightened. What happened?"

"A man. A foreign man. I don't know his name. He...he accosted me in the street one day when I was completing some errands for the duchess."

Dashkov. Rafe should have guessed the man would go to any lengths to carry out his warped plan of revenge. Anticipation thrumming through his veins, he asked, "What did he say to you?"

"He told me I must give him an account of the duchess's daily schedule, every single day—her appointments, social engagements, excursions, anticipated visitors. Everything. Of course, I said no. I would never, ever do such a thing, give a complete stranger that sort of private information about my employer. The duchess is the loveliest woman... Oh—" Constance pushed her kerchief against her mouth and screwed up her eyes as if attempting to stem another flood of tears.

Rafe gave the girl a few moments to compose herself. This *was* the missing piece. It explained how Dashkov had been able to keep track of Georgie's movements without being detected. But he needed more details. "If you didn't want to give this man the information he asked for, why did you, Miss Lovedale? Did he threaten you?"

The maid's eyes widened. "Yes," she breathed. "How... how did you know?"

"I know who the man is and his nature. He is Russian. A baron by the name of Dashkov." Rafe softened his tone. "If you don't mind my asking, how did he threaten you?"

"It wasn't me that he threatened so much. It was my family," she said, her voice quivering. "My sister, Faith—she's widowed with a young son—and my younger brother, Thomas who lives with them. Faith owns a milliner's shop in

Grafton Street, just off Bond Street. Her Grace purchases most of her hats from there."

Rafe frowned. He knew the shop. Had been there with Georgie. "What did he say he would do?"

Constance bit her lip and her eyes filled with tears again. "Well, he had already done something. Something terrible. The day before he spoke to me in the street, my sister found her cat..." She sucked in shaky breath. "Her cat had been slaughtered, cut open. Gutted like a fish and left on the doorstep at the back of the shop. My sister lives upstairs so if one of the boys had seen it..." Constance shuddered and her face grew as pale as her white linen kerchief. "The man— Dashkov, you say?—he said that if I didn't do as he instructed, then my sister and the boys would end up just like the cat. And...and I believed him. I'm so, so sorry, my lord."

The maid began crying in earnest again, but Rafe didn't have time for her tears right now. Not when he was so close to finding out something truly useful. "Miss Lovedale, I can see this is difficult for you. And believe me, I understand that you felt you had no other option than to comply with this man's demands. However, I need to know more."

Rafe offered Constance his own handkerchief as hers was clearly sodden. She accepted it with thanks, and after she'd blown her nose and swiped at her eyes, he continued with his questioning. "You mentioned you give Dashkov an account of the duchess's schedule, every day. How do you do this? Do you meet with him somewhere? Does he send someone to collect it?"

She shook her head. "No. My brother, Tom—he's twelve —he's been coming to Dudley House very early, well before sunrise, and I give the schedule to him at the servants' door."

Rafe tried to keep the sharp note of impatience out of his voice. He was getting so close to the information he needed to find Georgie, he could feel it. "And how does Tom get it to Dashkov?"

"He delivers it to an address in Marylebone. Pushes it under the door. It's only about a mile from here and Tom is fast, being a link boy and all. But if something happens, a change in Her Grace's schedule, I have to send a message straightaway. Or...or there are consequences. For instance, the last time I failed to provide the correct schedule, a brick was thrown through my sister's shop window. And another time, just last week, my nephew found a beheaded rat by the door. Last night, I know that I shouldn't have eavesdropped on Her Grace, but I could tell something was afoot. When I heard she was going to Battersea-fields at first light, I knew I had to get word to Dashkov, or something bad would happen again. Perhaps something even worse than dead cats and rats and broken windows. So I delivered the note myself. And I knocked very hard on the door to make sure the man, Dashkov, knew it was there. Please forgive me, my lord. I know I should have come to you, or Sir Jonathon, or gone to the Bow Street Runners, but I was too terrified, and—"

The maid was rambling and close to tears again, so Rafe cut in. "Miss Lovedale, you just said you've been to this man's residence. Do you know the exact address in Marylebone?"

"Why, yes. It's number 14, Gloucester Place Mews."

Hallelujah! Rafe strode to the door and called Cowan and Lumsden. Could it really be that easy? Could Dashkov really have taken Georgie to an address that was so close to Hanover Square?

God, he prayed with everything he had within him that it was so.

CHAPTER 23

Georgie would have dozed all day if she could have possibly managed it; then she wouldn't have to face the waking nightmare she was presently in. But the unrelenting pain radiating through her body was reaching a pitch that could only be described as intolerable—a state not conducive to sleep at all. Her back and shoulders and *derriere* ached, her throat was as dry as a desert, and her forehead pounded every time she moved her head. She hadn't noticed it earlier when she'd first awoken, but the room was bitterly cold. Her fingers were frozen, her feet like blocks of ice. She couldn't stop shivering. How ironic that her soubriquet, the Ice Duchess, seemed very apt at the present moment.

Her only consolation was that Dashkov hadn't returned.

Every time her thoughts strayed in that direction, she quaked even harder, her stomach churning with sheer terror. Focusing on what she could do to save herself seemed to be the only way to keep herself sane.

She'd rubbed her wrists raw trying to loosen the ropes, but they hadn't budged in the slightest. If she could dislodge her gag and call out, someone might hear her. Dashkov was clearly concerned about that. The intermittent sounds of human activity in the alley below were both comforting and frustrating.

Yes, if she could just get the blasted gag off, she would scream and scream and scream.

Someone would definitely hear her.

Help would arrive.

Oh, please, God, send help.

Send Rafe.

A vision of him, handsome and strong, capable and fearless—a man like no other—sprang into her mind. Since Rafe had entered her life, she had so much to hope for. To live for. A future filled with love and laughter and untold joy.

She had faith in him. He had come through the duel unscathed, and he was searching for her at this very moment. This couldn't be the end.

For Rafe and herself, she wouldn't give up.

Her gaze darted to the window. Perhaps if she were closer, she could attract someone's attention across the street. There was a window opposite this one, she was sure of it. She began to rock and wiggle in the chair and it moved a little on the wooden floor. *Yes.* She applied herself to the task with vigor, jostling and jiggling as hard as she could, until she was sweating and panting with exertion. But after a few minutes, she realized it was a futile exercise. The chair was too heavy and her bonds too tight. All she'd managed to do was shuffle around in a half circle so that now she was facing toward the door with the window behind her.

Tears of frustration welled, burning her eyes and blurring her vision. Hope faded and cold, dark fear returned to keep her company once more.

Please find me, Rafe.

The heavy clomp of footsteps on the stairs and then in the hallway outside made Georgie start so violently, her chair moved again. Her gaze riveted on the door, she held her breath.

Not Dashkov. Please, God, not Dashkov.

The key grated in the lock and Georgie clamped her eyes shut. She was too terrified to look.

"Ah, *moya dorogaya,* I see you have been busy in my absence." She heard Dashkov cross the room. He stroked her cheek with his finger. If she could have bitten it off, she would have. "You are just like my Anna," he crooned. "Very brave. I like that about you."

Georgie forced herself to open her eyes. To give Dashkov an imploring look. She made a noise around the gag. If he removed it, even for a second...

Dashkov smiled down at her, his pale gray eyes as cold as arctic ice. "No, no, my pet. I cannot remove it. I cannot risk you making a single sound."

And that's when she saw it. The knife. The wicked-looking steel blade caught the light filtering through the window, and it was like a living thing. Winking at her.

Mocking her.

Dashkov bent forward and whispered, "Your Lord Markham ruined my beautiful Anna's face, and so I will ruin yours."

Bile rose in Georgie's throat.

She closed her eyes. She couldn't look...

Dashkov's fingers touched her ear. Pinched hard.

Oh, God save me.

∽

Hold on, Georgie. I'm coming, my love.

Pistol in hand, Rafe eyed the door of number 14, Gloucester Place Mews. The dull green paint was peeling, and the hinges and doorknob were rusted. It would be child's play breaking in.

He nodded at Cowan. "Pick the lock if you would."

While he was all for kicking down doors—and he had so much rage pounding through his veins right at this moment he would like nothing more than to do it—he didn't want to startle Dashkov into taking rash action.

As expected, the lock tumbled quickly and Cowan stepped back. "I'll keep a watch, milord, whilst you an' Lumsden check inside."

Rafe gave him a curt nod. Taking a fortifying breath, he pushed on the door.

It creaked open on its rusty hinges, revealing a dim, filthy hallway. A narrow set of stairs. A door to the right and left. He nodded at Lumsden who'd already drawn his own pistol. Together they entered and quickly checked each downstairs room, taking care not to make a sound.

The tiny room to the left was bare of furniture but the next showed definite signs of occupation. Dirty glasses, plates and food scraps littered a scratched deal table. A misshapen tallow candle and a cracked spill jar of tapers sat on the roughly hewn mantel beside a dented teapot. A pile of potatoes sat by the hearth where the remnants of a fire smoldered, and a black greatcoat hung lopsidedly off the back of a rickety wooden chair.

Rafe caught Lumsden's eye and gestured with his head. *Upstairs.*

But for the occasional creak of a floorboard, the shabby townhouse was silent as the grave as Rafe led the way to the next floor.

That did not bode well.

Like downstairs, one room was deserted whilst the other contained signs of habitation. A pallet bed, roughly made up with threadbare sheets and a scratchy woolen blanket, stood against one water-stained wall. More men's clothes were piled over the back of a worn leather armchair and spilled out of a battered traveling trunk onto the bare wooden floorboards.

"Milord," murmured Lumsden. He held out a sheaf of papers. Ivory parchment. Good quality and covered in neat, feminine handwriting.

Rafe's heart leapt.

Georgie's schedule.

This was definitely Dashkov's bolt hole.

But where the hell were Dashkov and Georgie?

Shit. Rafe blew out a breath in frustration. He was so close to finding his duchess. Of course, he could lie in wait for Dashkov, but how long would that take? The monster was probably with Georgie right now, doing God knew what to her. He crossed to the window and rested his forearm against the splintered frame, gazing out the grime-crusted pane to the alley below and the building opposite.

What next?

A movement in the window directly across from him caught his eye.

A figure. A man.

Tall and dark-haired. Broad-shouldered.

It couldn't be...

Rafe sure as hell wasn't going to wait a moment longer to find out.

He bolted down the stairs and sprinted across the mews, his pistol drawn, Lumsden close on his heels. The dull green door gave way with a single kick and then he was taking the stairs, two at a time to the floor above.

The door on the right.

Another explosive kick to the lock and the door splintered. Swung open.

And there was Georgie—his beautiful Georgie—gagged and tied to a chair, her blue eyes as wide as saucers while

Dashkov stood behind her, a maniacal grin contorting his face as he pressed a knife to her throat.

Blood welled over the blade.

Fuck the bastard.

Rafe fired and the shot hit Dashkov right between the eyes. The knife clattered to the floor and the Russian toppled backward, his head hitting the windowsill before he slumped to the floor.

It was over.

Thank, God, it was over.

~

Rafe is here. He's alive and so am I.

Georgie had never felt such sweet, blessed relief until the moment Rafe burst into the room like a furious god of vengeance. Now as he knelt before her, murmuring she was safe and that he loved her, checking the cut on her neck and using his own neck cloth to bandage it, she could barely see his adored face through the tears falling thick and fast onto her cheeks.

He removed the gag and she tried to speak. Croaked, then tried again. "Thank you," she rasped, her voice starchy from misuse and from a lack of anything to drink.

"No. Don't thank me, Georgie. Not when I brought this evil to your door."

"But—"

Rafe leaned forward and kissed her forehead. "We will talk of this later. Let me take you home. Your wounds need attending."

Georgie wasn't about to disagree with him on that score.

Once her bonds were cut, Rafe helped her to stand, but her legs buckled. Rafe immediately swept her into his arms and bore her from that most hellish of rooms, down the stairs and into a waiting carriage that had appeared, as if by magic, outside the door.

"How is Jonathon?" she asked as soon as the carriage door closed. Rafe hadn't relinquished his hold on her; draped across his lap, she had to draw back to see his face.

His mouth twitched into a wry smile. "He has an impressive lump on the back of his head, and a devilish megrim. Aside from being worried sick about you, he is all right."

Georgie nodded and relaxed into Rafe's strong arms again, her head on his shoulder. The cut on her neck stung, her wrists burned, but she didn't care. She closed her eyes and rubbed her cheek against Rafe's black coat, breathing in his familiar scent—musk and leather, and the bergamot cologne he favored. The scent of home and heaven.

Rafe's hand gently kneaded the back of her head. She had so many questions she wanted to ask him—about the duel, how he'd found her in time—but her mind began to wander. She was so, so tired.

Lulled by the steady beat of Rafe's heart and the rise and fall of his chest, she drifted to sleep.

Georgie was barely awake when Rafe carried her into her bedroom in Dudley House.

Exhaustion and the lingering effects of the laudanum made her so drowsy, she could barely keep her eyes open. She had a vague impression that Rafe kissed her forehead before he left her in the care of Dudley House's housekeeper and a chamber maid. It seemed that Constance was still indisposed. Georgie's wounds were cleaned and dressed, she was offered barley-water to ease her thirst, and then, after being helped to don a loose cotton night rail, she was tucked up in her bed.

Alone.

As Georgie slipped into sleep again, she wondered why Rafe hadn't stayed with her. *He must have business to attend to...*

She wasn't sure how long she slumbered, but when she awoke it was with a start. Momentarily disorientated, her heart pounding, she blinked at the festoons of pale blue silk forming a canopy above her head.

You are home, you are safe, she repeated to herself until her breathing and pulse returned to a pace approaching normal. *The nightmare is over.*

Sitting up gingerly, Georgie winced when the bandage at her neck pulled and the cut beneath stung. She sensed it was late in the day given how dark it was, and a quick glance at the mantel clock confirmed she was correct—it was close to five o'clock. The curtains at the windows had been drawn and a fire crackled brightly in the grate, but she didn't feel cheered by the sight.

She was unsettled. She wanted Rafe.

Scanning the cluster of chairs before the fire, and then all the dark corners of her room, her heart sank when she realized she was indeed alone. But perhaps Rafe was in the sitting room. She slid from the bed and after putting on slippers and wrapping a silk dressing gown about herself, she padded to the door.

"Jonathon," she cried, her voice cracking with emotion when she saw her brother sitting by the fire.

He jumped to his feet and within a moment had enveloped her in a gentle hug. "Oh dear Lord, Georgie-bean. What are you doing out of bed?"

"I could ask you the same question. You could have been killed." She drew back to study his face. "Tell me how you are. Does your head still hurt? What did the physician say?"

An affectionate smile lit her brother's eyes as he chucked her under the chin. "I've been officially diagnosed with a 'sore head'. Apart from a tender spot at the back, I am well." He led her over to the shepherdess chair on the hearthrug and urged her to sit. "I will ring for tea and supper, and then, if you feel up to it, you can tell me your version of this morning's events."

"So you have spoken with Rafe?" Georgie couldn't hide the note of melancholy in her voice when she added, "I'm surprised he isn't here..."

Jonathon rang the bellpull then returned to the fireside, taking the chair beside hers. "Yes, I have spoken with him..." He spoke slowly, as if choosing his words with care. "He... I understand he's had to tidy up some loose ends. With the Bow Street Runners and the Foreign Secretary's office. As you would expect."

"Of course." Georgie plucked at the lace edging of her robe. Her brother had been assaulted. She, a duchess, had been kidnapped. And a man had been shot—a former spy, a traitor to his own king and country. A mad man.

She closed her eyes and shivered as a memory of feeling utterly helpless with a knife at her throat intruded into her thoughts.

"Here, drink this, sis." Jonathon offered her a sherry, which she accepted with thanks. "As I said, if you'd like to talk about it..." He resumed his seat and then stared into the fire, leaving it entirely up to her to continue. Or not.

"I would." She had questions too, and she was certain her brother would be able to fill in the gaps. She took a large sip of sherry to bolster her courage and then began her story at the point where Jonathon had been knocked out and Dashkov had kidnapped her. By the time she'd finished, she was trembling again and Jonathon's scowl was as black as a thunder cloud.

"I could kill him for what he's put you through, Georgie."

Georgie frowned in confusion. "What? Dashkov? But he's already d—"

"No. Bloody Markham." Jonathon's blue eyes flashed with anger. "If it weren't for him—"

Georgie leaned forward and touched his sleeve. "If it weren't for him, I'd still be a sad, lonely widow, hiding myself away with nothing to look forward to. Simply existing and never really living. I don't regret anything. Not a single thing."

Jonathon's gaze sharpened on her face. "You really love him so much that you can forgive him for putting you in danger?"

"Yes. I do love him that much, Jonathon. There's nothing to forgive."

Jonathon puffed out a sigh and leaned back in his chair, his fingers steepled beneath his chin. "So be it. I was intending to give Markham his marching orders when he returned, but if he really makes you that happy, I suppose I can hold my tongue."

"Thank you. Although, there's something that's been perplexing me. How on earth did Rafe find me?"

Jonathon hesitated for a moment before responding, "I gather your maid Constance provided him with the information."

Georgie's brows shot up. "Whatever do you mean? What on earth has my maid got to do with any of this?"

"It seems Dashkov was coercing her, threatening her family with physical harm if she didn't divulge a detailed account of your daily schedule," explained Jonathon. "That's how Dashkov always seemed to be lurking in the wings, ready to pounce out at odd moments. Like this morning."

When Jonathon explained the exact nature of Dashkov's threats, Georgie felt sick with horror. Poor Constance. No wonder the girl had been looking so unwell these past few weeks. "Where is Constance now? Is she all right? She must be riddled with guilt."

"She's distraught, as you'd expect," replied Jonathon. "I've given her a few days to recuperate. She's staying with her sister and younger brother in Grafton Street."

Georgie nodded. "That's probably for the best. However, I would like to send word to her tomorrow to reassure her that her position is safe. None of this is her fault."

"Of course."

Georgie sighed. "I still don't understand how Rafe found me. How was Constance able to help?"

"Apparently Constance and her younger brother would deliver your schedule to an address in Marylebone. When Markham went to investigate, you weren't there, but then he was lucky enough to sight Dashkov through the window across the street. And you know the rest."

Indeed she did. If Rafe hadn't seen Dashkov... Georgie shuddered. No, she didn't want to think about it. Instead, she turned the conversation in another direction. "Did you hear...?" Her voice quivered so she took a fortifying breath before continuing, "What was the outcome of the duel?"

"Markham felled Craven with one shot. A leg shot, according to Phillip. But he'll live." Jonathon grimaced before adding, "More's the pity. As mad as I am at Markham, it's clear he loves you too."

A knock at the door made Georgie's heart leap, but disappointment swept through her when she saw it was only one of the maids responding to Jonathon's call. Tea, a light supper, and a bath were ordered. Jonathon also informed her that he'd summoned Madame Choffard, her usual hairdresser to attend her. The woman waited downstairs and would style Georgie's hair whenever she was ready.

"Thank you, Jonathon," Georgie said, her eyes brimming with grateful tears. "You are too good to me."

"Nonsense. You deserve to be spoiled considering every-thing that's happened." He rose and leaned down to kiss her cheek. "I'll take my leave now. I'm sure Markham won't be long." As he straightened, he ruffled what remained of her hair. "I look forward to seeing your new *a la Titus* locks in the morning. Goodnight."

As the door closed, Georgie couldn't help but wonder when Rafe would return.

The longer he stayed away, the more she began to worry that something was wrong. When he'd rescued her from Dashkov, he'd told her not to thank him. He'd even intimated that he was responsible for everything that had befallen her.

Was some odd sort of misplaced guilt keeping him away?

She frowned at the bandages on her rope-burnt wrists. *Surely not.*

A knock at the door roused her from her tangled and alto-gether useless musings and heralded the arrival of a small army of servants—a maid bearing a supper tray, another with a tea tray, and several footmen who, under the supervision of the housekeeper, set up a bath in front of the fire in her bedchamber.

After Georgie had partaken her fill of supper—a simple repast of bread and butter, and white soup—she bathed then dressed in a fresh white night rail and robe with the help of a chambermaid. At last, she was ready to receive Madame Chof-fard. Of course, appearances could be deceiving.

The moment the middle-aged French woman produced her scissors, Georgie gripped the arms of her chair steeling herself for what would happen next. As she expected, the metallic clip of the blades and the soft fall of her curls all around her brought the memory of what she'd endured earlier in the day flooding back. Her pulse raced and her whole body trembled. Turning her thoughts to Rafe and how he would smile at her helped a little.

Fortunately, Madame Choffard was efficient. Within a quarter of an hour, Georgie had a stylish new coiffure of cropped, bouncy curls.

"You have worked a miracle," Georgie declared as she examined the hairdresser's handiwork in the looking glass.

The middle-aged woman beamed at her as she fastened a pale blue ribbon about Georgie's crown. "*Bien sûr, madame.* You will be the toast of *le bon ton.*"

Georgie summoned a smile to acknowledge the compliment. However, attending Society functions was the last thing on her mind. If truth be told, she'd much prefer spending most of her time with Rafe and Rafe alone. Given it was nearing the Yuletide season, life in London would be growing quieter anyway.

She wondered where she would spend Christmas. With Rafe of course, but at Harrow Hall in Lincolnshire or at Rivergate? Perhaps she might even be invited to meet Rafe's father, the marquess, at his estate, Avonmore Park.

An entirely appropriate course of action if Rafe proposed...

She smiled again, only this time it wasn't an effort at all.

Once Madame Choffard departed, Georgie settled herself in her favorite sitting room chair. A glance at the mantel clock made her frown. Eight o'clock and still no sign of Rafe. Just like last night, she was clock-watching, an activity she despised. With a gloomy sigh, she took up *Emma*. She could send for more tea. A poor substitute for Rafe's company, but comforting none the less.

Half an hour later, as she attempted to stifle a yawn, she heard the sound she'd been longing to hear—the click of her door opening.

Her heart racing with anticipation, she cast her book aside and rose as Rafe walked in. Even though his hair and attire were uncharacteristically disheveled—he hadn't replaced the neck cloth at his throat, the one he'd used to staunch the bleeding at her neck—he was as breathtakingly handsome as always.

"Georgie," he said, crossing the room, his mouth tilting into a half-smile. He took her hand and kissed her cheek. "I am so very sorry I took so long. I had a few matters to attend to."

Ignoring her injuries, Georgie threw her arms about him, hugging him tight, relishing his warmth and strength. "I understand," she murmured against his throat before kissing his ear, then his stubble-clad jaw. She slid her lips toward his mouth...

"Thank you." Rafe placed a kiss on her cheek then gently unwound her arms from his neck, setting her away. "Would you mind terribly if I got myself a drink? As you well know, it's been a trying day."

Without waiting for her to respond, Rafe went to the carved mahogany sideboard and poured himself a sizeable brandy before turning back to her. "Your hair looks lovely." His gaze wandered over her from head to toe, but his smile seemed forced and his examination felt cursory, not apprecia-tive at all despite his compliment. "You wear that style much better than Caroline Lamb ever did."

Georgie's face heated and she touched the curls at her neck, suddenly self-conscious. And annoyed. Part of her wanted to take Rafe to task for rebuffing her kiss, but she simply said, "Thank you."

Rafe was definitely different. Distant. Even now he was staring into the fire, avoiding her eyes. The firelight high-lighted the fine lines about his eyes and the grim set of his wide mouth. A muscle worked in his jaw.

A frisson of unease slid over Georgie. After what they'd both been through today, why was Rafe acting this way? Had she been right to think he still warred with personal demons she couldn't even begin to fathom? He loved her, but right at this moment, she felt she was standing in the room with a complete stranger.

"Won't you...won't you take a seat?" she suggested, hating the fact she felt both awkward and resentful. This was not how she'd imagined this meeting would be. "I could ring for a supper tray. Or tea..."

"No, I'm not hungry," Rafe said, still not meeting her gaze. He swirled the brandy around in his glass. "This will be sufficient."

"Rafe..." Pushing aside her bruised feelings, Georgie approached him. "Tell me what's wrong. You are not yourself."

He ran a hand down his face; he was clearly exhausted. "I know. I'm sorry." His mouth twitched into an approximation of a smile. "I'm making a hash of this evening, aren't I?"

"Well, I rather think the whole day's been a bit of hash. But you're here, I'm here, and it's over now."

Rafe's smile grew a little wider but shadows lingered behind his dark gray gaze. "Yes."

Encouraged, Georgie continued, "Jonathon spoke to me earlier. He told me about Constance, and how you were able to find me. And about the duel."

Rafe's wide shoulders heaved with a great sigh. "Yes, about that..." He looked directly at her, searching her eyes. "This morning you tried to stop me."

Georgie reached for Rafe's hand. She was relieved he didn't sound angry with her. "I was terrified you would be hurt, or if you killed Craven, you would be held to account. I couldn't bear it. Living without you. So I did what I felt I had to do."

Rafe raised her hand and kissed her knuckles. "You are nothing but brave." He released her hand and swallowed another mouthful of brandy before asking, "Did Jonathon tell you what happened?"

"Yes. You shot Craven in the leg. But not only that, you've ruined him. To punish him, for what he did to me."

"Yes, I did…" Something flickered in Rafe's gaze. A flash of emotion Georgie didn't immediately recognize. "Craven's dead."

"What?" Georgie gasped and clutched Rafe's arm. "But how? If he only suffered a leg wound…"

Rafe put down his brandy and laid a warm hand over hers. "The Bow Street Runners investigating his death believe he took his own life with a pistol. This afternoon. He was found in his rooms in Gerrard Street in Soho. Of course, suspicion fell on me, but as I was with Phillip, John Townsend and the Foreign Secretary himself at the time of Craven's death, the matter was resolved fairly quickly."

Georgie reached out and touched Rafe's cheek, a brief, tentative caress. "I'm relieved beyond measure you haven't been blamed. And I should thank you. I've feared and despised Lord Craven for what seems like a lifetime." She took a deep breath, mustering her courage to make an admission that weighed heavily upon her heart. "Ever since I found out that you've been plotting to destroy that sorry excuse for a man, I've been struggling with how I felt about it all. What he did to me was wrong. So wrong that words often fail me when I try to describe the gaping hole he left inside me. I do understand why you wanted to punish him so badly. I really do. And this may sound shocking to you, but I've only just realized I'm relieved that he is dead." She dragged in another steadying breath and lifted her chin. "No. It's more than that. I'm glad he is dead. I hope he rots in hell."

Rafe's turbulent gaze softened. "I know how difficult it can be to acknowledge such emotions, Georgie. And honestly, I'm not shocked at all to hear you feel that way about Craven. But," his mouth twisted into a wry grimace, "I can also see that *I've* shocked you by my actions. In many ways, I'm not a good man either."

"No, don't you dare say that," Georgie said fiercely, gripping his arms. "You are noble and kind-hearted. The very best of men." Before he could stop her, she kissed him. Reaching up, she grasped the back of his head and pushed her mouth against his. Her movements were frantic and clumsy but that didn't matter. She was determined to show Rafe how much she loved and admired him. How much she wanted him despite his imperfections and his dark past. And how grateful she was to have him in her life.

Rafe groaned, a primal, guttural sound and kissed her back. Spearing his fingers into her short curls, he effortlessly took control of the kiss, plundering her mouth with such fervor, she was soon dizzy with lust. She pushed her hips against his and slid her hands beneath his coat, began to fumble with the buttons of his silk waistcoat. And that's when Rafe ripped his mouth away.

"Georgie," he rasped. "I'm sorry, I can't."

For the second time tonight, he set her way from him, and the pain lancing through her heart hurt more than the press of Dashkov's knife. "I don't understand," she whispered.

Rafe pushed his hands into his hair. "I know you see me as some sort of hero after today. A man worthy of your love. But I'm not, Georgie. Not at all."

Anger flared inside her. "Of course you are."

Rafe shook his head, backing away from her, his expression bleak. "I've killed men...and worse." He could barely meet her gaze. "I've tortured them to extract information, manipulated them, and betrayed others. I've lied, stolen, cheated, lured women to my bed with impunity, broken hearts. Name a sin, I've probably committed it. And I haven't felt the remorse I know that I should a good deal of the time... Like today. I didn't feel one iota of guilt when I shot Craven. Or Dashkov."

"Yes, you shot two men today, one to avenge a heinous wrong and the other to save me." Georgie closed the distance between them again and caught Rafe's hand. "Not many men would do, or *could* do what you have done."

"Perhaps not, but it *is* my fault that Dashkov entered your life. I thought I could put my messy, sordid, ugly past behind me, but it seems that I cannot. *I* put you in harm's way, Georgie. Me. And *that* is something I regret with my entire being." Rafe's throat convulsed and his eyes glimmered with tears. The tender despair in his voice made Georgie want to weep also. With trembling fingers, he touched the bandage on her neck. "Look what he did to you, my love. You almost died today. And for that, I can never forgive myself."

And that's when Georgie knew. This treacherous guilt clawing Rafe to pieces, it wasn't just about her.

She drew a deep breath. "Tell me about Solange."

CHAPTER 24

R afe bowed his head and closed his eyes. *Solange.* Of course, Georgie would see that she had something—perhaps everything—to do with the unrelenting guilt he carried about inside him. And after everything Georgie had been through, she had a right to know about the memory that haunted him the most. She'd witnessed his nightmares. He suspected he would suffer nightmares about how Dashkov had treated Georgie too.

"I'm sorry if I'm asking too much of you," she murmured.

"No, you're not." Rafe offered her a weak smile. "Of course you're not." He gestured toward the arrangement of chairs before the fire. "Come, let us sit down."

Georgie chose the settee and against his better judgment, Rafe sat beside her. Her leg brushed his and it was pure torture. He wanted her so badly, yet she would never be safe if he remained in her life. There were too many other men like Dashkov out there in the world. He'd been naïve to think someone like him—a spy—could ever live a normal life. His past was like a canker that he would never be able to cut away.

And he had to make Georgie see that.

"At the start of the Peninsular War, eight years ago, I was sent to Spain by the Foreign Secretary, Baron Hawkesbury, to gather intelligence on the activities of the French," he began. "Old Boney had invaded and had made his older brother the new King of Spain."

Georgie squeezed his hand. "Yes, I recall that. King Joseph. There was much fear at home that Bonaparte was going to conquer all of Europe."

Rafe nodded. "Quite so. Posing as a French servant, I found employment as a footman within the household of a French officer of interest, a General Duchamp who'd just been posted to Madrid. It was believed he was within Bonaparte's inner military circle. And he had a wife. A much younger, quite beautiful wife. Madame Solange Duchamp took care of her husband's household affairs including the hiring of staff."

"She offered you the position?"

"I spoke excellent French and was armed with an impeccable, albeit false, set of references." Rafe didn't care to add that the footman he replaced had been injured in an "accident" on the street only several days before he'd arrived on Duchamp's doorstep on the Calle de Alcalá. Georgie needn't know about every violent act he'd committed in the line of duty. What she was about to hear would condemn him easily enough.

"As you can imagine," he continued, "Duchamp spent a considerable amount of time away. But when he was home, I would eavesdrop whenever I could, and scour any documents I came upon so I could pass the information on to another contact. That man would then send the intelligence onto our British officers who were leading the campaign."

"You mentioned Solange was younger than her husband," prompted Georgie. "You fell in love with her."

Rafe had denied it once before, but he couldn't deny the

truth now. "Yes. Although I told myself at the time it was only lust that I felt for her. I was four and twenty and I knew from the very beginning Solange was attracted to me." The memory of how her large, dark brown eyes would shine whenever he'd walked into the room would stay with Rafe forever.

When he looked at Georgie, she was smiling. Thankfully, there was no censure in her expression. "I can imagine," she said softly. "I am sure you were quite a sight in your livery."

Rafe almost laughed. "Well, I don't know about that. Powdered periwigs do tend to make any man look ancient. But I digress." He blew out a sigh, preparing himself to relate the next part of this sorry tale. "I've never spoken of this to anyone before, Georgie. So please forgive me if I'm not particularly eloquent."

"I understand."

The light of compassion in her eyes made it possible for him to continue. "I had been employed but a month when Solange and I embarked on our affair. She was quite lonely and desperately unhappy in her marriage. You see, Duchamp was a despicable man—he had exacting standards and a blazing temper, which only became worse when he drank, which was often. Although she denied it, I had strong suspicions Duchamp actually struck Solange if she did something to anger him. In private I saw marks on her—bruises on her arms and other places on her body and once she had a swollen lip— but she was reluctant to talk about it. She always had a ready excuse to hand to explain her injuries away."

Georgie blanched. "Oh, my Lord, Rafe. That's terrible. Did they have children?"

"No. That was another source of tension in the marriage. Solange told me they'd been married six years but were child-less. She suspected she was barren. And Duchamp was not happy about it."

"It must have been very difficult, working within that household, knowing what was happening to the woman you cared about."

As always, Rafe was amazed by Georgie's understanding. "Yes. It was a tense, troubled time to say the least. There I was, a young man, flagrantly stealing confidential military information from a French general, and all the while, I was having carnal relations with his beautiful wife. I kept telling myself that I wasn't falling in love with Solange but of course I was. I was such an idiot to think I could handle the situation. I wasn't careful enough and poor Solange paid the price."

Georgie raised a hand to her throat. "What happened?"

"Solange discovered what I was doing. She caught me going through her husband's papers in his study one day. Fortunately, she didn't care. She just wanted to be with me. In fact, she wanted us to run away together as soon as we could manage it. I understood of course but I just couldn't give her what she asked for. It wasn't as simple as that. There was no foreseeable end date to my mission... You may condemn me for this, Georgie, but I believed I had a job to do. There was so much at stake—the lives of hundreds if not thousands of British soldiers. And as much as I cared for Solange—and as much as I hated the mistreatment she endured at the hands of her husband—I felt my duty to England was far stronger. I promised Solange that when I was able to, I would help her leave Duchamp. But it turned out I grossly underestimated the general and what he was capable of. And in doing so, I completely misjudged Solange's situation."

Georgie's face was as pale as her night rail. "You told me after your nightmare at Rivergate that Solange died."

Too agitated to sit any longer, Rafe stood and paced over to the fireplace. Bitter self-loathing swirled around inside him. He didn't want to tell Georgie the next part of Solange's story, but he must. He drew in a deep breath and forced himself to go on. "One night, during dinner—I was always one of the attendant footmen—General Duchamp snapped at Solange because he didn't like the wine that had been served or the quality of the food. It was Solange's usual habit to try and placate her husband, but this particular evening, she'd taken a little too much wine. It was, in fact, only a few days after she had discovered I was spying on him, and in hindsight, I believe the knowledge weighed heavily upon her mind. Perhaps that's why she drank more than usual. At any rate, instead of accepting her husband's criticism, she spoke back to him. She told him she was tired of his behavior. Of course, her words were akin to waving a red flag at a bull. Duchamp became enraged. He slammed his fist on the table and dismissed her, ordered her to their private apartments. And then he followed."

"What did you do?" Georgie whispered, her eyes wide with horror.

Rafe turned his back on Georgie and gripped the mantel. He couldn't face her. "Not enough. The wrong thing entirely. I was such a bloody fool. Telling myself yet again that my duty, first and foremost, was to my king and country, I took the opportunity to search Duchamp's study. He'd just returned from the barracks and I knew he probably had papers of importance related to troop numbers, movements and supplies—which was indeed the case. In fact, I found invaluable information about the twenty-five thousand strong force that had been amassed under another French general, Junot. I stole away and made my way to the residence of my contact so he could pass the information onto Castlereagh who was, at that time, the Secretary of War. Even though I found out later the intelligence was key in helping our forces defeat the French at Roleia, our first battle on the Peninsula, it has never alleviated my remorse or my guilt, that I was to blame for everything else that happened that night."

He felt Georgie at his side. "You don't have to go on," she murmured. "I can see how the memories pain you so."

He shook his head. He still couldn't bear to look at her. "No, it's better this way. You have a right to know." He had to make Georgie see that he wasn't the noble man she supposed him to be. "When I returned to the Duchamps' townhouse but a half hour later, I found there was a commotion outside in the street. The maids were sobbing outside the front door. Leclerc, one of the other footmen, sat on the doorstep. He was shaking and couldn't tell me what was wrong. But I knew..." His heart thudding erratically with cold dread, Rafe had entered the townhouse and had gone straight to General Duchamp's bedchamber.

He closed his eyes and tried to swallow down the acrid nausea as the recollection hit him with the force of a bullet. He sensed that Georgie held her breath.

"Her husband killed her...didn't he?" she whispered.

"Yes." Rafe at last met her gaze, opened his mouth to tell her what the general had done, but he couldn't find his voice, couldn't formulate the words to describe that scene of blood and horror. When he'd burst into the room, it was to find Duchamp sitting on the edge of the bed beside Solange's life-less body. Dazed, the Frenchman sat as motionless as a statue with a knife in his bloodied, raw-knuckled grip. Until he saw Rafe.

Then he exploded into action, leaping to his feet as he roared, "*Bâtard! Espion dégoutant!*" *Bastard. You filthy spy.*

And all Rafe had been able to do was flee.

"It's my fault, Georgie." His throat was tight, his voice ragged with pain. "I should have known Solange was in danger. I shouldn't have pushed my concerns aside. Duchamp beat her—most likely tortured her, and then cut her throat. I am just as culpable as he is."

"Rafe." Georgie reached out to touch his shoulder but he

flinched away. He didn't deserve her kindness let alone her love. "You didn't know it would go so far," she persisted. In the firelight, her eyes shone with tears. "How could you know? You're not accountable for Duchamp's actions any more than you are accountable for Dashkov's. Evil men do evil things. They are everywhere and you can't always stop them."

Rafe turned to face her. "And that's my point, Georgie. I can't stop them. I tried so very hard to stop bloody Dashkov from hurting you and look what happened. It could happen again." He dragged in an unsteady breath. "But I won't let it."

"What are you saying?" Georgie breathed, eyes wide with dawning horror.

Rafe swallowed his own tears and made himself look her in the eye. "For your safety, we have to end this. Us. I have to go. It's the only way I can truly protect you."

"No. You cannot be serious." Georgie's face was ashen but for two flags of high color on her cheekbones. "You can't just leave me. Not after today. Not like this."

"I'm deadly serious. Who knows how many more monsters are lurking out there, just waiting to strike out at me and my loved ones when I least expect it? I love you too much, Georgie. I won't let you suffer any more than you already have."

"Rafe, this is madness." Georgie reached for him but he stepped away. The anguish in her eyes at his rejection was almost his undoing. Until he recalled how she looked with a knife at her throat.

Somehow, Rafe hardened his heart and found the strength to continue. "Castlereagh wants me to come back. He's offered me another position. And I've accepted it."

Georgie's eyebrows shot up. "What? When?"

"I can't say."

A harsh sound escaped Georgie, somewhere between a

bitter laugh and a choked sob. "Of course. How silly of me to ask."

Rafe took a step closer wanting so very desperately to take everything back. To touch Georgie. But if he did, he'd capitulate so he clenched his fists instead. "I have to do this. It's the only option that will guarantee your safety."

Georgie searched his face. Her expression had changed. The longing and agony had been extinguished. She was in the process of hardening her heart too, and he was nothing but proud of her.

"You've really made up your mind, haven't you?" she said. Her voice was edged with frost and accusation. It wasn't really a question, but he'd answer it anyway.

He held her gaze. "Yes."

Coldness turned to incandescent fury. "Rafe Landsbury. I cannot believe that you are doing this. Treating me so...so cruelly for the sake of some warped sense of honor. You make me love you and then—" Georgie broke off and paced away from him, fuming and oh, so beautiful. When she spun back, her eyes were aflame with cold, blue fire. "You dared me to take a chance. To give myself to you. And I did. Heart and body and soul. You told me you wanted a love that would last forever. And now you want to throw it all away. Throw *me* away because *you* aren't brave enough to take a chance. Because you are scared of shadows." She lifted her chin. "How dare you?"

"Georgie—"

She held up a hand. "Get out. Go. While I still have a little pride left."

He inclined his head and dredged up a voice that was passably even—which was no mean feat, considering his own heart had split in two. "Goodbye, Georgiana. I wish you well."

As Rafe shut the door, he was certain he heard something smash against the wood paneling, and he almost smiled. In the end, Georgie would be all right. She would ache and bleed for a while, but eventually she would heal and find love again with some other lucky bastard who could give her everything she deserved.

Whoever he was, Rafe wanted to kill him.

CHAPTER 25

South Audley Street, Mayfair
21st December 1816

R afe groaned and pulled a pillow over his face, but it didn't help to muffle the violent pounding on the door that seemed to match the rhythmic pounding in his head. *Christ and all his saints.* Who the hell was trying to beat his way into his bedroom?

He lurched into a sitting position and when the room stopped spinning, snatched up his pocket watch from the bedside table and squinted at the time. One o'clock in the afternoon. He supposed he should get up if only to dispose of the bastard on the other side of the door.

"Markham, answer me for God's sake. Or do you want me to break down this door?"

Shit. It was Phillip. He'd half expected his friend would try to dig him out of his rooms eventually. It had been well over a month since he and Georgie had parted ways, and he'd only ventured out of his townhouse on a handful of occasions. Mostly to get blind drunk so he could try to forget what he'd done to Georgie. Especially the deep hurt in her eyes when he'd told her that they could never be together.

Rafe's stomach lurched as he slid out of bed. Over the last few weeks, he'd no appetite for anything but alcohol and self-pity. Casting his gaze back over the twisted sheets he'd just vacated, he rather suspected guilt and nightmares would be his only bedfellows for a long time to come. Perhaps forever.

He'd ruthlessly cut things off to keep Georgie safe. But what if he'd been wrong to do that? He wanted her. He *loved* her.

He missed her so much his chest ached.

But whenever Rafe felt like he was on the brink of seeking Georgie out—of groveling on hands and knees and begging for her forgiveness—a picture of her bound and gagged with Dashkov's wicked blade at her throat intruded into his mind and then he hardened his resolve.

Keeping her safe from his past was paramount.

Staying away *was* the only option. Because if anything ever happened to her...

"Bloody hell, Markham." Another knock came, louder and more insistent. And then a jarring thud. No doubt Phillip had aimed a kick with a booted foot near the door jamb.

Rafe sighed as he pulled on a robe and cinched it around his middle. "All right. I'm coming," he called.

It was time to face the firing party.

He unlocked the door, admitting his friend. "I suppose Castlereagh wants something," he grumbled. The head of the Foreign Office had indeed offered Rafe another position, but he'd yet to assign him any duties. The man had undoubtedly received intelligence from Phillip that Rafe needed time to pull himself together.

Phillip looked Rafe up and down with undisguised disgust. "Enough of this wallowing in self-indulgent misery. Even if Castlereagh *did* want something from you, you are worse than useless in your current state." He wrinkled his nose. "Christ, Markham. When did you last bathe?"

Rafe pushed a hand through his hair and frowned, trying to remember. "Don't recall."

Phillip arched a brow. "I'd wager it was probably last week when I saw you at White's."

Rafe shrugged. "Why don't you make it the subject of this week's club wager then?"

"Not funny, Markham." Phillip crossed the room and thrust back the blue damask curtains before throwing the casement window open. "Where's your valet?"

Rafe groaned again and massaged his throbbing forehead. "God knows. Probably in the kitchen drinking the cooking sherry with the butler. Why the bloody hell are you here anyway if it's not at the behest of Castlereagh?"

Phillip leaned against the windowsill, crossing his arms over his chest. "Helena and I want to speak with you. She's downstairs in your drawing room so you'd best not dawdle over your toilette. You know what she's like when she's kept waiting."

Rafe wiped a hand down his face, the bristles on his jaw abrading his palm. "Your wife is downstairs?" His gut began to roil with unease as well as nausea. "What's wrong? Is it Georgie?"

"Of course it's about Georgie, you dunderhead. But you don't get to find out the details until you clean yourself up. You've got half an hour." Phillip strode to the door, adding as he left, "I'll order coffee."

Twenty minutes later, a washed, freshly shaven, and suitably attired Rafe stepped into his own drawing room.

Helena immediately rose from the settee and greeted him with her infectious smile. "Rafe, it's been far too long. Come and sit by me and I will pour your coffee." She turned to her husband who stood by the fire. "You shall only have tea this time, Phillip. You've already had enough coffee for one day."

Rafe cocked an eyebrow at his friend who gave a resigned shrug. Phillip had told him on many an occasion that it was a silly man indeed who opposed his wife. Rafe had the distinct impression he was about to find that out first-hand.

He took his place beside Helena on the claret velvet settee and accepted his coffee with thanks, but declined a sandwich. Once Phillip was armed with his permitted cup of tea, Rafe gathered his patience together and addressed his friends. "While I anticipate taking luncheon with you both will be quite pleasurable," he said glancing between Helena and Phillip, "I believe you have something you wish to tell me. About Georgie."

Helena put down her cup and saucer on the oak table with a precise click. "Yes." She fixed her gaze on him, studying him for a brief moment. "I know these past few weeks have been very difficult for you, Rafe. And I understand your decision to end things with Georgie was for the very noblest of reasons. But"—her gaze flitted to Phillip as though she was seeking his reassurance before returning to him again—"Phillip and I thought it was best you hear the news from us, rather than from another, less reputable source."

Rafe felt the blood drain away from his face. His heart thudded oddly in his chest as he put down his coffee. "What news?" *God, if anything had happened to Georgie...*

Phillip cleared his throat. "Georgie is to be married."

"*What?*" Rafe lurched to his feet, nearly upsetting the tea table. "You have got to be joking." His gaze darted between Helena and Phillip. "Please tell me this is some sort of sick joke."

Helena put out a hand and touched his sleeve. "It's not a joke, Rafe. We would never jest about something as important as this."

Rafe pushed his hands into his hair and began pacing up and down the Turkish hearthrug. Was he really awake or was this another one of his twisted nightmares? He'd had so many of late... "Who? Who is she marrying?" he demanded as he came to a stop in the middle of the room. "And when? Where?"

Phillip and Helena exchanged a speaking look. Phillip cleared his throat again. "To answer your first question, Lord Farley."

Rafe's mind spun with the sheer incredulity of the idea. "Farley? *Winterbourne's* Farley?"

Helena nodded. "I'm afraid so. We"—she gestured toward her husband—"have been asked to attend the wedding at Harrow Hall. Three days hence, on Christmas Eve."

Rafe dragged a hand down his face. Georgie was going to marry Lord Farley. Another man who preferred the company of men. There had to be a very good reason for such a monumental decision. *Surely she isn't...* "Please forgive my indelicate question, Helena, but do you think Georgie is with child?"

Helena held his gaze steadily. "She hasn't shared such a confidence with me, Rafe. But I rather think *you* might know if that were a possibility."

Phillip coughed. "Our carriage is waiting outside, Markham, if you would like to make the journey to Lincolnshire with us."

Rafe strode toward the bellpull to ring for his valet. "Give me ten minutes."

CHAPTER 26

Harrow Hall, Harrow-on-the-Wold, Lincolnshire
24ᵗʰ December 1816

Georgie sat in the window seat in her bedroom at Harrow Hall and tried to pay attention to Constance's endless prattle about her wedding attire. If truth be told, she didn't give a fig about the arrangement of her curls, or which ribbon or comb Constance would use to secure her hair, or anything at all to do with her impending marriage to Ambrose, Lord Farley.

Oh, dear God, am I really going to go through with this?

Georgie clutched her hands together as a fresh wave of despair washed over her. She took a shuddering breath and blinked away tears. Being this upset all the time couldn't be good for the baby. *Rafe's baby.* A baby he would never know.

She cast her gaze over the snow-blanketed view outside her window and fervently wished she were numb inside, frozen to hardness like the lake by the denuded willow copse. But she wasn't numb. Far from it.

Her heart ached and her belly churned with doubt even

though her ever-practical mind insisted there was only one sensible course of action for her to take, and that was to marry Lord Farley.

When she'd realized she was pregnant—a fortnight ago— she had confided in Jonathon. He'd immediately suggested the most expedient and logical way to solve her predicament: enter another marriage of convenience. Jonathon confessed that whilst Ambrose could never replace Teddy in his heart, he had fallen very much in love with the young earl. And like Teddy, Ambrose required a wife and heir.

Still reeling from Rafe's rejection, Georgie had straight-away agreed to the proposal. There was no way on earth she would let her son or daughter be born into this world with the ignominious label of "bastard." Nor was she willing to be labeled a fallen woman. Of course, she could always steal away to the Continent to have the babe, but then she couldn't tolerate the notion of giving the child to someone else to raise when she returned to England.

She wanted this baby with her entire being.

It was all she had left of Rafe.

She'd briefly contemplated the idea of seeking Rafe out to tell him that he was going to be a father. However, he'd made it abundantly clear—despite the fact that he loved her —that there was no place for her, or *any* loved ones, in his life. And so, in the end, she'd discarded such a foolish plan. She certainly wouldn't beg him to take her back. For better or for worse, she had too much pride within her to do such a thing.

Marriage to Lord Farley was the only way forward for her and this baby.

"Shall I make arrangements for your bath, Your Grace?"

Georgie started at Constance's question. "I..." She glanced at the ormolu clock. It was eleven o'clock, and she was still dressed in only a pale blue satin robe. Her gaze darted to the bed where her wedding gown lay, a confection of silver muslin and white satin, beaded with seed pearls.

"Not yet," she said. "I have plenty of time." Ambrose had obtained a special license and they were to be wed in Harrow Hall's private chapel at three o'clock. "Besides," she added, "I would like to wait for Lady Maxwell before I begin to get ready. I trust she will arrive soon."

Constance curtsied. "Yes, ma'am..." Her brow furrowed with concern. "I apologize if I seem forward, but if there is anything else that I can do for you, anything at all, just let me know and I will do it straightaway."

Georgie inclined her head. "Thank you."

Since returning to service, Constance had carried out her duties with unquestionable dedication and with the utmost discretion. Considering Georgie had missed her courses and had been sick every morning for the past fortnight, Constance must know her mistress was pregnant. Yet her maid had remained tight-lipped on both matters.

And Georgie was nothing but grateful. Despite Constance's involvement in Dashkov's scheme, Georgie still trusted her. Constance and her family had been the baron's victims too.

As Georgie drew another breath to dismiss her maid, she heard the distant crunch of horses' hooves and wheels on gravel.

Glancing out the window, she confirmed it was the Earl and Countess of Maxwell's carriage. She watched the glossy black coach follow the curved drive until it drew to a stop before the main wing of the gray-bricked Restoration-style manor. Phillip had sent a message via courier earlier this morning indicating he and Helena would arrive at Harrow Hall by noon at the very latest. And true to his word, here they were.

The corner of Georgie's mouth twitched. It was the closest

she'd come to smiling in days. She was both heartened and thankful her friends had accepted the invitation to attend her wedding; she regretted she'd hardly seen them in the past month. The day after Rafe had ended their affair, Helena had come to see her at Dudley House to coddle her—as only Helena could—and to commiserate. However, a week later, she had decamped to Harrow Hall. Remaining in London when Rafe was so close was pure torture. If she ever saw him again, she knew she would be completely undone.

But then, what if she *never* saw him again? There was certainly every chance he was already gone, sent on a mission to some far-flung place by Lord Castlereagh.

She gripped the edge of the window seat and squeezed her eyes shut. The pain that she had been trying so hard to suppress every single minute, of every single day, suddenly sliced into her heart, and she had to bite her lip to stifle a whimper of distress.

No. Don't think about him, Georgiana Dudley. He's gone. There is nothing you can do and you have a wedding to prepare for.

"Your Grace?" Constance was at her shoulder.

Unable to speak, Georgie waved her away. "Please arrange for tea to be served to our guests in the drawing room," she said eventually, her voice husky with strain. Swallowing hard, she somehow regained a semblance of control before adding, "And when Lady Maxwell is ready, please direct her to my rooms."

"Yes, ma'am."

As soon as the door closed, Georgie rushed to the wash basin and splashed cold water over her face to stem the flood of scalding tears she could feel gathering behind her eyelids. Perhaps in time she wouldn't feel this way. So angry and broken and utterly desolate.

As far as she was concerned, that day couldn't come soon enough.

~

"Oh, God, I thought you'd left the country."

Rafe finished handing his hat, gloves and greatcoat to the attendant footman before turning to address a glowering Sir Jonathon. "It's a pleasure to see you, too," he said with a sardonic lift of an eyebrow.

"Now, now, Jonathon," soothed Helena. She crossed the polished parquetry floor of the entry hall and laid a placating hand on his arm. "You know, as well as I, that bringing Rafe here was the right thing to do."

Jonathon snorted. "Unless you've had a genuine change of heart where my sister is concerned, Markham, I'd leave straightaway. I'm more than willing to set the dogs on you."

"Steady on," said Phillip. "I'm sure this situation can be resolved satisfactorily—"

"What situation?" At that moment Lord Farley stepped into the hall and when he saw Rafe, he paled. "Oh, I see... I must say, I wasn't expecting you to turn up, Markham." Frowning, his gaze traveled to Jonathon. "Does Georgie know he's here?"

"No."

Rafe addressed Georgie's brother. "I need to speak with her. In private. Where is she?"

"Now, wait one minute," Jonathon fumed. "You cannot just come charging in here on my sister's wedding day and expect to be welcomed back with open arms. You broke her heart for God's sake."

Farley put a hand on Jonathon's shoulder. "Enough, my friend. Everyone deserves a second chance." He turned back to Rafe. "I think I know why you've come, and I won't stand in your way. The duchess is upstairs in her room. Third floor, north wing. Second set of doors on the left."

Rafe inclined his head. "Thank you."

He strode across the hall and took the stairs two at a time until he reached the third floor. His heart pounding, he paused in front of a set of oak-paneled doors, trying to catch his breath as well as compose his riotous thoughts.

Groveling wouldn't be enough.

He had to get this right.

Deciding not to knock, Rafe opened the door and stepped into a tastefully decorated, very feminine sitting room. The chamber was devoid of occupants; a fire crackled in the gray marble fireplace, but the ivory silk upholstered wing chairs before the hearth were empty. So too was the window seat. A door to the right of the fireplace stood ajar and he could see another wide window dressed in dusky blue brocade curtains.

Georgie's bedroom no doubt.

The plush Aubusson rug deadened Rafe's footsteps as he crossed the room. Taking a deep breath, he put his hand on the door, and then paused on the threshold when he heard something that made his heart twist with agony—a muffled sob.

Oh, God, no. Georgie was crying. And it was all his fault.

She was sitting on the edge of the four-poster bed, her head in her hands. The sound of her weeping, the sight of her so wretched and bereft, made his heart fracture all over again. What a bloody, gutless, pathetic fool he'd been to end things with her, this beautiful, intelligent, courageous woman.

"Georgie?" he whispered, but she didn't hear him. He risked taking a few steps closer and tried again. "Georgie, my love. Please don't cry."

She raised her face and blinked at him. Blinked again and then she gave a sharp cry, a hand flying to her mouth. "Rafe?"

He rushed to her and dropped to his knees. Gathered her

into his arms and held her so very tight. For the briefest moment she stiffened, her hands braced against his shoulders as if to push him away, but then she sagged against him with a shudder and buried her face in his neck.

"I'm so sorry, Georgie. You'll never know how much," he said against her hair, his own voice thick with tears. "Please tell me you'll forgive me."

This time when she pushed against him, he released her. Even with disheveled hair, a tear-stained cheeks and a red nose, he was struck anew by her incomparable beauty.

She dashed the tears away from her eyes with a trembling hand and frowned at him. "What are you doing here?" she demanded.

He swallowed, taken aback by the hostility in her expression. "Phillip and Helena told me you were to be married to Farley this afternoon. I cannot let you go through with it."

"Why?" Her blue eyes were as cold as the winter sky as she searched his face.

"Because you deserve so much more from life. A real marriage to a man who you love and who loves you in return." Rafe reached out to touch her cheek but Georgie flinched away.

Her mouth flattened into a hard line. "Well, twice in my life I thought that was a possibility. But on both occasions it seems I was mistaken."

This time it was Rafe who flinched. "I understand you're angry with me, Georgie. And you have every right to be."

She lifted her chin. "Yes. Yes I do." She slid away from him then stalked over to the window. "I still don't really understand why you've come," she said with her back to him. "Don't you have somewhere else you need to be? I thought Lord Castlereagh would have sent you halfway across the world by now."

"Castlereagh can go hang himself." Rafe climbed to his

feet and followed Georgie across the room, taking up a position on the other side of the window. "I have another, more important duty right here in England."

Georgie swallowed but she kept her gaze steadfastly fixed on the snow-shrouded grounds of Harrow Hall. "I can't imagine what that might be."

"I'm sure you can," he said softly, drawing closer. "Georgie, I know you're with child... My child."

She sucked in a startled breath and her gaze whipped up to his face. "How could you possibly know that?" she whispered.

He curved his mouth into a gentle half-smile. "Why else would you agree to marry Farley?"

Her face paled but she didn't look away. "I'm still going to marry him, Rafe," she said, a militant light in her eyes. "You being here, it doesn't change anything."

He took one step closer. Then another. He was now close enough to touch her. "Of course it does," he murmured.

She cast him a fulminating glare. "Why? The last time I saw you, you were adamant you could never lead a normal life. And I won't marry you—even if you care to offer—because you feel it is your duty."

He reached out and grasped her chin with gentle fingers so she couldn't escape his gaze. "Then marry me for love."

Georgie bit her lip to stop herself saying "yes" when everything within her demanded she do just that.

"Why the sudden change of heart, Rafe?" she asked, pulling away from his hold. She was too hurt, too raw to tolerate his tenderness, let alone a proposal. "You talk of marriage and love, and of spending a lifetime together—yet not that long ago, you were loath to take such a risk. A baby will only make the burden of care worse for you."

"The guilt I felt, it made me too blind to see there could be another way, Georgie. I wasn't thinking clearly. But I sincerely believe we *can* make a life together."

"How? How will it work?" she demanded. "Will you keep me and our child under lock and key? Hire an army to protect us around the clock just in case something should happen?"

Rafe grimaced. "If I have to... I know I ask a lot of you. The question is, would you be willing to try? For us? For our child?" He grasped her shoulders. "I love you, Georgiana. I need you. These last few weeks have been the most miserable in my life. And I can think of nothing worse than living without you. Or never knowing my child... Our child." Again he cupped her face. "Marry me. Say 'yes.'"

"I don't know, Rafe..." She searched his dark gray eyes. His expression was so sincere, full of naked expectation, yet still she hesitated. Could he really have changed that much? Vanquished the monsters inside him? And could she live with all of the constraints he was insisting upon? "I trusted you, and then you deserted me when I needed you the most. How do I know you won't do that again? Leave me because you feel you are not worthy enough? Or because you believe that you are somehow poisonous, too dangerous to know?"

A muscle jerked in his cheek. "You doubt me. I understand that." With a suddenness that startled her, Rafe shrugged off his black superfine tailcoat and threw it onto the window seat. His fingers then worked at the knots of his cravat.

Georgie frowned in confusion. "What are you doing?"

"Proving my love." He pulled off the loosened neck cloth and dropped it on the floor.

"Stop that," she said. Butterflies danced wildly in her belly.

"No." His gaze fixed on hers, he started to undo the buttons of his charcoal-gray silk waistcoat. "If you won't trust my word then I will show you how much you mean to me."

"You're being ridiculous." She took several steps away from him but then stopped. She didn't dare go near the bed. A strange combination of panic and lust made her feel giddy and hot all over as she watched Rafe discard his waistcoat then pull his white linen shirt from the waistband of his tight, buckskin breeches. "I want you to go. I have to get ready for the wedd—"

"No. You don't." He ripped off his shirt and she gasped at the sight of his naked chest and torso. The defined lean muscles of his upper body rippled as he tossed the garment way.

He prowled closer.

"What about Lord Farley and the other guests?" she asked in a breathless, high-pitched voice as she circled away from him. But her retreat was to no avail. He followed her until the back of her legs bumped against the window seat. "Helena and Phillip?"

"I don't care about them." Rafe was so close, she could feel the heat radiating from his body. His hands rose and gently cradled her face like she was the most precious thing in the world. "I only care about you."

Oh...

He bent his head, his lips brushing across hers. "Say you forgive me," he murmured against her mouth, his breath teasing her just as much as the satiny caress of his lips. "Tell me you love me." He bestowed another kiss, the press of his mouth firmer, hotter. When he spoke again, his voice was a low, seductive rumble she felt all the way to her toes. "Marry me."

Oh, dear God, how could she resist him? Of course she wanted to be with him, for better or for worse. But perhaps they shouldn't... He shouldn't...

Her hand fluttered to her stomach. "The baby," she whispered.

He pushed her robe off her shoulder and kissed her bare neck. "I'll be gentle. Let me love you, Georgiana."

"Yes." She clutched the back of Rafe's head and pressed her body against his, offering herself to him. *Surrendering*. Sweet, Lord how she'd missed this. *Him*.

With a groan, he slid an arm around her waist and lashed her closer still, claiming her mouth with a gentle ruthlessness that made her pulse race and moisture pool between her thighs. As he palmed her breast with his other hand, he pushed his hips against hers, his impressive erection jutting into the softness of her belly.

She wanted him so badly it hurt. She reached for the fall front of his breeches and stroked his rock-hard length through the soft leather, wanting to enflame his need to blazing proportions, but he stilled her fingers. "Not yet, my love," he rasped. "Take off your robe."

Georgie couldn't deny him, or herself. She loosened the tie at her waist and after the blue satin garment slid to the floor, Rafe eased her down onto the cushioned window seat amongst the silken pillows. Then he spread her thighs.

Georgie watched his face. Rafe's gaze was focused, sharp with undisguised hunger as he stared at her throbbing quim. She bit her lip and moaned. "Please," she begged, rolling her hips. "I need you."

Rafe smiled. His gaze met hers. "I know." His thumb circled the pulsating center of her sex. Once, twice, then stopped. "But I'm still waiting to hear if you'll accept my proposal."

"You are too cruel."

His smile widened to a thoroughly rakish grin. "Agreed. But then so are you."

She arched a brow. "Perhaps. However, I thought you wanted to demonstrate how much you loved me first before demanding an answer."

"Wench." Rafe's searing gaze traveled down her body, melting her will to resist him just that little bit more. "Now, where was I?" He buried his face between Georgie's thighs and pleasured her throbbing nub and juice-slickened folds with his tongue and lips until she did not think she could endure such sweet, sweet torment a second longer. At last she was swept away in a whirlwind of sublime sensation, hurtled up, up and up to the dizzying heights of ecstasy, a place she never thought Rafe would take her to again.

Panting, bittersweet tears gathering in her eyes, Georgie barely had time to catch her breath before Rafe freed his member from his breeches and began nudging her wet, swollen entrance. She cried out as he slid inside her, not with pain but with joy. The sensation of him filling her, stretching her, *loving her*, was exquisite.

This was what she had been missing. This was what she wanted.

This wondrous feeling of completeness and connection she could only achieve with Rafe.

Lord, she would do anything he wanted, to hold onto this, *to him*, forever.

She gripped his wide shoulders then slid her hands beneath his breeches, cupping his firm buttocks as he began to pulse in and out of her slick passage, teasing her with gentle strokes. When he laved one of her nipples into a tight aching peak, she arched her back and gasped with sheer pleasure.

Her reaction seemed to spur Rafe on. His thrusts grew longer, deeper, faster, driving her ever closer to the brink of bliss. She began to pant and writhe, undulating beneath him, rocking her hips, taking him deeper. Her inner sheath rippled. Quivered. She was close, so very close, she almost couldn't bear it.

"Love me, Rafe," she demanded hoarsely, wrapping her legs about his hips.

"Always." He bent his head and plundered her mouth with such a searing, possessive kiss, it was the catalyst that at last sent her spinning heavenward.

Crying his name, Georgie climaxed. Devastating pleasure like nothing she had ever known before pulsated through her body, carried her away to the stars. She was barely aware of Rafe's cry as he found his release as well. His body slick with sweat, he shuddered then collapsed on top of her, whispering her name like a prayer.

When Rafe at last raised his head she saw there were tears upon his cheeks and his face was etched with stark longing. "I'm in agony, my love. You haven't given me an answer yet," he said hoarsely. He brushed a strand of hair away from her face and his smoke-dark eyes stared intently into hers. "So, Georgiana Dudley, I will ask you again. Will you do me the incomparable honor of consenting to be my wife?"

Georgie bit her lip as her heart clenched. Rafe had said earlier she was being cruel and he was right. And she really had no reason to be. Not when this man had bared every part of his soul to her. He'd move heaven and earth for her if she asked him to. Protect and cherish her until his dying breath. And here he was, all but begging her to be with him. Forever.

She'd be a fool to refuse him.

She reached out and stroked his lean jaw. "Yes, Rafe. The answer is 'yes.'"

Rafe's answering smile, brighter than the summer sun, made her heart swell with unadulterated happiness. "Thank you," he whispered. He leaned over her and kissed her with such ardent, tender reverence she wanted to weep. "I love you, Georgie."

"I love you too," she whispered huskily, her vision blurred by tears. "I've missed you so much. Don't ever leave me again."

He dropped another kiss on her lips. "Never."

EPILOGUE

Rivergate, Richmond
One year later...

The wedding of Georgiana Dudley, the Duchess of Darby, to Rafe Landsbury, the Earl of Markham, had not taken place at St George's in Hanover Square in December 1816 as many of the *ton* might have expected. Instead, a private ceremony followed by an intimate wedding breakfast shared with close family and friends was held at Latimer House, the Earl and Countess of Maxwell's Mayfair residence, on New Year's Eve.

During their first year of complete happiness, Georgie and Rafe divided their time between Rivergate House at Richmond and Landsbury House, an elegant and spacious townhouse in Portman Square. The townhouse—unexpectedly beautiful—was a property Rafe's father Henry, the Marquess of Avonmore, had gifted to his son and heir as a wedding gift. As much as Georgie had enjoyed living with Jonathon at Dudley House, she was more than happy to hand the run of the place over to her brother and his love, Lord Farley.

When their first-year wedding anniversary arrived, Georgie could scarcely believe how swiftly time had flown.

Or blissfully.

Especially after their baby boy, Henry Theodore Jonathon Landsbury, Viscount Woodford—or Harry, after Rafe's late brother, for short—arrived in the world in August. Georgie was thrilled beyond measure that she'd been able to carry and safely deliver a healthy child who was so utterly adorable. It helped to heal the lingering scars in her heart left there by the loss of her first baby through miscarriage, all those years ago. And of course, she was doubly happy that Rafe had a healthy son.

Indeed, so content were they as a family, both Georgie and Rafe had decided to politely decline most of the invitations they received to attend numerous Yuletide house parties at their friends' country estates, or balls or soirees thrown in London.

"Why should we go out when we can spend a quite evening at home with our favorite person in the whole world?" remarked Rafe, his voice as soft as velvet as he cradled his four-month-old son in his arms.

They were presently in the nursery of Rivergate House, and the fire dancing in the grate bathed the room and its furnishings—a study in muted shades of blue—in a warm golden light. It might be snowing outside but it was nothing but cheerful and cozy in Harry's room.

Georgie caressed the silky, light brown locks on Harry's small head. When she looked up to meet Rafe's gaze, the love she felt was reflected in his gray eyes. "I agree completely, my darling husband," she murmured. "There's no place I'd rather be tonight."

Rafe smiled down at her. "There's not a day that goes by that I don't thank God that you and I are together. And that we now have Harry in our lives. I never thought a man like me could be so blessed."

A man like me...

Georgie reached up and caressed his cheek. "Yes. A man like you deserves all this and more."

A shadow flitted across Rafe's handsome countenance. "Do you really think so? Heaven knows I'm not an easy man to live with." His mouth tilted into a small, crooked smile. "You put up with a lot."

Georgie's heart clenched with a bittersweet ache. Yet again, she had to reassure him that he was exactly what she wanted. "What a load of rot, Lord Markham," she said in a gently rebuking tone. "If putting up with 'a lot' means spending every single day and night with the man I love and creating a family with him, then I'll take my medicine, and gladly." She softened her voice. "Being with you—loving you—*is* easy. I couldn't imagine a life without you."

Even though Dashkov's cruel and calculated vengeance campaign had ended over a year ago, Georgie knew that Rafe continued to be concerned about her safety—and everyone else he held dear, including baby Harry—but he was learning to manage his not inconsiderable, and perfectly understandable fears. His life as a spy had made him instinctively look for danger around every corner, compulsively watching the shadows. To lessen his anxiety, he'd employed a small army of well-trained, burly footmen, stable hands, and coachmen to keep watch over Georgie and Harry. But she never felt caged or confined or restricted in any way. She only felt protected and cherished.

And in time, she prayed that Rafe would come to realize that he no longer had anything to fear. That his past wouldn't come back to haunt him. That another monster like Dashkov wouldn't snatch away his wife or anyone else he cared about.

More than anything, Georgie hoped Rafe could forgive

himself for the things he'd done during his service to King and country. That a life filled with peace and joy and love could, indeed, be his.

While Rafe settled a sleepy Harry in his cradle, Georgie summoned the nursemaid, and then the happy parents repaired to their own suite of rooms, a short distance away down the hall.

As soon as the door to their bedchamber snicked shut, Rafe gathered Georgie into his arms. "I can't believe that I'd convinced myself to give you—and all this—up," he murmured thickly. His gray eyes were aglow with adoration, and something else brighter and hotter that Georgie suspected might be barely contained desire. He brushed a lock of her hair behind her ear. "What was I thinking? I must have been mad."

"You were afraid, and you thought you were doing the right thing for love." Georgie tugged on the lapels of her husband's satin banyan, suddenly wishing it and the clothing beneath it were gone. Her mouth quirked with a smile. "I'm glad you came to your senses though, my lord."

His expression turned rueful. "Eventually. I fear that I'm forever indebted to the Maxwells, particularly Helena, for helping me to see the light. When I turned up at Harrow Hall, I'm glad you didn't reject me outright for being such a dunderhead."

"Dunderhead or not, I love you." Georgie fixed her husband with a determined look. "Rafe Landsbury, you are the most patient, kind, and caring man that I know. Without you, I would never have found love. We would never have had our beautiful baby boy. We have so much joy in our lives, sometimes I can scarcely believe it. Indeed, I have to regularly pinch myself to make sure I'm not dreaming." She cupped Rafe's strong lean jaw that was already rough with his night beard. "You are my everything. Happy anniversary, my darling."

Rafe's hands lightly skimmed up Georgie's back, and through the silk of her robe she shivered with sweet anticipation. He gently cradled her face. "I love you too. With my entire heart and soul. Happy anniversary, Duchess."

Georgie smiled as Rafe's heated gaze dropped to her mouth. She loved that Rafe still called her "Duchess" even though she'd taken the unconventional route of eschewing her former title to take up her husband's. "Let's make another baby, Lord Markham," she said, pulling him down for his much-wanted kiss.

Desire immediately sparked and flared between them, just like it was always did, and it wasn't long before Georgie was swept away on a tide of heat and glorious pleasure.

So much pleasure. And love.

Indeed, Georgie and Rafe made languid, exquisite love until the New Year rang in. As she lay warm and sated in her husband's arms, listening to the thud of his heart, steady and true, Georgie would readily acknowledge she'd never been more satisfied.

No, satisfied wasn't quite the right expression. *Perfectly replete with bliss.* Georgie smiled sleepily and beneath the covers of their bed, snuggled contentedly against Rafe's side. *Yes, that would do. Everything's perfect.*

In fact, Georgie knew right down to her very bones that with Rafe in her life, it would always be like this. Forever.

The End

AUTHOR'S NOTE TO READERS

Thank you so much for reading **The Ice Duchess**! If you have the time and inclination, please do consider leaving a review wherever you bought the book. I would greatly appreciate it!

Read on for an excerpt from Chapter One of **A Most Unsuitable Countess**, Book 3 in the Scandalous Regency Widows series!

ENJOY A SAMPLE OF A MOST UNSUITABLE COUNTESS

BOOK 3 IN THE SCANDALOUS REGENCY WIDOWS SERIES...

Chapter 1

Winthorpe House, Mayfair, London
October 1811

"Catherine, you cannot be here." Adam St Clair, the Earl of Dalton, ran a hand down his impossibly handsome face, his expression caught somewhere between exasperation and despair.

At least, Catherine hoped it was despair. Because that was the emotion churning about inside her heart and making her throat tighten with the effort not to cry. That, and a good dose of apprehension.

"I know." Her voice was so hoarse, the words came out as a croak. She licked dry lips and continued. "But...there's something I need to tell you." Her trembling hand fluttered downward over the skirts of her lilac silk ballgown to her belly.

Adam blew out a sigh as he raked a hand through his tousled light-brown hair. His pained gaze darted to the French doors leading to the crowded, chandelier-lit ballroom of

Winthorpe House, then back to her. Oh God, he *was* frustrated with her.

"We said goodbye a month ago." His deep voice was low yet tinged with an unmistakable undercurrent of urgency. "I thought you understood. You being here tonight... It's too..."

Dangerous. Inconvenient. Pitiful? The bitter words hovered on Catherine's lips but somehow she swallowed them down along with her tears. How could she tell her former protector—the man she loved with her entire foolish heart even though he couldn't possibly love her in return—that she was with child?

His child.

"I know," she repeated uselessly. "I know I shouldn't be here." It would be futile to remind him that he had instigated the parting of ways, not her. Men discarded their mistresses all the time, and it was Adam's prerogative after all.

But he was going to be a father and she had to tell him, come what may.

The sound of merrymaking—laughter, chatter, and the strains of a small orchestra—traveled clearly on the damp cold night air, filling the taut silence stretching between them. Lord and Lady Winthorpe's ball was in full swing but the October night was so chilly, the stone-flagged terrace was deserted...except for her and Adam.

"How did you gain admittance?"

Adam's gruff question cut Catherine to the bone. It was to be expected, but nevertheless, it hurt. Narrowing her eyes to mask her pain, she fired back, "I didn't slink in the back door like a common sneakthief, if that's what you're implying."

"Of course not—"

She raised her chin. "I came here with Sir Louis Fortescue."

Adam nodded. The light spilling through a nearby window revealed a muscle pulsing in his lean jaw. A flash of jealousy in his eyes? His reaction gave her courage. But not hope. She dared not hope he would change his mind about her and a longed-for future that was well-nigh impossible.

Noblemen didn't fall in love with whores and then marry them—especially bastard brats who'd grown up in the gutters of revolution-torn Paris. It was simply the way of the world. And hadn't he once told her that he didn't believe in the idea of love? That romantic love made both men and women lose their minds? Caused them to make foolish decisions and take rash actions? That he would never let himself fall victim to such a senseless, volatile emotion that often ruined hearts and lives?

But he has a right to know I'm pregnant, doesn't he…?

Before she could drag in a breath to say what she needed to, Adam spoke again. "God help me, Catherine," he muttered through clenched teeth. "I'm trying to do the right thing here."

She shook her head, bewildered. *Right thing for whom?* "I don't know what—"

She got no further as Adam seized her, crushing his hot mouth against hers. He pushed her into the dark velvet shadows up against the cold brick wall, his strong arms crowding her in, trapping her so she couldn't escape, even if she'd wanted to. The kiss was rough, brutal.

Desperate.

His teeth nipped, his lips grazed, his tongue invaded her mouth and lashed against hers. And she loved it. Welcomed it. Clinging to his wide shoulders, she kissed him back with equal ferocity.

Yes, her heart sang. *Remember this, Adam, Remember us. Don't cast me aside. Don't abandon me.*

His hands were in her hair, gripping the back of her head, then cradling her jaw. At her throat where her pulse pounded. On her breasts…

Then all at once Adam dragged his mouth away. His wide chest rose and fell with his jagged breaths. He shook his head and released her from his embrace, his hands clenching and unclenching at his sides as he stepped back toward the French doors. "This is madness. I..." A wash of bright candlelight illuminated his piercing blue eyes as they locked with hers. "I can't do this."

"But why not?" She reached out a hand but let it fall when Adam took another step away from her. "You want me. I know you do. And besides—"

Another emphatic shake of his head. "Wanting isn't enough. I have responsibilities. A duty—"

"Adam? What on earth are you doing out here?" An attractive, fair-haired young woman appeared in the suddenly open doorway. "I've been looking everywhere..." Her sharp gaze slid past Adam's broad shoulders and landed on Catherine. "I don't believe we've met," she said in a voice dripping with icicles.

With a jolt, Catherine recognized her—it was the daughter of the house, Lady Sybil Gower. She couldn't have been older than twenty. A mere slip of a thing. *A debutante*. A ripple of unease passed over Catherine's skin, making her shiver.

Adam moved toward the scowling younger woman. "Sybil, Miss Delacourt is a former acquaintance of mine. And a friend of Sir Louis Fortescue's," he said in a voice so smooth, Catherine blinked in astonishment.

How could he be so calm, so urbane when only a moment ago a wild storm of passion had consumed him?

"I see." Lady Sybil turned her attention back to Adam and reached for his arm. "Come, my darling. Papa wants to make the announcement after the next cotillion finishes."

My darling? Announcement?

Catherine's stomach pitched as sharp realization slapped her in the face.

I have a duty...

"You're getting married," she whispered through numb, frozen lips.

Adam turned back to her, his expression wooden. "Yes."

"Yes, indeed we are." Lady Sybil stared up at Adam with such adoration, Catherine thought she might lose the contents of her stomach.

How could he do this? Of course, Adam needed to marry someone from his own class, but why choose someone like Lady Sybil? Someone so young and inexperienced? He'd grow bored with her within the space of a few weeks. She just knew he would.

Wouldn't he?

Surely Adam hadn't fallen in *love* with Lady Sybil. Not when he was so cynical about that particular emotion. Or so he'd always claimed...

Unless he simply can't love you, *Catherine...*

A sob gathering in her throat, Catherine swallowed hard and somehow made her voice work as she stepped out of the shadows. At times like this, she was grateful she'd inherited her mother's gift for acting. "Then may I be the first to offer my congratulations, Lady Sybil?" Plastering a false smile on her face, she blinked away her tears and forced herself to look Adam in the eye. "Lord Dalton."

Lady Sybil's expression was a combination of smugness and a civility so false it matched her own. "Why thank you, Miss..." She trailed off then affected a small laugh. "Goodness, I've already forgotten your name."

"Delacourt," Adam supplied. He offered a gentlemanly bow and another smooth smile. "Thank you, Miss Delacourt. Your good wishes mean a great deal to me."

Lady Sybil shot him a suspicious look but Adam ignored it. Tucking her gloved hand into the crook of his arm, he inclined his head in farewell again before escorting his haughty betrothed back inside.

Catherine staggered backward toward the edge of the terrace. Gripping the white marble balustrade, she closed her eyes as dark anguish engulfed her. *Adam is to be married. I've truly lost him. I didn't tell him he's going to be a father. And now he'll never know...*

Burning tears welled and this time Catherine let them flow unheeded. Their child would forever be tainted by the stain of illegitimacy. It was a stain she knew all too well.

A match most unsuitable. A love that's undeniable...

Catherine, the widowed Lady Rosemont, is considered a most unsuitable countess by polite society. Whispers about her checkered history follow her wherever she goes. Was she once a courtesan? Is her young son really the late Earl of Rosemont's child or a by-blow? And worst of all, is she a murderess? Despite the scandalous rumors, Catherine navigates high society's treacherous waters with her head held high. For the sake of her beloved son, Louis, she must never sink. But when she receives threatening letters and young Louis's life is endangered, she desperately turns to a past paramour for help...the man who once left her heartbroken. The far-too-honorable Earl of Dalton...

Adam St Clair, Lord Dalton, has always been one to adhere to family duty no matter the cost. Five years ago, he set aside his all-consuming desire for his mistress, the beautiful and mysterious Catherine Delacourt, and took a conventional ton bride. Now, newly widowed, fate decrees he should cross paths with Catherine once again. When she shares a stunning secret and implores him for protection, Adam is torn. With danger lurking around every corner, keeping Catherine and her son safe is undoubtedly the right thing to do. Nevertheless, Adam must decide whether he'll risk his reputation—and his family's—for the only woman he's never been able to forget... The one woman who might just steal his heart...

DON'T MISS AMY ROSE BENNETT'S OTHER
ROMANCES
Visit www.amyrosebennett.com to find out more...

SCANDALOUS REGENCY WIDOWS

Lady Beauchamp's Proposal, Book 1
The Ice Duchess, Book 2
A Most Unsuitable Countess, Book 3

~

IMPROPER LIAISONS

An Improper Proposition, Book 1
An Improper Governess, Book 2
An Improper Christmas, Book 3
An Improper Duke, Book 4 (Out Jan 2024)

~

THE BYRONIC BOOK CLUB

Up All Night with a Good Duke, Book 1
Curled Up with an Earl, Book 2
Tall, Duke, and Scandalous, Book 3

~

THE DISREPUTABLE DEBUTANTES

How to Catch a Wicked Viscount, Book 1
How to Catch an Errant Earl, Book 2

How to Catch a Sinful Marquess, Book 3
How to Catch a Devilish Duke, Book 4

STANDALONE TITLES

All She Wants for Christmas
Dashing Through the Snow
The Duke Who Came to Christmas Dinner
My Lady of Misrule
Long Gone Girl

COMING SOON...

HIGHLAND ROGUES
The Master of Strathburn, Book 1
The Laird of Blackloch, Book 2

LADY MEETS ROGUE
The Lady and the Libertine (**FREE** for newsletter subscribers)
The Lady and the Privateer (Out July 2023)
The Lady and the Duke (Out January 2024)

ABOUT THE AUTHOR

Amy Rose Bennett is an Australian author who has a passion for penning emotion-packed historical romances. Of course, her strong-willed heroines and rakish heroes always find their happily ever after. A former speech pathologist, Amy is happily married to her very own romantic hero and has two lovely, very accomplished adult daughters. When she's not creating stories, Amy loves to cook up a storm in the kitchen, lose herself in a good book or a witty rom-com, and when she can afford it, travel to all the places she writes about.

Sign up for Amy Rose Bennett's newsletter via her website at www.amyrosebennett.com to receive all of her latest book news! When you subscribe, you'll also receive an exclusive FREE copy of her hot but sweet novella, *The Lady and the Libertine!*

When bluestocking Lady Angelina Pembroke decides the only way out of an impending but unwanted engagement is to ruin her reputation, she approaches London's most notorious libertine —a former naval officer dubbed the "Tattooed Viscount"—to ensure her plan is a resounding success. But sometimes, the road to ruination isn't all plain sailing...especially when love gets in the way...